ARACHNID
PRESS

CW00515878

HIDE
AND
SEEK

Ken
Lussey

Other books by Ken Lussey

Thrillers featuring Bob Sutherland and Monique Dubois
and set in Scotland and beyond during World War Two:
Eyes Turned Skywards
The Danger of Life
Bloody Orkney
The Stockholm Run

For younger readers:
The House With 46 Chimneys

First published in Great Britain in 2023 by
Arachnid Press Ltd
91 Columbia Avenue
Livingston EH54 6PT
Scotland

www.arachnid.scot
www.kenlussey.com

ISBN: 978-1-8382530-6-6

Cover design and photography by AuthorServices.scot.
Printed and bound in Great Britain by Inky Little Fingers Ltd,
Unit 3, Churcham Business Park, Churcham, Gloucester, GL2 8AX.

For my grandsons Alistair and Alexander.
One is now almost old enough to read my stories about Bob
and Monique. The other will have to wait a little longer.

PROLOGUE

'You may think of me as old and decrepit, ladies, but it's not as simple as that. Yes, I'm sixty this year. You've been with me before, Maude, and you know my flesh is always willing.

'The truth is that I've spent too much time today in an inn on the Grassmarket and I've drunk far too much ale. I was with two old friends, drinking to the new king's health and good fortune and the old one's eternal damnation. God knows, the young King James is sorely in need of good fortune. He is but a boy like his father was when he became king. We can look forward to arguments or worse over who holds his power for him in the coming years.

'And the old King James, if you can call 29 years of age "old"? You both probably think of him as a great and virtuous king because that is what he has become. At least, that is what he had become until he stood too close to a cannon outside Roxburgh Castle that misfired and killed him. But I knew him when he was younger. In those days I was the master of the household, a close adviser to the king. He had a terrible temper and, at that time, did little to control it. That was how he gained the name we knew him by. Yes, he had a large birthmark on the left side of his face. But that wasn't the real reason he was known, behind his back, as "James of the Fiery Face".

'It was the way he let his temper rule him that warrants his eternal damnation. I was there at Stirling Castle on that dreadful night when he murdered the Earl of Douglas. You may both gasp, but that is what happened. The story of his struggle for power with the Douglases is a long one, but James was wrong to strip the Earl of Douglas of titles and lands to help pay for his own marriage to Mary of Guelders. Against my advice, I should add. The earl tried to defend himself by forming a bond with important men who held power in much of northern Scotland. That was a threat to the king's hold on the country. Hoping to rebuild trust between them, King James invited the earl to Stirling Castle for Shrove Tuesday feasting under a letter of safe conduct.

'1452 seems such a long time ago now, even though only eight years have passed. The first night of feasting went well, but on the second night the discussion became more serious. After the food had been eaten and a great deal of wine and ale had been drunk, James demanded that the earl break his bond with the northern magnates. The earl refused. Their argument went back and forth, growing ever more heated. It ended when James flew into a rage. I tried to calm him but was too slow. James pushed me aside and drew a dagger. He used it to stab the earl, who had been caught by surprise, in the neck and then in the body. I thought he was going to attack me too.

'Most of the other nobles present were as drunk and as hot-headed as the king. Under orders from James, one of them used a poleaxe to cleave the earl's head, which spread his brains over the table and over all of us who were close to him. Other men at the feast then stabbed the earl's already dead body again and again. The strength of my objections caused the king to dismiss me from his service there and then. I never saw him again and can be thankful I emerged with my life and my titles intact. The murder caused serious conflict with the Douglases and, while the king did finally prevail, it was all so unnecessary.

'Very few people know what really happened. Now the king is dead it is time the story was told. One of the men I was drinking with earlier is writing a history of the late king's reign and I have agreed to contribute an account of that night. I will never forget the horror and I will never forget the names of the nobles who wielded the weapons. It is fitting that they should be remembered for what they did.

'But while that is why I was drinking today, it isn't why we are here, is it? It might help, Maude, if you and Margaret pleasure each other. If you can make me believe your enjoyment is not feigned, and if that revives my ale-sapped interest, I will pay you both double the usual amount.'

*

The intercom crackled into life. 'I can see land. That's Scotland ahead!'

On hearing Hans's voice, Rudolf Hartmann, Rudi to his few friends, twisted round to his right, then his left, trying to get a glimpse of their destination from his rear-facing seat in the back of the cockpit. He couldn't see far enough to the front, so he unstrapped his harness and stood up, turning to his left, careful to avoid the unforgiving rear of the MG 131 machine gun. This left him standing a little awkwardly with his head slightly bowed to avoid the cockpit canopy. At least it meant he was able to get a clear view ahead, past the right side of the top of the armoured pilot's seat, past Hans's leather-helmeted head and over the top of Wolfgang's, sitting in the lower right-hand flight engineer's seat.

Wolfgang seemed to be straining against his harness, leaning forwards. Then he sat back and pointed, ahead and slightly to their left. 'Yes, I see it too. I suppose it's too late to ask if this is a sensible idea?'

Oberleutnant Hans Weber looked round from the pilot's

seat. 'It was too late from the moment we radioed fighter HQ in Denmark to tell them the starboard engine was on fire. They'll have aircraft out looking for us by now. They might even have found the empty life raft we dropped. There's no going back. Not unless you like the idea of standing in front of a firing squad.'

From behind him, Rudi patted Wolfgang on the shoulder. 'Don't worry. We've talked this through. We'll be fine.'

Wolfgang turned in his seat and smiled nervously in response.

Rudi reminded himself that Wolfgang was little more than a boy, just 20. He was right to be nervous. Rudi was frankly terrified of what they were about to do. If they survived the next fifteen minutes, they would be fine. But he didn't know what their chances were of surviving the next fifteen minutes.

Hans looked round again. 'Can we have less chat please, gentlemen? Our lives could depend on seeing the fighters they send up before they see us. As you say, Rudi, the time for talking is behind us. Now we need to turn words into actions. Wolfgang, have you got the flare pistol ready?'

Wolfgang held up the pistol in response.

'Good,' said Hans. 'Make sure you only fire red flares and, once I give the word to start, keep firing them as quickly as you can until I tell you to stop. We can only be a couple of kilometres off the coast. I'll go into a gentle left-hand orbit.'

'What's our altitude?' asked Rudi.

'50 metres. That's higher than we've been for most of the crossing, certainly since we pretended to ditch in the Skagerrak.'

'Will the British radar have picked us up?'

'This close to the coast, I think so. I'll climb a little to give them a better view. I'll also let our orbits move slowly west, as far as the coast. Both of you keep a constant lookout. Visibility is quite good so we should see them coming. Unless we've drifted well off course, we should be between the RAF airfields at Dyce to the south and Peterhead to the north. But the fighters could approach from any direction.'

There was a tense silence in the cockpit. With just the noise of the engines as background, Wolfgang scanned the sky to the rear and the sides of their Junkers Ju 88 heavy fighter. It was a role he was well used to as the part-time rear gunner in the aircraft.

'A Spitfire is coming from the south!' The tone of Wolfgang's voice in Rudi's headphones suggested he was very scared. 'No, there are two of them! A little high and a little inland.'

'I see them,' said Hans. He seemed to Rudi to be trying to keep his voice calm, without completely succeeding. 'Right, Wolfgang, start firing those red flares. I'll lower the undercarriage and waggle the wings.'

Rudi could do nothing except watch the two fighters close rapidly with them. 'This is a view of a Spitfire I always prayed I'd never see,' he said.

'You can keep on praying,' said Hans, 'only now you should pray they don't open fire. If anyone sees either of them firing, shout and I'll do what I can to get us onto the beach down there, though I'm making no promises.'

There was a moment, just a moment, when Rudi thought that the nearest Spitfire was going to fire at them, but then it turned to match their course and moved in closely on their left, waggling its wings in reply to the movement of the Ju 88. It was close enough for Rudi to see the Spitfire pilot make a 'going down' gesture with his hand to Hans, who echoed it.

'Stop firing the flares, Wolfgang,' said Hans 'He's moving in front of us. He wants us to follow him. He's a brave man, he must know we could blow him out of the sky in seconds. Where's his wingman?'

'He's taken up position behind us,' said Rudi. 'We could get one of them, but the other would certainly get us.'

'Whatever you do, don't touch the machine gun back there,' said Hans. 'The last thing we want is for the pilot of the second aircraft to see it move and think we are about to open fire.'

The thought had already crossed Rudi's mind.

'I've got the undercarriage back up,' said Hans. 'He's taking us south, so I think he wants us to land at RAF Dyce.'

Rudi's attention was fixated on the front of the wings of the Spitfire behind them, where the aircraft's gun muzzles were. He felt paralysed by the overwhelming certainty that at any moment he'd see flashes and sparkles as the guns were fired.

But it didn't happen and after what seemed like an age, but couldn't have been many minutes, Rudi felt and heard the undercarriage being lowered again, then the aircraft's flaps coming down.

As they got close to the ground, the following Spitfire moved to their right, Rudi assumed so it could fly past as they landed. Suddenly there was a flash from the rear of the Ju 88 and a bang that reverberated through the aircraft.

'What was that?' shouted Hans.

'We've been hit!' said Rudi. 'I think someone on the ground opened fire on us.'

'I can't see any signs of flak so if they were firing, I think they've stopped now. What did they hit?'

'The tailplane, I think.'

'The controls seem all right.'

Rudi felt himself exhaling deeply. He wasn't sure how long he'd been holding his breath.

Nothing more was said in the cockpit during the landing, not until they had come to a complete halt.

'They're moving lorries to block the runway ahead of us,' said Wolfgang.

'And behind us,' said Rudi.

'OK,' said Hans. 'I'll stop the engines. Let's get the access hatch and ladder lowered. Make sure we leave our personal weapons in the aircraft. Remember what we discussed. The hard part is behind us. We survived the interception. It will be a lot easier and safer from now on.'

Rudi followed Hans and Wolfgang out of the aircraft, clambering down through the hatch. Several men were standing by the parked lorries on the runway ahead of them. Hans raised his hands and walked slowly over towards two of them, men wearing RAF uniforms with white tops on their hats and pointing submachine guns at him.

Hans's English was much better than Rudi's. As he walked, he called out clearly, 'Hello, we are surrendering. Can I speak to your commanding officer, please?'

A sudden roar made Rudi look up as a Spitfire passed fast and low overhead before pulling up and doing a victory roll. He smiled. The pilot deserved his moment of glory for holding back and not killing them when he so very easily could have done.

CHAPTER ONE

The young woman paid the taxi driver and put her leather suitcase down on the busy pavement beside the station cab road. She returned her purse to the handbag slung diagonally across her body but then had to pick the suitcase up again to get out of the way of an elderly man who was trying to get a large bag into the taxi she'd just vacated.

'I'm sorry,' she said, smiling.

The man merely grunted, barely looking at her as he pushed past.

Princes Street Station was busy. The steam and the smoke from the engines produced an atmosphere that was compounded by the more personal smells of people smoking cigarettes and pipes and, in some cases, those who had been too long without a bath.

People were either on the move or just milling around. Most seemed intent on catching trains or were heading in the other direction, towards the station exit and Edinburgh beyond it. Many of the younger men, and some women, wore uniforms of different services and nations. Some people seemed to be waiting, perhaps for friends and relatives or for their trains to be announced.

Add in the noises of the trains, of whistles, of porters' carts, of people talking, of the news vendor shouting out his incomprehensible headlines and this really was a scene of chaos.

Helen Erickson was wearing a beige raincoat and black beret. Her wavy blonde hair fell to below her shoulders and, as so often when she turned her head, she had to push it back from the right-hand side of her face.

She was worried, though she tried not to show it. Her mother had taken her to the Ritz Hotel in London for a light dinner the previous evening. During the meal, she'd seen a woman at a table a little distance away glance at them several times. The woman was sitting across the table from a man whose back was turned towards them.

Helen was used to attracting attention, but this was different. The woman's glances, despite being veiled, sent unpleasant shivers down her spine. Usually, it was men who looked at her and usually she found it amusing.

She'd been told often enough that she looked very like the young American film star Veronica Lake. When she found out that Veronica Lake was born on the 14th of November 1922, exactly a week before Helen's date of birth, she began to cultivate the likeness. She was off to a good start with her blue eyes and blonde hair and the shape of her face. Helen had also grown her hair so it quite closely replicated Veronica Lake's 'peek-a-boo' style, though without recourse to the expensive hairdressers she suspected were used by Veronica. Where Helen differed most was in her height, which was a good six inches more than Veronica Lake's 4 ft 11in. But height apart, the likeness was now remarkable.

The younger sister of an old school friend had asked why she wanted to copy someone else's appearance when she was beautiful in her own right. Helen replied that she found it fun. She did, but the truth went further. She often found that aspects of her everyday life made her anxious or, on a bad day, unable to cope. Having Veronica to help and, at times, to hide behind, allowed her to assume a confidence that too often deserted her as Helen.

When her mother was seeing her onto the *Night Scotsman* at King's Cross Station the previous night, Helen saw the woman from the Ritz on the platform, a couple of carriages along, with a man she thought was the one who'd been with her earlier. She saw them both look at her briefly before the man got onto the train.

She'd said nothing to her mother, who'd seemed distracted throughout their time together. Anyway, her mother would probably just have given her a complicated lecture about the chances of bumping into random strangers, probably backed up by an equation written on a napkin or a cigarette packet.

Her mother had paid for a single berth first class compartment for her and, on the journey north, she'd locked herself in and tried to sleep. The compartment had cost 24/6, on top of the train fare, but she'd never been so grateful. She was woken at one point in the middle of the night by someone rattling the door as if they were trying to get in. Then she heard a guard out in the corridor telling them they weren't meant to be in that part of the train. She didn't get much sleep after that as she was worried that whoever it was would come back.

Then she thought she saw the man and the woman together again at Waverley Station after the train arrived earlier that morning. She found a back way out of the station and climbed up some steep steps that seemed to go on forever. At the top, she hailed a taxi, which brought her around the back of the castle to Princes Street Station.

Helen already had her onward ticket, so walked round the end of a pair of railway lines to a deep doorway marked 'private' in the run of buildings along that side of the station. This seemed a good place to watch from without being too obvious.

She'd seen on an information board that the train she wanted was due to leave from platform 3 at 9.25 a.m. Platform 3 was only a short distance away. It seemed her train was on one of the tracks she'd walked round the end of.

Helen was taking a last careful look at the people in the main body of the station before making for platform 3 when her breath caught in her throat. The woman she'd seen at the Ritz and at King's Cross and Waverley stations was standing at the near end of the island ticket office. The man was with her. Both had light-coloured overcoats and the man had a dark hat. The woman had blonde hair. They appeared deep in conversation but then Helen saw the man look up and catch her eye.

There was an indistinct announcement over the station's loudspeakers. Helen thought it was about the impending departure of her train. She felt a rising panic. A policeman was standing nearby and she thought of asking for help. But getting involved with the police, even hundreds of miles away from London, was the very last thing she wanted to do just now. She caught the eye of a young naval officer as he walked past. He smiled and for a moment Helen thought he was about to come over and talk to her but, instead, he walked on.

There was another announcement over the speakers, this time clearer.

Helen could see that platform 4 was on the opposite side of the same platform to the train she wanted. She picked up her suitcase, took a deep breath, and marched off towards the trains. Platform 3 was on her right, occupied by the Perth train, the one she needed to catch. To her left was platform 4. According to the second announcement, the train on that platform was due to leave three minutes before the Perth train and was going to a place called Carstairs to connect with a train from Glasgow to London Euston.

The carriages of the train were formed from a series of individual compartments, each with an outside door on either side. She looked behind her and could see the couple who'd been following were hurrying after her.

She picked a compartment that looked full and had a door with its hinges towards the front of the train. On opening the door, she had the impression of people looking back at her. There was probably a seat available if the people on her left shuffled together a little, though they showed no immediate signs of wanting to. That wasn't what Helen had in mind, anyway. She pulled the door closed behind her using the half-open window as a grip and stood with her shoulder against it, so she could watch for the couple passing. If they got into the same compartment she'd be completely stuck, but she hoped that standing by the door added to the impression of how crowded it was.

She saw the woman and man walk past and then heard the slam of the door of the next compartment towards the front of the train.

Whistles started to be blown on the platform almost immediately and Helen heard the engine at the front of the train toot its whistle in response. She still had her suitcase in her left hand and turned towards the door.

She knew she had to time it just right. As the train began to move, she released the shielded latch on the inside of the door and pushed the door open. She saw a young man sitting on the compartment's rear-facing bench reach for her left arm but shook him off, while a woman behind her gasped. Then Helen stepped down onto the platform, having to run a couple of steps to slow down while swinging the compartment door closed with a louder slam than she'd hoped for.

Almost immediately, she saw the man who'd been following her, now without his dark hat, lean through the window in the door of his compartment and look back at her. She got the impression he was about to try to get off the now more quickly moving train until second thoughts or the woman intervened. The odd smile that crossed his face was one she knew she'd remember.

Helen crossed the platform towards the Perth train, just as whistles started to blow again. A porter who'd been standing nearby tried to say something to her.

Helen smiled at him. 'I'm sorry, I got on the wrong train. Please don't stop me from catching the right one this time.'

The porter stepped back, looking bemused. She opened the nearest door and boarded.

The carriages of the Perth train each had a corridor that ran along one side, connecting the compartments, and appeared to be far from busy. She found an empty third class compartment and after placing her suitcase in the overhead luggage netting, sat down. Then she lit a cigarette with badly shaking hands.

Outside, she heard the station announcer say that the first stop for this train would be Falkirk Grahamston. She hadn't listened carefully to the intermediate stations for the Carstairs train but was sure that wasn't one of them. Whoever those people were, she didn't think they were going to be able to follow her any further.

Helen's mother had planned the journey and provided the tickets. She had also given her daughter a copy of the current edition of *Bradshaw's Guide* while they were at the Ritz. This was, she had said, so that Helen could keep track of what was going to be a complicated journey and so she'd be able to cope with any unforeseen problems that might arise. Helen had laughed. Railway timetables were the sort of thing that appealed to her mother's mind, and it was typical of her not to consider whether Helen might have any interest in what, by any standards, was a thick and impenetrable tome.

After she'd been awakened on the sleeper train during the night, Helen had tried to distract herself by tracing the route that her mother had planned for her across several different tables in the guide. One thing that puzzled her was why her mother had decided Helen should change stations in Edinburgh and catch a train via Stirling to Perth. She'd hoped that her journey north might involve a crossing of the Forth Bridge.

Thanks to her *Bradshaw's Guide* she found there was a train that left Waverley Station and went over the bridge and via Dunfermline to Perth in plenty of time to catch the Aberdeen train from there. Taking that train would have saved her having to get to Princes Street Station from Waverley. On the other hand, it was shown as a local service on the timetable, and it gave less of a margin than the one her mother had chosen if the sleeper from Kings Cross had been delayed. But it gave Helen pause for thought to realise that her mother, genius that she was, might simply have overlooked the existence of the alternative train. That wasn't like her at all.

CHAPTER TWO

Monique thanked Bob for retrieving her overnight bag and coat from the boot of the car, which he'd parked near the control tower at RAF Turnhouse. The momentary look of surprise on his face as he looked past her was enough to cause her to laugh. She realised he'd forgotten.

'You had taken to calling it "my Mosquito", Bob,' she said. 'Now it undisputably is!' After accepting Bob's offer to carry her bag, Monique set off towards the aeroplane in question, parked on a nearby area of concrete. Bob walked beside her.

'I know,' he said, 'but what Eric Gill had his people at RAF Leuchars do to it during our second visit to Stockholm wasn't exactly subtle. I'm the deputy head of Military Intelligence 11, for God's sake. It doesn't feel right to be broadcasting where I am to all and sundry like that.'

'Wing Commander Gill spoke to me before we left for Stockholm,' said Monique. 'As he saw it, they couldn't leave the code letters of the squadron that previously owned your Mosquito on the side of the fuselage, and it didn't seem right to put his squadron codes in their place. According to him, it's quite common for senior RAF officers to have their initials on their personal aircraft. He asked me what your full initials were and I realised I didn't know, which was a little embarrassing given we're engaged.

'Anyway, although it was only a very brief trip, while we were away, he found out that you're "Robert Andrew Sutherland" and, thanks to him, so did I. That's why both sides of the aircraft that stands before us have "RA" to the left of the fuselage roundel and "S" to the right of it. I suggested he put a

"B" on both sides to make "BOB" if you include the roundel but he said that the RAF would consider that too informal.'

Monique was pleased to hear Bob laugh.

'I suppose it could have been worse,' he said. 'I'm still getting used to the other additions he made to the markings, which seem a little immodest, to say the least.' He pointed towards the nose of the aircraft they were approaching.

Monique looked again at the red and blue triangle below the front of the cockpit canopy and the small black crosses, each outlined in white, on the side of the nose, in two rows of ten with two more starting a third row. 'The group captain's pennant, as Eric called it, and the 22 kill markings? He thought they were essential additions to your aeroplane. He said it wasn't usual to mark unconfirmed kills, so the 23rd and 24th that I know you should have been credited with can't be shown. He and I also talked about the flying boat you captured in Caithness but decided against marking it up.'

'That was mostly down to you anyway, Monique, so I'm glad it's omitted. But this is an unarmed bomber version of the Mosquito. Kill markings seem out of place.'

'Eric said they are credited to the pilot rather than the aircraft, so it's right you should have them on your plane, whatever it is. Let's face it, if the markings belonged to the aircraft and not the pilot, then you'd have lost all yours when you were shot down in November 1940.'

'That's a fair point, but somehow it all feels so ostentatious.'

Monique laughed again. 'So says the man with four rings on each arm of your uniform jacket and a collection of medal ribbons that broadcasts your achievements almost as clearly as the German crosses on the nose of your aircraft? If you really want to be anonymous, you're going to have to start wearing civilian suits and travelling by train.'

'I was never going to win this argument, was I?' said Bob, smiling. He climbed up the first two rungs of the access ladder before reaching into the aircraft and passing down Monique's sheepskin-lined leather flying jacket, leather helmet and yellow life vest. 'You've done this often enough to know the drill by now, but I'll run through everything again before we take off. When we've got our kit on, follow me in as usual. I'll put your travel bag and your raincoat in the nose. Once we're in the air, remember to keep a lookout for other aircraft and tell me if you see any at all. Don't assume I've seen them. Three eyes are much better than one and these are busy skies.'

As Monique donned the leather flying jacket, she felt a twinge in her right side, not nearly as sharp as it had been at first, but still enough to catch her by surprise when she forgot.

Bob must have seen her wince. 'We'll need to be a bit careful about how we strap you in, Monique.'

'I'll be fine, Bob, so long as the pilot flies like a grown-up.'

He smiled. 'I promise.'

*

Bob took off to the north-west from Turnhouse. After the wheels had retracted and the speed built up, he took a deep breath. Once they were over the distinctive landmark of Hopetoun House he turned north and then north-east, watching out for any barrage balloons protecting the Forth Bridge and the naval dockyard at Rosyth before climbing through a sparse layer of fluffy cloud.

Monique tapped him on his right arm and Bob half-turned

in response to look at her. She pointed to their right. 'There are two aircraft beyond the bridge, lower than us.'

'Thank you.' Bob had seen the two naval training aircraft flying in formation but was grateful Monique was also scanning the skies around them.

'There's something I want to ask you. Bob. Since you let slip that the takeoff in a Mosquito is dangerous, I've noticed just how tense you get for a few moments after we're in the air. Should I be worried?'

'I'd have preferred it if you'd not heard that conversation,' said Bob. 'But you might as well know the full picture. The aircraft's takeoff speed is lower than the speed at which it can safely fly on a single engine. Added to that is the problem that the speed only really builds up after the undercarriage is fully retracted, and that seems to take forever when you're waiting for it.'

'What happens if an engine fails just after you've taken off?' asked Monique.

'As ever, you've spotted the really important question. Overall, it's best not to find out.'

'You must be able to turn back to the airfield and land using the one remaining engine?'

'No, that would simply ensure you crashed while trying to turn, which is likely to be much worse than just flying straight ahead and looking for the smoothest available field to come down in.'

'Ah, I see. You're right. Sometimes it's best not to know.'

Looking round, Bob could see from Monique's eyes above her oxygen mask that she was smiling, despite the seriousness of the conversation. There was a comfortable silence between them for a while.

It was Bob who broke it. 'You've been very secretive about where you're going to be until Thursday afternoon. It's obviously important. When I asked you to come on this trip you emphasised the need for me to get you back to RAF Grangemouth by 4 p.m. this afternoon. The idea seems to be that you then simply disappear for two nights, reappearing at some point on Thursday. What's going on?'

'I'm sorry, Bob, I know very little and I can't share even that.'

'Would it help if I told you that I know you're going to Stirling Castle?' asked Bob.

'How did you know that?'

'I didn't, not for sure. Not until now, anyway. But I can add two and two. I tried to ring Commodore Cunningham in London before we set off this morning to let him know about today's little jaunt. I was told he was tied up in meetings away from his office this morning and was then travelling directly to RAF Northolt for the flight that would take him to Scotland for the Stirling Castle meeting. I think his secretary assumed I was involved. I'm guessing you need to be at RAF Grangemouth this afternoon so you can go from there to the castle for the same meeting.'

Monique laughed. 'I'm genuinely pleased to see that what I've been telling you about not trusting anyone is beginning to sink in, Bob.'

Bob didn't respond.

'Perhaps I should change the subject,' said Monique. 'We're getting a good view of the ground through the breaks in the cloud and, according to this map, we passed Dundee a little while back and that's Montrose ahead of us. You've told me nothing at all about where we are going or why; or why you need me along rather than anyone else from the team. When I asked, if you remember, you said you'd tell me on the way. We are on the way, yet I still know absolutely nothing about what's going on.'

'That's true, Monique. Earlier this morning a Luftwaffe aircraft turned up off the Aberdeenshire coast north of Aberdeen and began circling. When it was intercepted by two Spitfires, its pilot convinced theirs that he was intending to surrender and they escorted him to RAF Dyce, a little to the north-west of Aberdeen. I'm told there's something rather special about the aircraft and the crew of three are saying that they have defected to help the allied cause. One of them speaks fluent English but the other two speak it much less well.

'I was contacted by a senior officer in RAF Fighter Command based near London and asked, given that I'm on the spot when seen from his distant perspective, to go and make a preliminary assessment. That's when I tried to clear my lines with Commodore Cunningham and found he was coming north for an altogether different reason. When we get to Dyce, I hope we can have a look at the aircraft, but I'm no expert on anything more complex than the one we're flying in now. The main purpose of the trip is to interview the crew and make an initial recommendation about whether they are to be treated as defectors or as prisoners of war.'

'And you want me along because you want a fluent German speaker so we can interview all three of the crew?'

'Partly, Monique. But also because I can't think of anyone better qualified to judge their real motivations.'

'They are hardly likely to have arrived in Scotland by accident, are they? The fact they are here at all is a fairly clear indication of what they have in mind.'

'Probably, but not necessarily. There have been cases of German aircraft simply losing their way, perhaps because of instrument failure or because their pilots had become confused and were following a reciprocal course on their compass. Last June, one Luftwaffe pilot in a high-performance fighter became so disorientated during combat over Devon that he then flew north instead of south, mistook the Bristol Channel for the English Channel, and landed his aircraft at an airfield in south Wales rather than the one he had in mind in northern France. What matters here is whether this is an intentional defection, or simply a crew that got lost and chose to pretend they were defecting when they were intercepted.'

'Are you saying that I get to decide their future?'

'Not just you, it will be a joint recommendation between the two of us and others will then review our recommendation. But you know that my German is less than fluent and that puts me at a disadvantage in understanding the finer nuances. And as you are always saying, you are less trusting than I am. We'll find out soon enough. I think that's Aberdeen we can see ahead. We'll pass inland of the city to avoid tempting fate and any bored anti-aircraft gunners. That should position us nicely for our arrival at Dyce.'

*

After landing, Bob followed radio instructions and parked the Mosquito between two Lockheed Hudson marine patrol aircraft on a concrete area close to one of the large, camouflaged aircraft hangars.

As he clambered down the access ladder, he saw Monique shaking hands with a squadron leader, who then turned and saluted him.

'Hello, sir. Thank you for coming so quickly. I'm Simon Whelan, the intelligence officer here at Dyce. When I saw what we'd got this morning, I made sure we put it under cover in the hangar here, away from prying eyes on the ground or in the air. I speak reasonable German and I understand the crew falsely declared engine trouble over the Skagerrak and ditched a life raft before heading this way at sea level. There's every chance the Luftwaffe have no idea that we have their aircraft, and it seems best to try to keep it that way.'

'Thank you, squadron leader. That does seem very sensible. I'm Bob Sutherland, deputy head of Military Intelligence 11, based in Edinburgh. We have a responsibility for military security. As she's probably already told you, this is Madame Monique Dubois, who is part of my team. We're here mainly to form a view about the motives of the crew and make a recommendation about their future. Having talked to them, do you have any initial thoughts on that?'

'You'll obviously want to form your own opinion, sir, but I interviewed them together and then separately and it looks to me very much like a genuine and carefully planned defection. And that's before we begin to think about the potential value of the aircraft they were flying. The Royal Aircraft Establishment are hoping to get a team here by this evening to take a closer look, but I thought you might want to do so yourself before talking to the crew.'

'Lead on, I'm intrigued.'

After the sunshine outside, it took Bob's good eye a little while to adjust to the relative darkness of the hangar. It seemed quite empty. There were several Spitfires in various stages of disassembly at the far end while, at the near end, one corner had been curtained off with green tarpaulins hung by ropes from the inside of the roof structure of the building. The only person in sight was an RAF policeman with a submachine gun standing by the curtained-off area who came to attention and saluted as they approached.

The squadron leader returned the salute and then bent down and picked up the corner of a tarpaulin, pulling it up to form an entrance into the area beyond, which he went through. Bob stood back to let Monique follow Whelan, then did so himself.

Beyond the tarpaulin, Bob found Monique standing next to the squadron leader, looking up at the front of an imposing twin-engine aircraft painted light blue on its lower surfaces and dark green everywhere else.

'What is it, Bob?' asked Monique.

'It's a Junkers Ju 88. It's quite like the one I shot down off the coast of Caithness last September. Only that one was a bomber and I rather think this one is a fighter variant. Is that right, squadron leader?'

'Yes, sir, it's a Ju 88R. Instead of the glass nose of the bomber, it's got what you can see here, a solid nose, with forward-facing guns and cannons, both in the nose and below the fuselage.'

'But what are those things sticking out of the nose?' asked Monique, pointing at a complex and rather ugly set of four thick metal prongs, each carrying a collection of four 'H' shapes made of much thinner metal.

'I'm guessing those are radar aerials,' said Bob. 'Am I right?'

'Yes, sir,' said Whelan. 'That's the obvious part of the FuG 202 Lichtenstein airborne interception radar that's fitted to this version of the aircraft. When I spoke to a wing commander at the Royal Aircraft Establishment, he at first flatly refused to believe we could have one. When I described the antenna to him, I could hear the excitement in his voice. If this is what it seems to be, it could be a hugely important coup, revealing exactly what capabilities the Germans have developed to intercept our bombers. That's why the RAE plan to get here so quickly to have a look themselves.'

'And that's why you think the aircrew are genuine defectors,' said Monique. 'The other side would never risk something as valuable as this just to convince us that a fake defection was real.'

'Precisely, ma'am.'

'We'd better meet the crew, then,' said Bob. 'Where have you got them?'

'We offered them breakfast after they arrived, which they declined, then gave them a chance to catch up on some sleep in the medical centre. They'd been flying since the early hours of the morning. I interviewed them when they were rested. They are under guard, of course, until you've decided whether we should treat them as guests or prisoners. For convenience, I've currently got them in a small canteen that forms part of the run of offices along the side of this hangar. You can talk to them together there, or individually in a room just down the corridor from it.'

'It all seems remarkably quiet here at the moment,' said Monique.

'Yes, ma'am. When I agreed with the station commander that I would have the crew brought here to meet you, he felt it best if the maintenance shift that would normally be working in the hangar and the attached offices was temporarily moved to help in the neighbouring hangar. That way we ensure complete privacy.'

'Lead on,' said Bob. 'We'll talk to them one at a time. I'm happy if you want to sit in but I'd be grateful if you would let us take the lead. My German's good enough for me to follow what's going on, but Madame Dubois will do most of the questioning of the two who don't speak fluent English. I think we should start with the most junior member of the crew and work our way up to the aircraft commander.'

CHAPTER THREE

The sound of the train quickly died away after it had pulled out of the station, though it was possible to see the plume of steam from its funnel for quite some way along the track as it diminished into the distance. The silence that followed was disturbed only by the sound of birds singing, then by a lorry on a nearby road. Helen looked around. Only one other person, a man in a dark coat and hat, had got off her train and he'd headed straight for a footbridge at the end of the platform that crossed the lines to what looked like the station buildings and car park. Coupar Angus station seemed otherwise deserted.

Helen knew that she now had an hour to wait for the 1.00 p.m. train to Blairgowrie. She was frustrated because she knew from her nocturnal reading of *Bradshaw's Guide* that it was only a ten-minute journey. She unfolded the map of Scotland her mother had also given her. It wasn't very detailed, but it showed enough to confirm that Blairgowrie was only a short distance from Coupar Angus.

It wasn't as if the connection was timed for passengers coming the other way on the main line, from Aberdeen. Helen looked along the line in the direction her train had gone. The steam from its engine had barely had time to dissipate before being replaced by the plume from a train coming towards her. That was the train from Aberdeen. Anyone on it who wanted to connect with the train to Blairgowrie would need to wait almost as long as her.

She knew that Uncle George and Aunt Jemima's farm was a few miles on the other side of Blairgowrie, but still wished they could have come to meet her here. On the other hand, she knew she should just be grateful that they'd agreed to take her in over Easter.

The train from Aberdeen stopped, but no one got off. It then pulled away, leaving the station quiet and deserted once more; though not entirely deserted. Helen realised that the man who'd got off her train was standing at the foot of the stairs down from the footbridge, near the station buildings, apparently looking at her. He was some distance away because the buildings were set in the angle between the railway line behind her and some goods sidings that curved off to one side, so she couldn't be sure. She took a few steps along the platform in that direction and when she looked again there was no one there. After what had happened earlier it still caused her to shiver.

She told herself that she shouldn't be frightened by shadows. The man who'd got off the train wasn't the one she'd seen with the woman. The idea of three people following her was completely absurd. Though perhaps not that much more absurd than the idea of two people following her, and she was sure that had happened.

Her concern was that if she was being followed again, then the man must know she was waiting for the Blairgowrie train and would be able to find out when it got there. He'd also be able to get to Blairgowrie ahead of her if he took a taxi. She smiled as a thought struck her. If she took a taxi herself, direct to Easter Crimond, anyone hoping to follow her from Blairgowrie would be disappointed.

Helen walked to the end of the platform and then crossed the iron footbridge to the main station buildings. From the footbridge, she could see that the car park beyond was, apart from one parked car and a grocer's lorry with no one in it, empty.

She went into the wooden ticket office.

A moment later a porter appeared through a door on one side. 'Can I help you?'

'Hello. I was wondering if there might be a taxi available?'

'You've missed it, I'm afraid. Sandy and his taxi are usually here to meet the two main line trains. But I know he's gone to Blairgowrie. A foreign gentleman asked me how to get there without waiting for the 1.00 p.m. train and I directed him to Sandy, who was parked outside.'

'Aren't there any others?'

'I'm sorry, no. And I'm sure Sandy won't come back here afterwards. There would be no point.'

After the porter had gone back through the door he had emerged from, Helen walked out into the car park. She sat on a wooden bench and opened her suitcase to extract a writing pad and an envelope. Despite her concern that she might be causing unnecessary alarm, she wrote a letter to her father setting out what had happened and letting him know how worried she was. She knew that she could have sent him a telegram from Coupar Angus or possibly telephoned him instead, but somehow that seemed much more serious. She didn't want to appear to be panicking and, above all else, she didn't want her father to think she was just being a silly young woman. Setting things out carefully and rationally seemed the best way to allow him to make his own mind up about what was going on.

Helen found a postage stamp in her purse and stuck it on the envelope. She then walked over to a post box outside the station and, before she had time to talk herself out of it, posted her letter.

*

Her arrival in Blairgowrie should have felt like the welcome end of an awfully long journey. But Helen had found herself becoming anxious as soon as her train left Coupar Angus and her anxiety only grew as it reached the end of the branch line, ten minutes later.

Once off the train at Blairgowrie station, she found herself looking around nervously. There were a few people, railway staff and others, inside the station, but Helen didn't get the sense anyone was waiting to get onto the train to go back to Coupar Angus and wherever it went beyond there. She couldn't remember from looking at the timetable whether it made the return journey immediately or later. She was very relieved not to see the man in the dark coat and hat.

Outside the station, it was much busier than it had been in Coupar Angus. Again, Helen looked around carefully and could see no sign of the 'foreign gentleman'.

She only hazily remembered what her Aunt Jemima looked like. She'd last seen her when her uncle and aunt and her cousins Andrew and Benjamin had stayed with Helen and her parents in Cambridge. But that must have been five or more years earlier, certainly well before the war started. This time when she looked around it was more hopefully.

'Are you Helen Erickson?'

The voice came from above her and Helen looked up, surprised, at the young man in a pony and trap she'd paid little attention to. Pulled by a black horse, the trap had a faded green body mounted on four equally faded yellow wooden wheels. The driver seemed to be in his late teens.

She smiled. 'Yes, I am. Are you Benjamin Moncrieff?'

The young man's face lit up as he smiled back. 'I much prefer "Ben". I'm here to take you to Easter Crimond. Why don't you get up here beside me? There ought to be enough room under the seats for your suitcase.'

Helen did as Ben had suggested. 'What's the horse's name?' she asked.

'We call him Raven.'

'Is that because he's black?'

'I suppose so,' said Ben. 'I've never actually thought about it very much.' He encouraged the horse into a walk, and they pulled away from the station and into the heart of Blairgowrie itself.

Helen again found herself scanning the faces of the people she could see.

'Mum says that you're a medical student in London and that you're training to become a doctor,' said Ben.

'That's right,' said Helen. 'I'm studying at the London School of Medicine for Women.'

'I don't think I've ever met a woman doctor,' said Ben.

'And you've not met one yet. I'm only twenty and have plenty of studying ahead of me.' Helen left unsaid the end of the sentence: '...*if they don't expel me when they find out.*'

She tried to put the thought out of her mind and carried on. 'There aren't as many female doctors as there ought to be. A lot of medical schools won't take women on as students. How about you, Ben?'

'I'm seventeen,' said Ben. 'I'm eighteen in September and will join the army as soon as my birthday comes round. I've already tried, at the beginning of the year. I went down to Perth to sign up with the Black Watch, but someone must have realised I was too young.'

Helen didn't know how to respond to that so changed the subject. 'It's quite a while since you all visited us in

Cambridge. Don't you have an older brother, Andrew?'

'Yes, he's nineteen. He's serving with the Black Watch in Tunisia. Mum spends most of her time frantic with worry about him.'

'Is it far to the farm?'

'About three miles. I'm sure Mum would have liked to pick you up in the car, but we very rarely use it because of the petrol restrictions. She thought this was more suitable than the tractor and trailer.'

After they left the edge of the town, Ben clicked his teeth and shook the reins and Raven started to trot.

Not far outside Blairgowrie, they passed a bus and then a lorry going in the opposite direction but, though Helen checked from time to time, she could see no sign of anyone behind them.

The horse was startled at one point when what Ben said was a Wellington bomber came from behind and passed extremely low and extremely noisily over them, apparently following the line of the road they were on. He was quickly able to calm Raven down.

The road had quite steeply rising ground to the north, to their right. There were a couple of small farms and cottages close by and they passed a castle, which seemed to Helen to sum up Scotland beautifully. At one point the road ran alongside the edge of a small loch.

Helen started to relax. There was a chill in the wind, but the sunshine was warm. With her coat and a blanket that Ben had given her, she was quite comfortable. What was most surprising was, once the aeroplane had passed, just how quiet everything seemed except for the rhythmic sound of Raven's hooves on the road.

'I remember that visit to Cambridge with Andrew and Mum and Dad,' Ben said. 'I was about twelve. I think our mutual grandmother had died not long before. Afterwards, my mum said she'd been hoping to rebuild bridges with her sister Elizabeth, your mother. I suppose it says everything that our families haven't met again since then.'

'Do you know why our mothers drifted apart?' asked Helen. 'Until I saw her yesterday in London mine had seldom talked about it.'

'What did she say yesterday?' asked Ben.

'She seemed more reflective and worried than I think I've ever seen her. She said it was a shame she'd not kept more closely in touch with your mother, and it would be good for me to get to know you all better. I almost got the feeling she saw me as some sort of diplomatic envoy. Please don't tell your mother that. I don't want to give her the impression this is anything other than a simple visit by her niece.'

'I'll not mention it, though I hope you'll feel you can talk about it while you are with us. I'm sure she'll not say anything to you, but Mum is a little bitter about the way things turned out,' said Ben. 'She is older by a few years and had to cope with the idea that her younger sister was a mathematical genius who got a scholarship to Cambridge University and went on to teach there, then married a successful RAF pilot who's now a senior officer. Mum had done some secretarial training after leaving school and then married a farmer she met on holiday with her parents, and I suppose with your mother, in Scotland. They'd travelled up from London, where they lived, and were staying in Pitlochry. Mum and Dad met at a dance in the Atholl Palace Hotel.

'Dad inherited the farm when our grandad died, and

grandad had inherited it from his father before him. I sometimes think that Mum envies what she thinks is her sister's more exciting life. As far as I know, she's not met your mum since our visit to Cambridge.'

'Given all that, it's especially good of her to let me stay now,' said Helen.

'She's really looking forward to getting to know you properly,' said Ben. 'I must ask, though, don't you have anywhere else to go? I'm sorry, that didn't sound very welcoming. I'm simply curious.'

'Don't worry, I understand why you asked. I live in a not very nice flat I share with three other women in a not very nice part of London. It's all we can afford, even with help from our parents. Until last autumn, I went back to Cambridge whenever I had time off. But then my mother was asked to leave her teaching post at Cambridge University to do other work. She never says what she does and our house in Cambridge is now rented out to an academic she knows and his family, so I couldn't stay there even if I wanted to. Over the Christmas holidays, I went to stay with my father in Oban, on the west coast. He was stationed there at the time, and he rents a house there. My mother was able to spend a few days at Christmas with us, too.

'But Dad's been posted away from Oban for three months so there was nowhere that I could go to over Easter until your mother offered to take me in. I could have stayed in London, but the flat is simply somewhere to sleep between studying and working. It's not somewhere I want to spend more time than necessary.' Helen thought this was a good moment to change the subject. 'What do you do?'

'Until I join up, I'm working with Dad on the farm,' said

Ben. 'I'm praying that Andrew survives the war. For the obvious reason, of course. He is my brother, after all. But I also want him to be able to inherit Easter Crimond, which will leave me free to do something more interesting.'

'Have you any idea what?' asked Helen.

'Do you promise not to laugh?'

'Of course.'

'After the war is over, I want to study to become an architect.'

'That sounds fascinating,' said Helen.

A couple of miles along the road from Blairgowrie, they came to a junction with a side road that had a phone box standing on the corner. Ben slowed Raven to a walk and turned right onto a much more minor road that climbed through a heavily wooded landscape. They'd not gone far when they encountered a steep hill and Ben got down to walk alongside Raven and lighten the load the horse was pulling. When the slope of the hill eased, he climbed back onto the trap.

The slope changed from rising to descending at the point where they emerged from the woods. As the view ahead of them opened out, Ben called for Raven to stop.

Helen could see that the road descended into a shallow valley. The bottom of the valley was marked by a thick line of trees that meandered slightly as if it was following a stream. The fields on their side of the valley, on both sides of the road, were covered with bushes that had been planted in lines that ran up and down the slope, apparently aligned from north to south. The fields on the lower level of the far side of the valley were likewise covered, though as the ground rose the fields turned to what seemed to be pasture and as they reached the skyline a much browner colouration suggested moorland.

Standing a little way off to the left of the road, just as it reached the line of trees, was an attractive farmhouse built of honey-coloured stone and topped off with a slate roof. The windows that faced them from the upper floor emerged from the lower part of the sloping roof.

A track from the road went through an open gateway and then forked. One part ended in front of the farmhouse. Another headed further to the left and passed clear of the front of the farmhouse before ending in a farmyard. There were two barns on the far side of the farmyard and some wooden sheds closing in its left-hand side. Helen could see a red tractor standing in the farmyard amidst a collection of trailers and farming implements, but there were no other signs of activity.

On the opposite side of the road to the farmhouse was a row of three small cottages, one of which, the one furthest away from them, had no roof. Smoke was coming from the chimneys of the other two cottages and those of the farmhouse.

'Welcome to Easter Crimond,' said Ben.

CHAPTER FOUR

The room they were using for the crew interviews had a window looking out onto the airfield, while a bookcase at the end next to the door held what looked to Bob like technical manuals. The panes of the window were covered by the normal criss-cross of protective tape to reduce flying glass in the event of an air attack. When they'd first come into the room, Bob had looked out and seen that his Mosquito was being refuelled a little further along the concrete area outside.

Monique and Bob had taken seats on the long side of the meeting table, with the window on their left and the door to their right. Facing them was a wall carrying a large blackboard divided into horizontal strips showing what seemed to be aircraft servicing records. Whelan was seated at the end of the table nearest the door.

While they waited for one of the RAF Police corporals guarding – or protecting – the Germans to bring in the third member of the crew, Monique stood up and went to the window.

Bob could see the tension in the set of her back and neck. 'What's this one's name, Squadron Leader Whelan?' he asked.

'Oberleutnant Hans Weber, the aircraft captain.'

'His rank is roughly equivalent to flight lieutenant, isn't it, whereas the other two are what we'd call sergeants?'

'That's right, sir.'

Monique returned from the window to take her seat next to Bob. She briefly met his gaze and smiled. As usual, she was dressed smartly but rather plainly, today in a dark jacket and skirt. He knew she preferred to stay in the background at any gathering. This was made more difficult for her by her striking presence, which tended to work against her efforts to remain anonymous.

Monique's dark hair framed a face that was classically beautiful, but oddly flawed in a way that to his mind made her even more attractive. He knew she could be happy, joyful even. But not today. Sometimes, Monique's eyes could take on a dark, haunted look, as if they had seen too many things their owner wished they hadn't. She was 30, some seven months younger than him. She'd packed a lot of living into that time, by no means all of it pleasant. She had told him her dark and complex story while they'd been locked up together in the cellar of a shooting lodge in Caithness the previous September and Bob knew she carried with her more than her fair share of ghosts.

The darkness behind her eyes had seemed a more frequent presence since they'd returned from the second of their trips to Stockholm at the beginning of the month. Bob had come back with a new nightmare to replace the one that had dogged him since November 1940, while Monique had acquired two cracked ribs and more ghosts to add to her collection.

His thoughts were interrupted by a knock on the door.

The RAF policeman showed Oberleutnant Weber into the room then retreated into the corridor and pulled the door closed behind himself. Weber was a slim man of a little over average height with blond hair and blue eyes. Bob guessed his age as about 30. He was wearing a black leather flying jacket over an open-necked shirt. His grey uniform trousers were tucked into black flying boots and his head was bare.

Monique had done most of the questioning, in German, during the first two interviews. They'd agreed Bob would take the lead this time.

'Hello Oberleutnant Weber. Please take a seat.' Bob waved towards the two empty seats on the far side of the table. As Weber sat down on the one opposite Monique, Bob continued. 'I'm Group Captain Sutherland and I'm with military intelligence. My colleague here is Madame Dubois. I believe you met Squadron Leader Whelan earlier. I understand you speak fluent English. Are you happy that we talk to you in English now?'

Weber smiled. 'Yes, of course.'

'Can we offer you a cigarette?'

'No, thank you.'

'Very well. Can I start by asking how you come to be here? Can you talk me through the flight you made this morning?'

'We are part of IV Gruppe of Nachtjagdgeschwader 3, a night fighter unit based at Aalborg near the northern tip of Denmark. We took off from there at 3 a.m. We had been briefed to patrol to the north, over the Skagerrak, in the hope of intercepting a British civilian aircraft known to have taken off from Stockholm and almost certainly en route to Leuchars in Scotland.'

'Did you know what type it was?'

'No. They are changing the aircraft they use on the service from older types to the Mosquito. The Ju 88 is a lovely aircraft in many ways but, even with the Lichtenstein radar, I suspect that the most ardent of my comrades would stand little chance of intercepting a Mosquito. They are so much faster than us, even before you take account of the drag of the radar antenna mounted on the nose of our aircraft.'

'So not much happened?'

'No. We patrolled for over two hours, until well after the

aircraft we were looking for would have passed, then landed to refuel at Kristiansand in Norway. We had an early breakfast there, which we took our time over. After it was fully daylight, we took off again, supposedly to return to Aalborg. Over the Skagerrak, we made a radio call on the emergency frequency to say our starboard engine was on fire and I descended to extremely low level. We jettisoned a life raft, hoping to mislead anyone who came looking for us, and then we headed for Scotland.

'I imagine you know the rest, group captain. Could you please pass on my thanks to the Spitfire pilots who intercepted us for not shooting us down? The one who flew in front of us must have known we had forward-facing weapons. He deserves some recognition for his bravery. I was less happy when we were hit by ground fire while landing.'

Bob looked questioningly at Whelan.

The squadron leader leaned forwards in his chair. 'One of our anti-aircraft gunners had turned a deaf ear to the instruction over the loudspeakers across the airfield to hold fire. Fortunately, he only got a couple of rounds off with a Lewis gun before someone else stopped him. Even more fortunately only one round hit, and it hit the tailplane without causing significant damage.'

'I think that's covered what you did,' said Bob, turning back to face Oberleutnant Weber. 'Now I'd like to discuss why you did it.'

'It's been a long time coming. Oberfeldwebel Hartmann and I first met when he was part of my crew on Heinkel He 111 bombers in the Condor Legion during the Spanish Civil War. Have you ever been a bomber pilot, group captain?'

'No, I flew fighters.'

'In a bomber, you are even further removed from the effects of what you do than you are in a fighter. All you see are distant and usually quiet explosions on the ground. If you're looking ahead as the pilot, you don't even see them. It's easy to separate yourself from reality. Then, one day in the summer of 1938, we got the chance to visit a small Spanish town we'd bombed a week earlier, and which had subsequently been occupied. Stupidly enough, I was one of those who decided to go. From that moment to this, I've been looking for a way to remove myself from the war.'

'But that was five years ago,' said Bob. 'Why did it take so long?'

'You don't just resign from the Luftwaffe in the middle of a war. I'd have been shot or worse. And I had a wife and a young son to think about, and parents. That's why I took part in the Air Battle for England in 1940 as a bomber pilot. Since then, I've filled a mix of operational and training roles. I met Oberfeldwebel Hartmann again when I was posted to my present unit at Aalborg at the end of last year. I knew he was as disillusioned as I was in Spain, and it didn't take me long to realise that he still is. I'm sure you'll have asked him about that yourself. And it should be obvious to anyone who's not blinded by Nazi lies that since our defeat at the Battle of Stalingrad the war can only have one possible outcome.'

'What about your wife and son and parents?' asked Monique.

Bob could see she was thinking about her father. She'd discovered in Stockholm that he had died under interrogation by the Gestapo in Paris in 1941 because of what the Germans regarded as her defection to Britain the previous year. That she'd been an MI6 agent since a remarkably early stage in her complex life, so what she'd done wasn't technically a 'defection', wouldn't have helped save her father. He knew she'd found asking the other two members of the crew about the implications of what they were doing for their relatives back in Germany hard, and it was obviously no easier this time.

'My wife and son went to live with my parents in Bremen. All four were killed in a bombing raid on the night of 25-26 June last year.'

'I'm sorry about their deaths,' said Monique. 'Hearing that leaves me wondering why you want to defect to help the people who killed your family. I'd have thought you would want revenge on Britain.'

'At first, perhaps. That was why I applied to transfer from bombers to night fighters. But it didn't take long to realise that while it might have been someone like the group captain here who flew the plane that dropped the bomb that killed my family, it wasn't him who started the war. It wasn't a pilot just like me who was responsible for my family's deaths, it was Hitler and the madmen who surround him.'

There was a pause while Weber looked down at the table. Then he looked up at Bob. 'Do you think I could have that cigarette now?'

Bob looked at Squadron Leader Whelan, who pulled a packet out of his lower tunic pocket, offered it to Weber, and then lit the cigarette the German had selected with a stainless steel lighter. Whelan then offered the packet to Bob and Monique, who declined, before taking and lighting one for himself. He pushed one of the glass ashtrays on the table in Weber's direction while pulling the other towards himself.

'The room they are keeping us in has windows out onto the airfield like that one,' said Weber. 'I saw the two of you arrive in the Mosquito that's parked out there. It was difficult to see clearly because of the angle, but I got the impression from the markings on the nose that you were a successful fighter pilot, group captain.'

'Let's just say that you and I were on opposing sides in 1940 in what we call the Battle of Britain,' said Bob.

'It's obvious from the crosses on your aircraft and from your medal ribbons that you shot down many of those I flew with. Don't worry, I know you were just defending your homeland in what you believed was a just cause. I don't hold it against you and, in your shoes, I would have done the same if I were able enough. I must ask, though, how many aircraft do you think I've shot down as a night fighter pilot? I'll tell you. Not one. It quickly became clear to me that it was folly to do anything that prolonged a war being fought in the wholly unjust cause of the Nazis even by an instant. At first, that wasn't a problem but, after a while, people began to ask why such a highly experienced pilot and crew were so ineffective. This has become even more obvious now I'm flying an aircraft with the Lichtenstein radar fitted.'

'I am sure colleagues of mine who are experts in the field will want to talk to you about the radar,' said Bob, 'but give me an idea of how much it helps in practice.'

'You have to imagine an invisible cone projecting from the front of the aircraft which can reach out to over 4km if the target's as large as a Lancaster bomber, or less than 2km for a small fighter,' said Weber. 'If there's an aircraft in that cone, then the wireless operator, in our case that's Oberfeldwebel Hartmann, can talk the pilot onto the target. He uses a set of three cathode ray tubes that indicate the target's range, whether it's left or right, and whether it's higher or lower. Over

Germany, it's increasingly being used to shoot down allied bombers without them ever being aware of the presence of the night fighter hunting them.'

'And you feared your failure to shoot anything down, even with the radar, would give you away?'

'Yes, but our Ju 88s have a crew of three and Rudi Hartmann and I couldn't defect on our own. We'd talked about simply holding the third member of the crew at gunpoint until we'd landed. But unless we killed him, word would inevitably have got out about what we'd done. Then Rudi came across Oberfeldwebel Seidel. It seems that over one too many drinks in their mess one night, young Seidel let slip to Rudi that he was worried about a girl he'd had a relationship with at university in Munich, before breaking off his studies to join the Luftwaffe. She'd been arrested by the Gestapo in February for membership of the White Rose resistance group. Some of those arrested at the same time had been executed soon afterwards, but others, including this girl, were still being held. Rudi got Seidel talking about his views more widely and it became clear that we had our third willing defector as soon as I could get him assigned to the crew.'

'What do you think you will gain from defecting?' asked Bob.

'Just the obvious. Staying alive to see the end of the war. Our aircraft and its radar should be extremely valuable to your people, but you need us, especially Rudi and I, to show you how it works in detail. We also have several publications about the radar in the aircraft that we are not meant to carry in flight to avoid them falling into enemy hands. I hope that in return for what we are giving you, you will agree to provide all three of us with new identities. It goes without saying that if you simply put us in a prisoner of war camp then our lives will be over very quickly. We can be of much more value to you if you allow us to work with you.'

Bob turned enough to catch Monique's eye with his good one. The tiny nod of her head indicated her feelings to him. He looked back at Weber. 'I'm sure you understand that the final decision about your future will be made by others, but I have been asked to make a recommendation. In the short term, as you say, our experts will need your help to fully understand the Lichtenstein radar fitted to your aircraft. I believe they hope to be here later today. I will be recommending that if you and Oberfeldwebel Hartmann cooperate with them fully for as long as it takes to complete their work, then you should be viewed and treated as defectors and given new identities and new lives. I will be recommending that Oberfeldwebel Seidel is interviewed further but will say that my view, having heard what he has to say, is that he should also be treated as a defector. Until the radar people arrive, and probably for a little time to come, you'll be held under guard, though that will be as much for your protection as to restrict your movement.'

Weber sat back in his chair and exhaled a plume of cigarette smoke. He looked as if he'd shed five years in an instant. 'Thank you, group captain. You won't regret it.'

CHAPTER FIVE

On the return flight, Bob passed well to the north of Dundee, following a nearly straight line towards their destination.

'You should be there in plenty of time,' he said over the intercom. 'Who's meeting you at RAF Grangemouth?'

'I gather the army are laying on cars and drivers. Stirling Castle is the regimental depot of the Argyll and Sutherland Highlanders. They are providing a secure venue for the meeting you've discovered Commodore Cunningham is attending.'

'With you,' said Bob.

'Yes, with me. I understand that the commodore and I are not the only people arriving at RAF Grangemouth today requiring transport to Stirling Castle so I'm sure I'll have no trouble getting there. What are your plans for the evening?'

'I've not thought about it. Having Michael and Betty living with us in the bungalow complicates matters a little and I've no desire to play gooseberry. With you not there, my dining options would normally be a walk to the fish and chip shop on St John's Road or something a little more formal at the officers' mess at RAF Turnhouse. First, though, I need to go to the office to write up a short report about today and give my recommendations.'

'I thought you resolved that before we left Dyce when you phoned that air vice marshal in Fighter Command?'

'I did, but it seems best to back that up in writing so there's no misunderstanding. It shouldn't take too long. It will also ensure Commodore Cunningham knows I'm keeping busy. I'll send a copy to his office.'

They lapsed into silence for a while. Bob had chosen to fly

below the scattered cloud, and they were approaching Loch Leven at quite low level when Monique spoke again.

'Have you had any thoughts about the wedding, Bob?'

It took a split second for Bob's brain to engage, but at least he avoided uttering the words *'what wedding?'* that had begun to form.

'Just that I'd like there to be one,' he said, 'and without too much delay. As Dad said to me when we visited them on Sunday, I need to make sure you don't have time for second thoughts.'

'That's why I'm asking. I suppose I'd had in mind a registry office wedding as the only realistic option. But your mother took me to one side when we were there to suggest you and I visit a little church she knows in a place called Dalmahoy. It's not all that far from the edge of Edinburgh or their house in Cramond. She said it would be a lovely place for us to get married. She also said that the attitude they are likely to have at the church to past entanglements like my two dead husbands might be more relaxed than some. And that's before we start to unpick the complications caused by my changes of identity.'

'Didn't you say you could produce a set of documents that would allow you to get married as Monique Dubois?'

'Yes, and I'm sure I can. But my colleagues in MI5 still think of me as Vera Duval and as you know I've had many other names too. What your mother said led me to think that this church might not want to create problems for me, while others perhaps would.'

'I'm pleasantly surprised to hear that Mum's pushing us in that direction. Her family were Presbyterians. Not Church of Scotland, but one of the smaller denominations that have split off over the past couple of centuries. The church she's talking about is St Mary's Dalmahoy. It's part of the Scottish Episcopal Church which, as she rightly told you, takes a less rigid view of the world. Dad's family were Episcopalians. I've been to a wedding at St Mary's, and it does have a nicely intimate feel. It's a really good idea.'

Bob saw Monique's eyes light up.

'It would certainly make my third wedding very different from the first two,' she said. 'It would also give it a sense of authenticity and permanence that I find appealing. Let's visit the church as soon as I'm back from Stirling. By the way, I asked your father on Sunday if he'd give me away and he said he'd be very happy to.'

'I was sure he would be, but it's great to have confirmation.'

'Bob, religion has never really formed part of my life and I'm a little confused by what you just said about Episcopalians. I thought Scotland was traditionally divided into Protestants and Catholics?'

'Up to a point, it is. But there must be half a dozen or more different denominations on what you'd call the Protestant side of that. The biggest by far is the Church of Scotland, but schisms caused by various disagreements have caused others to split off from time to time.'

'And the Scottish Episcopal Church is one of those?'

'No, it isn't,' said Bob. 'The Scottish Episcopal Church is an Anglican church, a sort of sister church to the Church of England and other churches in many other countries. Something that sets it apart from the Church of Scotland is that it is governed by bishops, while the Church of Scotland and its various splinters are Presbyterian churches governed by representatives of their congregations.'

'Does that make much difference?'

'You wouldn't think so, would you? But if you look at Scottish history it was King Charles I's efforts to impose government by bishops on the Presbyterian Church of Scotland that led to a riot in St Giles' Cathedral in Edinburgh in 1637. This in turn led to a series of escalating conflicts culminating with what is wrongly known as the "English" Civil War, with the execution of Charles I, and with the occupation of Scotland by Cromwell. The conflict didn't end until the restoration of Charles II in 1660, 23 years after it had begun. There was a time when a difference of opinion about church governance could quite literally be a matter of life and death.'

'Perhaps it's best if I add that to the list of things that I shouldn't mention to them,' said Monique. 'That's the River Forth we can see ahead. It's not far now, is it?'

'No, it's not. RAF Grangemouth is just beyond the far side of the river. That's where my squadron was moved to with our Spitfires in October 1939, just after we'd been mobilised. We only stayed a month before moving to an airfield in East Lothian, beyond Edinburgh. That was where our real war began, defending eastern Scotland and the Newcastle area from Luftwaffe air raids.'

'It will be interesting for you to see how it's changed,' said Monique.

'I know already,' said Bob. 'I accompanied our RAF colleagues on one of their routine security visits the day before you and I made our second trip to Stockholm. You were in London at the time. The grass strips of late 1939 have been replaced by tarmac runways. I was pleased to see that the main features I remembered, an impressive pre-war watch office and two enormous hangars built in its days as the Central Scotland

Airport are still there.'

Bob landed at Grangemouth from the east and taxied round to a large 'D' shaped area of concrete not far from the attractive watch office, which extended forwards like the superstructure of an ocean liner from between the two hangars. Here he was directed to come to a halt next to an Avro Anson light transport aircraft that he'd seen land ahead of them.

After the Mosquito's engines had stopped, Monique unstrapped herself and then bent down, slightly awkwardly, to reach through into the nose compartment for her overnight bag and coat.

'I don't think you're going to have a problem finding someone to take you to Stirling Castle,' said Bob.

'I didn't expect to. But what makes you say that?'

'Look who's just climbed out of the Anson that came in ahead of us.'

'Commodore Cunningham?' asked Monique.

'No, see for yourself.'

At that moment Major General Sir Peter Maitland, the Director of Military Intelligence, turned to look at the Mosquito. Bob caught his glance and raised a gloved hand in greeting. Sir Peter nodded in response. If he was surprised to see Bob, he didn't show it. There was a man in civilian clothes standing with the general, who was in full uniform.

'Good God, what's he doing here?' asked Monique.

'I'm not a great believer in coincidence, so I imagine he's taking part in the meeting you are attending. Didn't you know?'

'No, absolutely not!'

'We need to get the hatch and ladder lowered. If you're going to ask him for a lift, you'd better not keep him waiting.'

'I want a kiss, first. We have just been discussing our

wedding.'

'OK,' said Bob, 'but briefly, and here in the cockpit. I'd feel a bit awkward taking you into a passionate embrace while standing on the concrete with Sir Peter and his chum watching.'

'He'll be able to see anyway,' said Monique.

'I don't mind him seeing. I just don't want to give the impression I'm forcing him to watch.'

Bob came up for air after a rather longer kiss from Monique than he'd expected. When he looked out of the cockpit again, Sir Peter and the man with him had gone.

'It looks like you're going to have to find another car to get you to Stirling,' he said.

'To be honest, the idea of making small talk with the general wasn't very appealing. I'm sure I'll manage.'

Bob had seen the effect of Monique's smile on any male she turned it on and was in no doubt she would find transport without any difficulty.

CHAPTER SIX

Helen thought that Aunt Jemima looked quite like her sister Elizabeth, Helen's mother. Her blonde hair was much shorter, but it was easy to see they were related. It had soon become obvious to Helen after her arrival that in other ways the sisters were very different. Aunt Jemima bustled around in a very no-nonsense way, asking when Helen had last eaten and preparing a pot of soup in what seemed a remarkably short time. Helen's mother tended to be more detached from the practical side of life. If a relative had arrived at their house in Cambridge in the days they still lived there, it would probably have fallen to Helen to think about feeding them.

Aunt Jemima cheerfully brushed aside Helen's suggestion they discuss how to use her ration book to ensure no one went short during her stay. There was plenty of time for that, she said, before they made their next shopping trip into Blairgowrie.

After lunch, her aunt sent Ben to pick vegetables from the kitchen garden and walked with Helen to the right-hand end cottage in the row of three across the road, one of the two with roofs on. This was where Helen would be sleeping, she explained. It was just large enough to have a small sitting room and a kitchen downstairs and two bedrooms upstairs.

There was a toilet in a little lean-to building just outside the back door and water could be heated for washing on the stove in the kitchen or she could wash in the farmhouse. There was a fire lit in the sitting room and, to Helen, everything about the cottage felt wonderfully cosy.

The long journey and the anxiety about being followed,

something she'd decided not to mention to her aunt or Ben, caught up with Helen. She spent the rest of the afternoon sleeping.

It was early evening when she had her tea, sitting at the large wooden table in the even larger kitchen of the farmhouse with Ben and Aunt Jemima. The room had a range on one side and her aunt had prepared venison, potatoes and cabbage, with gravy. Helen thought it was delicious.

The sound of the back door banging open caused Helen to jump.

'Boots!' shouted Jemima, loudly. 'And remember we have a guest.'

There was some muttering from the lobby between the back door and the kitchen door and sounds of movement, then Uncle George came into the kitchen with socks on his feet and a flat cap on his head. He was otherwise wearing tweed trousers and a green cardigan.

Helen had a memory of him as a large man and, as he entered, she saw that she'd not been mistaken.

'Perhaps I should have said "boots and hat",' said Aunt Jemima.

Uncle George smiled warmly back at her and removed his hat. 'Hello. It's a long time since I've seen you, Helen. How are your mother and father?'

After her uncle sat down for his meal, Helen passed on the latest news, such as it was, about her parents.

'I'm pleased you're here. You know that you're always welcome. You'd be especially welcome in July and August, of course, when we harvest the raspberries and need every hand we can get. But I'm pleased to see you even when I'm not looking for a source of cheap labour.' He smiled.

'You said you were going to be back in time for tea, George,' said Jemima.

'I know, I'm sorry love. Angus and I were on the track of a large stag on Cochrage Muir, not far from the old road to Bridge of Cally.'

'Did you get him?' asked Ben.

'Yes, I did, but it took time. Then we had to gralloch him and put him on Missy. Angus is hanging him over in the shed now.'

'George, please remember we have a visitor who might not want to hear too much detail about how the venison she's just been eating is prepared.'

'Sorry, yes, of course.'

'Angus would be welcome to join us.'

'He knows. That will be him now.'

Helen heard the back door close and a few moments later a man with a lined face and grey hair wearing a tweed cap and a black donkey jacket came into the kitchen. He smiled when he saw Helen and she liked the way his dark eyes twinkled.

Jemima stood up, also smiling. 'You're as bad as George, Angus. I don't want to give our visitor the impression we eat in a barn. Give me your coat and hat and I'll hang them up. Have you washed your hands? Helen, this is Angus, as you'll have worked out.'

Angus was wearing a tweed waistcoat beneath his jacket, above well-worn brown corduroy trousers. He reached over to shake Helen's hand before taking a seat at the table.

George looked at Helen. 'Angus helps us out here on the farm and lives in the cottage next door to the one we've put you in. I'm sure you won't mind but he has difficulty sleeping and spends most of each night practising his bagpipe playing.'

'George!' said Aunt Jemima. 'Don't tease!'

Helen smiled to show she'd realised her uncle was pulling her leg. 'Who's Missy?'

'Our pony,' said Uncle George. 'She's ideal for carrying deer we've shot back to the farm. Hunting deer means we get to eat better than most people do in these dark days. It also provides a useful supplement to the farm income which is otherwise largely based on a frantic period in the raspberry season with not very much beyond some lambs and wool for the rest of the year. Which reminds me, first thing in the morning I'd like you to go out and shoot some rabbits, Ben.'

'Rabbits?' asked Helen.

'Yes, they're another good source of income and food for us as the land here has always suited them. Sometimes I think we get a larger weight of rabbits than raspberries during the year. It's especially good that they're not rationed. We can sell whatever we can shoot to butchers in Blairgowrie and through them to others further afield.'

'Would you like to come too?' asked Ben, looking at Helen.

Helen tried to hide her dislike of the idea. Ben seemed nice enough company, but while she recognised the need for animals to be killed for the table, she had no wish to get closer to the process than she had to.

'I'm sure Helen would benefit more from a lie-in,' said Aunt Jemima.

Helen shot her a grateful glance.

When everyone had finished eating, the two men and Ben opened bottles of ale. Jemima opened the ceramic stopper of a bottle of dandelion and burdock and both she and Helen had a glass while the five of them sat around the table and talked.

Helen found the chat that went back and forth enjoyable

and relaxing. She listened to George outlining his plans for priorities on the farm for the next month, with suggestions and discussion from the other three. Helen told them about her studies and how, as a medical student, she'd been exempted from conscription. When asked, she went into a little detail about how she spent her time. Then the discussion moved on to how the war was going.

The warmth of the room and the comfortable conversation eventually left Helen feeling quite drowsy.

'Come on, I think it's time we brought the evening to a close,' said Jemima. 'I can see that Helen needs her bed.'

'Aye, so do I,' said Angus. 'I'll just get my coat and hat and then walk you over to your cottage on the way to mine.'

'I think you'll find everything you need there,' said Jemima. 'We thought you'd appreciate the relative quiet of the cottage compared with a room in the farmhouse. Your mother said in her letter that she thought you'd want to use some of your time to study for exams, so that seemed best.'

Helen smiled. Given what had happened, she had decided against bringing anything more than two files of lecture notes with her on her journey. She honestly believed that time spent studying during her stay would be time wasted, though she didn't say so.

She was surprised to find that it was still quite light when she and Angus emerged from the farmhouse to walk across to the cottages. On the short walk, he pointed out to her some of the landmarks in the glen.

Then Helen realised he'd stopped walking and when she turned, she saw that he was looking up the hill that she and Ben had descended to the farm when she arrived.

'What is it?' she asked.

'Nothing, I think. Just for a moment, I thought I saw someone standing up there, just where the road comes over the crest and then starts down into the glen. But there's no one there now, I'm sure. For my age, my eyes are pretty good, so I'm surprised I'd make a mistake like that.'

Helen felt like she'd been hit in the stomach and thought she was going to be sick.

'Are you all right, lassie? You look like you've seen a ghost.'

Helen looked at Angus and felt she could trust him. 'There's something I want to tell you, Angus, though only if you promise not to tell my aunt and uncle. Can we go into my cottage and sit down?'

She saw Angus looking at her with concern. 'Of course, Helen. I'll just pop into my cottage first, but I'll be with you in a moment.'

Helen went into her cottage and lit an oil lamp in the sitting room, where the fire had died right down. She sat in a deep armchair that seemed very old, very worn and very comfortable. It was still warm in the room. She heard Angus open the front door a moment later. He entered the sitting room and sat on a small sofa and placed two white tin cups with blue rims on the small table in the centre of the room. Then he poured them both drinks out of a bottle of whisky he'd also been carrying.

'I'm not really keen on whisky, I'm sorry.'

Angus held the mug out to her. 'From the look on your face just now, this might be a good time to acquire a taste for it. What did you want to tell me?'

Helen took a deep breath, then a larger sip than she'd intended of the drink. When she'd stopped coughing, she told

Angus all about the couple who'd been following her, and the man she'd seen at Coupar Angus station.

'Aye, well the person I thought I saw could have been wearing a dark overcoat. Or they could have been a figment of my imagination.'

'Do you think what I've just told you about being followed is a figment of my imagination?' asked Helen.

'Well, it was obviously very real to you, which is what matters. Why don't you want to tell George and Jemima what you've just told me? I think it might be wise to call the police from the phone at the farm.'

'That's why I don't want to talk to them about it,' said Helen. 'I really don't want to involve the police.'

Helen saw the curious look that Angus gave her and went on. 'It's all very complicated, but something happened in London, and I don't feel I can go to the police, even here.'

'I can see you don't want to tell me more than that and I can also see you're not an axe murderer, so I won't pry. How would it be if we simply told George and Jemima that, being a city girl, you were having second thoughts about the idea of spending the night in a cottage on your own in the middle of nowhere? They could find you a room in the farmhouse. At least you'd be sharing a roof with others.'

'No, thank you, Angus. I don't want to be a nuisance to them. It's helped to be able to talk to you about it. Are there keys for the locks in the cottage doors? I would sleep more soundly knowing that the doors were locked.' She took another drink from the mug. 'You are right about it tasting better if you give it a chance!'

Angus smiled, though she could see he was still worried about her.

CHAPTER SEVEN

Monique felt that the food itself, served at a long and highly polished wooden table in the Argyll and Sutherland Highlanders officers' mess dining room, was extremely good. The room was decorated with a series of paintings on the walls depicting battles and there was a wood and glass cabinet in one corner with an impressive collection of silverware on display.

Sir Peter Maitland seemed to have taken the dining room over in its entirety and Monique found herself wondering where the displaced regimental officers were eating their dinner. She'd seen a sign pointing towards the 'canteen' on first entering the Palace and wondered if they had been reduced to eating with the non-commissioned officers or junior ranks.

More distracting, though, was the unresolved question of why she was there, or why any of them were there for that matter. As far as she knew, she was the only one of those present who was based in Scotland. That suggested most, or perhaps all, of the rest had travelled from London, which seemed hugely wasteful of their time.

Other than Sir Peter himself, who was sitting in the centre of a long side of the table, there were 20 people around it. She knew Sir Peter, of course, and during the meal she sat next to Commodore Cunningham, who deflected her questions about the purpose of the gathering, preferring to talk instead about her and Bob and their wedding plans. This gave her a chance to gain his support in arranging concocted documentation that would allow her to marry as Monique Dubois. The man sitting on her other side had introduced himself as a deputy head of Military Intelligence 9, helping resistance organisations in parts of occupied Europe. After that, he mainly talked to the man beyond him.

There were three other women present at the dinner, which struck Monique as an unexpectedly high number for a gathering of this sort. She'd met one of them when she was working in MI5 and knew another by sight, but not by name, as a female official in the Foreign Office, one of the vanishingly few who worked there who were entrusted with anything more important than a typewriter.

Perhaps because her career in British intelligence had been so short, certainly the part of it spent in Britain, Monique only recognised two of the men present, other than the general and the commodore. She had worked alongside one of them after transferring to MI5 and had found him unimaginative and dull in the extreme, but conveniently easy to ignore or circumvent. The other was the man who had inducted her into the Secret Intelligence Service, known to many as MI6, after she'd come ashore with two German spies at Port Gordon on the Moray Firth in September 1940.

Bill Douglas was a loathsome creature in his mid-thirties with a moustache, slicked-back black hair, and a vastly over-inflated sense of his attractiveness to women. After Monique's arrival in Britain, he had tried hard to exploit her rather ambiguous status and consequent vulnerability to his advantage. His efforts to charm his way into her bed soon gave way to subtle and then less subtle attempts to blackmail her to the same end.

Things had come to a head in a pub not far from Victoria Station in London where he'd given her an ultimatum. Either she went to bed with him, or he'd report invented suspicions that her true loyalties lay with the Abwehr and Germany rather than with SIS/MI6 and Britain. Monique had picked up his nearly full pint of beer and poured it over his head, then walked out.

True to his word, he'd tried to label her as a suspected enemy agent, but more senior figures in SIS/MI6 chose to believe her account of why he was trying to ruin her reputation. Perhaps he'd done it before, though if that was the case his being given responsibility for her seemed perverse. Nonetheless, the ill-feeling caused by Bill Douglas's allegations was part of the reason she then transferred to MI5.

Monique hadn't seen Douglas earlier or noticed him before the meal started and it was only once it was under way that, from his seat some way along the opposite side of the table, he caught her eye, smiled broadly, and raised a wine glass in greeting.

Monique tried to conceal the anger he still roused in her and simply ignored him.

'Is he a friend of yours?' Commodore Cunningham asked.

'Only in the sense that Maximilian von Moser could be called an "old flame",' Monique said.

'The German SD agent you encountered in Sweden? Ah, I see. Well, we know what became of him.'

At the end of the dinner, the general asked the waiting staff to leave and ensured the doors to the dining room were closed. Monique assumed that he, or more likely someone following his orders, had checked there were no hidden microphones in the room. Then he asked those present to say who they were.

Monique could detect no pattern. Attendees seemed to be a random mix from various arms of the military intelligence community and the Foreign Office, plus a man sitting next to Sir Peter who said he was with the Cabinet Office.

Then Sir Peter stood up and spent perhaps fifteen minutes explaining why they were there.

Looking round the table as he spoke and in the silence that followed, Monique had the sense that she was not the only one shocked by what he had said.

It fell to the general to end the silence his words had prompted. 'I think that concludes the dinner. You are welcome to drink in the officers' mess bar. That's one floor up in the Prince's Tower, which protrudes from the west end of this side of the Palace. There's a staircase along the corridor. Please remember not to discuss what I've just said as there are likely to be regimental officers present. Please also remember that I expect to see you all at 9 a.m. tomorrow in the education centre, which is in the old Chapel Royal, the building on the far side of the Inner Close from the Palace. In the meantime, thank you.'

Everyone stood as the general walked out and then the hum of conversation started.

'Are you going to have a drink, Monique?' asked Commodore Cunningham.

'Thank you, sir, but no. I wouldn't mind getting some fresh air and collecting my thoughts. I may pop back later.'

It was still light when Monique emerged from the Palace, through an archway in an upper corner of the large sloping courtyard known as the Inner Close. She nodded to acknowledge the sentry standing outside, who had come to attention. She wondered if he was bored.

There were few positives about the war but, to her mind, the introduction of double daylight saving time in the summer half of the year was a real bonus. She looked at her watch. It was a little before 9.20 p.m. The sun was due to set within the next ten minutes, but she knew that she had at least three-quarters of an hour of reasonable daylight left, especially on a fine evening like this one. She stopped briefly and looked at her surroundings, scarcely able to believe the depth of history around her.

A young soldier had been detailed to give her a quick tour of Stirling Castle after she'd arrived earlier. The castle had probably been even more glorious before the army had converted it for use as a barracks in the early 1800s. They had inserted extra floors into the Great Hall, on the lower side of the Inner Close, to allow it to accommodate 400 troops. The Chapel Royal, where Sir Peter wanted everyone to meet the next morning, was now the education centre. The Palace provided, as she'd seen, everything from the junior ranks' canteen to the officers' mess. Other buildings had become officers' or senior NCOs' quarters, regimental offices, a medical centre, equipment stores, armouries, or any of the many other things an army regimental depot needed so it could function. They'd even, she noticed on her arrival, built a gym block in the broad ditch in front of the castle's outer defences and, on her tour, she'd seen a firing range in the Nether Bailey, the lower part of the castle at its northern end.

Despite all these changes, it was still a remarkable place. She wished that Bob could be here to share her enjoyment of it. She also wished he could have been here to hear what Sir Peter had said after dinner. She knew that was something she'd never be able to share with him, for his protection as well as her own.

There were a few soldiers in view, most apparently heading towards the Great Hall, plus two more on sentry duty, one by the Palace entrance she'd exited from and one down by the gap between the Palace and the Great Hall that gave access to the Inner Close from the Outer Close.

Monique had been disappointed on her arrival that afternoon to find that except for a couple of the officers she'd seen, the soldiers didn't wear kilts while on duty in the castle. When she'd asked, she'd been told that the Argyll and Sutherland Highlanders she'd met guarding the king in Caithness the previous September were exceptions because of their ceremonial duties. The ordinary soldiers at the castle wore what she had been told were called Balmoral bonnets, like floppy berets with a broader top and a small pom-pom on the crown that was, like the hat itself, khaki in colour. Other than their hats, all that set them apart from all the other khaki-clad army soldiers she'd seen in London, Edinburgh or anywhere else was a red and white chequered badge on the upper left arm.

Monique spent a moment debating whether she could manage without a coat before deciding it was too cold. She turned and headed for the slightly anonymous door close to the near end of the building that ran along the high side of the Inner Close, to her left. This, according to her guide earlier, was called the King's Old Building. The door gave access to some of the officers' accommodation and Monique had been allocated a room on the first floor. Her room was at the rear of the building and on arrival she'd seen that the view from its window was simply magnificent, extending from a high vantage point over a broad plain to distant mountains.

A few moments later she re-emerged into the Inner Close, now wearing her beige raincoat. She turned left and headed for the upper end of the Chapel Royal. She knew from her earlier tour that there was a rather quaint passage there that made its slightly indirect and rather uncertain way between the chapel and its neighbour, a continuation round the corner of the close of the King's Old Building she was staying in.

The gardens beyond had seemed a lovely oasis when she had first seen them on her tour, and she wanted more time to enjoy the views she'd only glimpsed earlier from the raised wall walk that ran round the perimeter of the gardens.

Monique paused for a moment on emerging from the archway at the far end of the passage onto the paved area beyond it. The gardens were deserted and easily quiet enough to allow her to hear birds singing. She turned half-right past the rear of the Chapel Royal and crossed to a set of stone steps leading up to a higher part of the wall walk, then slowly followed that round, taking in the views of distant mountains to the north and then to the west, where the aftermath of the sunset was still clearly visible on the horizon.

After a while, Monique began to feel cold, even with her coat on. She didn't want to give up the views but needed to move. She decided to go to the officers' mess bar for a drink with the commodore, if he was still there, before having an early night. She reluctantly descended from the wall walk to the gardens using a second set of stone steps.

As she walked back towards the passage, she got a strong sense that someone was nearby, watching her. She stopped and looked around, then scanned the windows overlooking the gardens from the north end of the King's Old Building. In what was left of the daylight there was no obvious sign of movement and all the windows she could see seemed to have closed internal shutters, but the uncomfortable feeling persisted. She turned and carried on.

Monique jumped slightly when a figure emerged from the end of the passage just as she approached it. With a sinking heart, she recognised Bill Douglas, now wearing an expensive-looking black overcoat, artfully left unbuttoned to show off what was obviously an equally expensive suit beneath it.

'Hello, Vera! It's lovely to see you again after all this time.'

'It's Monique these days, Bill. And I wish I could say I feel as warmly about seeing you as you apparently feel about seeing me. Did you follow me here?'

'Let's let bygones be bygones, shall we? Water under the bridge and all that. I don't hold a grudge against you for that pint of beer. It just shows the filly has a little spirit, which I really admire in a woman.' He had a final pull on the cigarette he'd been smoking and flicked the butt some distance away onto the grass.

'Can we get one thing straight, Bill? You obviously didn't get the message last time we met so I will try to be as clear as I can. If you were the last man on Earth, I wouldn't go to bed with you. That was true before I became engaged and it's even more true now.'

'Congratulations! Who's the lucky man? I see you're not wearing a ring, though.'

Monique only wore it when off-duty and wasn't about to explain herself to Bill Douglas.

'Just stand aside, Bill, I've somewhere else I want to be and other people I'd prefer to be with.'

'Are you going to abandon me in my gardens so heartlessly? To answer your earlier question, no, I'm not following you. I'm simply making use of an opportunity to spend some time in a place that is rather special to me. It's made this damn-fool meeting of Peter Maitland's worth the trip. Something of a pilgrimage, even, because I've not visited these gardens since I was at school. I had no idea you were here, though I'm glad you are.'

'What do you mean, your gardens?' Monique realised too

late that she shouldn't have risen to such obvious bait.

Douglas turned away from her and pointed up at a window she'd not previously noticed above the arch at the near end of the passage. 'That's the Douglas Window up there with the Douglas Room beyond it, and what you've been enjoying are called the Douglas Gardens.'

'It's a common enough name,' said Monique.

'True, but I'm descended directly from a man called James Douglas, who from 1452 was the 9th Earl of Douglas. He was the last of the branch of the family known as the Black Douglases to have an earldom. But while his titles were forfeited in 1455 and he went off into exile in England, the family retains significant estates in south-west Scotland, where I grew up. When my father dies, I will inherit them.'

'Do you find the "I'm really rich so you should sleep with me" approach works with many women?'

'You might be surprised. But you misunderstand. I was named William Douglas after the 8th Earl of Douglas, who was my many times great-grandfather's older brother. He grew powerful enough to be seen as a threat by King James II of Scotland and the two agreed to meet here at Stirling Castle in February 1452 to discuss their differences. The meeting didn't go well, and the king personally murdered my namesake with a dagger before another man bashed his brains out. It all happened up there, in the room beyond the Douglas Window. The king's courtiers then inflicted further wounds on the body before throwing it out of the window and into the gardens, just here, where we are standing. It was the unsuccessful revolt that my ancestor, the 9th Earl, raised in response that led to him being stripped of his titles.'

'Is that true?'

'Up to a point. This building, the King's Old Building, was only built in 1496 and seems to have replaced the one in which the murder took place. And what you see today owes much to a major rebuild after a serious fire less than ninety years ago. It follows that what is called the Douglas Window can't be the actual window they threw the 8th Earl's body from or the room beyond the window the one in which the murder took place. But the paving we are standing on is in the place where the body is believed to have ended up and the rest of the story is completely true.'

'It's a shame it wasn't the 9th Earl, your ancestor, who was murdered, and preferably before he'd fathered any children. Then you'd not be here spoiling my evening walk.'

'Oh, come on, Vera, Monique, or whatever you want to call yourself this week. Don't be like that. How about a quickie just for old times' sake? We can do it here if you must, but I'd prefer it if we went back to one of our rooms.'

'Go to hell!'

Monique tried to push past Douglas. She saw him glance back along the passage as if judging whether they could be seen by anyone in the Inner Close. Then he caught her arm and swung her round before throwing his weight against her and driving her a couple of steps backwards into a corner formed by the walls of the building. She felt her back and head hit what felt like a drainpipe as he leaned in, presumably to kiss her. He was physically larger than her and she'd not expected him to resort to force so quickly, so was caught off-balance.

'Let me go!'

'You always did have far too high an opinion of yourself, Vera. I know what a slut like you needs. Come on, you know you want to.'

Monique regained her balance and brought her right knee up, driven by the power of her anger and fear, into Douglas's crotch. Her coat impeded her movement a little, but she still made satisfyingly solid contact. The man doubled up and, as he did so, she punched him in the throat. He collapsed to the ground, gasping for breath.

Monique stepped over him as her only way out of the corner she was in. Douglas was lying on his side and still doubled up and he seemed to be having real difficulty breathing. His back was to her, and she resisted the temptation to kick him as a parting gift. Instead, she turned and walked through the passage to the Inner Close beyond. The idea of a drink no longer appealed but she did walk across to the sentry by the entrance to the Palace.

The soldier came to attention again.

'There's a man in the Douglas Gardens who seems to have fallen ill,' Monique said. 'You had better get someone to check on him.' She then turned and headed towards her room.

CHAPTER EIGHT

Back in her room, Monique tried to calm herself down. She could feel the adrenalin slowly draining from her system, leaving a much sharper pain in her ribs than she'd felt for some days.

She thought it might help to read and opened her bag to take out a book that Bob had suggested she try: *Murder on the Orient Express* by Agatha Christie. Then she sat down in the armchair next to the bed, wishing she'd visited the officers' mess bar for just long enough to enjoy one strong gin and tonic.

It was a short time later when she heard hurried footsteps in the corridor and was startled by a loud rapping on her door.

Surely Bill Douglas couldn't have recovered enough to have come after her? She removed her pistol from its holster and went to stand beside the door.

'Hello?'

'Monique, it's Maurice Cunningham. Can you open the door, please?'

It certainly sounded more like the commodore than Bill Douglas. Monique opened the door a little, holding her pistol behind her back with her right hand. It was the commodore, and she opened the door fully.

'Can I come in?'

'Yes, of course, sir.'

The commodore came into the room and closed the door behind himself. 'You weren't happy to see Bill Douglas at dinner. Have you met him since?'

'Yes, sir. Our paths crossed in the Douglas Gardens, which he told me are named after an ancestor of his.'

'What happened?'

'He tried to rape me.'

'What did you do?'

'I kneed him in the balls and punched him in the throat. He went down on the ground and stayed there. I doubt if he's going to be interested in sex for a while.'

'That's certainly true,' said the commodore. 'What happened then?'

'I came back here, though on the way I took a detour to tell the sentry outside the Palace entrance that someone had fallen ill in the gardens. I suggested that they should check on him.'

'What were you wearing?'

'This blouse, with the jacket over it that I was wearing at dinner. As well as my beige raincoat as it was cold. Why?'

'Can I see the raincoat? And please put your gun away.'

Monique lifted the raincoat off the hook on the back of the door and handed it to the commodore. She watched as he went over to stand under the room's electric light and examined the fabric.

'Are you sure that this is the coat you were wearing when Bill Douglas attacked you?'

'Yes, sir. What's this about? The sentry I talked to will be able to confirm I was wearing that coat.'

'Put your jacket on and then your coat and come with me. Leave your shoulder holster and pistol here.'

Monique was beginning to feel worried about whatever it was that the commodore wasn't telling her. She followed him down the stairs and out of the door into the Inner Close. Dusk had advanced and the last of the light was draining away. The sentry had moved, she guessed at the commodore's request, so he was waiting outside the door as they emerged.

'Was this the lady who spoke to you about a man falling ill in the gardens?' asked the commodore.

The sentry flashed a torch in the commodore's direction and then in Monique's.

'Yes, sir.'

'Did she come to speak to you directly from the gardens?'

'Yes sir. She emerged from the passage over there and came straight over to speak to me, then she doubled back to this door and went in.'

'What was she wearing?'

'The same as she has on now, sir.'

'Are you sure it's the same coat?'

The sentry shone his torch at Monique again. 'Or one identical to it, sir. It was lighter than it is now, so I had a good view. And she's the sort of lady you take notice of and remember.'

Monique felt herself blushing.

'Were there any marks on her coat when she spoke to you.'

'Nothing noticeable sir. It was fastened, unlike now, so I'd have seen anything significant.'

'Very well. Thank you. Can you follow me please, Monique?'

Cunningham turned and strode in the direction of the passage and Monique followed. It was now quite dark between the buildings and although the commodore used a torch to light their way, she half-tripped over a low step halfway along the passage that she'd forgotten about and didn't see. She reminded herself there were two more further along, where that end of the passage passed under what was called the 'Douglas Room'. She could see figures standing in the slightly better light beyond the end of the passage, plus a flickering of torches that only seemed to confuse things.

As he emerged from the archway, the commodore stepped to the right. Three other men were standing on the paved area, with at least two of them shining torches at something on the ground, in the corner where she'd left Bill Douglas.

Monique felt momentarily sick. Douglas was still there, pretty much as she'd last seen him, still doubled up on his side and facing into the corner, with his feet pointing towards the end of the passage and his head away from it. The difference now was that he was lying in what she was sure, even in the dim light, was a large pool of blood. As she looked at his body in the torchlight it appeared that Douglas had suffered multiple wounds and, when she moved round and looked just a little more closely, she saw that most of the top of his head was missing.

'I understand you were here a little while ago, Madame Dubois?'

Monique recognised Major General Sir Peter Maitland's voice and realised he was one of the three men.

'Yes, sir. The last time I saw Bill Douglas he was lying on the ground pretty much where he is now. But he was alive, if not feeling at all happy.'

'Why was he lying on the ground?'

'He attacked me, sir, and I got the better of him. He had very sore balls and possibly a damaged windpipe. But all this blood was most definitely still inside him.'

'What do you think, Maurice?' asked Sir Peter.

'I've confirmed that the man she spoke to before returning to her accommodation saw no blood on her coat, sir. Whoever did this is going to be covered in the stuff. It can't be Monique.'

'Thank you, I tend to agree. You'll understand that we had

to check, Monique. As I recall from your report and the one written by the SIS people who found you, the man you killed in Gothenburg ended up with nearly as little blood in his body as our unfortunate Mr Douglas.'

'That's probably true, sir, but that time it did end up all over me, quite literally, and even with help it was quite hard to clean it off.'

*

After writing his report, Bob had driven the couple of miles from the MI11 offices at Craigiehall to RAF Turnhouse, where he'd had dinner in the officers' mess. He'd then driven to the bungalow in Featherhall Crescent in Corstorphine before it got dark. He avoided driving at night whenever possible, just as he'd made an unbreakable rule never to fly at night. He knew that his 'acquired monocular vision' meant he'd never again be able to benefit from proper stereoscopic three-dimensional sight.

When Bob had been shot down over Kent in November 1940, he'd suffered an injury to the left side of his head that damaged the optic nerve and left him functionally blind in his left eye.

In the two and a half years since his injury, he'd found that he was increasingly able to unconsciously recognise a wide range of depth cues that meant he could drive or fly nearly as well as he had before he'd been shot down, but only in daylight. At night it was quite different.

Driving at night in the blackout was a nightmare for everyone. In the early part of the war, vehicles on Britain's roads had only been allowed to use a single masked headlight at night, and Bob had never driven after dark. Since September 1941, two masked headlights had been allowed on vehicles and Bob had found that at a push he could manage, though usually uncomfortably and rather slowly. And not when he had a choice.

Michael Dixon - Lieutenant Commander Michael Dixon - was Bob's deputy in his northern outpost of Military Intelligence 11. Michael and his fiancée, Betty Swanson, had been staying with Bob and Monique in the bungalow since Betty's arrival from Orkney a few weeks earlier. As an interim measure, until they found somewhere of their own, the arrangement had worked well.

When Bob returned to the bungalow, he found a note saying that Michael and Betty had gone to see a film at a cinema in Edinburgh. Bob added coal to the burned-down fire in the lounge and settled down to read some reports from the southern part of MI11 that he'd been finding reasons to avoid in the office. He put the radio on in the background. He soon put the reports on one side and instead picked up his much-read copy of John Buchan's *The Thirty-Nine Steps.*

The sound of the telephone ringing in the hall brought him back to wakefulness with a start. The clock on the mantelpiece said it was 10.45 p.m. Bob went through to the hall, almost bumping into Michael Dixon wearing a dressing gown. He and Betty must have returned from the cinema without waking Bob.

Michael stood back to let Bob get to the phone.

'Hello.'

'Hello, is that Bob?'

He recognised Commodore Cunningham's voice, wondering why he was ringing from, presumably, Stirling Castle. Then he realised there was an obvious reason.

'Is everything all right, sir?'

'I'm very aware we are talking via at least one public switchboard so I will be guarded. But yes, everyone you care for is fine, so you have nothing to worry about there. Nonetheless, a problem has arisen, and we think it would be helpful if you could make your way here as soon as possible. Don't name it, but do you know where I mean?'

'Yes, sir, your office mentioned your intended whereabouts when I spoke to them this morning.'

'Ah, did they?'

Bob wasn't proud of potentially stirring up trouble for the commodore's secretary, but he wanted to avoid his boss assuming that Monique had revealed the location of the meeting to him.

'Do you want me to come on my own, sir?'

'No, I rather think a few extra pairs of hands might be helpful too. How many can you manage?'

Bob's Royal Air Force team of two was visiting airfields in north-east Scotland to check on their security and would be away for the next two days. And the junior member of his Royal Navy team was on leave, as was the office's driver.

'If I leave my secretary in charge, sir, I can muster three plus myself.'

'Good. As soon as you can, Bob.'

The line went dead, and Bob replaced the receiver in its cradle.

'What's up, Bob?' asked Michael.

'I don't know,' said Bob, 'but something is. Please pass my apologies to Betty, but you and I need to get to Stirling Castle as soon as possible. As you'll have seen outside, I've got my staff car here. You can drive us to Stirling.'

'Any idea how long we'll be there?'

'No, sorry, though an overnight bag might be prudent. I've taken to leaving one permanently packed. While you're getting dressed, I'll ring Anthony Darlington at the officers' mess at Craigiehall and get him and Gilbert Potter to make their way direct to Stirling.'

Captain Anthony Darlington and Sergeant Gilbert Potter were Bob's army team. Whatever had caused Commodore Cunningham and, presumably, Sir Peter Maitland to decide to call Bob in, he hoped he would have enough 'extra pairs of hands' to do the job.

*

Helen wished that she'd been out to the toilet before she'd gone upstairs to her bedroom. No sooner had she tried to settle down after reading a chapter of Aldous Huxley's *Brave New World* than the need arose.

She didn't like the idea of using the chamber pot that was under the bed and carrying it out to empty it into the toilet in the morning. She turned on her torch to find the matches and lit the oil lamp. Then she put on her dressing gown and slippers. She carried the lamp down the stairs. She'd not noticed earlier, but the third and then the second stairs from the bottom creaked extremely loudly. She paused, then remembered she was alone in the cottage and there was no one to disturb.

At the bottom of the stairs, Helen turned left into the kitchen. She realised that the blackout curtains weren't closed on either the front window or the one at the back. It would be all right, she told herself. There probably wasn't an Air Raid Precautions warden this side of Blairgowrie to see the light from her lamp and complain or report her.

She crossed to the stout green wooden back door and slid open the heavy bolts at the top and bottom, then used the large age-blackened key kept on a hook on the wall to unlock it. Once outside, shivering, she pulled the back door closed behind herself, then turned to her right and opened the door of the toilet. The cottage's smallest room was cold and had a very distinctive smell. Not actually unpleasant, but there was a strong sense of many decades' use of bleach and Vim. Probably not together, she thought, remembering something from a school chemistry lesson.

The green-painted cistern was decorated with the maker's name set into the casting and was positioned just below the ceiling. After doing what she'd come to do, Helen pulled the wooden handle on the end of the long and heavy chain to operate the flush. Then she picked the oil lamp up off the shelf intended for it before going back out into the cold and turning towards the kitchen.

As Helen pushed open the back door, she realised there was a figure standing and facing her in the centre of the darkened kitchen. She gasped and dropped the oil lamp, which went out.

CHAPTER NINE

The light from the full moon and the clear skies helped, thought Bob. So did the scarcity of other traffic. From Corstorphine, Michael had driven along Turnhouse Road, passing through the heart of RAF Turnhouse with the airfield on one side and most of the accommodation on the other. The plan then was to drive through Kirkliston, Linlithgow and Falkirk before taking a right turn towards Stirling.

'You'd think that with the prospect of invasion by Hitler long gone, they'd get around to replacing the road signs,' said Michael. 'You say you know this road, Bob?'

'I've certainly been along it plenty of times in the past, though not very recently. And not at night in the blackout, which makes everything look so different. Effectively we're following the A9 from its start, which was back where we turned off the road to Glasgow.

'Before the war, you just followed the A9 and it found its way through these places to Stirling and then beyond, all the way to John o' Groats if you wanted to go that far. But back then you always had the road signs for confirmation. Even without them, it's a road you can follow without really thinking about it, but only in daylight. I've got a map, but again it's not a huge amount of help without the odd road sign for confirmation of where you are. I can tell you that we're going the right way, though, because this is Linlithgow we're coming into. The large building on the left we've just passed is the distillery. There should be a railway bridge just ahead, and we go under it and then through the town. There it is.'

Despite what had seemed to Bob to be an awfully slow journey, he and Michael arrived at Stirling Castle before Anthony Darlington and Gilbert Potter. The guards at the top of the approach road had clearly been told to expect them. They were directed to drive over a wooden bridge and through the main entrance before taking a sharp right through a narrow stone arch and then following the road through another arch not far beyond it.

'I can see why they park their lorries in the area below the main gate,' said Michael. 'These stone gateways are pretty tight, even for a car. They said to turn right in the open area beyond the second arch. Yes, there's a line of cars and other small vehicles parked over there.'

'And someone's waiting for us,' said Bob.

It was cold outside. Bob opened the back door of the car and pulled out his RAF officers' greatcoat, just as Michael was putting on his naval equivalent.

'Could you follow me please, sir?'

Bob turned to see the soldier who'd been waiting for them waving his torch towards a nearby building. Though he'd lived not all that far away for much of his life, this was the first time Bob had been inside Stirling Castle and he wished he could see more than just the looming shapes in the moonlight. Their guide entered the building, where he stopped in a hallway and indicated they should go through a door on the left.

'I'll let them know you've arrived, sir.'

Bob found himself in a wood-panelled meeting room with maps of Scotland and the local area on the walls. Heavy curtains covered the only window, which Bob realised was at the front of the building.

'A cup of tea might be nice,' said Michael.

'True,' said Bob, after removing his greatcoat. 'I wonder what's keeping Anthony Darlington?'

A few minutes later the door opened. Major General Sir Peter Maitland came in, followed by Commodore Cunningham, and then Monique, a civilian in a dark suit, and an army lieutenant colonel wearing a kilt. Bob recognised the civilian as the man he'd seen with Sir Peter at RAF Grangemouth.

Monique smiled when she caught his eye but, to his mind, she looked troubled. He returned the smile.

'Thank you for coming, Bob,' said Sir Peter. 'Let's all sit down.'

The meeting table wasn't large, and Sir Peter sat on one side flanked by the commodore and the civilian, while Bob sat on the other, flanked by Michael and Monique. The army officer sat at the end.

'I'm expecting my army contingent,' said Bob, 'but I don't know how long they'll be.'

'I'm not sure how much of what you are about to hear I want to be shared with them anyway,' said Sir Peter. 'You can tell them what they need to know afterwards.'

'As you wish, sir,' said Bob.

The door opened again, and two soldiers came in with trays.

'Given the time of night, we thought we should break out some decent coffee,' said the lieutenant colonel.

Bob sipped from his cup and thought it wasn't bad at all.

Sir Peter put his coffee cup back in its saucer. 'Bob, sitting on my left is Paul Gillespie who is from the Cabinet Office, while at the end of the table is Lieutenant Colonel Ian

Ferguson, who commands the Argyll and Sutherland Highlanders' training depot here at Stirling Castle. You know Maurice and me, and Monique of course. Can you introduce yourself and your colleague for the benefit of those who don't know you?'

Bob did so.

Commodore Cunningham then recounted the events of the evening, leading up to the murder of Bill Douglas. Then Monique gave an account of what had happened between her and Douglas. Bob reached to his left under the table and squeezed her hand.

With his other hand, he put his coffee cup down. 'If I've got this right, sir, this man, Bill Douglas, was murdered by someone who seems to have been re-enacting the murder of another William Douglas in the castle nearly 500 years ago? And the man who was killed tonight was a direct descendant of the younger brother of the man murdered by King James II back in 1452?'

'That's pretty much it,' said the commodore.

'That's rather weird. But setting that aside, all this took place some little time ago now. What's been done since discovering the body, other than phoning me?'

It was the lieutenant colonel who spoke. 'Sir Peter and the commodore took immediate steps to ascertain whether Madame Dubois could have had anything to do with the murder. As she had been seen coming from the gardens and told a sentry that something was wrong with Mr Douglas, it was an obvious possibility that had to be excluded.

'By that time, I had already ensured that the gardens were secure. There are two ways in or out, plus two doors at the end of the King's Old Building and quite a few windows, including some on the ground floor. There's also a building used as a store in the corner of the gardens and steps down from the gardens to an enclosed defensive point in the wall beyond it. There's only so much we've been able to do in the dark, but I've got men guarding the possible exits and positioned outside the rooms from which the gardens could be accessed. I have aimed to ensure no evidence is compromised before the morning when things might be a little clearer.'

'Thank you, lieutenant colonel,' said Bob. 'Can I ask, do you know if there's likely to be a book about the history of the castle available anywhere? I'd rather like to know a little more about the 1452 murder as it's so obviously connected with what happened tonight.'

'We've got a small library in the Chapel Royal, which serves as the depot's education centre. I'll get someone to see if we've got anything that might help.'

'No, could you simply seal the library off, like you have the scene of the murder? I'll have a look tonight.' Bob turned back to the commodore. 'I will also need to know about the meeting that Bill Douglas was attending. Who else is attending? What's its purpose? What was his role? It has to be a possibility that his murder is connected to the meeting or someone else attending it.'

Sir Peter Maitland coughed. 'That is exceptionally sensitive information, group captain. I am prepared to tell you and Lieutenant Commander Dixon as I accept it's essential that you know the background; though only because Commodore Cunningham argued strongly in favour of my doing so when we agreed he should ask you to take on the investigation. But I would ask that you do not pass what we are about to tell you to anyone else in your team or beyond it. Madame Dubois already knows, of course. For the same reason, I'd like to ask Lieutenant Colonel Ferguson to leave the room. Ian and I have known one another since before the war, which is why I chose this as a suitably invisible location from a London perspective. He has been very generous in agreeing to accommodate our meeting here at Stirling Castle, but he does not know its purpose.'

The lieutenant colonel smiled and stood up. 'I think I'd prefer to keep it that way, sir. I'll check on the sentries I've posted and get another to secure the library.'

'Would you mind also looking out for my MI11 army team?' asked Bob. 'Captain Anthony Darlington and Sergeant Gilbert Potter should be here soon if they've not already arrived. If you could brief them on what we've discussed here so far, it would save some time.'

'Yes, of course, sir.'

There was a silence after Ferguson closed the door behind himself.

Bob looked round, waiting for someone to speak.

'I think that perhaps this falls to me,' said Paul Gillespie. 'Sir Peter briefed the meeting about its purpose after dinner, but this is really my show.

'My home department is the Cabinet Office, but I work in Sir Peter's office to coordinate intelligence gathering and distribution across the various arms of military intelligence. As you are probably aware, they have not always pulled in the same direction in the past, to put it mildly.

'This conference involves our spending two nights at the castle before everyone leaves on Thursday morning, wrapped round a series of meetings and discussions tomorrow. It is intended to explore the scope for cooperation and joint working. Counting Sir Peter there are only 21 attendees, though that's 20 now, of course.'

'There has to be more to it than that,' said Bob. 'Nothing you've said gives any reason for holding this meeting quite so far from London or in conditions of such secrecy.'

'I was coming to that, group captain. There is a particular focus for the discussions we will be holding tomorrow. Which, I should add, Sir Peter has decided should go ahead despite what has happened tonight. I am aware that your part of MI11 has had a series of interactions with Soviet agents since you arrived in post, mainly negative. I am sure you do not need me to convince you that we are rapidly approaching the point, if we have not already reached it, where the Soviet intelligence agencies are more of a threat to the UK's long-term national interests than the German intelligence agencies.

'Against that background, we were deeply concerned to receive a recent report from a trusted source within Soviet intelligence that there is a group of Soviet spies working within our intelligence agencies and the Foreign Office. We've had nothing specific enough to identify individuals, but the suggestion is there are up to half a dozen men involved, though no women, apparently, and that they were recruited at the University of Cambridge a decade ago or more. It was also said that they all had socialist or communist leanings in their younger days. Though it seems they were not sufficiently socialist or communist to turn down the opportunity of studying at Cambridge.'

'Are you sure this isn't just a way to get us chasing our tails?' asked Bob. 'Like getting us to fly people up to Scotland for a meeting that diverts them from other duties.'

'That was very much my thought, Bob,' said Sir Peter

Maitland. 'That's why we kept our response subdued when we received the first report of this sort of thing going on, over a year ago. And the second, from a separate and trusted source a few months after that. But when a third source popped up, as far as we know unrelated to the first two, and told a remarkably similar story, it seemed time to take notice and take action.'

'Surely all you need to do is work out who you have who's been in service over ten years, studied at Cambridge, and leaned to the left in their youth?'

'That was of course something that occurred to me,' said Sir Peter. 'The problem is that a lot of our more senior men were recruited in the right sort of timeframe; a lot of them studied at Cambridge; and a lot of them, a surprising number of them, I must say, had political leanings to the left when they were younger. When you try to identify those who fit into all three groups, you end up with a list that has on it a significant portion of all senior officers in military intelligence or the Foreign Office.'

'Which of course is no help at all,' said Bob. 'Do I take it that you are coming at it from the other end, instead?'

Sir Peter smiled. 'Yes, we are starting on a modest scale by assembling a group of people from across the different parts of military intelligence and the Foreign Office whose backgrounds suggest they cannot be members of this group of Soviet spies. The aim tomorrow will be to establish an informal network coordinated by Paul Gillespie that allows comments and suspicions to be fed back to me without any chance of their crossing the desks of any of the Soviet spies. Over time I'd hope to broaden that out and consequently narrow down the list of possible suspects, ideally allowing us to identify one or more of them.'

'How did Bill Douglas fit into this?' asked Bob.

It was Paul Gillespie who answered. 'His background made him a good SIS/MI6 candidate for the group. There were questions in his record about his attitude and behaviour towards women and other aspects of his character, arising from his supervision of Madame Dubois after she landed in Britain and for other reasons. But he went to university in Edinburgh and appeared to have no interest in politics. We're not looking for nice people, just people we can be confident aren't Soviet spies.'

'Thank you for being so open with me,' said Bob. 'It's perhaps time that we got things moving. It seems to me that what was done to Bill Douglas was premeditated and planned. It feels like the manner of his murder was deliberately chosen for some symbolic purpose, given how it echoed the murder of his almost ancestor. Subject to views from round the table I propose to have my army team look at the longer-term residents of the castle, the Argyll and Sutherland Highlanders, while Michael, Monique and I initially focus on those who are here for your meeting. We will talk to everyone we can tonight, but I'm aware it's now very late and much of the work will need to wait until the morning.'

'I know she's sitting here,' said Sir Peter, 'but I must ask whether in the circumstances you feel it appropriate for Madame Dubois to play an active role in your investigation?'

'I may have had good reason to dislike Bill Douglas,' said Monique, 'and I'd be lying if I said I'm sorry he's dead. But I will do everything I can to support Bob in finding the murderer.'

'I'm happy to move forward on that basis, sir,' said Bob.

'Very well. You'd best get on with it then,' said Sir Peter.

'And please remember what I said about the sensitivity surrounding the purpose of the meeting.'

CHAPTER TEN

'I'll see how much of the tour I can remember,' said Monique.

Bob was standing with her and Michael outside the building where they'd met Sir Peter and the others. They'd put their coats on before exiting the front door.

After emerging from the light of the meeting room and hallway, Bob could see even less of their surroundings than he had when he'd arrived. As his right eye started to adjust, he again became aware of the dark shapes of the buildings in the moonlight.

'We should start by visiting the murder scene,' he said.

'Yes,' said Monique. 'They're waiting for you to see it for yourself before they remove the body. We need to head over to the far corner of this courtyard, which is the Outer Close. The large building ahead and slightly to our right is the Great Hall, which is now a barracks for hundreds of troops. Ahead and slightly to our left is the Palace, now used for the officers' and sergeants' messes and canteen for other ranks, as well as other communal spaces.'

Monique led the way under the stone bridge linking the corners of the Palace and Great Hall. The sentry stationed just beyond it saluted and checked their passes in the light of his torch. Then she continued retelling what she'd learned earlier, this time talking about the Inner Close and its surroundings. She took them directly to the entrance of the passage near the close's furthest corner, encountering another sentry as they arrived. Bob could see other men posted by doorways around the Inner Close.

Beyond the arch at the far end of the passage, Monique

stopped and shone her torch down at the bloody corpse of Bill Douglas. Bob saw he was lying on his side with his legs drawn up and his hands over his groin, facing away from them.

Bob flashed his torch around. Lieutenant Colonel Ferguson was there, as were Captain Anthony Darlington and Sergeant Gilbert Potter. There was also another captain, while in the darkness a group of four soldiers stood a little way away, the tips of their cigarettes lighting up brightly as they puffed on them. He guessed they had been detailed to carry the body away. Then he shone his torch down at the body.

'Was this the position he was in when you last saw him alive, Monique?' he asked.

'Pretty much so.'

'That suggests he made no effort to defend himself from his killer. Perhaps he had too much on his mind already to realise what was happening, or just didn't see them approaching from behind him.'

Bob looked at Ferguson, 'I appreciate it will be difficult to say while he's still in situ, but is it safe to assume that he died from the wound to the head? To say his head injury is serious is an understatement.'

It was Anthony Darlington who replied. 'This is the medical officer, Captain Butler. He's had a look and is best placed to give an opinion, sir.'

Captain Butler appeared to be about forty and looked uncomfortable to be the centre of attention.

He coughed. 'Thank you, yes. As far as I can see without moving him, sir, he suffered perhaps a dozen or more stab wounds on the back and side of his torso, and there was at least one very heavy blow to the head. The head wound would have killed him instantly, but I don't know if it was done before or after the knife wounds. I'm afraid I've never studied forensic medicine. The knife wounds appear to have been made by a narrow non-serrated blade, a little less than an inch wide and thicker in the middle than at the edges. The one wound I've been able to look at closely, on the side of the neck, has a diamond cross-section where the skin is pierced.'

Bob saw Captain Darlington bend down and reach for his lower right leg. Then he stood up and held something out to the medical officer.

'Could it have been a knife like this one?'

The medical officer took it, and then looked at it from different angles in the light of his torch.

'I'd say it was a knife very much like that one that inflicted the wound I looked at.'

'It's a Fairbairn–Sykes fighting knife, standard issue to men who have passed their commando training,' said Captain Darlington.

He took the knife back from the medical officer and replaced it in what Bob now realised was a sheath attached to the outside of his right calf under his trouser leg.

'What about the blow to the head?' asked Bob.

The medical officer knelt and shone his torch at what was left of the top of Bill Douglas's head. 'You can see he's lying on his side in a foetal position, probably in reaction to the injuries he'd suffered shortly before. I'd say that someone came up from behind him with something like a hand axe, the sort of thing that might be used for chopping firewood. They then hit him with extreme force with the sharp edge of the axe. All the blood, brains, hair, and fragments of the skull make it difficult to see, but there's what looks like a fresh scar on the concrete of the paving slab directly beneath the top of the head, just where it would have been struck by the blade of the axe.

'I might be able to tell you more if I can get him moved to the medical centre, but as I said, this isn't my area of expertise. You might be better seeing if the local police have a doctor who knows more than I do about murder victims.'

'Should I see to that, sir?' asked Lieutenant Colonel Ferguson.

'Yes, please,' said Bob. 'I think we can move the body now, though do you have anyone who could take some flash photographs of it, and the area around it, before we do so? Can you also get its outline marked in chalk so we can be sure of its position in the morning?'

'Yes, of course.'

Bob had crouched down to follow what the medical officer was saying and now stood up. 'It seems to me that Bill Douglas stayed on the ground after Madame Dubois left the scene. At some point very soon afterwards, certainly before the help she asked for arrived, someone took advantage of his incapacity to stab him multiple times with a fighting knife and chop his head open with an axe, though we're not sure which was done first.'

'It sounds like the killer came prepared to murder the victim, sir,' said Michael.

'Indeed, it wasn't someone who just happened to stumble across him and just happened to have a knife and an axe on their person. Monique, did you see anyone else in the gardens while you were here, either before or after you encountered Bill Douglas?'

'I didn't see anyone, but I had a strong sense someone was watching me when I walked back from the steps down from the wall walk over there.' She gestured into the darkness. 'I stopped and looked. I saw no one but still felt uncomfortable.'

'Which means it's possible someone was already here, perhaps waiting for Bill Douglas,' said Bob. 'It would be useful to know how long the killer had between you leaving, Monique, and the body being found in its current state. You said you walked across the Inner Close to speak to the sentry over by the entrance to the Palace. Do we know what happened next?'

'I may be able to help,' said Captain Butler. 'I take my turn with the other officers here to act as orderly officer. Tonight, I was on duty. The orderly officer works from a couple of small rooms in the King's Old Building, which are reached by one of the doors along the upper side of the Inner Close. It's not actually all that far from the other end of this passage. I became aware of a problem when the sentry your colleague spoke to burst in, saying that he'd been told that someone was ill in the Douglas Gardens. I told him to return to his post and asked another private who was there to accompany me. I may have delayed a moment to put on my uniform cap and greatcoat, but it was only a moment. I noticed that the clock on the wall was showing a minute or two before 9.50 p.m. as I left. When we emerged from this end of the passage and saw the body it was obvious that "ill" was something of an understatement and I sent the man who had accompanied me to alert Lieutenant Colonel Ferguson.'

'Did you see anyone else when you arrived in the gardens?' asked Bob.

'No, and it was still light enough for me to have seen if anyone else was about. I was of course rather distracted by what I'd found but I did look around quite carefully, and nervously, I must admit, in what felt like rapidly gathering gloom.'

'How about when you were approaching the far end of the passage?' asked Monique. 'You only need to be a few steps this side of the body and you'd be visible along the passage from the Inner Close. I think that was why Bill Douglas pushed me into the corner. Did you see anyone then?'

'Sorry, ma'am,' said the captain. 'I came straight here from the office, which meant I approached from the uphill side and couldn't see along the line of the passage until I got to it. And the sentry you spoke to would still have been returning to his post at the Palace entrance at that point, so would have had his back to the passage entrance.'

'Thank you,' said Bob. 'I don't think we can do much more here until it gets light. Once the body's been photographed and its position marked, it can be moved to where it can be examined by a police surgeon. In the meantime, perhaps Anthony and Gilbert could start talking to all the sentries on duty and anyone else who might have been about at the time to see if anyone saw or heard anything. The sooner we can talk to them the fresher things will be in their minds. First, though, I want you to retrace Monique's steps to where she told the sentry that Bill Douglas was ill, then walk swiftly from there to the office where the sentry spoke to Captain Butler, then back here, and time the excursion. Give or take how long it took to don coats, that ought to give us a rough idea of how long the killer had between Monique leaving here and Captain Butler arriving. It would be helpful if Captain Butler could first show you where the orderly officer's rooms are, and if Monique could point out where the sentry was standing.

'We also need to talk to all those who are here at the castle to attend Sir Peter's meeting. Michael, could you and Monique speak briefly to each of them now, mainly to establish basic details and to find out who had come out of the Palace before this happened and whether they saw or heard anything? I think it may be particularly useful to find out who knew Bill Douglas, whether because they worked with him or had done so in the past, or because they simply talked to him at dinner. If there's one thing that we can be sure of, it's that this wasn't a random attack. Someone wanted Bill Douglas dead, and they wanted it done in a very particular way.'

'Most of those here for the meeting will probably have gone to bed by now,' said Monique.

'I know, but I want that basic information tonight, even if it means knocking on bedroom doors and waking people up. It will give us something to work with in the morning.'

'What about Sir Peter, the commodore and the man from the Cabinet Office?' asked Michael.

'You can pass on my apologies, but you need to talk to them too.'

'What are you going to do, Bob?' asked Monique.

'I want to do some historical research,' said Bob.

CHAPTER ELEVEN

Lieutenant Colonel Ferguson arranged for Bob to be met by a Sergeant MacMillan outside the education centre in the Chapel Royal. He worked in the centre and was also the regiment's part-time librarian. He unlocked the main door, now with its own sentry, and led Bob inside.

'I was a teacher in a primary school in Clackmannan until I joined the regiment, sir. It's nice to be doing much the same sort of thing here, not all that far away.' He led the way along a dimly lit corridor. 'The library, such as it is, is on shelves along one side of the reading room in the corner of the building on the ground floor. This is it.'

'When is it normally open to readers?'

'8 a.m. to 9 p.m., sir. The men are worked hard during training, and some like to come here in the evenings to read and relax.'

He turned on the lights and went to check the blackout curtains covering the window were doing their job.

'Were you looking for something specific, sir?'

'I want to know more about the murder in the castle by King James II of a man called William Douglas in 1452.'

'Ah, the 8th Earl of Douglas, who came to a very brutal end. Your best bet might be the standard history of the castle, written by Eric Stair-Kerr in 1913. It's a book we encourage the men passing through here to read, as the castle is important to the Argylls. It's so well-read that we've got three copies.'

Sergeant MacMillan walked over to one of the sets of shelves. 'Someone must have one out, but there are two copies here.'

'Don't touch anything, sergeant. I've got some rubber gloves in my pocket and will have a look myself. Bob donned the gloves then pulled one of two brown hardback books off the shelf and opened it.

'It's in chronological order, which helps,' he said, riffling through the pages. 'I've overshot a little. This is it: *"the King twice plunged his knife into Earl William's body. Sir Patrick Gray, Sir Alexander Boyd, Stewart of Darnley and other courtiers soon dispatched the helpless noble, and having finished the work of butchery, rudely flung the corpse out of the window."* You say there are normally three copies?'

'Yes, sir. The library is only staffed for a few hours each day, and the men sign out any books they borrow in the loans book here. I've been looking through while you were finding the right page and can't see any mention of that book, not in the last month, anyway.'

'Which means that there's a copy missing?'

'Yes, sir, but I've no idea when it went missing. I'll tell you what is interesting, though. The story as it's told in that book isn't quite as I remember it. I thought that after the king had stabbed the earl twice, one of the courtiers finished him off with a poleaxe, a fighting axe on a long pole, which he used to slice open his head. Then others stabbed the body before they threw it out of the window.'

'I don't suppose you've got anything here that might tell that alternative version of what happened?'

'It's a long shot sir, but we do have a copy of John Hill Burton's eight-volume *The History of Scotland*. It's on the bottom shelf down there and is not one of our most popular reads. I assume you don't want me to touch it?'

'That's right,' said Bob. 'I might want to get these books

fingerprinted, which is why I'm wearing these gloves.'

He pulled out one of the old-looking books from the middle of the row of nine, counting the volume containing the index. He opened it and flicked through, then replaced it. It took two more attempts before he found what he wanted. '1452 falls right at the end of Volume II. Here we go: *"and he twice stabbed his guest"*. It goes on to say that another man *"came up and felled him with a pole-axe. His body was cast from the chamber-window into the court below."* That sounds closer to what you remember.'

'It is, sir, but again it only tells part of the story because it omits the subsequent stabbing by others present. I honestly can't remember where I read my version, but I'm quite sure I remember what I read correctly.'

'Thank you, sergeant, that's extremely helpful. Is it possible there's another book here that tells the complete story?'

'I don't believe so, sir.'

'OK, thank you. Do you have a box I can put these books in so we can check them for fingerprints without needing to keep a guard on the education centre overnight? It will need to be big enough for the full set of Scottish history books and the two copies of the castle's history. And you're sure there's no way of checking who took the third copy of the history of the castle?'

'I can help with the box and will certainly have a more careful look through the loans book, but it's a simple system that works on trust and I'm sure I'd have seen an entry for it if there was one. I've known popular fiction books to disappear without a trace from the library, but never a history book. And I ought to warn you that if you are fingerprinting the books, you are likely to find mine on most of them.'

'If we do fingerprint them, I'll get someone to take your

prints so we can exclude you.'

*

'These beds weren't made for two,' said Bob.

'I think you'll find that's why they are called single beds, my love. If you don't like it, you can always go to the room you were allocated and sleep on your own.'

'No, I prefer the company. I'm sorry if I seem preoccupied. I'm trying to work out if we did everything we could before giving up for the night.'

'I think so,' said Monique. 'We got a picture of everyone's whereabouts while things were still fresh in their minds, and I think we can map out who from amongst those involved in Sir Peter's meeting knew or had ever met Bill Douglas. Or at least who is prepared to admit to it. I was pleased we found Sir Peter still up and about with the commodore. I didn't want to have to knock on their bedroom doors and wake them up. We still need to cross-refer what we've been told, but we've at least got something to work with.'

'That's true,' said Bob. 'To my mind, the top priority in the morning will be to take a proper look at the scene of the murder and try to work out what happened after you left the gardens.'

'You mean later this morning,' said Monique. 'We're not going to get much sleep before we need to get moving again.'

'There is one thing you could do for me first, Monique.'

'Are you being serious, Bob? You know I'm as enthusiastic as you are, but is sex really the most important thing on your mind just now? Besides, my encounter with that bastard Bill Douglas did nothing to help my ribs heal.'

'I'm sorry about your ribs, but that wasn't what I meant.

While it's still fresh, can you tell me what Bill Douglas said to you about the 1452 murder?'

'I told you earlier.'

'I know, but I need to know as exactly as possible what he said.'

'Well after he'd spun his yarn about the gardens being a place of pilgrimage for him that he'd not visited since he was a schoolboy, he went on to talk about the murder itself. He said something about the king personally murdering the earl with a dagger before another man, and I quote, "bashed his brains out". He then said that other men had inflicted further wounds on the body before throwing it out of the window, and it ended up where we were standing at the time. Which was only a few paces from where Bill Douglas's body ended up.'

'Nothing else?'

'He went on to say that the building standing there now had replaced the one that was there in 1452, in which the murder took place, so the window there now isn't actually the one the earl was thrown out of. But that was about it. Why does it matter, Bob?'

'I'm not sure. I've now read or heard four accounts of that murder. One book, the one we're missing a copy of, had him stabbed by the king and then by others, and a second had him stabbed twice by the king and then felled by a poleaxe. The sergeant in the library, who used to be a teacher, remembered that the story he'd read was that the king stabbed the earl twice, then another man sliced his head open with a poleaxe, then others stabbed the body, and then they threw it out of the window.'

'I'm still not following you.'

'It seems to me that other than the sergeant in the library

and the murderer, no one agrees on those three elements. Even Bill Douglas talked to you about the earl having his brains "bashed out", which to my mind doesn't really imply the use of an axe. Yet in recreating what happened for Bill Douglas's benefit, the murderer knew about the multiple stab wounds and the axe. They couldn't have got that information from either of the books in the library that mention the incident, and they are apparently the only ones that do. What I'm feeling my way towards is the sense that the murderer already knew the story and had no need to go and look it up.'

'Where does that get us?' asked Monique.

'Again, I don't know. But I'm wondering if it means we're looking for someone who knows Bill Douglas's family history, perhaps even better than he did; as well as someone who disliked him even more than you.'

'Of course, you have met one person who knows the same version of the story as the murderer.'

'Who? The librarian? He didn't strike me as the type. And I'm sure he wouldn't have revealed what he knew about the 1452 murder if Bill Douglas's death had anything to do with him.'

'Really?' asked Monique.

There was silence for a few moments.

'Bloody hell! I'm going to have to get up and have someone put Sergeant MacMillan in custody until we can interview him more fully, aren't I?'

'Perhaps that's better than waking up in the morning to find he's disappeared.'

'Keep the bed warm for me, Monique.'

'Of course, Bob.'

*

Monique seemed to be asleep when Bob returned to her room, but she turned towards him as he climbed into the narrow bed in the dark.

'God, Bob, you're cold. Is everything sorted?'

'I can't say I feel very proud of myself, having a man locked up for the rest of the night simply for trying to help us. But as you said, it's better to be safe than sorry. As you also said, we need to get some sleep.'

'We do, but I've been thinking about my ribs,' said Monique.

'What about them?' asked Bob.

'If you lay on your back and I get on top, I think I can avoid hurting them any further.'

She had one arm wrapped round him and Bob felt her hand move down his back.

'Your bum is really cold, Bob.'

He eased away from her to give her more room as she moved her hand round his side to his stomach, and then lower.

'But other parts of you are very much warmer. Roll on to your back, Bob. I've been thinking about this since you went out and I don't want to have to wait any longer.'

CHAPTER TWELVE

Sergeant MacMillan was still on Bob's conscience when he awoke, so he and Monique went to talk to the man before going for breakfast. It seemed the entire garrison was up and about early, with groups of men marching in one direction or running in the other, all under the scrutiny of non-commissioned officers shouting commands. There were no regimental officers in sight and Bob wondered whether they were allowed to sleep in later than their men.

It turned out that the sergeant was being held in a cell in the guardhouse in the lower, northern, part of the castle. The Nether Bailey it was called, according to Captain Butler, who was still on duty as the orderly officer and had directed them.

It was a beautiful late April morning. Despite the early hour, the chill of the previous night seemed to be receding quickly. Bob thought it was good not to have to wear a coat.

Access to the Nether Bailey was via the North Gate, which formed a slightly descending curving tunnel under a building and had a sentry posted who asked to see their identification. The guardhouse was not far beyond the gate. The corporal on duty in the guardroom looked startled when Bob entered. He jumped up, saluted, and stood to attention.

'At ease, we've come to see Sergeant MacMillan.'

'He's in the end cell, sir.'

'Is there anywhere we can talk to him?'

'You can use this room, sir. I'll wait outside.'

Sergeant MacMillan looked rather dishevelled when the corporal brought him from the cell but smiled when he saw Bob. Bob invited him to sit at a small square table and he and

Monique took two of the other sides. Bob had thought MacMillan seemed to be in his mid-thirties the previous night. He looked nearer forty this morning.

'I introduced myself when we met last night,' said Bob. 'This is my colleague, Madame Dubois, who works with me in Military Intelligence, Section 11. I'm sorry to have had you brought here in the middle of the night. Have you had breakfast, by the way?'

'Not yet, sir. There's no need to apologise. I did rather let myself in for it. When we spoke, I'd already heard that someone had been killed in the Douglas Gardens where the 8th Earl is traditionally believed to have ended up and that he had a similar range of injuries. I'd imagine that when you realised that at least one person in the castle knew what the 8th Earl's injuries had been, I had to be considered a suspect in what seems like an attempt to do something very similar.'

'That's right, sergeant. What you might find interesting is that the similarities go deeper than the gossip appears to suggest. The man who was killed worked for the Secret Intelligence Service, MI6 if you prefer, and his name was Bill Douglas.'

'That's quite a coincidence. Or is it?'

'Not really. The William Douglas, or "Bill", who was killed last night was a direct descendent of the 9th Earl of Douglas.'

'The younger brother of the William Douglas who was killed in 1452.'

'That's the one,' said Bob. 'It looks to me as if someone knew the modern Bill Douglas well enough to want to kill him and knew the story of the earlier murder well enough to be able to re-enact elements of it.'

'As you know, I qualify on the second count. But I'm sorry

to disappoint you. As far as I know, I've never met the man who was killed last night. I didn't even know he existed. Where's he from?'

'He talked about his family having estates in south-west Scotland and said he grew up there,' said Monique. 'I don't know where exactly. What about you? What's your background?'

'I was born and brought up in Clackmannan, not far down the River Forth from here. I did well at school and went on to study at the University of St Andrews. For family reasons I then had to return to Clackmannan for a while and ended up teaching in a primary school. I got married to a girl I'd first met when we were at school together, but she died of a brain tumour.'

'I'm sorry,' said Monique.

'Thank you. We had no children and my wife's death left me a bit rudderless. In 1937, the year after she died, I signed up for the Argylls, more properly known as the Argyll and Sutherland Highlanders. You'd have thought I'd have been able to see there was a war just round the corner, but it never occurred to me. For me, it was just a way of breaking free of my life in Clackmannan and seeing the world. I've ended up teaching much larger children in army uniforms, less than ten miles from where I started, but I really can't complain. I enjoy what I do, and I think I make a real difference to some of the men who are trained here.

'But I must repeat what I've already said. I'd never met your Bill Douglas and had no reason to want him dead. Whoever killed him, it wasn't me.'

'Thank you, sergeant,' said Bob. 'I'll get you released from here and let you get back to your duties. One thing does puzzle me. If the regiment recruits in Argyll and in Sutherland, how did a man from Clackmannan become involved?'

'The regiment came about through an amalgamation of two others in 1881, sir. Until then, the 93rd Sutherland Highlanders had recruited in Sutherland, while the 91st Argyllshire Regiment had tried to recruit in Argyll. In practice, most of the officers came from there, but they'd always had problems overcoming the natural tendency in Argyll for the sort of men they needed to prefer service in the navy to the army. As a result, they always had to make the numbers up with men from other parts of Scotland, especially the west side of central Scotland, and from England and Ireland. After the 1881 amalgamation, the areas of recruitment for the new regiment included Argyll, as before, but also a swathe of the country to the north of Glasgow extending as far east as Stirling, Clackmannan, and Kinross. Plus, especially since the war started, just about anywhere else. Our only real connection with Sutherland these days is in the name itself, and in the fact that our origins allow us to regard ourselves as a highland regiment rather than a lowland regiment.'

'Thank you,' said Bob. 'That's helpful.'

'I didn't get much sleep last night, sir, and had a lot of time to think. I'm wondering if I can be of more help to you.'

'In what way?'

'I wonder if it would be useful for you to know the origin of the story of the 1452 murder? Last night you found two different accounts in books in the library, and I knew a third. What really did happen and where was it recorded, and why are there different versions? I'd love to be able to satisfy my curiosity about that, but I think it might be of help to you too.'

'What do you suggest?'

'If you can get the regiment to allow me the use of a car, I can drive to Edinburgh and see what they've got in the National Library of Scotland. I'm sure they will have the definitive version of the story, whatever it is. There's another thing, too. If you're looking for people who knew the man who was killed last night, then it might help to find out more about him. If he's descended from an earl and his family has estates in south-west Scotland, then there will be publicly available records somewhere. Narrowing down where he came from might give you more to go on than you have at present.'

'Thank you,' said Bob. 'That's an excellent idea. I'll find someone to get you a car.'

'If you don't mind, sir, I'll get a shave and some breakfast before I go, but that shouldn't take long.'

*

The regiment had made a small office available to Bob, upstairs at the rear of the building in which he'd had his initial meeting. Given the weather was so good he chose instead to ask the team to meet in the gardens. First, though, he telephoned his secretary at Craigiehall to let her know where he and the others were.

The five of them stood in a circle near a large tree a little distance from the chalk-marked and blood-stained area of paving where Bill Douglas had been killed. There'd been a sentry at the Inner Close end of the passage and Bob could see another where the gardens narrowed at their eastern end, while a third stood outside the door of a single-storey building that ran along part of the western end of the garden.

'It all looks quite different in daylight,' said Bob. 'I want to discuss what we've done so far and decide what we should be concentrating on this morning. I'd like to start by asking Monique to talk us through your walk in the gardens after dinner last night and your encounter with Bill Douglas.'

'Yes, of course, Bob. When I arrived yesterday afternoon a soldier gave me a quick familiarisation tour of the castle. We passed through these gardens quite quickly and I was attracted by the idea of spending rather more time here after dinner.

'I came in via the passage over there, and then walked this way, across to our left, to the steps leading up to the higher section of wall walk that comes round behind us. I spent a bit of time enjoying the views and moving slowly round the wall and then over to the western side. Once I got too cold, I came down the steps over in the far corner, near the end of the King's Old Building, and walked back towards the end of the passage.

'That was when I got the strong feeling someone was watching me. I stopped and looked around but couldn't see anyone in the gardens, or in any of the windows on this end of the building. As you can see it's quite large and part of it rises to four storeys. The windows I could see clearly had closed internal shutters; I suppose to comply with blackout regulations. I didn't see any lights from any windows. The feeling persisted, but I couldn't establish its cause. I walked on and met Bill Douglas as he was coming out from the archway at the end of the passage. I asked him if he'd been following me, and he said not. I think he was telling the truth.

'I should add for those who don't know, for Anthony and Gilbert, that I've crossed paths with Bill Douglas in the past. In my early days in SIS in London, I was under his supervision and he tried to blackmail me into sleeping with him. When I doused him with beer in a pub, he tried to have me labelled as an enemy agent. You'll already have worked out that we didn't succeed in putting our differences behind us last night. When we met, he took a much more direct approach to what he wanted, and I had to defend myself. He ended up lying in the corner over there feeling extremely sorry for himself, with very sore balls and possibly a damaged windpipe.'

'Brava!' said Gilbert Potter, enthusiastically.

Monique smiled at him. 'We talked about what happened after that when we met last night.'

'We did,' said Bob. 'Anthony, how did your timed re-enactment go?'

'There's a bit of a margin for uncertainty, but I'd say our killer had perhaps three minutes from the time Monique left the gardens to the time Captain Butler came back into them.'

'Thank you. And in that time, they had to kill Bill Douglas and get sufficiently clear to be out of sight of the captain when he arrived. I say "they" as shorthand for "he or she", but I must admit that an axe feels like the sort of weapon a man would use. We should keep an open mind of course.'

'We should, Bob,' said Monique. 'I'm sure there are women out there who would be happy to kill Bill Douglas with an axe or with anything else for that matter.'

'You are right, of course,' said Bob. 'It would be helpful for us to identify ways into and out of the gardens for someone intent on murder, plus potential hiding places once they got here. We also need to think about possible means of disposing of the axe. I'm assuming the killer will have kept the commando knife. As Anthony demonstrated last night, they are quite easy to hide.'

'I know how I'd dispose of the axe,' said Monique. 'Part of the wall walk running round the edge of the gardens looks out over the Nether Bailey, where the army has its guardhouse and firing range. But from the corner beyond the small building over there to the end of the King's Old Building, it looks out over a sheer drop formed by the wall and the side of the rock the castle stands on. I tried to look down on my walk, despite the thickness of the parapets, and got the sense of craggy rocks with trees and bushes growing out of them, and then more trees where the gradient is less sheer. If it was me, I'd have thrown the axe over the wall and down the cliff.'

It was Michael who responded. 'I see the attraction, but wouldn't it take time to go over there, climb up the steps, drop the axe over the edge and then reverse the process? And we know that time was one thing our murderer didn't have much of.'

'Why be so measured?' asked Monique. 'You could just run over to somewhere close to the wall, then throw the axe clear over it. That might mean it fell somewhere beyond the sheer sections of the rock to where it might be more accessible, but it would still be well hidden if no one thought to look. With all the shutters closed, there'd be no chance of our killer being seen from inside the building.'

'That's one for me, I think,' said Anthony Darlington. 'I'll get the regiment to do a sweep for the axe along the castle rock below the wall, extending as far up it as possible.'

'I have something else in mind for you, Anthony,' said Bob. 'I'd be grateful if Michael could organise the search for the axe. And while the Argylls are down there, they might usefully also look for any indications that someone could have climbed down the outside of the walls. Discarded rope or that sort of thing. The same is true beyond the rest of the wall, where it drops to the Nether Bailey. Is there anywhere where someone could have looped a rope round something, then gone over the wall before unlooping the rope and pulling it down after them? Then we have the building in the corner, which needs searching, I get the sense there's an area behind it, between it and the wall. We should look there too. And the defensive outpost in the wall we were told about.

'There are other possibilities too, of course. I saw a blocked-off doorway in the passage, into the education centre, which rules that out, and there are no windows on this side of the building. But some of the windows on this side of the King's Old Building are on the ground floor and could perhaps have been points of entry or exit, though the shutters Monique saw would make that more difficult. There are also the two doors I can see, one at ground floor level and, a little nearer, one at first-floor level accessed by that odd set of external stone steps that takes a right-angled turn part way up.

'Finally, there's the narrow end of the gardens to our left. Do we know where that wall walk goes to after it disappears out of sight?'

'It passes behind the Great Hall,' said Monique. 'Then it curves round behind the building above the gateway to the Nether Bailey before ending up in the northern corner of the Outer Close.'

'Michael, could you liaise with Lieutenant Colonel Ferguson to provide enough manpower to check on all those possibilities and ensure that all the rooms beyond the doors or lower-level windows facing onto the gardens are searched? Meanwhile, Monique and I will interview in rather more depth the six people attending the meeting who last night said they knew or had met Bill Douglas.

'I should say for completeness that a man I identified in the middle of the night as a possible suspect is no longer one. His name is Sergeant Alan MacMillan, and he runs the library here. I've recruited him to do some research for us in Edinburgh into the original 1452 murder that was partly re-enacted here last night and to investigate Bill Douglas's background. If we know more about where Douglas was brought up, it might be easier to identify people who knew him in the past.'

'Anthony, could you and Gilbert meet the police surgeon? I'm told he is due to look at the body at 9.30 a.m. in the mortuary at Stirling Royal Infirmary. I understand that's where he's based. See if he has anything useful to add to what we already know. Then I'd like you to talk to the people who look after the service records here.'

'What are we looking for, sir?' asked Anthony.

'I wondered whether anyone currently based at the castle might in the past have trained at the Commando Basic Training Centre at Achnacarry Castle, perhaps not making the grade and being sent back on a "return to unit" basis.'

'You think we might find who owns that commando knife?' asked Anthony. 'They are highly desirable pieces of kit, sir, and more likely to have been come by in a game of cards than at Achnacarry. Remember, too, that the knife and the beret only get awarded to men who complete the training. But we will certainly look.'

'I agree, but we shouldn't dismiss the possibility. And an even longer shot might be for you to get a sense of how many men based here come from south-west Scotland, and so might conceivably have known Bill Douglas when he was younger. The regiment doesn't recruit there, so there may not be many. With any luck, we'll be able to narrow that down to a specific location later, but an initial idea would be helpful. Right, does anyone else have anything they want to say?'

'Just one thing, sir,' said Michael Dixon. 'Monique, can you go over to the steps you came down from the wall walk, then walk to where you met Bill Douglas? What I'd like to know is where you first had the sense that someone was watching you.'

'Of course, Michael.' Monique did as he had asked while the others watched. The steps from the door at first-floor level protruded out into the gardens and her route took her just past them.

'I think it was about here,' she said, stopping close to the steps.

'And last night you stopped and looked around when you were exactly where you are now?' asked Michael.

'I'm not certain, but perhaps I walked a few more paces before the feeling became strong enough to cause me to react.'

'Right, stay there.' Michael walked over to her. There are a few places you could have been watched from, even excluding the windows in the building. But a thought did occur to me.' He ducked down and shuffled beneath the angle of the turn of the stone stairs, obscured from Bob's sight by the supporting stonework.

'How about this for a hiding place for our killer?' Michael asked. 'There's an area beneath the lower flight of stairs that is large enough to take a crouching man. It's not obvious, but pretty handy for this end of the passage. If you were waiting for Bill Douglas to come to the gardens and didn't want anyone to know you were here, it wouldn't be a bad spot.'

Michael re-emerged, dusting himself down.

'I was only a yard or so away,' said Monique, 'but didn't see or hear anything. I can see into part of the space down there from here.' She took three steps towards the passage and turned round. 'But if I'd gone a little further before I looked, which I think I did, the angle would have changed. I can't see into the space from here. But how did the killer know Bill Douglas would be coming into the gardens when he did? It's not the sort of hiding place you'd trust for hours on end. It's not obvious, but it wouldn't have been completely invisible from some angles even though the light was fading at the time.'

'Well done, Michael,' said Bob. 'We should still explore all the other possibilities because even if our killer was waiting under the steps, we need to know where they went afterwards. And you're right, Monique, if we could work out how the killer knew Bill Douglas would be coming here when he did, we might be rather closer to identifying them. Right, let's get moving. We can gather again before lunch, but if you need me in the meantime, Monique and I will be conducting our interviews in an office in the education centre so we can call in our interviewees with minimum disruption to Sir Peter's conference.'

CHAPTER THIRTEEN

The first interviewee was Daniel Elliot, a portly dark-haired man in his fifties from the Foreign Office. He said he'd met Bill Douglas the year before to discuss staffing issues at a joint unit set up between the Foreign Office and SIS in New York, the details of which he declined to reveal to Bob and Monique. He was happy to tell them that he'd found Douglas to be 'rather full of himself' but it seemed they'd had a productive meeting. Letters had been exchanged afterwards, but there had been no need to meet again. That, it seemed, had been the extent of their interaction. After the previous night's dinner, Mr Elliot had stayed for drinks in the officers' mess bar.

Bob and Monique then talked to a short, wiry man in his forties called Gareth Keeble from Military Intelligence 2. He told them he dealt with intelligence gathered in several middle eastern counties but preferred to say no more than that. He said he had met Bill Douglas for the first time at dinner the previous night because they'd been seated next to one another. He'd not really liked Douglas and by the time the starters had been cleared away each was talking almost exclusively to their respective other neighbours. After dinner he had gone straight back to his room and stayed there, working on, he was at pains to emphasise, non-classified material he had brought to Scotland with him.

Their third interview was with Bill Douglas's other neighbour at dinner, an older man called Brian Jack. He had grey hair and appeared to keep himself fit. He said he worked in the personnel department of MI5 and that he knew Monique by reputation, as Vera Duval, even though they'd never met.

He'd also never met Douglas before the dinner, but he had an interest in history and found the story Douglas told about his family and his links with the castle fascinating.

'What did he tell you about the murder of the 8th Earl?' asked Bob.

'He'd had a couple of glasses of wine by this time and was really into the flow of the story. According to him, King James II tried to persuade the 8th Earl of Douglas to renounce a bond with other powerful earls that he saw as a threat to the crown. When that didn't work the king, who by this point was probably drunk anyway, lost his temper, pulled out a dagger and stabbed the earl twice, once in the neck. Then another man chopped his head open with a poleaxe and after that everyone else joined in with knives, apparently to keep on the right side of a king known for his fiery temper. What was left of the body was thrown out of a window into the gardens outside.

'Bill Douglas said that he'd not visited the place where his however many times great-uncle had been killed since he was 15 and that after dinner, if it finished while it was still light enough, he was going to pay his respects by visiting the Douglas Gardens for the first time in two decades. He asked me to go with him.'

'Did you?' asked Monique.

'No, sadly. If I had, then perhaps he would still be alive.'

'What did you do after dinner?' asked Bob.

'I went out for a walk I'd planned before coming to Stirling, out of the castle and down the hill into the town, and then back. I wanted to see the house used by Lord Darnley, the ill-fated second husband of Mary, Queen of Scots. I've always thought he was maligned by history.'

'Did anyone see you?'

'I spoke to the guards at the main gate as I left, just a greeting, and they checked my documents when I returned. There were also a couple of sentries about at that end of the castle who might have noticed me and a few soldiers who seemed to be returning from an evening in the town. But I was on my own, so otherwise no.'

Bob looked at Monique after Brian Jack had left the room. 'It seems that Bill Douglas did know all the details of the killing, even if he summarised them when talking to you.'

'Yes, and Brian Jack knows them too, which means we've got to consider him to be a suspect.'

'Agreed,' said Bob. 'But we'll be able to check his story about leaving the castle easily enough. If he's telling the truth, I see no way that he could have been in the gardens at the time Douglas was killed. I did have another thought, Monique. You were at the dinner. Do you think it's possible that if Bill Douglas was telling the story of the murder to his neighbour on one side, then the neighbour on the other could have overheard?'

'Gareth Keeble? If he did, then it becomes more interesting that he had no alibi after the dinner. Though the sentry I spoke to last night would have seen him coming and going, just as he saw me. That's something to check but, to be honest, I doubt if he would have been able to hear the story. Or the person sitting beyond Brian Jack either. There was quite a buzz of conversation around the table. Anyway, if someone only heard the story for the first time at dinner, they'd have had to get hold of an axe and a knife and get to the gardens and find a hiding place, all in the short time before I got there. It doesn't seem very likely.'

'I tend to agree,' said Bob. 'Right, who's next?'

Claire Summers had blonde hair and strikingly green eyes and appeared to be in her mid-twenties. Bob thought she seemed extremely nervous as Monique showed her in and asked her to sit on the other side of the office's small table.

'Hello, Claire,' said Monique after doing the introductions. 'Can you tell me how you know Bill Douglas?'

'I work in the Secret Intelligence Service registry. We manage papers and ensure that files are up to date and available when needed. Last Christmas I was with some friends from work in a pub near Trafalgar Square when Bill Douglas came in. He knew one of the people I was with and joined the group. We were introduced and spent a lot of time talking. He was rather old for me but charming, interesting and amusing. When some of the others left, he suggested we go to another pub. I ended up drinking much more than I was used to, and then we went back to his flat.'

She paused.

'What happened at his flat, Claire?' prompted Monique.

'To cut a long story short, he raped me there. He knew I was very drunk, and he ignored me when I made clear I wasn't happy with what he was trying to do and wanted to get a taxi home. He simply carried on until he'd got his way by force. I was in quite a state when I got back to the friend's house I stay at. She wanted me to call the police, but I didn't think they'd believe me. The same was true in the office. I wanted to report what had happened, but it would have been his word against mine and he was much more senior in SIS.'

'How do you feel about his death?' asked Monique.

'I probably shouldn't say this, but I feel deeply relieved. It's like a shadow that's been following me about for months has gone.'

'Did you kill him?'

'No. I wish I had, to be honest. But I don't think I'd have been able to, even if the opportunity had arisen. Do you know that he didn't even seem to recognise me last night? I sat almost opposite him at dinner, and he looked straight through me like I wasn't there.'

'What did you do after dinner?'

'I went to the officers' mess bar because I knew there would be other people there. At the end of the meal, Bill Douglas finished his glass of wine and left the room. I wasn't sure where he'd gone, and I followed some of the others to the bar. When I saw he wasn't there, I stayed for a couple of drinks. If he'd been there, I'd have gone back to my room and locked the door.'

'Thank you, Claire,' said Monique. She looked at Bob. 'I think that's all the questions we've got for you.'

'Can I ask you one, Madame Dubois?'

'Of course.'

'They are saying Bill Douglas attacked a woman last night and she injured him before he was killed. You were at the dinner. Was it you?'

'Yes, it was, but I didn't kill him either.'

'If you are still here tonight, can I buy you a drink in the bar? Just to say thank you.'

'What for?'

'For hurting him.'

Bob waited while Monique showed Claire Summers out.

When she returned to the room, she closed the door and leaned back against it. 'I think we can mark her up as having the first really strong motive we've come across, apart from mine of course.'

'That's true,' said Bob. 'But she's got an alibi we can easily check. If she was at the officers' mess bar last night after dinner, then she'll have been noticed, not just by the men at the dinner, but by any regimental officers who were present too.'

'Yes,' said Monique, 'she is extremely attractive.'

'Right, that's four down and two to go. Who's next?'

The next interviewee Monique showed into the room was a grey-haired woman in a dark jacket and skirt. Bob was unsure of her age but guessed she might be in her fifties.

After she sat down, she looked across the table at Bob, who had introduced himself and Monique. 'I suppose I'm here because I admitted last night to having met the man who was killed?'

'That's right,' said Bob. 'Could you start by telling us who you are?'

'My name is Edith Burns and I work in the Foreign Office, specifically in the part that looks after our relations with the United States.'

'And how did you come to know Bill Douglas?' asked Bob.

'I don't know him. I have merely met him, unfortunately.'

'Why "unfortunately"?'

'Because it means I'm sitting here talking to you rather than taking part in Sir Peter Maitland's meeting.'

'I hope we won't keep you long, Mrs Burns.' Bob had noticed the rings on her wedding finger. 'Can you tell us how you met Mr Douglas?'

'I arrived at RAF Northolt yesterday afternoon to find I was to share an aircraft with two men from the Secret Intelligence Service, Mr Douglas and a rather younger man, a Mr Warner. I got the sense that the two were not the best of friends. The journey to Scotland did not go well. Our aircraft developed a fault and we had to land at an airfield near Carlisle. It took some time to arrange a replacement. As a result, we arrived at RAF Grangemouth much later than originally intended. Although by that time the three of us had spent far longer than expected in each other's company, not much had been said between us. I'd lost myself in a book during the two flights and gone for a walk while we were waiting for the replacement aircraft to be arranged at Carlisle.

'But in the car from RAF Grangemouth to Stirling Castle, I ended up in the back with Mr Douglas while Mr Warner sat in the front reading a newspaper. Or pretending to. I got the sense he was simply trying to avoid having anything to do with Mr Douglas.

'I suspect that the journey by car wasn't a very long one, but it certainly felt it. I was already anxious about the prospect of being late for the start of the dinner. Being late is something I abhor. And then Mr Douglas took it into his head to tell me what felt like his life story. I didn't encourage him, and I tried to indicate I wasn't interested, but he wanted to talk and didn't care whether I wanted to listen.'

'What did he tell you?' asked Bob.

'He said that he was descended from the Black Douglases, a noble family who wielded great power until they fell out of favour and were deprived of their earldom in 1455. The family power base had been a fortress on an island in a river called Threave Castle, near a town called Castle Douglas in Galloway. His family helped found the town and still has extensive landholdings in the area, which he expected to inherit when his father died. That's a little ironic really, with hindsight.'

'Did he say anything about family connections to Stirling Castle?'

'Oh yes, he most certainly did. As he told it, he was directly descended from the 9th Earl of Douglas. That man's older brother, William Douglas, had fallen out with King James II and they had met at Stirling Castle to try to resolve their differences. It didn't work and the king murdered him. Mr Douglas's direct ancestor replaced him and rose in revolt. He failed and had to go into exile, no longer an earl.'

'Did he tell you anything about the actual murder?'

'It wasn't very pleasant but, yes, he did. I think he was trying to shock me. He failed. According to him, the king stabbed the earl twice with a dagger, in the neck and then in the body. Then one of the courtiers split the earl's head open with a large axe. And then the other courtiers present drew their daggers and joined in the carnage. Afterwards, they threw the body out of a window.

'Mr Douglas said that the site where the body ended up was still visible, in what became known as the Douglas Gardens. He'd visited when he was 15 but not since, and very much hoped the dinner wouldn't go on too long so he could visit again before it got dark.'

'What did you do after the dinner finished?' asked Bob.

'I went to the room I've been allocated to unpack and to read my book. And no, other than the sentry in the courtyard outside, no one will be able to confirm that.'

'Thank you, Mrs Burns. That will be all for the moment. You can return to Sir Peter's meeting.'

After Mrs Burns closed the office door behind her, Bob turned to Monique. 'I begin to think that everyone in the castle knows the story of the 1452 murder.'

'It does seem that way. What I'm not clear about is the timing of Bill Douglas's arrival in the gardens,' said Monique.

'Two people have now told us he was hoping it would still be light when the dinner ended so he could go there. He talked about it to me as a pilgrimage. Yet I was there well before him. I'd had time to see what I wanted to see and get cold before he arrived, by which time the best of the light had gone. Why didn't he go immediately after dinner? We know from Claire Summers that he didn't go to the bar. He'd obviously gone back to his room for his coat, but that would only have taken a couple of minutes.'

'That's one of a list of things we don't know at the moment,' said Bob. 'I'm assuming that our last interviewee is the younger SIS officer Mrs Burns told us about, "Mr Warner".'

'That's right, Bob. His name's Alastair Warner and I'll get him now.'

The young man who followed Monique into the room seemed in his mid-twenties. Bob noticed that he had a dark ring under his left eye that looked very much as if someone had hit him.

Bob invited him to sit down, wishing they'd arranged a cup of tea, at least between interviews, but it was too late to think of that now. Then he did the introductions.

'Could I start by asking you how you knew Bill Douglas?'

'When I joined SIS after completing my studies at Oxford, he was my first supervisor. That was late in 1938.'

'How was he as a boss?' asked Bob.

There was a long silence.

'That was meant to be an easy question to help you get into the interview.'

'I know, sir. It's just that what I'm about to tell you won't look particularly good given he was killed last night. The truth is that he was an abysmal boss. He had a habit of telling his superiors what they wanted to hear to further his career, and of being extremely unpleasant to those reporting to him. He was a demanding bully and I think it was worse for any young woman who worked for him. I heard that he had abused his position more than once. I found he belittled anything I did but would have no hesitation claiming credit for work of mine that he thought would make him look good, even if he'd already told me that it was rubbish.

'He damaged my confidence and nearly destroyed my career before it had started. Fortunately, I was transferred away from his section before it was too late. I have done considerably better since then.'

'And then you found yourself at RAF Northolt yesterday afternoon, getting on the same aircraft as him to come to Scotland,' said Monique.

'Yes, it made me feel sick when I saw him. But I tried to ignore him on the plane. On both planes as it turned out because we had to land near Carlisle to get a replacement after a fault. I could tell he was as unhappy to see me as I was him. I asked to visit the control tower when we were on the ground at Carlisle and that helped keep me away from him.'

'What about in the car from Grangemouth to Stirling?' asked Monique.

'I made sure I sat in the front, where I buried myself in a newspaper. It wasn't really possible to read because of the movement of the car, but it saved me from having to get involved in what was happening in the back.'

'What was happening in the back?'

'Bill Douglas regaled that poor woman from the Foreign Office with his life story and then rounded it off with a very unlikely tale about him being descended from the brother of a man who was murdered in this castle by a king. To be honest, I tried not to take any notice.'

'Did you see anything more of Bill Douglas after you arrived?' asked Bob.

'It was a bit of a rush, but I made it to dinner in time, as did the other two. I was relieved to find I wasn't sitting near him during the meal. After dinner, I was making my way to the officers' mess bar with several others when someone tapped me on the shoulder. I turned round to find it was Bill Douglas. We were standing close to a doorway that lets out onto some steps descending to a broad stone terrace built onto the south side of the Palace. He half dragged me down the steps and onto the terrace. Then, in a sort of loud whisper, he demanded to know why I'd told lots of lies about him after I'd worked for him. It was frankly mad, but I could see he was deadly serious and really angry.'

'What happened then?'

'I spent some time talking to him, trying to placate him, but nothing seemed to work.'

'Did anyone else see this?' asked Monique.

'I don't think so. People seemed to have moved away from the doorway that has the view along the terrace and it's a rather isolated spot. Anyway, Bill Douglas just kept on getting angrier and angrier as he ranted on, all in the same weird whisper. Then he grabbed me by my collar, and I brushed his hand away. After that, he punched me in the face. I've still got the mark to show for it.'

He moved his hand up to touch his cheek below his left eye.

'How did it end?' asked Bob.

'I hit him in the stomach and winded him. I left him crouched on the terrace, trying to catch his breath. I then went to the bar and had rather more to drink than I'd initially intended. I half expected him to appear and for hostilities to resume but wasn't sure because I'd heard him tell the woman in the car that he wanted to go somewhere else after dinner.'

'How did you feel when you heard he'd been killed?' asked Monique.

'How would you feel in the circumstances? The world is a better place without him. I've heard that someone decapitated him. I'll buy whoever did it a drink if I meet them. But before you ask the obvious question, no, it wasn't me who killed him. I can't account for my movements while I was outside on the terrace with Bill Douglas, but I now know he was killed in another part of the castle, and I was with people who I'm sure will remember me at dinner and then in the bar afterwards.'

Monique looked tired when she sat down again after showing Alastair Warner out.

'Another strong motive,' she said, 'and another person who knew all the details of the 1452 murder, even if he'd not wanted to listen. But he has another alibi that sounds convincing and will be easy to check. And it seems significant that though he knows about the 1452 murder he got an important detail wrong about last night's killing when he said Bill Douglas had been decapitated. That's not a mistake I'd expect the murderer to make.'

'I agree and I think that's a good summary,' said Bob. 'What is quite remarkable is that the murderer was the third person to have physically damaged Bill Douglas last night.'

'What we've just heard does at least answer my earlier question about why Bill Douglas didn't arrive in the Douglas Gardens until I was leaving them.'

'It does,' said Bob. 'It might also explain why he moved so

quickly to a physical attack on you. His adrenalin was already flowing.'

'The problem we have,' said Monique, 'is that we've only talked to the people who told us last night that they knew or had met Bill Douglas. What if Claire Summers hadn't been honest when we first spoke to her? We'd have no reason to believe she knew him at all. One thing that's clear is that Bill Douglas was an evil man who made a lot of enemies. What if someone else at the meeting is simply denying that they knew him? Which, if you think about it, the murderer would be well advised to do if they thought they could get away with it.'

'You're right of course,' said Bob. 'But we still needed to do what we've done, and I think it has added to what we know. Not least, we now know that Bill Douglas came from Castle Douglas, which might help Anthony and Gilbert when checking on the origins of the Argylls who are based at Stirling Castle.'

CHAPTER FOURTEEN

Bob and Monique left the education centre in the old Chapel Royal after their final interview and walked through the passage to the Douglas Gardens.

'I'd expected to see more activity,' said Bob.

'Remember we've been interviewing those people for some time,' said Monique. 'I'd imagine Michael would have started here, and in the King's Old Building, before moving the focus of the search for clues to the Nether Bailey and beyond the side wall to the cliff forming the castle rock.'

'I'm sure you're right,' said Bob. 'At least this gives us a chance to take another look at the place while it's quiet.'

'You've not been along the wall walk, Bob. It gives a different perspective on the gardens. If we start over to our left, climbing the steps I came down last night, we can follow it round past the back of the Great Hall and into the Outer Close. That will give us a chance to see if any of the others are back at the office we've been assigned.'

Bob followed Monique up the steps, and she then doubled back along the wall walk. He was struck by the views to the west, but then found himself paying more attention to the noises coming from below, from beyond the wall. 'I take back what I said about the level of activity. It sounds like Michael's got half the regiment down there beating their way through the vegetation.'

Monique smiled. 'And from a choice comment I just heard drifting up, some of them aren't too happy about being there. I do hope I've not set them off on a wild goose chase with my theory about the axe.'

'I see what you mean about a different perspective on the gardens,' said Bob. 'I think we can assume that Michael's made sure they've checked all the areas we identified. Let's carry on around the wall walk.'

At one point Monique stopped. 'I think this is about as far as you can see from where Douglas was killed, so if the murderer came this way, they'd have been out of sight of Captain Butler from here on.'

'Yes, it's quite narrow and constricted on this next stretch,' said Bob. 'This enclosed courtyard area behind the Great Hall is interesting. It looks a bit high to have jumped down from the wall onto the cobbles without injuring yourself though. There are a couple of places, like this lookout projecting from the wall by the corner of the building, where someone could have hidden temporarily, but not safely once the alarm had been raised. There's also a door on the right from the wall walk into this building.' He rattled the door. 'It's locked.'

Monique walked ahead. 'Once you are past the narrow part, it opens out again as you enter the corner of the Outer Close. Anyone coming this far and covered in blood would have probably been noticed by a sentry or anyone else going about their duties. It still wasn't completely dark by this time, remember.'

Bob looked along the line of old cannons pointing out through embrasures in the top of the wall and then at the Outer Close more widely which, in marked contrast to the gardens, looked quite busy, with soldiers coming and going singly or in groups.

'You're right,' he said. 'It seems we're once again trying to work out how the killer got away if they didn't follow the wall walk this far or go through the passage into the Inner Close.

Let's see if we can find Michael and hear if he's made any progress on that front.'

As the two of them walked in silence towards the building housing their office, a staff car came slowly through the stone gateway and turned towards the nearby line of parked vehicles.

'Here are Anthony and Gilbert,' said Monique.

'Good,' said Bob. 'Let's see if we can find anyone to get us a cup of tea in the office and run through how they've got on this morning.'

Lieutenant Colonel Ferguson's office was at the front of the first floor of the building theirs was in, and his secretary had a room between the lieutenant colonel's and the one they'd been loaned. When Bob asked, she was happy to arrange for a soldier to bring them tea.

Bob thought Sergeant Potter looked a little pale as he sat down. As offices went, theirs was utilitarian. It was wood panelled, like the meeting room downstairs, but the panelling had seen much better days and the walls were unadorned. A fireplace on one side had been boarded up and the only window was small and offered a view of a nearby slate roof. The furniture comprised a wooden table large enough to accommodate the six ill-matched chairs that surrounded it. The table looked like it had last been polished in the previous century and it carried numerous battle scars in the form of cup rings and cigarette burns.

'How did it go this morning, Anthony?' asked Bob.

'It was the first time I've ever attended a full post-mortem and it was fascinating,' said Captain Darlington.

'I'm not sure "fascinating" is the word I'd have used,' said Gilbert Potter. 'I've never thought of myself as squeamish, but there was something really cold and dispassionate about the way Doctor Ambrose just carved his way into the late Mr Douglas. Seeing gore in the heat of battle is one thing, but when the body is just laid out like that, well…'

Bob smiled. 'I'm not sure how I'd react either. What conclusions did the doctor come to?'

Anthony Darlington put his teacup down on its saucer. 'Doctor Ambrose is pretty sure the cause of death was a massive blow to the head with an axe, or something very like an axe, while Mr Douglas was lying on the ground on his side, pretty much as Monique left him and as he was found. He thinks the blow was struck with considerable force by a right-handed person standing behind Mr Douglas at an angle that effectively removed the top of his skull. He thinks the axe was extremely sharp and that its sharpened edge was a little over four inches in length.

'It seems that having struck just once with the axe, our murderer then got to work on what was already a dead man with a knife. The doctor identified fifteen separate knife wounds on the body. One was in the side of the neck, as we already know, and another was in the top of the shoulder nearby. The neck wound seems to have been inflicted quite carefully and may have been made before the others. The rest seem to have been done at random and hurriedly. Some wounds were inflicted by stabbing the knife into the back of the body, probably with the blade projecting from the front of the attacker's hand, with others probably caused by holding the knife the other way, projecting from the back of the hand, and bringing it down at an angle while leaning over the body to cause wounds in the left side of the victim's torso.

'I showed the doctor my Fairbairn–Sykes knife and he asked if I had an alibi for the time of the murder, as the wounds in the victim were made by something as near identical as makes no practical difference. He also noted the start of bruising on the left side of the stomach which was very fresh but apparently unrelated to the fatal attack on Mr Douglas.'

'I'll tell you about that when you've finished,' said Bob. 'Anything else?'

'Yes. The doctor identified damage to Mr Douglas's windpipe which I imagine was Monique's doing. He didn't mention an injury to the man's testicles, but perhaps it didn't occur to him to check. I certainly didn't suggest he should.'

'Thank you, Anthony. It seems we're probably looking for someone who is right-handed, which isn't a great help, and for an axe with a blade that's a little over four inches in length.'

As he spoke, Bob heard the office door open behind him and then Lieutenant Commander Dixon's voice.

'I'd say this blade was a little more than four inches long, wouldn't you?'

By the time Bob had twisted round far enough to bring his good eye into play, Michael had leaned past him and with a rubber-gloved hand placed an axe partly folded in a brown paper bag on the table. It had a shaped wooden handle and a black head with what was probably a shiny sharpened steel blade, though it was difficult to tell given the amount of reddish-brown staining on the business end of the tool.

'Where was it?' asked Bob.

'One of the trainees found it pretty much where Monique said it would be,' said Michael. 'Down below the wall and the cliffs, but far enough out from them to suggest it had been thrown in an arc from well within the wall rather than carefully dropped by someone on the wall walk. It's like a jungle down there and it gets progressively worse as you get nearer to the vertical cliffs. Frankly, we'd probably never have found it if the killer had taken more care and time and dropped the axe vertically from the wall. I'd instructed them not to handle anything they found and the lad who found this assured me he'd not touched it. On the other side, the handle has the usual broad arrow military issue mark cut into it.'

'Thank you, Michael. Gilbert, can you get this dusted for fingerprints, though I get the sense our killer wouldn't have been that careless? Could you then take the axe to Doctor Ambrose to ask him whether it made the initial head wound and whether what I assume is blood on the blade is likely to be Bill Douglas's?'

'Of course, sir. I've got a fingerprint kit in the boot of our car. I'll check the axe for prints at the hospital before handing it over to Doctor Ambrose.'

Sergeant Gilbert Potter stood up, pulling on a pair of rubber gloves he'd taken from his tunic pocket. He gathered up the axe in the paper bag so he could hold it in one hand and left the room.

'OK, you've brought us up to date on your side, Anthony. I assume there was no time to start digging through the service records of the men here?'

'I'm afraid not. Doctor Ambrose was quite thorough with his post-mortem, but he was by no means quick. We'd only just got back from the hospital when we saw you.'

'That's probably for the good,' said Bob. 'I think we can narrow the area of origin for the men we might be interested in. Earlier on, Monique and I interviewed the six people attending Sir Peter's meeting who, when asked last night, admitted to having ever met or known Bill Douglas. That's an important point because, when you think about it, if there was someone whose past contact with Douglas had led to their killing him, their best strategy would be to lie about knowing him and hope we never find out.'

'That's true but rather dispiriting,' said Michael.

'Nonetheless,' said Bob, 'the six people we talked to did provide some thought-provoking insights. One was a young man who had worked for Bill Douglas in SIS and nearly had his career ruined by him. An argument between the two after dinner resulted in Bill Douglas striking him in the face and being punched in the stomach in return. Rather incredibly, that means that the killer was the third person to have done damage to Bill Douglas in a very short period.'

'A truly popular man,' said Anthony Darlington.

'And that's before we take account of the feelings of the young woman in SIS who was raped by Douglas last Christmas,' said Monique. 'I believed her, I think we both did,' she looked at Bob, 'when she said she didn't kill Bill Douglas last night. She's got an easily checkable alibi anyway. But she said that she wished she had killed him.'

'I must admit that I came away from the interviews with a sense that the victim was a man who really might, as one of our interviewees said, have made the world a better place by dying,' said Bob. 'But it's our job to find the killer and what we were told did highlight two important things for me. The first is that if the six people we interviewed produced two with good reasons for wanting him dead, and others who had formed a clear dislike of him, then the number of people out there with motives for killing him might be quite large.

'The second thing we found out was that whatever Sergeant MacMillan discovers at the National Library of Scotland about the historical records of the 1452 murder, Bill Douglas had a very clear version of the story in his head that he was keen to broadcast to all and sundry, whether they wanted to hear it or not. He told it in detail to two of the six people we interviewed while another overheard but pretended not to be taking any notice to avoid engaging with him.

'I've been puzzled because versions of the story told in books in the library here don't quite tie in with Bill Douglas's injuries. But the story he'd been telling was that King James II stabbed the earl twice with a dagger, with one of those wounds being in the neck. Then one of the courtiers at the dinner split the earl's head open with a poleaxe. And then others present inflicted further stab wounds before they threw the body out of a window.'

Anthony Darlington sat forwards. 'Other than the order in which the wounds were inflicted, and perhaps the size of the axe, that's exactly what happened to Bill Douglas. The doctor thought the head wound came first, then the stab wound in the neck, then the other stab wounds.'

'Which means,' said Monique, 'that the killer didn't learn about the details of the earl's death from any of the books in the castle library. He or she probably heard the story directly from Bill Douglas and then set out to re-enact it, with him as the victim.'

'Logically,' said Bob, 'it's possible that the killer had picked up the story from the same source as Bill Douglas. But I have to admit it seems more likely it was his version of the story that was being acted out. If that's true, the important question appears to be who else he told the story to after he arrived at the castle.'

'He didn't have much chance to tell anyone other than the people we already know about,' said Monique. 'We know that the plane he and two of the others flew to Scotland on had problems and had to be replaced in Carlisle. As a result, they arrived here so late they had to rush to get to dinner on time. We might need to plot it out in detail, but I suspect that what we already know gives us a complete account of what Bill Douglas did and who he interacted with from the time he arrived at Northolt yesterday afternoon to the time he was killed.'

'That does narrow it down,' said Bob. 'But unfortunately, it narrows it down to people we are already inclined to exclude as suspects. Possibly more usefully, what we did find out was that, according to Bill Douglas, his family came from Castle Douglas in Galloway, and they still have extensive landholdings there which he hoped to inherit. That narrows down our geographical search for people who might have known him in the past.

'Let's put that thought on one side for the moment. What did you discover, Michael, apart from what seems very likely to have been the murder weapon?'

Michael coughed to clear his throat. 'Lieutenant Colonel Ferguson was very helpful, and we were able to thoroughly check all the rooms at the gardens end of the King's Old Building. They comprise the medical centre on the upper floors, a large meeting room and the office of the regimental clerks on the first floor, and a series of smaller offices and stores on the ground floor. We were told they enforce blackout regulations quite rigorously here and this ties in with what Monique said about shutters, which are fitted to the inside of most of the windows. It seems that any rooms actually in use at the time would probably also have had their blackout curtains closed.'

'Shutters and curtains?' asked Bob.

'As I said, they take the blackout very seriously. If they

didn't, it would be visible for miles around and they'd be getting complaints or perhaps even the odd German bomb.'

'What about the doors?' asked Bob.

'I looked at both,' said Michael. 'As you know, one is on the ground floor while the other is on the first floor at the top of the external stairs. The ground floor door leads onto a short corridor that in turn gives access to the rest of the building. The one on the first floor opens onto a small lobby, from which you can go through another door into the meeting room I referred to a moment ago. I was told that both doors are kept locked and that the keys are kept in the orderly officer's office, which is a little further into the King's Old Building when approached from the gardens, though it's normally accessed from the Inner Close. There's no indication either key was missing at the time of the murder, but no one checked. They were certainly there today. We searched the rooms at that end of the building without finding anything that might be connected to the murder.

'I had all the other possibilities we discussed checked. The building in the corner of the gardens is kept locked and there's a locked metal gateway preventing access to the defensive outpost we discussed beneath the wall of the gardens and above the Nether Bailey. We obtained the keys and searched both anyway. We also looked at possible places to loop a rope. To be honest, there are quite a few, which doesn't help us very much. There was no sign in the Nether Bailey of anyone having descended from the wall, but that's no guarantee they didn't.'

'Did you notice an enclosed area below the wall behind the Great Hall?' asked Bob.

'Yes, though there was no obvious way to get down into it from the wall. Again, though, I ended up thinking that if someone had time to plan the murder, they would have had plenty of options for getting out unseen. My money would be on their using one of the doors into the King's Old Building, probably the one on the ground floor, then using one of the smaller rooms there to change out of their bloodstained clothing into something they'd left there on their way out into the garden. We found no sign of anything like that taking place, but that would be the quickest escape for someone working against the clock. It would also tie in with their going in that direction after the murder to throw the axe over the wall, and it would mean they didn't have to cross the end of the passage and risk being seen by anyone approaching from the Inner Close. It's true that we can't dismiss any of the other possibilities we've discussed, but what I've suggested would be the simplest and best escape route.

'There's one more factor we need to consider. From what the orderly officer said last night, the murder must have taken place just before 9.50 p.m., as that was the time that he left his office before finding the body. I've been told that the regiment enforces lights out for all trainees, though less so for other personnel, at 10 p.m. If the murderer was a member of the Argylls, then the delay in Bill Douglas getting to the gardens means there's a chance they could have been late for lights out, or at least running it very close. That's something that might have been noticed by others.'

'Thanks, Michael.' Bob looked at his watch. 'Perhaps this afternoon we need to interview anyone who was in that part of the castle again, to see if they noticed anything consistent with what you've just described. I don't know about anyone else, but I suspect we might think a little more clearly with some lunch inside us. Let's head over to the officers' mess.'

CHAPTER FIFTEEN

The officers' mess was quiet. It seemed that those attending the general's meeting were dining elsewhere and Bob had the impression most of the regimental officers were also otherwise occupied.

The food was good but, to Bob's mind, the discussion was rather frustrating as they seemed simply to go round the same loops they had explored before lunch, without anything very new or helpful emerging. They agreed that in addition to pursuing Michael's theory about the King's Old Building as an escape route, they still needed to check the records of men based at the castle to find if any came from the area around Castle Douglas, and they also needed to check the alibis of the people Bob and Monique had interviewed that morning.

Beyond that, Bob had the sense they were running out of momentum and ideas, which didn't give him a warm feeling. He knew that on this case he was personally accountable to Commodore Cunningham and Sir Peter Maitland.

After lunch they returned to the office, to find Sergeants Gilbert Potter and Alan MacMillan eating sandwiches.

'You could have lunched in the sergeants' mess,' said Bob, trying to conceal his slight feelings of guilt.

'Don't worry, sir,' said Sergeant MacMillan, 'the sandwiches are pretty good, and we've been able to talk about ways of narrowing our search for men from Galloway and especially from the Castle Douglas area.'

'I fear I may have been wasting your time in Edinburgh,' said Bob. 'It emerged this morning that the victim had told people he was from Castle Douglas, so we already knew that.'

There was a broad grin on MacMillan's face. 'I bet he didn't tell people what else I found out this morning, sir. From what you told me about him, I doubt if he knew himself.'

'Hang on,' said Bob. 'Let's take this step by step. First, can I ask Gilbert to brief us on anything you discovered about the axe?'

'It will only take a few moments, sir. There were no fingerprints on the handle or head. I would guess that the attacker wore gloves. Doctor Ambrose thought the size of the blade on the axe fitted the wound exactly. And he said that the blood on the blade was the same type as the victim's. I think we can be fairly sure that what we've found is the murder weapon. I left it with the commanding officer's secretary in the next-door office as she said she could lock it away in a cupboard.'

'Thank you, Gilbert, that's some good news at last. We need to try to work out where the murderer might have obtained the axe when they were planning the murder. The regiment must have a tool store or something of the sort. Right, Sergeant MacMillan, you went into Edinburgh to look at historical sources of information about the murder of the 8th Earl of Douglas, and to find out what you could about Bill Douglas's family background.'

'I'll take them in that order, sir. It turns out that there is only one historical account of what happened in 1452. This has survived as part of a document called the Asloan Manuscript, an anthology of Scots prose and poetry dating from the early 1500s. It was probably copied from the work of multiple original authors but at least its date means that we know that the account of the murder was written within half a century of it happening, and possibly much closer to the event than that.'

'What does it say about the actual details of the murder?'

asked Bob.

Alan MacMillan looked at a notebook he'd opened. 'I've got photographs of the two pages of the original in Scots and a typed translation. But the key elements are that after he argued with the earl, the king drew a knife and struck Douglas in the *"collar"* and *"down in the body"*. Then a noble struck Douglas with a *"poll ax"* on the head and struck out his brains, and then some of the other nobles who were present each contributed *"a straik or twa"* with knives. According to the manuscript he ended up with 25 or 26 wounds, depending on how you choose to read a particular Roman numeral. It doesn't hold back on naming the murderers and you do get the sense that the author of the original account might have been present when it happened.'

He looked up from his notes. 'That's it, sir. Every other account that's ever been written or told is based on that original. What is most striking for me is that there is no mention in the original document of the body being thrown out of a window. It seems someone introduced that detail to embellish the original at some point, and everyone else followed their lead.'

'Thank you,' said Bob. 'That's very helpful. Talking to people who our modern Bill Douglas had spoken to suggests that what he was saying about the 1452 murder was fairly accurate: first, a wound in the neck and another wound also made by the king; then the head injury from the axe; then multiple further stab wounds. He then added the later embellishment about the body being thrown out of the window. The actual injuries were quite well replicated on the modern Mr Douglas. The police surgeon who did the post-mortem thinks the head injury probably preceded any of the stab wounds, which was most likely down to simple expediency, and there were fifteen knife wounds on the body rather than the 25 or 26 mentioned in the document you unearthed. To my mind, the murderer was working to a script based on Bill Douglas's version of events rather than from any of the documentary sources. That really ought to help identify them, but it hasn't so far.'

'You made it sound like you'd turned up something unexpected about Bill Douglas's background when you were talking just now,' said Monique.

The grin returned to MacMillan's face. 'Ah yes. This is the sort of thing that makes me love history so much.'

Bob found the man's enthusiasm infectious. 'I'm intrigued. What did you find?'

'I'll not bore you with the ancient history, but what you've heard about the 8th Earl of Douglas being murdered by the king and the 9th Earl of Douglas rising in revolt and being stripped of the earldom as a result, is true. Moving forward, though, things get more interesting. You said that the modern Mr Douglas talked to people about his family history. Can I ask what he told them?'

It was Monique's turn to consult a notebook. 'He said that he was descended from the Black Douglases, a family that included the two men you just mentioned. He said that the family power base had been a fortress on an island in a river called Threave Castle, near a town called Castle Douglas in Galloway. He said that his family helped found the town and that they still have extensive landholdings in the area.'

'Right, that's what I thought. Most of that is true, only not in quite the way he seems to have believed. The one part that isn't true is the part that the murder victim probably thought was the most important, and that changes everything else out of recognition.'

'Which part was that?' asked Monique.

'I've already told you that what you've heard about the 1400s is correct. You then need to wind the clock forward to the late 1700s. That was when William Douglas, the third "William Douglas" to feature in our story, arrived in a town then called Carlingwark in Galloway. This William Douglas had made a large fortune in the United States as a trader, though of what and with whom seems unclear.

'William Douglas expanded Carlingwark into a much larger town, complete with cotton mills, and this became known as Castle Douglas in 1792. He was granted a baronetcy and became known as Sir William Douglas in 1801. So far, so good. Where it becomes particularly interesting is that although Sir William Douglas claimed descent from the Black Douglas family who were closely associated with nearby Threave Castle, and although this was accepted as fact at the time, it seems he actually had quite humble origins and there is no known family link back to the Black Douglases. He was a self-made man who took advantage of the coincidence of his name to falsely acquire an entire family history going back centuries before his time.'

Monique laughed. 'Are you telling us that the modern Bill Douglas wasn't in any way related to the man who was murdered by King James II in 1452?'

'That's it exactly. He probably believed he was descended from the 9th Earl, though it wouldn't have taken much research to find out that was untrue. His family is wealthy and does have extensive landholdings in Galloway, and he was brought up near Castle Douglas. But the family's links with the area date back only to the late 1700s rather than to the 1400s and earlier.'

There was silence in the room as everyone digested this.

It was Monique who spoke first. 'Am I alone in seeing a huge irony here? If Bill Douglas hadn't gone round telling everyone he was related to the man killed here by King James II, and how that murder took place, then he might still be alive, if nursing sore balls, a bruised stomach and a damaged windpipe.'

'I'm not so sure about that, Monique,' said Anthony Darlington. 'To my mind, he was killed because he was an utter bastard who managed to get himself hated by a lot of the people who knew him. If he'd not been broadcasting his supposed family links with the 8th Earl of Douglas, he wouldn't have been killed in the way he was, but it wasn't those links that got him killed. Whoever wanted him dead would still have wanted him dead, and would probably have killed him anyway, though perhaps in a less theatrical way.'

'Bloody hell,' said Bob. 'Where does that leave us?'

'I don't think it makes very much difference,' said Michael Dixon. 'It might leave us better placed than we would have been. If you take the false history out of the equation, then whoever killed Bill Douglas would, as Anthony said, still have wanted him dead. Only they might just have stabbed him in the heart with their commando knife. They'd have left fewer clues that way. They wouldn't have had to source and then dispose of the axe, for example, and they'd probably have been less at risk of getting covered in blood.'

Monique still had a broad smile on her face. 'If it counts for anything, Sergeant MacMillan, you've really brightened up my day. The Bill Douglas I knew and despised would have been appalled by what you've unearthed. This is the first time since he was killed that I've felt in any way sorry about his death. I would have loved to see the look on his face if he'd been sitting in the corner of the room when you were telling us that.'

'Thank you, ma'am. I'm pleased I've brightened up someone's day. Group captain, now I'm involved I'm rather reluctant to let this go. I'm sure that if you asked Lieutenant Colonel Ferguson, he'd agree to my helping Gilbert go through the regimental records to find any men who are currently at Stirling Castle who come from the Castle Douglas area. As I told you, though, that's not where the regiment traditionally recruits from.'

'Thank you, sergeant,' said Bob. 'I'm grateful and I'm sure that would help. I'll have a word with the lieutenant colonel. While the two of you are at it, see if there's anyone at the castle whose service records reveal they've spent any time at the Commando Basic Training Centre. I accept what you said about the knife, Anthony, but we need to check anyway. Perhaps the two of you could also take on the job of working out where the axe came from and who might have taken it?'

Bob was about to say more when there was a knock on the office door, which then opened.

The lieutenant colonel's secretary put her head round the door. 'Group Captain Sutherland, I'm sorry to interrupt, but I've got your secretary on the line in my office, and she needs to speak to you urgently.'

Bob followed her to her office, linked by an open door to the lieutenant colonel's office at the front of the building. She indicated a telephone with its handset lying on a desk.

Bob picked it up. 'Hello, Joyce.'

'Hello, sir. I'm sorry to disturb you, but you've had a call from someone I think you'll want to talk to.'

'Who is it?'

'Group Captain Erickson.'

'The station commander at RAF Oban?'

'He said that's where you'd remember him from. He's now commanding RAF Stornoway in the Outer Hebrides. He asked me to pass on his apologies but said that he needed to speak to you extremely urgently.'

'Thank you, Joyce, I'm sure I can get back to him via the switchboard here. Is everything otherwise OK?'

'Nothing you need to worry about, sir.'

As he put down the phone Bob wondered why he'd never been able to convince his secretary to call him 'Bob' rather than 'sir' or 'group captain'. Joyce Stuart was an Edinburgh lady in her fifties and the very model of efficiency, but she seemed to feel the need to maintain a degree of formality where he was concerned.

CHAPTER SIXTEEN

Bob turned to face the lieutenant colonel's secretary. 'I'm sorry to trouble you, but would it be possible to get me put through to the station commander at RAF Stornoway?'

In the event, it took twenty minutes to make the connection.

'Hello, Group Captain Erickson?'

'Yes, it is. Is that Bob Sutherland?'

'That's right.'

'Just call me Tom. Thank you for returning my call.'

'How could I not? You taught me everything I know about flying boats.'

'Which I gather you made good use of with that Dornier in Caithness. Congratulations on the promotion, by the way.'

'Thank you, Tom.'

There was a pause.

'What I'm about to tell you is going to seem bizarre, Bob, but I think I need your help.'

'What's wrong?'

'I'm worried about my daughter.'

There was another pause.

'Sorry, Bob. That didn't sound very compelling, did it?'

'Can you tell me more?'

'My daughter Helen is a twenty-year-old medical student. In the past, while away at school in Cheltenham and then when studying in London, she's tended to spend any holidays at the family home in Cambridge though, for reasons I'll explain, she spent Christmas with me in Oban. I'm currently in the middle of a three-month posting to Stornoway to oversee the setting up of new units here before I return to Oban. Helen didn't want to remain in London over Easter so it was arranged that she would stay with my sister-in-law and her family on their farm near Blairgowrie in Perthshire.

'What prompted me to contact you was a letter I've received from my daughter. Mail gets here either by steamer or, if we're lucky, it gets flown over from Inverness. The letter I received must have come by air mail because it was posted yesterday at the railway station at a place called Coupar Angus. She was sure that she had been followed from London to Edinburgh. She took what seemed like extreme measures in Edinburgh to fool the two people, a man and a woman, who she thought were following her. But at Coupar Angus she encountered what a railway employee who had spoken to him described as a "foreign gentleman", a different man, who she thought was also following her.'

'I don't want to sound dismissive, Tom, but why would a young woman going on holiday be followed the length of the country? You said she's twenty. You and I have both sent young men out to fight, and be killed, at that age and younger.'

'I agree with you, Bob. But the "why" may be the important question. How secure is this line?'

'God knows, but I'm calling from the army barracks at Stirling Castle, so I hope we're avoiding any civilian switchboards.'

'I'll try to be circumspect. My wife Elizabeth, Helen's mother, is a genius who studied and then taught mathematics at the University of Cambridge. Last September she was, in her words, made an offer she couldn't turn down. She left her post in Cambridge and went to work for the government. We rented out our house in Cambridge and she went to live in a shared requisitioned house in Bletchley in Buckinghamshire. She was able to spend a few days with Helen and me in Oban over Christmas. Over a glass of wine one night, she told me that the work she is doing is of the utmost importance to national security. She then described it as "ultra secret" before getting flustered and asking me to forget she'd used the expression. I know you're now with military intelligence, Bob. Does that mean anything to you?'

There was a pause.

'Bob, are you still there?'

'Sorry, Tom, yes I am. And yes, that does mean something to me. Have you contacted your sister-in-law?'

'I've tried, but the phone line to the farm seems to be down. I also contacted the police in Blairgowrie and spoke to a Sergeant Christie. He told me in so many words that he had better things to do than trace faults on telephone lines or pursue the fantasies of a young woman's overactive imagination. When I asked him to check on the farm, he simply refused.'

Bob thought he knew the answer to the question before he asked it. 'How can I help?'

'Can you get someone to visit the farm and find out what's going on? I know this probably sounds highly irregular but, given my wife's work, I'm worried that German intelligence might be trying to use our daughter to get at her. I'm more than half inclined to fly over there myself, but this isn't my area of expertise. That's why I've turned to you for help.'

Bob knew he had no choice. 'I owe you a favour anyway, Tom. I'll get someone over there this afternoon. We're all in Stirling and I've not got a map handy to check how far Blairgowrie is, but I'll do what I can.'

'Thank you, Bob. Would it help if I flew over anyway?'

'Give us a chance to find out how things stand, and we can

take it from there.'

'Thank you again, Bob, I'm grateful.'

'Hang on, I need the address of the farm, the name of your sister-in-law, and a description of your daughter. First, though, have you talked to your wife?'

'No, she's difficult to contact except by mail and tends to telephone me once a week. Besides, she's even less well-placed than I am to do anything. I wouldn't want to worry her when it could all amount to nothing.'

As Bob finished the call, he found himself hoping that no one had been listening in to his conversation with Tom Erickson. There had probably been no other way to convey the urgency of the situation, but the group captain hadn't been quite as 'circumspect' as he should have been.

Bob remembered to clear the loan of Sergeant MacMillan with the lieutenant colonel before returning to join the others.

He found Monique, Michael and Anthony sitting around the table looking at a large plan of the castle they had acquired from somewhere.

'Hello, Bob,' said Michael. 'Gilbert and Alan have headed off to pursue the areas you asked them to look at. The three of us were just trying to tie down what else we need to do this afternoon.'

'I'm afraid that any plans we've made are about to be changed,' said Bob. 'I've got an unrelated job I want Monique and Anthony to take on. This may only be for as long as it takes to drive to Blairgowrie and back, or it might be for rather longer. I'd suggest you take your overnight bags.'

'How are the commodore and the general going to react to that?' asked Michael.

'I'm not going to tell them, not initially at least. If it only takes a few hours, then they'll never know anyway. If it takes longer, then I'll have no difficulty convincing them it was the right thing to have done.'

'You are making this sound very mysterious, Bob,' said Monique.

'Sorry, that's not by choice. Monique, I'd like you to come outside with me so I can brief you on what I want you to do. Anthony, can you find the castle armoury and persuade them to issue you with two Sten guns and plenty of ammunition? Use my authority if you need to. Michael, once these two are on their way, you and I can start checking the alibis of the people Monique and I interviewed this morning.'

Bob led Monique out of the building and over to the wall, where they stopped beside one of the old cannons that stood in a line pointing out towards long-gone enemies. This was a spot that offered stunning views across the Forth Valley and past the Wallace Monument to what he guessed was the western end of the Ochil Hills.

'What's going on, Bob?'

Bob told her about his conversation with Group Captain Erickson.

Monique leaned back against the wall. 'His wife should never have mentioned "Ultra" to him, and he certainly shouldn't have used the word on the phone to you.'

'Both of those things are true, but she did, and he did and, as a result, we have a much clearer idea of what we might be dealing with and what the implications could be. You may know more about the process behind Ultra than I do, but I suppose it's likely that they'd want to recruit the best mathematicians available to help break codes. And I suppose her sharing a house in Buckinghamshire tells us something about where that's done.'

'I don't think I know any more than you do, Bob. But we do both know that the quality of the intelligence from Ultra means we can be sure that there aren't three German agents following Helen Erickson around Scotland.'

'Yes, the fact that Tom Erickson thought they might be Germans confirms that his wife hasn't told him much about what comes out of Ultra.'

'They might be someone else's agents though,' said Monique.

'That's also true. It's still possible, of course, that Miss Erickson was imagining things yesterday when she wrote the letter to her father and that the telephone line to the farm has been cut by a falling tree branch. You could arrive to find there's nothing wrong and you've had a wasted journey.'

'Or we could be walking into something altogether more serious. That's why you asked Anthony to come with me, isn't it? And why you asked him to get hold of two Sten guns?'

'Yes. If things get nasty, I'd prefer it if you have someone with you who's seen real action. Anthony knows how to look after himself.'

'That's true, Bob. Michael is very good at his job, but I don't think he's ever actually killed anyone. Anthony has a look in his eye that says he has and that he wouldn't hesitate to kill again if he really needed to.'

'Just be careful, that's all,' said Bob.

Monique laughed. 'Don't worry. I'm not about to do anything that lets you off the hook of a church wedding!'

CHAPTER SEVENTEEN

Monique asked Anthony to drive, which allowed her to concentrate on reading the one-inch scale maps the Argylls had given her before she set off.

It was a beautiful day and the sun was largely behind them, showing the scenery off at its best. Despite the wartime absence of signposts, she had no difficulty navigating.

Anthony didn't seem in a very talkative mood. He was pleasant enough, but he tended to close rather than expand the conversations she started. After they left Auchterarder along the road towards Perth she tried again.

'I'm thinking about an invitation list for the wedding,' she said. 'I'm sorry, but I don't even know if you're married, Anthony.'

'No, there's no Mrs Darlington, if you exclude my mother.'

'Is there anyone else you'd want to bring with you to the wedding?'

Anthony smiled. 'I'm grateful for the thought, Monique, but no, there's no one who I'd want to bring with me.'

Monique looked down again at the map, wondering why she felt so uncomfortable, as if she'd been caught trying to pry into Anthony's private life. Perhaps because that's what she had been doing, she concluded.

They were driving into Perth when Anthony spoke again. 'There was a girl. It was in France in May 1940, in the utter chaos as we retreated towards the Channel coast. Her father had a farm just outside Lille. My unit, the 5th Battalion of the Gloucestershire Regiment, had suffered heavy casualties and had been pulled out of the immediate fighting. We were ordered to move back towards the coast and prepare defensive positions and the farm was the location someone had picked on a map. I met Annette the first evening we were there when she came to complain that some of my men had stolen two hens. My French is quite good, and we ended up talking for most of the night.

'It sounds ludicrous to say you can fall in love with someone so quickly, but I did, and I believe she did too. We were able to spend a second night together but, the morning after that, orders came through to abandon the positions we'd prepared and head for the coast as rapidly as we could. The Germans were coming our way in overwhelming numbers. From that moment on, we were no longer even pretending to defend France, just the ports and beaches we needed for an evacuation.'

'What happened to Annette?'

'I don't know. I left and she stayed. It was obvious from the moment we met how it would have to end. I feared that someone might tell the Germans she'd been with a British officer. A couple of the men realised what was going on, but I think, I desperately hope, that nobody else did.'

'And there's been no one else since then?'

'There have been a few women I've met along the way. Nothing that's lasted for very long. I think they've suffered because they've never measured up to my memory of the strength of the feelings I had for Annette. I've come to think that perhaps I fell so deeply in love with her partly because of the sheer desperation of the circumstances and my near certainty I wouldn't survive the retreat.' Anthony laughed. 'If that's true, then no one else has ever had a chance and no one is ever likely to.'

'I'm sure that's not true,' said Monique. 'You are bound to

meet someone. On the other hand, if you wanted, it might be possible to find out how Annette is doing. France is occupied, of course, but there's still a lot of information flowing backwards and forwards. I've got contacts who might be able to help.'

'I find that a terrifying idea, to be honest. What if she was killed because of me? What if she married a German? What if we did meet again and the spark that I've treasured for nearly three years just isn't there?'

'I understand, Anthony, honestly I do. But the offer's there if you ever decide you'd like to find out more.'

Silence descended again, but Monique felt it somehow seemed more comfortable than it had before.

They didn't go into the centre of Blairgowrie, instead turning left onto the road towards Dunkeld after they reached the edge of the town.

'We're looking for a minor road on the right,' said Monique. 'According to the map, there's a telephone box beside the junction. This is it, ahead. Hang on, can you stop?'

Anthony pulled over and Monique walked the few yards to the phone box and pulled open the door. She closed it again and then walked back to the car.

'Did you change your mind about making a call?' asked Anthony.

'I didn't go to make a call: I went because something didn't look right. Someone has cut the wire to the handset, which they've left on the floor. It was the lack of a handset that caught my attention.'

'That's impressive eyesight from a moving car,' said Anthony. 'While it could just be coincidence, that does seem a rather worrying find.'

'Yes, I agree.' Monique opened the back door of the car and lifted out one of the Sten submachine guns that they'd put in the rear footwells, then fitted a magazine and checked the cocking handle operated properly.

'That will even the odds a little,' said Anthony.

Anthony turned the car onto the minor road, which became very narrow and climbed a wooded hillside. Then the landscape opened out as the road began to descend.

'Hang on! Stop here, Anthony. According to the map, that's Easter Crimond, the sister-in-law's farm, in the bottom of the valley in front of us. Let's get out and have a look at the place.'

Anthony pulled off to the side of the road and onto the verge. Another vehicle could probably have got by at a squeeze, but Monique had the sense this wasn't a well-used road, apparently serving only the farm they had come to find and the three cottages on the other side of the road from it. No, two, she corrected herself, as the furthest one had no roof.

Monique stood beside the car and looked at the scene, trying to work out what wasn't right about it. Anthony was standing on his side of the car, on the road, looking down at the farm through binoculars.

'There's no smoke coming from any of the chimneys,' he said.

'It's a nice day. Perhaps they don't think they need a fire.'

'I'd have thought that any farmhouse worth the name would have a range constantly lit in the kitchen, for cooking and hot water even if not to heat the building. We ought to be seeing some smoke.'

'You're right,' Monique said. 'I'm not getting a very good feeling about this. Let's go down and say hello.'

Monique had the door of the car open and was about to get

in when she realised that Anthony was standing still and looking over the roof of the car and past her, into the trees on her side of the road. She turned round but couldn't see what he was looking at.

'Someone is sitting against a tree over there,' he said. 'I think your view is obscured by your angle on that nearer tree.'

Anthony opened the rear door on his side of the car and reached down for the second Sten gun, which he checked after fitting a magazine.

As she walked cautiously in the direction he had indicated, Monique realised that Anthony was right. The very obviously dead body of a man was sitting against a tree. His arms were pulled back behind him on either side of the trunk and when she checked she could see they'd been tied together by a rope looped round the tree. He'd also been gagged. The man wore a black jacket, and she got the sense he might have been elderly from traces of grey hair on his head.

Only traces, though, because someone had shot him in the forehead and most of his hair was matted with dried blood. That wasn't the only blood on view.

Anthony crouched down beside the man. 'Someone was very keen to get him to tell them something he didn't want to reveal. He's been shot in both ankles and both knees. There would have been no point doing that unless it was done before the shot to the head.' He lifted the man's left leg, then let it drop. I'm no expert, but he feels cold and stiff, so I'd say he's been here for over eight hours, perhaps a good bit longer as it's a warm day.'

'There's nothing we can do for him right now,' said Monique. 'Let's drive down to the farm.'

'What, just pull up in front of the farmhouse as if we've

been invited to dinner?'

'Whoever did this is long gone,' said Monique. 'But yes, I agree we need to be cautious. How would you feel about turning the car round at the end of the farm track and leaving it facing back this way on the road? That way we've got a line of escape, in theory at least. That would also allow us to split up and approach the farmhouse from two angles, though we'll both be very exposed as there's no cover near it.'

'I've not got any better ideas, Monique.'

Monique felt extremely tense as she walked towards the farmhouse, with Anthony some yards to her left. At one point she stopped after Anthony gestured toward something on her right. She realised he was pointing at a wire on the grass that trailed down from a telegraph pole beside the road. It looked like someone had cut the telephone line where it arrived at the house.

Monique found herself trying to see into the windows as she walked, though with the bright sunny sky behind her reflecting in the glass, she couldn't see much of the interior. She kept the Sten gun pointed at the downstairs window nearest her as that seemed to offer the greatest potential threat.

Monique was first to reach the front door which, rather ominously she thought, stood half open. She pushed it fully open and winced at the loud creak from the hinges. At least there was enough light flooding in to see that the hallway beyond the door was empty.

'You take the upstairs and I'll check the ground floor,' she said.

'Fine by me,' said Anthony, slowly climbing the stairs and peering upwards.

Monique saw a black telephone on a small table in the hall.

She picked up the handset to find it was, as she'd expected, completely dead. Then she visited the rooms one at a time. The sitting room at the front of the house had the feel of somewhere that wasn't used every day. The dining room on the other side had seen more use. Behind the sitting room was what was obviously the farm office. The last significant room was the kitchen, which was very large and well used. Despite the warmth of the day, it felt oddly chilly.

As Anthony had predicted, there was a range on one side of the room. She quietly walked over to it and cautiously reached out a hand. It was completely cold. Set into the wall nearby was a door that she thought must lead to some sort of pantry in the space between the kitchen and the dining room.

In the rear corner of the kitchen was another door which she pulled open, revealing a short passage almost full of coats on a line of hooks on the wall. There were boots on the floor and a stand for walking sticks and umbrellas. At the far end was the back door.

Monique turned and walked back over to what she assumed was the pantry. The door itself, like everything else in the farmhouse, looked like it had been built to last. There was a keyhole but no key. She turned the door handle and rattled it, trying to open the door, but it seemed to be locked.

As if in response, there was a sudden hammering on the locked door and Monique could hear voices shouting for help.

Out of the corner of her eye, she saw Anthony come into the kitchen.

Monique rattled the door again and then shouted. 'The door's locked, do you know where we might find a key?'

The banging and shouting stopped instantly. Monique looked quizzically at Anthony. 'Hello, did you hear me?' she shouted.

The silence seemed almost threatening. She looked at Anthony, who raised his eyebrows.

He walked over to stand beside her. 'Hello, this is Captain Anthony Darlington of British military intelligence. Who's in there?'

The noise from within resumed even more loudly.

'I can't make anything out,' he said. 'But if they've been deliberately locked in, there's not much point looking for a key. Any objections if I take the most direct route to getting them out?'

Monique shook her head.

'Please be quiet and listen,' shouted Anthony. The noise abated. 'Are you able to move well away from the door? You need to be to one side of it, and not just back from it. Just one of you shout yes or no.'

Monique heard a woman's voice shout out, 'Yes'.

'That's good,' shouted Anthony. 'Move as far to the side of the door as you can, and crouch on the floor. Now put your fingers in your ears as tightly as you can.'

Anthony looked at Monique and she moved behind him. The fewer targets for ricochets the better. He lifted his Sten gun and fired a single round into the woodwork of the door between the keyhole and the doorframe. Then he rattled the door before firing a second round into the door. It took a third round to shatter the lock sufficiently to allow him to pull the door open.

The room beyond had an unpleasant smell. Monique remembered that the people locked inside might have been there for quite some time.

A man and a woman in their forties emerged, wearing pyjamas and a dressing gown respectively, followed by a younger man, also in his pyjamas. The older man had a black eye.

Anthony lowered his Sten gun and stepped back. 'As I said a moment ago, I'm Captain Anthony Darlington and I'm with military intelligence. This is Madame Monique Dubois, who is a colleague of mine. Can you tell me who you are and what happened to you?'

The woman burst into tears and was comforted by, Monique assumed, her husband.

It was the younger man who replied. 'My name's Ben Moncrieff. This is my mother and father, Jemima and George Moncrieff. Last night we were woken up by two men and a woman with guns who had got into the house. They took us from our rooms onto the upstairs landing and said they were looking for my cousin Helen, who arrived yesterday to stay with us over Easter. Dad said that she wasn't in the house. One of the men hit him and asked where she was. Dad didn't reply. The woman stopped the man from hitting Dad again and asked where the most secure place in the house was. Mum said it was the pantry and they brought us down here and locked us in. I've no idea how long we've been in there. The light switch is outside the door, on the kitchen wall, so we've been in the dark the whole time. The woman who was in charge sounded like you, miss.'

'In what way?' asked Monique.

'Her voice was quite like yours and she had an accent that was a little like yours too. When you shouted just now, after you rattled the door, we thought they were back. That's why we didn't reply until the captain shouted. The two men also had foreign accents and the captain has an English accent, so we knew it wasn't them.'

'If your cousin wasn't in the house last night, where was she?' asked Monique.

'We put her in the end cottage across the road, the one you get to first as you approach the farm.'

'Who else lives or works on the farm?'

'At the moment there's only Angus Henderson, who helps us all year round. There are more people during the berry season. Angus lives in the middle cottage, next door to the one my cousin is staying in.'

'Can you describe Angus?'

'Quite old, with grey hair. He always wears a tweed cap.'

'Anything else? When did you last see him?'

'Yesterday evening. We all talked for a while after tea and then Angus walked Helen back to her cottage.'

'What was Angus wearing yesterday evening?'

'His cap as usual, and a short black coat.'

'Thank you, Ben, you've been very helpful. You should all know that the phone line to the house has been cut and the telephone box back at the junction with the main road has also been disabled. Is there another phone anywhere nearby that might still be working?'

It was George Moncrieff who answered. 'No, sorry. You'd have to go to one of the other houses or farms along the main road back towards Blairgowrie or the other way towards Dunkeld.'

'That complicates matters,' said Monique. 'Can I ask the three of you to get yourselves dressed and perhaps make yourselves a cup of tea if you can heat any water? We've got to summon help, but first Captain Darlington and I need to go and check on the cottages.'

'You won't leave us, will you?'

'No, Jemima, I promise. We'll be back in a few minutes.'

The front door of the end cottage stood open. It only took Monique and Anthony a couple of moments to establish that the building was empty. There was no one in Angus's cottage either. Its front door was closed but unlocked. They also looked at the roofless cottage, but it was just an empty shell.

They set off back towards the farmhouse, but Monique touched Anthony's arm, bringing him to a halt.

'We need to compare notes when we don't have the Moncrieff family listening to us,' she said.

'That's very true. What do you make of all this, Monique?'

'Three people, two men and a woman, followed Helen Erickson here. Last night they made their move. We know they locked the Moncrieffs in their pantry, and I think we can be sure that they tortured and then killed Angus up in the woods where we found him. What we don't know is whether they found and took Helen Erickson or not.'

'I've been thinking about that too,' said Anthony. 'It would be easy to assume they did, but two things don't seem to square with that. One is the complete absence of Helen's belongings from the cottage. To my mind that makes it more likely that she left under her own steam than that she was kidnapped. The other is what was done to Angus Henderson. If the three would-be kidnappers had taken Helen, then, at most, they'd have killed Angus. More likely they'd have locked him up with the Moncrieffs. Why were they trying to extract information from him if not because they thought he might know where Helen had gone?'

'I tend to agree,' said Monique. 'If you assume that someone followed Helen here then you'd expect them to have been watching the place yesterday, and to know that she was staying in the cottage. All they had to do was gain entry to the cottage, bundle Helen into a car, and that would be that. They'd never have to go near the farmhouse or the Moncrieffs and they'd certainly not have gone to the farmhouse to ask where Helen was. And, as you say, they'd have had no need to do what they did to Angus. It's clear we're dealing with some very ruthless people, but they didn't kill the Moncrieffs when they easily could have done, which suggests their treatment of Angus was done for a reason.'

'While we're here, Monique, do you think we ought to check on the farm buildings? There wouldn't have been anything to stop Helen Erickson from going there last night. It doesn't seem likely, I admit, but we need to be sure she's not hiding right under our noses.'

It didn't take long to establish that if Helen was in either of the barns or any of the farm sheds then she was very well hidden. Thinking about what Ben had said about her accent, Monique asked Anthony to call out Helen's name. If she was there, his BBC English accent and his army officer's uniform should draw her out. There was no response except from the horse they found, with a pony, in one of the sheds.

'We can leave it to the police to do a proper search,' said Monique. 'I think we have to conclude Helen isn't here.'

The Moncrieffs were still in the kitchen when Monique and Anthony returned to the farmhouse. Someone had lit the range, though Monique imagined it would take a while to heat up.

Monique saw Jemima look at her hopefully, and then bow her head in disappointment when it became obvious that she and Anthony hadn't found Helen.

'The absence of a telephone makes things very awkward,' said Monique. 'Do you have a way of getting into Blairgowrie to seek help?'

'We've got a car in one of the barns,' said George. 'We've stopped using it because of the problems getting petrol, but we do have some for emergencies.'

'The one under the tarpaulin?' asked Anthony. 'Does it run?'

'Yes, I keep it in perfect order,' said George.

'You've been injured,' said Anthony. 'Are you fit to drive?'

'I'll be fine.'

'Good,' said Monique. 'I need you to go and tell the police in Blairgowrie what's happened here. I'm sorry to have to tell you this, but the people who came here last night killed a man, I think it was your friend Angus Henderson. His body is in the trees just off the road where it starts to descend into the valley. Please don't go near him. Leave that for the police. You should also make sure that the police arrange to have you checked over in hospital. You've been through quite an ordeal and your eye needs to be looked at, George. And the police will have to start a search for the three people who came here last night. They could be a long way away by now, but I'm beginning to think they have unfinished business here.'

'What about Helen?' asked Jemima, with tears in her eyes. 'What's happened to her?'

'I'm not sure,' said Monique, 'but I think she may have got away before the people who locked you up arrived. Can any of you tell me if you can think of anywhere that she might have gone to, at night and on foot and carrying her belongings?'

'She only arrived yesterday and had never visited before,' said Jemima. 'She doesn't know anyone apart from us and Angus.'

'What if Angus was helping her? Is there anywhere he

could have taken her for safety? An old barn or a ruined cottage in a remote part of the farm? Something like that?'

'I can think of somewhere he might have taken her,' said Ben. 'I can show you.'

'Oh, no you don't, son,' said George Moncrieff.

'I'm sorry, Mr Moncrieff, but I have to insist,' said Monique. 'The life of your niece may well be in danger and Ben's offer may be the best chance we've got of finding her. I promise he'll come to no harm with us. Which way are we going, Ben?'

'It's a little way back towards Blairgowrie, but not far.'

'If we're going that way, then I want George and Jemima to drive in front of us. Then we can see you on your way. Right, let's get moving. Can you go and get the car from the barn, please? You can pull out in front of us on the road and we'll follow for part of the way. Don't stop for anything until you get to Blairgowrie police station.'

CHAPTER EIGHTEEN

Bob looked at his watch.

Michael smiled. 'Stop fretting, Bob. It must be about fifty miles and you know that could take a while, depending on the roads. They'll be fine. I'd not want to cross swords with either Monique or Anthony.'

Bob had given Michael an outline of where Monique and Anthony had gone, and why he'd sent them, though he'd made no mention of the nature of Mrs Erickson's work as Michael wasn't cleared to know about Ultra. Bob was aware this left the rationale for splitting his team looking very threadbare. Perhaps Michael sensed there was more to it than Bob had told him because he hadn't pressed the point.

'I just hope they are having a more productive afternoon than we are,' said Bob. 'So far, we've established that the alibis given to us by the people who Monique and I interviewed this morning stand up. Those who had alibis, anyway. That rules them out, though I'm not surprised. And we've interviewed two of the four men currently based at Stirling Castle who Gilbert and Alan identified from their service records as having origins in, or next-of-kin listed as living in, the Castle Douglas area. Without finding anything very revelatory, I should add. And the final bit of bad news is that we aren't going to be able to narrow things down via the source of the axe. With the tool store apparently open to all-comers, the axe could have been taken by just about anyone.'

'I don't think we should consider our interviews of the men from Castle Douglas to have been completely pointless,' said Michael. 'The second one, the older man on the catering staff in the officers' mess, did say he'd heard of Bill Douglas years ago, though he also said he didn't know he'd arrived at the castle yesterday. I don't think it will take us long to confirm that his alibi for the time of the murder stands up, or that of the first man we talked to, for that matter, as both say they were in barracks with others at the time of the murder. But it was interesting to hear that Bill Douglas's tendency to abuse women was nothing new and that it was only his family connections that stopped him from being arrested for rape during the school summer holidays when he was seventeen.'

'I find myself wondering more and more whether we should be thanking rather than detaining the murderer when we find them,' said Bob. 'Perhaps I should say *if* we find them.'

'There are still the other two men,' said Michael, 'though as one of them has been on leave for the past three days, he is also in the clear. The last one's picking up supplies in Edinburgh and we can talk to him later. And it would appear no one at Stirling Castle, other than those of us in MI11, has ever been to Achnacarry Castle, so that's a dead end too.'

'We still need to talk again to the people Anthony and Gilbert found to have been around the King's Old Building in the initial interviews last night,' said Bob. 'I get the feeling I'm going to have to report what amounts to a total lack of progress to Commodore Cunningham and Sir Peter Maitland. In their shoes, I'd not be very impressed. Let's get out of this office. I know you've put your money on one of the doors into the King's Old Building being the killer's escape route, but I'd like to look again at the other place that, for me, felt somehow significant when I saw it this morning.'

Bob led the way out of the building and past the line of old cannons on the path running alongside the wall in the Outer

Close. The weather had held, and it was a lovely afternoon. He followed the wall walk behind the buildings at the north-east corner of the Outer Close, and then round to the rear of the Great Hall.

Bob stopped and Michael nearly walked into the back of him.

'It's this section of the wall walk here,' Bob said. 'Because of the curve of the wall, you are out of sight of anyone in the gardens ahead of us or in the Outer Close behind us. The shape formed by the east end of the Chapel Royal and the north end of the Great Hall and the wall itself gives a narrow tapering triangular courtyard that seems completely secluded. I'm not sure I fancy the idea of dropping down to the cobbles from this height, though.'

Michael leaned over the parapet on the inside of the wall walk. 'I had a look down there earlier when we did our sweep of the area looking for clues. It's accessed from the Outer Close if you want to have a look yourself.'

'Lead on.'

This time Bob followed as Michael led the way back into the Outer Close and then cut across to the side of the Great Hall.

'It's through this arch here,' said Michael. 'Then round the corner of the Great Hall and into the cobbled area that we saw from above. As you say, it's completely private here.'

'The narrowness of this end of the triangle shows just how close the wall is to the hall,' said Bob. 'I know that you took a careful look at the end of the King's Old Building overlooking the gardens this morning. What about rooms on this side of the Great Hall? There are several windows on view, plus two doors into the hall and one into the Chapel Royal from this area. I think it might be worth having a look at what's beyond them, just in case.'

'I can get it organised immediately, Bob.'

'Yes, please do.'

CHAPTER NINETEEN

'Your father was right about the car being in perfect order,' said Anthony as they followed George and Jemima down the hill towards the main road. 'That Rover 10 looks like it's his pride and joy.'

'It is,' said Ben, from the back seat. 'He was heartbroken when they stopped the petrol ration for private cars last year. He still gets it out and polishes it once a month.'

'From what you said, I'm guessing we need to turn left when we get to the main road?'

'Yes, that's right.'

'Can I ask where we are going?' asked Monique, turning round in her seat.

'Angus has got a lot of friends in the travelling community. Ah, I mean…'

Monique saw the young man's eyes fill with tears. 'I'm sorry about Angus,' she said. 'He was a good friend of yours, wasn't he?'

Ben nodded.

After they turned onto the main road, Monique asked Anthony to stop the car and, before she turned round again, watched George and Jemima continue out of sight ahead of them towards Blairgowrie.

Are you able to talk now, Ben?' she asked.

He nodded again.

'You said that Angus had friends in the travelling community.'

'Yes, the berry farmers round here have always relied on seasonal labour in the summer, and travellers have always been important in helping with the harvest. There's a camp in the woods near here that they use all year round. I knew kids at school who said bad things about travellers, but I think they are friendly and interesting. Angus always had a lot to do with them.

'My elder brother Andrew, who's serving with the Black Watch in Tunisia, told me that Angus had a wife once, but she died, and they never had children. Andrew said he'd heard Mum and Dad talking about Angus becoming close to the widow of a man from the travelling community after he died. They never married and she died last year. But she had a large family and they accepted Angus. I've been with him to the travellers' camp lots of times and some of them treat him like their father. Or did, anyway.'

'You think that's where he will have taken your cousin?' asked Monique.

'I think so,' said Ben. 'It depends on who is there, as they come and go a lot, but Angus could be fairly sure that someone staying there would help.'

'Where's the camp?'

'It's quite close. There's a road off to the right in a hundred yards or so and then, after another hundred yards, we follow a track into the woods. I hope that someone there will know me, though they might react oddly to you at first and especially to the captain. I know why you've got those Sten guns you've been carrying but I don't think you should take them into the camp. I also think you should park the car near the end of the track, and that we should walk from there. As I said, it's not far.'

'That sounds like good advice,' said Monique. 'We'll put the Sten guns in the boot of the car now. Just so you know, that won't leave us defenceless if we do run into the three people who locked you up last night.'

Ben had been right about how near they were to the camp. Anthony pulled the car off the road just short of the turning for an obvious track.

'I can smell wood smoke,' he said, after getting out of the car.

'Me too. Let's take that as a good sign,' said Monique. 'I imagine we walk down this track, Ben?'

'That's right. The track curves round to the left. The camp is quite close to the main road from Blairgowrie to Dunkeld, but the trees mean it's not visible from the road except sometimes in winter.'

'Perhaps it would be best if you and I lead, Ben, and the captain stays a few steps behind. I don't want to alarm anyone with his uniform and hopefully you'll be recognised before anyone starts to wonder why there's an army officer here.'

As they walked along the track, Monique could hear noises from ahead of them, of someone with an axe cutting a log, of a metal utensil clattering against a metal pot, of a small child crying, of other children's voices as they played. Meanwhile, the smell of wood smoke was getting stronger.

Monique hadn't been sure what to expect and the scene that revealed itself as they entered a small clearing in the wood was some way from anything she'd been imagining.

Half a dozen, no, seven, tents were standing around the edge of the clearing. Each was perhaps two or three times as long as it was wide, and each structure had curved sides and a curved roof. They made her think a little of the corrugated iron Anderson shelters, the government-issued air raid shelters that were a feature of so many people's gardens. Only, these tents stood on the ground rather than being dug into it like Anderson shelters. From the framework visible of one tent that stood off to the right, half constructed, it seemed they were made from a series of bent sticks with a tarpaulin stretched out over the top and the whole thing was then held down by large rocks placed on the edges of the tarpaulin. Each tent had an entrance, some on the side and others at an end of the structure. Each also had a cooking fire, set in a ring of stones, that was topped off by a means of suspending a pan or a kettle over the fire, mainly using what seemed to be old metal fence posts.

There were carts near some of the tents, some looking as if they were intended to be pulled by horses while others were rather smaller. Four horses were tethered to trees in the wood to the right of the camp.

Monique thought she could see perhaps thirty people in the camp. There were about ten women of varying ages from old down to quite young. As far as men were concerned, she could only see five, two of whom were elderly, two perhaps in their fifties and one in his thirties. There were about as many children as adults in the camp, evenly divided between boys and girls.

Her appearance with Ben and Anthony on the edge of the clearing caused all activity to cease and she realised how quiet it had become, quiet enough to hear the crackle of the fire nearest to her, though it was some distance away. Every person in the camp stood or sat completely still, looking at the new arrivals. Then a young girl standing nearby giggled as an even younger boy standing beside her said something too quietly for Monique to hear.

'Hello everyone,' said Ben, loudly. 'These are friends of mine.'

There was an uncomfortable silence and Monique found herself holding her breath.

'Hello Ben, how are you?' Monique saw the speaker was a young woman, probably in her early twenties, sitting on a stool and holding a baby outside a tent on the far side of the clearing.

People started to move again, and the level of sound began to return to nearer what it had been, though it was clear that many of the residents remained interested in the new arrivals. Monique followed Ben across the clearing towards the woman's tent. She looked round to catch Anthony's eye. He smiled, then also followed.

'Hello Betsy,' said Ben. 'How's little Duncan?'

Betsy smiled. 'He's teething so we're not getting as much sleep as we'd like. He's asleep at the minute, though. Who are your friends?'

'I'm Monique, and this is Anthony.'

'You're not here to pay a social call, are you?'

'No, Betsy, we're not,' said Monique. 'We're here because we're looking for Ben's cousin, Helen. She's missing and we wondered if anyone here might be able to help us find her.'

'What's she to you?'

'The man Anthony and I work for is a good friend of her father. Yesterday, Helen sent her father a letter saying she thought she was being followed. After he got the letter earlier today, her father couldn't reach George and Jemima Moncrieff by telephone at Easter Crimond, so he phoned my boss and asked us to help. We think Angus Henderson may have helped Helen escape last night, and Ben thinks he may have brought her here. Did he?'

'You should ask Angus.'

Monique had seen this moment coming. 'I'm afraid we

can't. We think Angus has been killed by three people who were looking for Helen.'

Betsy went as white as a sheet and then let out a loud wail. Her son woke up and joined in. Monique walked over and crouched down next to Betsy, then awkwardly tried to put her arms around her without crushing the baby between them.

Monique saw an elderly woman approaching out of the corner of her eye.

'You've upset her.'

'I didn't want to,' said Monique.

'She's saying Angus has been killed by the people looking for Helen,' wailed Betsy.

The woman took the baby off Betsy and handed it to an elderly man who had been following her. Then she lifted Betsy to her feet and drew her into a deep hug, giving Monique a look, as if to say, *'That's how it should be done.'*

The man cradled the baby in his arms. 'Is it true that Angus is dead?' he asked, looking at Monique.

'We are fairly sure the body we found was Angus's.'

'And you think the people who are looking for Helen did it?'

'It seems very likely. They broke into Easter Crimond last night and locked up Ben and his parents. We think it's possible that they wanted Angus to tell them where he had taken Helen and that they killed him when he wouldn't.'

'Why are you involved?'

Monique explained again.

Betsy's wails had subdued to sobs.

The man turned to her. 'Betsy, love, I think we need to tell her.'

Monique was relieved to see Betsy nod. It seemed she had

the final say.

'I'm Peter, by the way,' the man said. 'This is my wife, Jessie. We are Betsy's aunt and uncle. Angus was a very good friend to Violet, Betsy's mum, after Betsy's dad died. He helped her, and us, a lot. He thought of Betsy as his daughter and Duncan as his grandson.'

'Is Helen Erickson here?' asked Monique.

'No, but she was,' said Betsy.

'Do you know where she is now?'

'I think you should tell her the whole story, Betsy, love,' said Peter.

Betsy took little Duncan from her uncle and sat back down. She put the tip of a forefinger in the baby's mouth, and he sucked on it vigorously before falling asleep. Monique looked around and the camp appeared to have returned to life as normal, as if she and Anthony weren't there.

'Yes, that's best,' said Betsy. She paused as if to gather her thoughts. 'It was well after midnight last night and I was asleep in our tent with my husband Duncan and with little Duncan. Duncan, my husband, woke me up and said he'd heard someone outside. He went out and came back with Angus. Angus told us that Ben's cousin was in danger from a woman and two men who were looking for her. He had left her waiting outside the camp, in the wood. We said we'd help, of course we did, and Angus went and brought Helen back. She seemed nice enough, but I got the feeling she'd been brought up to believe she might catch something nasty just by being around us. Angus talked to her about us and explained his links with travellers and told her she'd be safe with us.

'Then Angus said he had to return to Easter Crimond and that Helen should stay with us until he came back and told her it was safe to return to the farm.

'This morning we got up as normal. Helen had some breakfast, then got a map and a thick book out of her suitcase and spent part of the morning looking at them. She seemed surprised when I asked what a *Bradshaw's Guide* was. I got the sense she hadn't expected me to be able to read what it said on the cover. I found her nice enough, but it was obvious this was a very different world from anything she'd ever seen. I doubt if she'd ever had reason to think about travellers before. Certainly not in a good way.

'Anyway, she was happy to talk to me about her *Bradshaw's Guide*, which she said her mother had given her before she set off to come to Scotland from London. It gives all the railway timetables for the whole country and they produce a new edition each month. Helen told me she was looking at it to try to decide which trains were best to get her back to England, where her mother lives. I told her that Angus would sort things out here and she had no need to go anywhere. Helen insisted she'd only be safe if she could get to her mother. She said that people had been following her all the way from London and Angus had seen one of them while walking her to her cottage from the farmhouse last night.

'Helen said that later last night, Angus came to her cottage to say that three people were watching the glen and they had a car blocking the only road in or out. He'd been up to where they were without them seeing him. She'd agreed with Angus that she needed to go somewhere safer in case the people planned to harm her. She said she quickly packed her suitcase and Angus led her out of the back of the cottage into the shelter of the garden, then along a path a little away from the road. They were able to keep out of sight of the watchers, even in the moonlight. He brought her here.'

'Where is she now?' asked Monique.

'About mid-morning, one of the boys, Simon, whose family have the darker green tent you can see over on the far side, came running into the camp. He said he'd seen a car stop at the end of the track and three people had got out of it and were coming towards the camp. Duncan got Helen into our tent and told her to stay silent and out of sight.

'When the people arrived, it was like when you came into the camp. It all went very quiet. The two men stood near the entrance to the camp while the woman walked into the middle. She spoke loudly and had an accent a little like yours. She said they were looking for a young woman missing from a nearby farm. She asked if we had seen her. No one said anything. Then she said she had £5 if anyone could tell her anything about this woman and held a note up above her head. Again, no one said anything. She turned round and had a conversation I didn't understand with one of the men, and the three of them left.'

'What did they look like?' asked Monique.

'The woman and one of the men wore beige raincoats even though it was already quite warm by then. The other man wore a dark raincoat. Both men had dark hats on. The woman had no hat and had hair a little like yours but blonde. She was about the same age as you. I think the men might have been a little older.'

'What happened then?'

'After they'd gone, Helen came out of the tent and told Duncan and me that she had to leave. She was frightened that the people had found the camp, though Duncan told her they'd probably seen the smoke from the fires drifting across the road. She was also frightened that someone here would betray her for the £5 because it was such a lot of money.

'We tried to tell her there was nothing to be afraid of, but she insisted. When we had a moment alone, I even suggested that she should call the police if she was that scared. She made me promise not to tell anyone else – I know I'm breaking that promise now – but she couldn't go to the police. She said she was in trouble with them in London for doing something she believed was right. She didn't want anyone in her family to know about it and felt she had to avoid having anything to do with the police, even in Scotland.'

'Did she say what had happened?' asked Monique.

'No, but I got the impression it was quite serious. Anyway, then Uncle Peter agreed with her that she might be safer somewhere else.' Betsy glared past Monique at her uncle. 'Duncan asked where she wanted to go, and she said she wanted to go to Dunkeld and Birnam railway station to catch the train that's due to leave for Perth just after 7.30 tomorrow morning. That would allow her to get down to her mother in England. Duncan said Blairgowrie station would be nearer, or Coupar Angus station if she wanted to be on the main line, but Helen said she'd come that way and the people looking for her would expect her to go there.

'Duncan agreed to take Helen to Birnam on his pony and cart. He said he knew places where they could spend the night that were close enough to get to the station in time for her train. He would then return here tomorrow. He said that if there were trains to Perth this afternoon or evening, she might be able to catch one of them and get away from the area sooner. Helen said that it was important that she caught that particular train tomorrow morning. I don't know why. Perhaps she didn't want to travel overnight tonight by train. She had something to eat here and then left.'

'Won't she be in danger on the road to Dunkeld if the three people who came here are still in the area?' asked Monique.

'Helen asked that. Duncan said there were lots of back roads and tracks he could choose from, and it was only about ten miles whichever route he picked. He didn't think there was much danger of meeting them.'

'Thank you, Betsy, you've been very helpful. Do you know where Duncan intends to spend the night?'

'No, sorry, but I know he'll have somewhere good in mind.'

'Thank you again. We'll be on our way now. Please buy something nice for little Duncan.' Monique took a 10 shilling note from her purse and gave it to Betsy.

'We didn't help Helen for the money!'

'I know you didn't, Betsy. I just want to thank little Duncan for being so quiet while you were talking.'

Monique said her farewells and turned to follow Anthony and Ben, who were already walking towards the start of the track back to the road.

'Can I walk with you for a moment?' asked Peter.

'Of course,' said Monique. 'Before I leave, could you point Simon out to me and ask if I can talk to him?'

Peter beckoned to a boy who had been standing beside a tent, watching them. He came over.

'Hello, are you Simon?' asked Monique.

'Yes.'

'Betsy said you saw the car the three people who came here earlier were in. Can you describe it? Did you see the number plate?'

'I'm sorry, miss, I can't tell you much. It was black and looked like most of the cars you see. A bonnet at the front and four doors and a solid roof. I know more about horses than cars, to be honest. I only saw the car as the people were getting out and didn't think to look at the number plate.'

'Thank you very much.' Monique gave the boy a shilling. 'Perhaps you can get some carrots for your horse?' She wondered if she was revealing the depth of her ignorance about horses.

The boy took the coin, smiled his thanks, and ran away, apparently happy. Peter turned towards the track that led back to the road and Monique did likewise.

'You might be able to answer a question I should have asked Betsy,' said Monique as they walked. 'How long will it take Duncan to cover ten miles in his horse and cart?'

'It depends if he's in a hurry or not. They could be there already, or they could still be on the road for an hour or two more. In the circumstances, my guess is that he'd want to get there as soon as he could and settle down somewhere out of sight.'

'If that's true then my chances of finding them this evening aren't good.'

'Duncan knows what he's doing. I'd say that you stand no chance of finding them. You ought to know that Duncan is a good man who was prepared to go to fight when he was conscripted. But a childhood brush with polio left just enough of a limp for him to be rejected on medical grounds.'

'I'm sure Betsy and little Duncan are grateful for that,' said Monique. 'And at least I know where Helen Erickson is planning to be just after 7.30 tomorrow morning. Look, I've got a description of Helen that her father gave to us, but it would help if you could tell me what she was wearing when you last saw her. I'm told she looks like Veronica Lake, only taller.'

'The film star?' asked Peter. 'I'm not what you'd call a regular visitor to the cinema, so can't comment. I can tell you that she's an extremely attractive young woman with blue eyes and long wavy blonde hair that seems to fall across one side of her face a lot. When she left, she was wearing a beige raincoat and a black beret and she had a brown leather suitcase with her.'

'Thank you, that's helpful.'

Monique saw Peter look over his shoulder as if to check that the camp was out of sight and out of hearing. Ahead of them, Anthony and Ben were also out of sight along the curving track

'There's something else I should tell you,' he said. 'But first I need to know who you and the captain work for.'

'We're with military intelligence, though what I told you about my boss being a friend of Helen's father is true.'

'OK. Betsy told you the woman had a conversation with one of the men after she'd tried to bribe everyone, as they were leaving. They spoke in Russian, and the woman said, "We're wasting our time here, let's go". The man replied with something like, "If I had my way, I'd shoot them all." The woman smiled at him and said, "You've had enough fun for one day, Viktor, go back to the car".'

'How did you learn to speak Russian?' asked Monique.

'I'd almost forgotten I could,' said Peter. 'It's been 25 years, but it all came back when they started talking. I was with the Royal Scots who landed in Archangel in northern Russia in September 1918 as part of international efforts to stop the Russian revolution. I read once that Britain put tens of thousands of troops into Russia and nearly a thousand of them were killed. It was obvious by the end of 1918 that we were wasting our time, but I suppose at least I learned enough Russian to get by. It just came naturally to me. I picked it up so quickly that they wanted me to stay on as an interpreter, but I got out of Russia and out of the army as quickly as I could.'

'Spasibo,' said Monique.

Peter smiled. 'You speak it too. I'm not surprised Betsy thought you sounded a little like the blonde woman, though her accent is Russian and yours is something else. That's not the only likeness. That woman had a look in her eyes that made me think I didn't want to get on the wrong side of her. That's why I was keen for Helen to get away from here to somewhere she'd be safer. You have the same look. You could almost be sisters, apart from the colour of your hair.'

CHAPTER TWENTY

Bob wondered what the Great Hall at Stirling Castle had looked like originally. Presumably, it had been what the name implied, a large hall for feasting and entertaining in an age when the castle had often served as a residence for Scottish kings and queens.

That was very hard to imagine now. He got the sense that it must have been altered very significantly when the army converted it into barracks in the early 1800s. With multiple floors inserted and then divided and subdivided, even the small part he'd seen made him think of a rabbit warren.

'The officer who has been overseeing the search is Lieutenant Shaw,' said Michael as he led the way down a spiral staircase.

They'd entered the north end of the building through a door from the Inner Close. Bob initially wondered why they needed to descend, then realised that the sloping site of the castle meant that levels might be deceptive.

This was confirmed a few moments later when Michael led him into a room that was largely occupied by racks full of folded bedding.

'This is Lieutenant Shaw,' said Michael.

The lieutenant turned round as they entered. 'Hello, sir.'

'Can you tell me where we are in relation to the triangular courtyard at the end of the Great Hall?' asked Bob.

'If you come over here you can see for yourself, sir.'

Bob followed and looked out of the window the lieutenant had indicated. 'Am I right in thinking that this is the ground floor on this side of the building?' he asked.

'That's right, sir. This is the bedding store, which accounts for two of the windows and one of the doors you see from the cobbled area outside. We've had a good look down here and can't see anything out of place, though unless you feel it's necessary, we've stopped short of moving each item to check nothing's been pushed between two folded blankets.'

'No, I don't think that's necessary. There are two doors leading into the building from the courtyard. What's the other one?'

'There's a second storeroom like this one just along the corridor you entered from. It's the uniform and personal equipment store. Again, a thorough search would take a lot of manpower, but a reasonably good look suggests there's been no disturbance.'

'What about the doors from the courtyard?' asked Bob. 'Are they kept locked?'

'Normally, yes. When we're restocking or rotating stock, we use the doors to bring stuff round from the side of the building. But otherwise, the doors are locked, and the keys are kept in a key safe in the quartermaster's office. The internal doors from the corridor to both stores are also normally locked.'

'Which makes it unlikely that someone could have entered the building this way,' said Bob.

'Very unlikely sir. Additionally, if the person you had in mind was on the wall walk, as I understand is the case, I think they'd easily break a leg dropping down to the courtyard.'

'There's also a door from the courtyard into the Chapel Royal.'

'Yes, sir. It leads into a boiler room in the basement. It's kept locked, though we looked inside and found nothing of interest.'

'What about the floor above us, which has a row of windows on this side?' asked Bob.

'The windows there are roughly on a level with the wall walk,' said the lieutenant. 'But you'd have the problem of getting from the wall walk's inner parapet to any of the windows, which means jumping across the rather intimidating drop to the cobbles outside, then gaining a purchase on the windowsill and opening the window to gain entry. I've taken the liberty of pacing the width of the gap and the end window, which is closest to the wall walk, is only about seven feet from the wall walk parapet. However, the diverging angle of the wall of the hall and the wall walk means that distance increases quite rapidly as you consider successive windows in the row. I'd say it was just about possible to leap across the gap to the first window, and perhaps the second, but not the others.'

'What are the rooms up there used for?'

'There are two twin bedrooms used by junior non-commissioned officers, while the room behind the two windows with the shortest gap to the wall walk is currently being used as a store for kit and material being used to redecorate all the barrack rooms in the hall. Paint, brushes, ladders, and dustsheets, you know the sort of thing. I've asked my men to take a closer look at that room than the others.'

'Can we see for ourselves?'

'Of course, sir. Follow me.' The lieutenant led the way out into the corridor and up the spiral staircase that Bob and Michael had descended and then through a door into a rather dingy corridor where he bumped into a soldier coming out of another door.

'Look where you're going, man!'

'Sorry, sir. It's just that we've found something I think

you'll want to see.'

'Go on then, show me,' said the lieutenant.

'Actually, can you show me, please?' asked Bob.

Lieutenant Shaw looked momentarily annoyed before stepping back.

'This way, sir,' said the soldier, who Bob thought seemed to be trying to conceal a smile. He turned and went back through the door he'd emerged from.

Bob followed the man into the room and found himself in a space that looked like a dumping ground, not just for the trappings of a large-scale redecoration but just about anything else too. There were folding ladders and dustsheets, piles of tins of paint, and brushes standing in open tins. But there were also two chests of drawers piled one on top of the other against one wall, with perhaps a dozen folding chairs leaning against the side of the lower one. Against another wall, next to a wardrobe with a missing door, were enough disassembled metal pieces of bedframe to make two or three complete beds.

As well as the man who had led Bob in, there were two other soldiers in the room, standing and looking at him expectantly.

'Over here, sir. There's a drawer in the base of the wardrobe.' The man bent down and pulled it open.

'I'm not sure what I'm looking at,' said Bob.

'It looks like a standard issue battledress blouse and trousers, sir, roughly folded and pushed into the drawer. We were told not to touch anything we found so I can't be sure, but I think that's a bloodstain there, and another one there.'

'Thank you, that's very good work. Could the three of you leave the room, please?'

After the soldiers had exited, Bob put his head out into the corridor. 'Michael, can you come in here? You too, Lieutenant Shaw. By the way, do you know if this door is normally locked?'

'I don't think so, sir,' said the lieutenant.

Bob returned to the wardrobe and, having put on rubber gloves, carefully lifted out two pieces of khaki-coloured clothing from the drawer. Both the jacket and the trousers were heavily spattered and stained with what did look very much like blood.

'There's a pair of green woollen gloves in here too, also stained,' Bob said. 'I think we now know where our murderer came after they'd killed Bill Douglas. We need to get a bag to put these things in, then we should get them tested to see if it's the same type of blood as Bill Douglas's. We also need to see whether this uniform can tell us anything about the person who wore it. I'm not expecting to find a name tag, that would be too easy. But we might at least work out how large our killer is from the size of the uniform.'

'I'll get that organised,' said Michael.

'The labels should tell us,' said Lieutenant Shaw. 'There should be one in the blouse and one in the trousers.'

Bob pulled open the battledress jacket. 'There is quite a lot of blood on this. The label says it's a size 12.'

'That equates to a man with a 40 to 41-inch chest and between 5 feet 9 inches and 5 feet 10 inches in height. What about the trousers?'

Bob carefully put the jacket down on a pile of dust sheets and turned his attention to the second garment. 'These are size 10.'

'They are intended for a man of the same height but with a comparatively narrow waist, of 31 to 32 inches.'

Bob laid the trousers on top of the jacket. 'How careful are you to fit the men with the correctly sized uniforms?' he asked.

'Your question implies you know that can be a little hit-and-miss, sir. It depends on what's available when the recruit is kitted out, but we do try to issue correctly sized uniforms if possible.'

'There's another thing,' said Michael. 'We must remember that this man planned to discard this uniform after the murder. We don't know if it's his or one he stole from somewhere for this purpose. The size might therefore be misleading.'

'That's true,' said Bob. 'But this is the closest we've come to a description of the killer. If the uniform is to be believed, he's a little on the upper side of average height and quite athletically built, with a broad chest and narrow waist. That's more information than we had fifteen minutes ago. We also need to know how our killer got into this room from the wall walk.'

One of the windows was partly obscured by two folding metal ladders. The other, which Bob realised would be the one that was closest to the wall walk, was more easily accessible. He walked over to it, released the catch, and lifted the sash.

'What are you thinking, Bob?' asked Michael.

'That if you were very athletic and very fearless you could jump from the parapet of the wall walk to the windowsill. But the sash would have needed to be open to start with to stand any chance of then getting into the room.'

'We think this was a planned attack,' said Michael, 'even if perhaps planned at fairly short notice. To my mind, the killer came in here to put a spare clean uniform on one side. Then he crossed from the window to the wall walk, while carrying an axe. Then he murdered Bill Douglas, disposed of the axe, and came back the same way. Once in the room he closed the window, changed into the clean uniform, and left the bloodstained one in that drawer, perhaps for later retrieval when things had quietened down.'

'I'm still not convinced by the idea of the killer jumping across the gap, even if it is only seven feet,' said Bob.

'Perhaps they used one of these folding metal ladders to form a bridge?' asked Anthony.

'That seems more likely than simply jumping,' said Bob.

'What about this?' asked Lieutenant Shaw. He was crouching down at the end of the room furthest from the window and pointing at a sturdy wooden plank lying on the floor. 'The men use planks like this supported between two ladders when painting ceilings. I've paced this one out and it's about ten feet long.'

Bob smiled. 'Thank you, lieutenant. I find that altogether more convincing. Michael, do you think you can find your way out of the building and round to the wall walk over there?'

'Of course, Bob. Give me a few minutes.'

After Michael left the room, Bob turned to the lieutenant. 'Lieutenant Shaw, I'd like you to help me with an experiment. Can you pick up the end of the plank and move it so it's resting on the windowsill, please?'

'Of course, sir.'

Bob watched as the lieutenant struggled slightly with the plank.

'Thank you. Now I want to see if one man can push the plank out far enough for the other end to rest on the wall walk parapet. Keeping control of the plank as more of it moves beyond the window and less of it is this side might be difficult.'

This was clearly a much harder task, but the lieutenant

managed. 'I think we may be looking for someone a little more strongly built than I am, sir. The trick was to use some of my weight to hold down this end of the plank as it got shorter, as a counterweight for the longer part outside.'

'Thank you, that's useful to know.' Bob saw that Michael had arrived on the wall walk. 'Right, Michael, it seems to me that leaving a bridge like this in place and in full view while the murderer was waiting in the gardens for Bill Douglas was asking for it to be found, which would have unravelled everything. Are you able to pull it over from your side, then perhaps lay it down on its edge at the side of the wall walk, where it isn't too obvious?'

Michael managed a little more easily than the lieutenant had done. He smiled. 'I see what you mean, Bob. You can't see from where you are, but the plank doesn't look too badly out of place down here. I'm betting you now want me to get it back into place between the parapet and the windowsill, don't you?'

'Yes, that re-enacts the murderer making their escape.'

'Try holding your end down with your body weight,' said the lieutenant, from behind Bob.

This was obviously a much harder task than pulling it in and at one point Bob thought Michael had lost control of the plank and was in danger of catapulting himself over the parapet and into the courtyard, but again he succeeded.

'I'm out of breath,' said Michael. 'And I've not just murdered someone in a particularly brutal way, then run to where I could throw the axe over the wall, then run the length of the gardens and back to here. On the other hand, I'm doing this dispassionately. It might have been easier if I'd had some adrenaline and rage and fear to help. Is that all you want, Bob? I'm always happy to oblige, but if you want someone to demonstrate crawling along the plank and into the window, it's not going to be me. It does look quite a long way down when there's a realistic prospect of you falling.'

'No, that will be fine, Michael. Can you come back by a safer route? Would you pull the plank back into the room, please, Lieutenant Shaw? We're going to need to check it for evidence, though if there was any to start with, I suspect we've rather compromised it by now.'

By the time the lieutenant had put the plank back where he'd found it, Michael had returned to the room.

'I'd call that a reasonable success,' said Bob. 'I think this experiment suggests we probably now know how the killer reached the gardens and then made his escape which, if the blood matches Bill Douglas's, is strongly supported by the discarded uniform. We also have a possible physical description of the killer. We are probably looking for someone with a broader chest and more muscle development than either of you.'

'One thing I think is now absolutely clear is that our murderer is connected to the Argylls rather than to the general's conference,' said Michael.

'I agree,' said Bob. 'Lieutenant Shaw, once the murderer went out through that door, I assume they could have gone anywhere in the Great Hall or beyond?'

'If it was one of the men then yes, they could have just faded into the background of all the other men. I'm not certain of the exact current numbers but several hundred men are living in this building while they undergo their training or as members of staff. One thing you must remember, though, is that lights out is at 10 p.m. sharp, and that applies to many of the men living here. From what I've heard, the murder in the gardens took place only a few minutes before then.'

'Yes,' said Bob. 'That was something that Lieutenant Commander Dixon raised when we thought the killer had escaped via the King's Old Building. It seems even more relevant now. The murder probably took place just before 9.50 p.m. Let's assume it was twelve minutes before lights out. The killer really must have felt pressed for time when he came back along the wall walk after disposing of the axe. Then he had to re-erect the plank bridge, cross it and remove it, then change his uniform and hide the bloodstained one before returning to wherever he was meant to be. Anyone getting back to their barrack room after lights out last night or appearing particularly out of breath when getting back just before 10 p.m. must be considered a suspect.'

'We seem to be agreed that the killer got away via this room,' said Michael. 'We need to begin the process of interviewing possible witnesses again, but this time talking to anyone who might have been in or around the Great Hall at the time of the murder, with particular reference to anyone coming back late for lights out.'

*

Bob asked Michael Dixon and Sergeant MacMillan to begin the process of looking for witnesses, while Gilbert Potter took the bloodied uniform and gloves, now wrapped in a torn-off piece of dustsheet, to be tested for blood type by the police surgeon.

With Monique and Anthony away, Bob was grateful that Alan MacMillan provided an extra pair of hands they could call on.

Bob went back to the office they were using and started to

make notes he could use later as a basis for a verbal report to Sir Peter Maitland and Commodore Cunningham. He felt they had at last begun to make progress and was relieved he would have something positive to report. If nothing else, the fact they no longer regarded any of the meeting attendees as suspects meant there would be no difficulty with any of them leaving to return to London the following day.

A sound in the doorway made Bob look up as the large presence of Sergeant Gilbert Potter came in, looking slightly flushed, as if he had hurried to be there.

'That was quick, Gilbert.'

'I've not been to the hospital yet sir. When I was signing out a car down in the hut they use as a motor transport section, the warrant officer there asked whether a Corporal Peter Kerr had come to see us. I said I didn't think so and he suggested I check. Do you remember that earlier on we identified four men based at the castle who came from the Castle Douglas area?'

'Yes, we interviewed two, while one has been on leave and the fourth was in Edinburgh.'

'That's right, sir. The fourth man had taken a lorry to pick up supplies and I left a message that when he got back, he should be told to come and see us. The fourth man is Corporal Kerr, who works in the quartermaster's office here at the castle. He got back from Edinburgh a little earlier and was told by the warrant officer who spoke to me to report to "the people from military intelligence". According to the warrant officer, he went white, as if he had seen a ghost, but then said he would come straight here.'

'Let's check with the lieutenant colonel's secretary whether he turned up while we were out and about,' said Bob.

'I've already done that sir, just now. She's seen nothing of him.'

'What do you make of his disappearance, Gilbert?'

'There could be any number of reasons why a soldier might not be happy to be asked to visit military intelligence,' said Gilbert. 'But given there was a murder here last night and I am sure everyone in the castle knows you are leading the investigation, there's one really obvious reason why Corporal Kerr might not want to talk to you.'

'We could do with knowing whether the bloodstained uniform we found is likely to have fitted Corporal Kerr,' said Bob.

'You want to find out whether the glass slipper really would fit Cinderella? I've already done that too, up to a point, anyway. From the description given to me by the transport section warrant officer, Corporal Kerr is probably about the right height and about the right build to fit the uniform.'

'That's excellent work, Gilbert!'

'There are two problems we need to consider, sir.'

'What are they?'

'If Cinderella had been in the army, the glass slipper would only have fitted where it touched. You'd expect a corporal working in supplies to have a better chance of a well-fitting uniform than a raw recruit, but that brings us to the second problem.'

'What's that?' asked Bob.

Gilbert leaned forwards with one shoulder and used the other hand to touch the three stripes on his arm.

'Ah, of course. A corporal has two stripes on his arm and the bloodstained uniform has none. That suggests that if our killer was a corporal, he chose to use a uniform that concealed the fact.'

'Which would certainly make him less conspicuous,' said Gilbert. 'Unless he met someone who knew him, in which case the absence of stripes could raise all sorts of questions. On the other hand, a corporal working in supplies might not find it too hard to acquire a spare uniform. And if he did, he'd probably acquire one that fitted well enough to be sure it wouldn't get in his way while he was killing Mr Douglas.'

'I accept we've only got suspicions,' said Bob. 'But it seems to me that finding Corporal Kerr must be our top priority. I'll pop down the corridor to ask Lieutenant Colonel Ferguson to launch a full-scale search.'

'Right, sir. And I'll be on my way to see the police surgeon.'

CHAPTER TWENTY-ONE

Blairgowrie police station was an imposing white-fronted building close to the centre of the town. Michael parked on a road that ran along one side, behind the Moncrieffs' Rover 10.

Monique turned round in her seat in the stationary car. 'You've been a great help and I'm truly grateful, Ben, but do you remember what we've agreed?'

'That I'll not tell anyone about the travellers or Dunkeld and Birnam station or the train tomorrow morning.'

'That's right, you promised. It's very important. From what Betsy said, if Helen sees any police there, she'll change her plans and disappear again. I've got to have the chance to talk to her without scaring her off and tell her that her father sent me. That means the police can't know about what she's planning. It also means that your mother and father shouldn't know about it because they might want to tell the police.'

'If I came with you to Dunkeld in the morning, Helen would know you were there to help,' said Ben.

'That's true, but I promised your parents I'd keep you safe and after what happened last night, I think they need to have you with them now.'

'I keep my promises too. I won't tell anyone.'

Monique led the way into the police station with Anthony and Ben following. The main desk was unmanned, but a constable came out of a rear room after Monique pinged a small bell on the counter.

'Hello,' she said, 'I'd like to speak to whoever is in charge, please.'

'That would be me.'

Monique swung round to her right to see who had spoken and realised that a tall dark-haired man in a police inspector's uniform was standing at the end of a corridor that led to that side of the building.

Monique smiled and the man responded.

'Hello, I'm Monique Dubois from Military Intelligence 11 and this is my colleague Captain Anthony Darlington. And this is…'

'Ben Moncrieff, yes, I know. I've got his mother and father in my office, being checked over by the police surgeon. He's a GP whose practice is just around the corner. I'm Inspector Stuart Kennedy, by the way. Before we go any further, though, could you show me your identification?'

Monique and Anthony complied.

'Thank you. I don't know what a Military Intelligence 11 identity card is meant to look like but, as you released the Moncrieffs, I'll accept you're on the side of the angels. I'd like to take Ben to join his parents and see the doctor, and then I think we should talk.'

Monique and Anthony were shown by the constable to an interview room while the inspector took Ben further along the corridor. Monique and Anthony sat on one side of the table in the otherwise bare room that smelled of stale cigarette smoke. Monique thought that probably had something to do with the overflowing ashtray on the table.

'Do you think Ben will keep his promise?' asked Anthony.

'I hope so,' said Monique. 'We know Helen isn't stupid and she is sure to find a way to check the area around the…' She stopped and looked around the room.

'Are you concerned someone might be listening?' asked Anthony.

'I very much doubt it, but let's assume they are. That means I've got to ask you to follow my lead with the inspector and I'll fill you in on the background afterwards.'

The constable returned with two cups of tea and a moment later the inspector came in carrying a mug and sat down on the other side of the table.

Inspector Kennedy looked across the table at Monique. 'I don't know what I'm dealing with here, beyond a missing woman, a family being assaulted and imprisoned in their own home and, apparently, a murder. I don't have very many men at my disposal, but I've currently got some of those who are on duty going around and bringing in others who are not meant to be. I have also sent a sergeant and three constables out to Easter Crimond to locate the body you told the Moncrieffs about. In the circumstances, I armed them with revolvers and rifles. I need you to tell me what the hell is going on, Miss Dubois.'

'It's Monique, please, or Madame Dubois if you want to keep it formal. And as for what's going on, I can let you have what I'd describe as a strong working theory.'

'That's more than I have.'

Monique put her teacup back in its saucer. 'As you doubtless know from the Moncrieffs, their niece Helen Erickson arrived yesterday to spend Easter with them. What I think will be news to you is that Helen believed herself to have been followed on her journey, all the way from London.

'While she was waiting for a train at Coupar Angus station, she wrote a letter to her father, who is a senior RAF officer stationed in the Outer Hebrides. It arrived today. He knows the man Anthony and I report to and rang him earlier to ask if MI11 could help. He had previously rung here and spoken to your Sergeant Christie, who was not prepared to help or to visit

Easter Crimond to check how things were when directly asked to do so.'

'Ah, I didn't know that. But that's not what's most important right now, is it?'

'No, that's correct, inspector. Much more important, and urgent, is the need to track down the three people who locked up the Moncrieffs last night. I am fairly positive they were also the people who were following Helen yesterday and I'm just as sure they also murdered Angus Henderson last night.'

'We also have to find Helen Erickson,' said the inspector.

'I'd like to suggest we divide the problem between us. I would be grateful if you could leave finding Helen to me. I've been told that, for reasons I only partly understand, Helen might be trying to avoid anyone in a police uniform as much as she's trying to avoid her pursuers.'

'You phrased that very nicely Madame Dubois, but it was more an order than a request, wasn't it?'

'Should we keep it at the level of a request for the moment inspector? But yes, if you were unhappy with my proposal, then I had dinner in Stirling last night with Major General Sir Peter Maitland, the Director of Military Intelligence, and I am sure I could get him to telephone your chief constable about my preferred approach to this investigation.'

Monique was surprised to see Inspector Kennedy smile in response to her blatant threat.

'There will be no need for that, Madame Dubois. I'm more than happy to leave you with the responsibility for finding the missing woman. Could I ask you to tell me what you know about the three people you referred to?'

'It's possible there may be more than three. But the three we do know about comprise two men and a woman. The woman may be about thirty and the men may be a little older. I am fairly sure that they are Soviet NKVD agents based in the UK and that they are trying to kidnap Helen Erickson because her mother is involved in highly sensitive war work and the Soviets want leverage over her.

'I understand they are driving a black four-door saloon, with unknown number plates. I know that's not much help on its own. The woman looks a little like me, but with blonde hair, and she sounds a little like me, though with a Russian accent rather than mine, which is more complex in origin. I also understand that one of the men is called Viktor and it is likely that it was him who killed Angus Henderson, though with the involvement of the other two.'

'How do you know all this?' asked Inspector Kennedy.

Monique could see that Anthony was wondering much the same thing.

'You don't need to know that. What you do need to know, inspector, is that if you get close to any of these people, there is a fair chance they will simply raise their hands and claim diplomatic immunity. Which, I should say, they are entitled to. If that happens, then I need you to ensure that it proves impossible for any of them to communicate with one another or with anyone else until the end of tomorrow at the earliest. I should warn you, however, that it's also possible that if you corner one or more of these people then they might forget about their diplomatic status and the fact that the UK and the Soviet Union are meant to be allies and start shooting at you.'

'Is that really likely?'

'It happened late last year when a Soviet agent being arrested in Leith tried to kill a senior military intelligence officer.'

'Did he succeed?'

'No. I shot and disabled him before he could shoot the man he was intending to kill.'

The inspector looked rather shocked and hesitated before he replied. 'Right, we'll take care then. As you've had more time than me to think about this, do you have any suggestions about how we find these people?'

Monique sat back in her chair. 'To my mind, there's a good chance they will be keeping watch on the railway station at Blairgowrie and the one at Coupar Angus, which I believe is on the main line. Helen came by train, and it might be reasonable to believe she is trying to leave the same way. In your shoes, I'd find a way of keeping a discreet lookout for anyone watching the stations. I also think it would be helpful for you to keep a presence at Easter Crimond in case the Soviet agents return, though I don't honestly believe that's likely. And it would be helpful if, when you have the manpower available, you do a full search of Easter Crimond.'

'What for?'

'Anything of interest. We established earlier that Helen wasn't hiding in the barns or farm sheds, but we could only take a superficial look. And, finally, we need a way of keeping the Moncrieffs safe.'

'I'm ahead of you there. Mr Moncrieff's brother has a farm in Alyth, and I've asked the family to spend a couple of days there. I've said I'll get their car filled with petrol, which was enough to persuade them to accept the idea.'

*

'You caught me on the wrong foot back there, Monique,' said

Anthony.

They'd driven out of Blairgowrie on the now almost familiar road towards Dunkeld.

'I'm sorry, Anthony. I had no opportunity to warn you. I only put the pieces together in my head while you and Ben were walking back to the car. Uncle Peter had a quiet word and suddenly everything made a little more sense.' She went on to relate what Peter had told her. 'And it was one of the children at the travellers' camp who told me about the car.'

'That's fair enough, Monique, but it still seems a bit of a leap to decide we are dealing with NKVD agents simply based on the language they were using.'

'Not really, Anthony. I can't think of any other explanation. And I've encountered the NKVD enough times to know that this sort of thing is right up their street. The Soviets may nominally be our allies, but I can see that stopping rather quickly as soon as Germany is defeated.'

'One thing that troubles me a little is whether we should have suggested that the police keep a discreet watch on the travellers' camp in case the Soviets return there.'

'I don't think they will return to the camp,' said Monique. 'I know that what they did to Angus was appalling but, in their minds, they had a good reason to do it. I don't believe they would try to harm a group of thirty people, no matter what "Viktor" apparently said to the woman. Besides, I don't want to draw the inspector's attention to the camp in case, by whatever route, that in turn draws his attention to Dunkeld and Birnam railway station.'

'How did Group Captain Sutherland seem when you spoke to him on the phone from the police station? Hang on, here's the turn to Easter Crimond. Do you want a quick detour to make sure the police have found Angus's body and know they are meant to search the farm?'

'I think we can leave that to Inspector Kennedy. Besides, we need to be elsewhere. All I was able to tell Bob was that things had taken a serious turn and that the insecurities of the public telephone network were such that you and I were returning to bring him up to date.'

'So, the idea is that we drive to Stirling Castle, brief the boss, and then drive back this evening?'

'Yes, but we also need to call in at Dunkeld though, actually, I think I mean Birnam, on the way. That's also where we will be returning to later.'

'Wouldn't it be better to make an early start from Stirling Castle in the morning?' asked Anthony.

'I thought of that. The problem is that we'd be driving in the dark with only blackout lights on the car for at least part of the way, whereas there's enough daylight to get us to Stirling and back tonight without difficulty. And I don't want to take the chance of being delayed in the morning and failing to get back before Helen Erickson arrives to catch her train.

*

Monique looked up. 'According to the map, that was Dunkeld we passed through on the other side of the bridge over the river. On this side, we pass through Little Dunkeld before coming into Birnam. This must be Birnam now. Can you take the road on the right and then drive up the hill to the top? That should bring us to the railway station.'

'Why do we need to call in now?' asked Anthony.

'I want to check something at the station. That's it, just over there. Can you pull up outside? I'll only be a couple of minutes. You can stay in the car if you like.'

Except for a small dark blue van and a derelict bus with flat tyres at one end, the station car park was deserted. Anthony stopped right outside the station entrance.

Monique was back at the car in not much longer than she'd predicted and found Anthony standing beside it, smoking a cigarette.

'That was very interesting,' she said.

'Are you going to keep what you've found a secret again?' asked Anthony.

'No, I'm happy to tell you. I've also just noticed a sign saying that the building at this end of the road leading up from the village is the Station Hotel. Some of the windows give a view of the railway station, if a slightly uphill and rather oblique one. It might be a good place to spend the night.'

'So long as it's open and they've got vacancies,' said Anthony. 'I don't know if you saw it, but there was a large hotel down in the village that looked like it was completely closed. Should we book rooms now?'

'No, let's get back in the car and head for Stirling.'

'Your wish is my command, Monique. But before we go anywhere, I want you to tell me what you've discovered.'

Monique smiled. 'I wanted to look at the timetable for trains from here to Perth. Something I've been puzzled about was why Helen was so certain she wanted to get what turns out to be the 7.34 a.m. train tomorrow morning. Duncan was correct in guessing there are other trains Helen could use to begin her journey south.' She looked at her notebook. 'There was one at 2.50 p.m. this afternoon, which might have been before they got here. There was another at 4.09 p.m. And then there are two still to leave, at 6.00 p.m. and at 7.52 p.m. Helen would have known about them from her *Bradshaw's Guide*. If her intention was just to get safely away from the area as soon as possible, why not catch one of those trains?'

Anthony flicked his cigarette end away. 'Here's a thought, Monique. We're working on the understanding that Duncan has found somewhere within a fairly short distance of the station for Helen to spend the night. What's becoming obvious is that she is a very bright young woman. What if this thing about catching a train tomorrow morning is some sort of feint? What if she really intends to catch a train today, to keep ahead of anyone following her?'

'If she was on the 4.09 p.m. train, we've not only missed her, but we are also too late to have had the train met when it arrived in Perth at 4.45 p.m.'

'There's nothing we can do about that,' said Anthony. 'What's worrying me is that if we go to Stirling as planned, we lose any chance of intercepting Helen at the station if she intends to catch one of the two remaining trains today.'

'Hang on a moment,' said Monique, before turning and walking back into the station.

She returned a few minutes later. 'I saw a porter when I was checking the timetable. I've just spoken to him. He says that no one at all boarded either of the Perth trains that stopped here during the time we are interested in this afternoon.'

'That's a relief,' said Anthony.

'It is. As Inspector Kennedy was keen to point out, I've taken on the responsibility for finding Helen. It wouldn't have been good if I failed quite so quickly. But we've still got two more trains this evening to think about. We're going to have to split up. Let's book rooms in the Station Hotel to start with, hoping that at least one of them offers a view of the station. You can then keep a look out for an attractive blonde girl in a beige raincoat and black beret arriving at the station or waiting for either of the two remaining trains today. If you see her, your uniform ought to allow you to get close enough to tell her that her father sent you to find her. If you do find her, get her back to the hotel until I return, which might be rather later.'

'Are you happy driving to Stirling and back on your own?'

'I'll pretend you didn't ask me that, Anthony. Wrap one of the Sten guns up in your coat so it's not obvious and get your bag. Let's get our rooms organised.'

CHAPTER TWENTY-TWO

'I appreciate being kept up to date, Bob, but I don't have much time.' Major General Sir Peter Maitland looked at his watch. 'I'm due to be hosting dinner for the meeting attendees in the officers' mess shortly. Commander Cunningham and Paul Gillespie also need to be there.'

Bob had a slight sense of déjà vu. The same people were sitting in the same chairs around the same table in the same room as they had in the meeting at the castle late the previous night. With one notable exception. Bob looked at his watch and wondered why Monique wasn't back yet.

'I hope not to take too much of your time, sir,' he said. 'We are making good progress in our search for Bill Douglas's killer. We've found the weapon, one of them anyway. The axe very probably used to slice the top off Douglas's head was thrown by the killer over the castle wall, where it was found this morning thanks to assistance from Lieutenant Colonel Ferguson. We have also worked out how the killer escaped, and we've identified a suspect, who has unfortunately disappeared. The lieutenant colonel is conducting a search for him.'

'Do I take it that your suspect is a member of the garrison here and not one of the attendees at my meeting?'

'That's right, sir. While I described the man we are looking for as a suspect, I am now quite confident, even if he turns out not to be the murderer, that it was one of the Argylls who killed Bill Douglas and not one of your people. Other than the search I mentioned, our main task at present is interviewing the large number of men who were in or around the Great Hall at the time the murder took place, in the hope that by cross-referencing what we are told, we can come up with a clearer picture of who was where and be more confident about the identity of the murderer.

'I should perhaps add that though I believe that your attendees are in the clear, Bill Douglas was such a popular fellow that two of them have said how pleased they are that he is dead. One is a young woman he raped last Christmas and the other is a young man whose career he tried to ruin. This is particularly relevant because we suspect that Mr Douglas may have had a habit of cultivating enemies. We have been told of a rape during the school summer holidays when he was seventeen that was swept under the carpet because of his family connections. When we can establish the link, I'm quite sure we will find that the murder was an act of revenge for something he'd done during a lifelong career as an utter bastard.'

Sir Peter Maitland sat back in his chair. 'You're not mincing your words, are you Bob?'

'There seems no point, sir. Now, given your need to be elsewhere, do you want me to lead you quickly through what I believe happened last night after your dinner finished?'

'Yes, please.'

'Most of your people arrived at Stirling Castle yesterday afternoon. Bill Douglas and two others were on a plane that developed a fault and had to land near Carlisle so a replacement could be found. As a result, they arrived late and had to rush to get to your dinner in time.

'Either on the journey or over dinner, Bill Douglas boasted to several other attendees about his family links to the 8th Earl of Douglas and related the story of the earl being killed by King James II at the castle. He also told those people of his intention to visit the Douglas Gardens if there was enough daylight left after the dinner finished.

'One of the people he'd flown up with was the young man whose career he had tried to ruin. After dinner, Bill Douglas provoked a confrontation with this man and it developed into a fight on a terrace outside the Palace. I only have the other man's account of what took place but find it convincing. He left Bill Douglas winded on the terrace and went to the officers' mess bar for a drink.

'Once he had recovered, Bill Douglas went to his room to get his coat, and then to the Douglas Gardens, where he met Monique, who was just leaving after taking in the views. You know what happened between them. Monique then left the gardens, told a sentry that someone was unwell and went to her room. The sentry alerted the orderly officer, who found Bill Douglas dead, as far as we can work out, about three minutes after Monique left him.

'I believe that the killer was already hidden under a stone staircase in the gardens waiting for Bill Douglas when Monique arrived. I do not know how the killer knew Douglas intended to visit the gardens after dinner as I've accounted for everyone who he told. That's an extremely important gap in my knowledge.

'After Monique left the gardens, the killer came out of hiding and killed Douglas in what appears to have been a theatrical recreation of King James II's killing of the 8th Earl of Douglas. The killer then ran over towards the wall at the west end of the gardens and threw the axe over it. He then doubled back and ran to the east end of the gardens and along the wall walk. There he used a plank he had left earlier to bridge the gap to a first-floor window at the end of the Great Hall that he had left open. Once inside, he pulled in the plank and changed out of his bloodstained uniform into a clean one he'd left there for the purpose. Then he made his escape into the rest of the building.'

'The killer did all that in three minutes?' asked Paul Gillespie.

'No, but he must have been out of sight of where he'd left Bill Douglas's body within the first three minutes. The place where he'd left the plank can't be seen from there, so that part of what I've just described could have been happening after the orderly officer found the body. But the killer was still up against another pressing time constraint. Bill Douglas had been delayed by his fight after dinner and then his need to get a coat. Based on the time on the clock in the orderly officer's office when he was alerted to a problem, our best estimate is that the murder took place at about 9.48 p.m. As that is so central to our understanding of what happened, I have today checked that the clock is telling the correct time. Lights out for the garrison is at 10 p.m. If he was subject to it, then our killer had just 12 minutes to do everything I've just described and then get back to wherever he was meant to be.'

'That seems very tight,' said Paul Gillespie.

'It does, but it fits with everything we know.'

'I might be able to help a little,' said Lieutenant Colonel Ferguson. 'If the murderer was one of the trainees passing through the depot, then the lights out would be very strictly enforced and it would most certainly have been noticed if he was late getting back to his barrack room. On the other hand, we are rather less rigorous when it comes to others who are stationed here on a more permanent basis. There's a degree of flexibility even for other ranks who are on the staff, who don't sleep in the same barrack rooms as the trainees. And there's certainly more flexibility for non-commissioned and commissioned officers.

'The man you have asked me to look for is a corporal so might not have been quite so tied to a 10 p.m. deadline. We are still looking for him, by the way. I've established that instead of reporting to you as instructed he was seen heading down the hill into Stirling. We are doing all we can to find him and have broadened the search given that he might have caught a train.'

'Thank you, lieutenant colonel,' said Bob.

'Thank you, too, Bob.' said Sir Peter. 'I'm grateful for the progress you've made on this. Now, is that everything? We don't want to be late for dinner. Incidentally, why isn't Monique at this meeting?'

'Something came up and I had to ask her and Captain Darlington to look into it,' said Bob.

'It doesn't appear to have impaired your ability to investigate Bill Douglas's murder, so that's up to you. I'd ask you to join us for dinner, but I get the sense you have other things to do.'

Sir Peter stood up. As Commodore Cunningham and Paul Gillespie followed suit, Bob saw the meeting room door open behind them and was relieved to see Monique come into the room.

'I'm sorry I'm late,' she said.

'We were just leaving,' said Sir Peter.

'I promise not to take up too much of your time, Sir Peter, but I think you will want to hear what I've got to report.' Monique looked around the room, past the standing men to Bob and Michael. 'All of you, in fact, except perhaps the lieutenant colonel and, with apologies, Lieutenant Commander Dixon.'

'We're going to be late for dinner, Madame Dubois.'

'I think you'll want to hear about three NKVD agents imprisoning and killing people here in Scotland as part of an operation intended to breach the highest levels of national security.'

There was a pause. Then Sir Peter Maitland sat down. 'You do have a very persuasive way of coining a phrase, Monique. Very well, could I ask Lieutenant Colonel Ferguson and Lieutenant Commander Dixon to leave the room, please.'

Michael stood up, looking puzzled, and made for the door. Monique smiled apologetically at him as she came round the table to sit beside Bob.

After Sir Peter, the commodore and Paul Gillespie had retaken their seats on the other side of the table, Monique turned to look at Bob. 'I think you'd better set the scene.'

'Yes of course. Could I start by asking if Mr Gillespie is cleared to know about Ultra?'

Sir Peter sat forwards in his chair. 'Yes, he is. Now you really do have my attention. Carry on.'

Bob recounted his telephone call with Group Captain Erickson. Monique then gave a brief account of what had happened in and around Blairgowrie and Birnam.

'There's one more thing you need to know,' she said. 'Before I came into the room, I went upstairs to telephone Inspector Kennedy at Blairgowrie police station who was helpfully open with me on what must have been a public line. It seems his men arrested a gentleman called Viktor Ivanov late this afternoon at Coupar Angus railway station. He'd been seen acting suspiciously and when approached by two constables tried to escape in a black four-door saloon car. He got as far as the entrance to the station car park before colliding with a coal delivery lorry coming the other way. He cut his face on the windscreen and broke a wrist but is otherwise OK. He drew an automatic pistol on the constables as they approached him after the crash, but that was when he found out about his broken wrist so it ended better than it might have done.

'Two things are of particular interest. The police searched the car. In the boot, they found what they believe is a high-frequency wireless transceiver intended to allow Mr Ivanov to keep in touch with his friends over fairly short distances. The police also found a second weapon in the car, under the front passenger's seat. Inspector Kennedy described it to me as a revolver, but with two cylinders, one where you'd expect it to be and the second at the business end of the muzzle.'

Commodore Cunningham sat back in his chair. 'A Nagent M1895 revolver fitted with a Bramit device!'

Bob was pleased to see that Sir Peter Maitland and Paul Gillespie looked as puzzled as he felt. 'Can someone explain?' he asked.

Monique smiled at him. 'A Nagent M1895 is a revolver that looks at first sight much like any other revolver. It was developed in Russia at the end of the last century, as the name implies, and is still used by the Soviets and others. What makes it rather special is that as it fires, the cylinder is moved slightly forwards, sealing the flash gap that on other revolvers allows some of the high-pressure gas to escape. Because it is sealed in this way, it is possible to fit sound suppressors of various designs to it, allowing it to be fired much more quietly than other revolvers.

'The Bramit device is a particularly effective way of silencing the Nagent M1895 revolver though, having fired one, I can tell you that it also makes the gun very slow to operate. It uses special ammunition that you can think of as a 6mm bullet housed within a 7.62mm outer casing, which is itself contained within the cartridge case. When the gun is fired the outer casing only travels along the barrel as far as the front cylinder, where it is trapped, allowing the 6mm bullet to fly free but preventing any gases from escaping and dramatically cutting down the noise. You then need to clear the outer casing before firing again by revolving the front cylinder. It's quite awkward to use. I understand why, when he was confronted by the police, Viktor Ivanov pulled out an automatic pistol and left the Nagent M1895 in the car.

'For me, this solves a puzzle, which is how at least five shots could have been fired in the middle of the night where Angus Henderson was killed without being heard at the travellers' camp, which is not all that far away, or at Easter Crimond, though I suspect the Moncrieffs were already locked in their pantry by that time. The Soviets silenced Angus by gagging him while shooting him and between opportunities to tell them where he had taken Helen.

'I've suggested to Inspector Kennedy that he has his men search the area just in front of where Angus was found, both for spent 7.62mm cartridge cases and for the discarded outer casings of the bullets, which would be less obvious.

'I understand from Inspector Kennedy that Mr Ivanov is saying he is a diplomat with the Soviet embassy in London and has the paperwork to back that up. He is demanding that he be allowed to contact the embassy.'

'Have the police allowed him to?' asked Paul Gillespie.

'No. I left instructions with the inspector earlier that if he captured any of the Soviets, he should not allow them to contact anyone until the end of tomorrow. The police have had him seen by a doctor but are keeping him locked up in a cell and are complying with my instructions.'

'Let me see if I've understood what you've said correctly,' said Sir Peter. 'You think you know where Helen Erickson will be early tomorrow morning and hope to take her under your protection. Meanwhile, the police know nothing about where she is, and you've tried to keep it that way to avoid scaring Helen off because, for reasons that are not clear, she is unhappy about involving the police. In the background we have three NKVD agents, now two, who are probably still looking for Helen and might still be in the area. And if they are, we no longer know what vehicle they are using.'

'That's a fair summary, sir,' said Monique.

'I do hope you are right about where Helen Erickson will be, Monique. There's a lot at stake.' Sir Peter turned in his seat. 'Paul, can you inform the appropriate people that there may be a security problem with Mrs Erickson? You can tell them that we hope to contain and resolve it, but for all we know the Soviets might already have contacted her. As things stand, she's not in a position to know they haven't taken Helen. Bob, I think you need to contact the father. You should sound cautiously positive that we can resolve this, without getting his hopes up too much yet. If there's one thing I've learned from you, it's that senior RAF pilots tend to flit around the country at the drop of a hat. I do not want Group Captain Erickson finding his way to Perthshire and complicating things for Monique.

'As for you, Monique, do you feel you have enough support in Birnam to handle this? Remember there are still two, at least two, NKVD agents unaccounted for.'

'I am sure we will be fine, sir. Helen Erickson appears to be both very wary and very bright. If we are heavy-handed, we could scare her away ourselves. If we do run into the Soviets, then I am sure Captain Darlington and I can manage.'

'Can I ask a question?' asked Bob

'I think you just have,' said Sir Peter.

'I understand why Monique has instructed the police to prevent Mr Ivanov from communicating with anyone. But given the circumstances we are now facing, is that the best way to proceed?'

'What do you mean, Bob?' asked Monique.

'The Soviet operation strikes me as having been rather ramshackle throughout. But as soon as they killed Angus Henderson and locked up the Moncrieffs last night, they must have known the authorities would become involved and their chances of success were disappearing fast. Even if they are now able to locate and kidnap Helen Erickson, they must know that we will realise what they are up to and take the sort of steps Sir Peter has just outlined to prevent Mrs Erickson from becoming a threat to security.

'If we allow Mr Ivanov to contact the Soviet embassy, or anyone else he wants to contact, then word will inevitably reach the rest of the team, probably sooner rather than later, that the game is up. Whether they are keeping in touch by radio or by telephone or however, they will realise they have no option but to call the whole thing off. That will give you and Anthony rather less to worry about when you meet Helen in the morning.'

'I see the sense in that,' said Monique. 'Do you want me to contact Inspector Kennedy again before I leave?'

'I agree,' said Sir Peter, 'and I think it must be you who talks to the inspector, Monique. He should insist that any phone calls made by Mr Ivanov are in English and the inspector should also monitor them and report back on the content. I understand why you want to drive straight back to Birnam in the remaining daylight, but when did you last have something to eat?'

'Er, at lunch sir.'

'Bob, when Monique has telephoned the inspector, you take her to get a sandwich and some coffee, then see her on her way before contacting Group Captain Erickson. Paul, you find a secure way of letting our friends in Buckinghamshire have the bad news and then join us for dinner.' Sir Peter looked at his watch. 'I'm hoping someone has had the sense to lay on some drinks for everyone and keep the food warm. Maurice, you and I need to get the dinner underway.'

*

'You've got plenty of time before it gets dark,' said Bob. 'You could sit and eat those sandwiches before leaving.'

Monique looked across the roof of the car at him. 'I know, Bob. But if I'm honest, finding my way across country without road signs and without someone to read the map proved rather harder than I expected. It should be better now, as this will be the third time today that I've been through most of these places. But I still want to give myself as much time as I can. There's also the possibility that Anthony has already met Helen. I need to get back as soon as possible in case he has.' She looked at her watch. 'Actually, he's due to be meeting the last train of the day about now.'

'You're also worried in case Anthony is on his own and our two Soviet friends appear on the scene, aren't you?' asked Bob.

'Yes, that too, though he has one of the Sten guns hidden under the bed. I'm more worried that he's going to be hungry.

That's why I've bagged up so many sandwiches.'

'Are you sure you don't want to take Gilbert Potter with you in case things get nasty?'

'No, I'm sure. Besides…' Monique grinned at him.

'Besides what?'

'Against the background of our planning to get married, there is something I need to tell you, Bob.'

'What's that?'

'We found out earlier that the main hotel in Birnam is closed. As a result, although Anthony and I were able to secure the view that we wanted from the Station Hotel of the station itself, it is from the only room they had left, which is a double.'

Bob laughed.

'You're not meant to find it funny that your wife-to-be is going to be sharing a bed with a younger and very attractive man,' said Monique.

'Do you really think he's attractive? You've got to remember that at 26 he's not just younger than me, Monique, he's also younger than you! I laughed because although Anthony is the man who I'd want alongside you if things become dangerous, there are other ways in which I don't see him as being on the same planet as you. I'm guessing he'll be terrified of the idea of the two of you sleeping in the same bed. I'll bet you half-a-crown he says he should sleep in a chair.'

Monique smiled. 'You might be right, Bob, though I was hoping for just a hint of jealousy from you. Anyway, from what he told me earlier, no one's ever measured up to the love of his life and I doubt if I would either.'

'Really, who's that?'

'A girl he met in France, before Dunkirk. He doesn't know if she's alive or dead, though she definitely lives on in his heart.'

'Like you do in mine, Monique. Please take care and please let me know how things go in the morning.'

CHAPTER TWENTY-THREE

When Monique got back to their room in the Station Hotel, Anthony was sitting in an armchair he'd pulled to one side of the twin windows and was looking through binoculars up the street, towards the railway station.

He lowered the binoculars and turned to face her. 'The view of the station from here is pretty good, but the angle of the front of the hotel means we can't see anything to the south-east of the station building itself. If someone approached from that side, we could easily miss them from here. Not that anyone's likely to now, of course.'

'How long have you been sitting there?' asked Monique.

'A while. As we agreed, I walked over to the station to see off the two trains we'd talked about. There's a waiting room that's quite handily placed to keep a discreet watch on the platform used by trains heading towards Perth.'

'You must be hungry.' Monique placed a brown paper bag on the corner of the bed. 'Sandwiches all the way from Stirling Castle.'

'Thank you, Monique. I'd resigned myself to doing without anything as they're not offering evening meals here.'

'You're very welcome, Anthony. I'll join you. I'd half hoped I'd get back to find we needed to share the sandwiches between three mouths rather than two.'

'I know. I'd convinced myself that Helen was intending to travel today and was quite disappointed when the second train came and went with no sign of her. What made it worse was the sense that someone else was interested in who might be getting on the train.'

'Really? How sure are you about that?'

'Not very, to be honest. After the 7.52 p.m. train pulled away towards Perth, I left the station to walk back here. That was when I noticed a man who'd not got off the train walking towards a small and rather dirty dark blue van that was parked a little way along the car park. He didn't look back, but I got a sense he knew I was watching him. The van was parked with its rear towards the tracks, and he got into the nearest side, the left-hand side, and it started immediately and pulled away, then drove off down into the village. There must have been a driver waiting for him in the van. I didn't notice either the man or the van when I checked on the 6.00 p.m. departure, but I do think I saw it earlier, parked at the far end of the car park when you and I first arrived.'

'There might be an innocent explanation,' said Monique. 'The problem is that it's our job to assume the worst. What did he look like?'

'I only saw him from the back, and I didn't see the driver at all. He had brown trousers and a tweed jacket and a flat hat, also made of tweed. He'd have fitted in well round here, but it seemed a little odd that he got into a van like that.'

'Did you see a registration number?'

'The number plate on the back of the van was obscured by grime and there were no "Hamish MacTavish Plumber" signs, of the sort you might expect on a van of that type.'

'There's nothing we can do about it now and while the binoculars are useful, it's going to be properly dark before long. We'll need to be vigilant in the morning. What you don't know is that Inspector Kennedy arrested one of the Soviets, a Viktor Ivanov, this afternoon at Coupar Angus railway station. After a discussion back at Stirling Castle, I telephoned the inspector to ask him to allow his prisoner to contact anyone he wanted, though in English and with the content of any phone calls monitored. Mr Ivanov was driving the black saloon car, so we know that's also out of the picture. It's of interest that the car had a high-frequency wireless transceiver in the boot.

'We don't know for sure how the Soviets are communicating with whoever is directing the operation, but the hope is that when the rest of the NKVD team realise that we are on to them, they will give up their efforts to abduct Helen and head back to London or wherever they are based.'

'That would make life a lot simpler,' said Anthony. 'The sooner they realise the better. Anyway, it's getting dark. We seem to have a choice between the room's main gas light, the oil lamps on the bedside tables, our torches, or sitting in the dark.'

'I don't mind keeping the curtains open and the lights off,' said Monique. 'We can't afford to oversleep in the morning. Sunrise will be at about 7.00 a.m., and I want to be in position over at the station a good twenty minutes before the 7.34 a.m. train is due to leave. With that in mind, it's probably time we thought about getting some sleep.'

'I agree,' said Anthony. 'You have the bed and I'll sleep in this chair. It's very comfortable. I can pull the other one over to put my feet up.'

Monique laughed.

'What's so funny?' asked Anthony.

'You just cost me half-a-crown. When I told Bob the Station Hotel only had a double room available, he bet me half-a-crown that you'd want to sleep in a chair.'

'You told the group captain?'

'Most certainly, Anthony. We're engaged and if there's one

thing that I've learned from two disastrous marriages it's that you don't keep personal secrets from your spouse. If I'm honest, I think you'll sleep better in the bed than in a chair. We're both responsible adults. I think we can be trusted to sleep in the same bed without allowing our baser instincts to overcome us, don't you?'

'Yes, of course. But I'm simply going to be more comfortable in the chair than I would be in a double bed with any woman I'm not intimately involved with. There are extra blankets in the bottom of the wardrobe over there, I looked earlier. I really will be fine.'

Anthony turned his back while he got undressed and donned a set of striped flannel pyjamas. He was obviously uncomfortable with the situation, even though he was sleeping in the chair. Monique thought he'd be more uncomfortable if he realised her nightwear extended to the dressing gown she used if she needed to go out to the toilet, and nothing else. She considered leaving her underwear on before deciding she'd sleep better without it.

If Anthony realised that she was naked when she slipped out of her dressing gown and got into the bed, he said nothing. It was now much darker. The room wasn't large, and his chair was close to the foot of the bed, still positioned off to the side of the windows.

'Can I ask you a question, Anthony?'

'If you want, Monique.'

'You didn't tell me what happened to the hens.'

'What hens?'

'The two hens your men stole. The ones that Annette came to you to complain about.'

'I don't know, to be honest. I imagine they were swiftly

killed, cooked, and eaten. After I got talking to Annette we forgot about the hens.'

'I meant what I said, earlier, Anthony. I know people who might be able to find out where Annette is and what she's doing. I can't make any promises, obviously, but we could try.'

'Thank you. I need to think about that. As I said, part of me, a large part of me, is afraid to know what's become of her, for all the reasons I gave. Is that all right?'

'It has to be your decision, Anthony. I won't mention it again, but the offer is always there.'

'Can I ask you a question now?' asked Anthony.

'That seems only fair.'

'I know a little about your past and I know you've seen and done things you'd prefer to forget. I'd know that, even if nothing had ever been said. When you've been through extreme experiences you come to recognise the mark that leaves on others who have been through something similar. I can see it on you, mainly in your eyes.'

'Yes, that's true. That's why Bob asked you to come with me to Blairgowrie. I think he knew I could be getting involved in something dangerous and we both see the same thing in you.'

'That rather neatly leads me to the question I wanted to ask. Something happened to the group captain when you went back to Stockholm, didn't it? I know he was a very successful fighter pilot during the Battle of Britain and that means he must have killed many of his adversaries. But there's a sense in which that's not very personal. I've also heard him say that last year he'd shot and killed the officer commanding a Brandenburg Regiment raiding party that landed in northern Scotland. But until you went to Stockholm for a second time, the group captain seemed to have escaped that shadow or mark, or call it what you will. He had a sense of innocence about him, like Michael Dixon. That had changed by the time you came back.'

Monique was quiet.

'I'm sorry if I've spoken out of turn, Monique.'

'No, it's not a problem. I was just trying to decide what to tell you and how. I will answer your question, but I'll first say that Bob and I both came face to face with ghosts from the past in Stockholm. His was meeting the German pilot who shot him down in November 1940. Mine was meeting a man called Maximilian von Moser who I had known in a previous life before the war. At the time I worked for the German intelligence agency, the Abwehr, as well as for MI6, and was married to a senior and rather elderly German intelligence officer. Maximilian and I had a brief affair which ended when he tried to strangle me. I stopped him by cutting his face open with a broken bottle.

'There was a genuine reason for Bob and I going to Stockholm, but it had been set up by Maximilian von Moser as a trap. He was betraying the Abwehr to the SD, the intelligence agency of the SS and the Nazi Party, and he was hoping to capture me and use me as a weapon against the Abwehr. He did capture me, by using another ghost from my past, and I ended up in Gothenburg, having to pretend I still carried a flame for him that had never existed in the first place.

'Things came to a head when I told Maximilian I knew that he'd been feeding me lies. I was naked in bed at the time, doing my best impression of Manet's *'Olympia'*. He had been planning to use my body one last time for his gratification before taking me to Denmark and handing me over to the Gestapo but, instead, he rose to the bait and attacked me. I'd left a knife under the pillow and after a struggle in which he nearly strangled me, I eviscerated him with one slash. I was on my back, and he was sitting astride me, so you can imagine where his guts ended up. Then I slashed his throat and was entirely covered in his blood. After that, I shot and killed a second SD man who was so horrified by my appearance he froze when he should have been firing his gun. I've killed before, but I've never experienced anything like that.'

'My God, I'm sorry to have brought those memories back.'

'No, it's OK, really. It helps to talk to someone I sense can understand what it was like. But it was Bob and the second trip to Stockholm you were asking about. Things were difficult between us when we returned from the first trip. Bob was wonderful, but I reacted quite badly to what had happened with von Moser.

'Now I'll answer the question you originally asked. For this next part, you need to know that I was, in private, forever criticising Bob for what I called his lack of a killer instinct. He's a good shot but when faced with a crisis he'd always think of something else to do before getting his gun out. I think he'd become especially tired of my going on about what happened on the walkway round the top of the tower of St Magnus Cathedral when we returned to Orkney last November.'

'Yes, I remember you talking about it at the time. He lowered his pistol when facing an armed man and was nearly killed as a result.'

'That's right. He told me afterwards that he wanted to "talk sense into him" and if it hadn't been for a miraculous long-range rifle shot by someone else at the scene, Bob would have died that day. My doubts about his limitations as a cold-blooded killer meant I nearly refused to have him involved in the Stockholm trip, but I knew that would be the end of our relationship and I didn't want that.'

'I think that's what I meant by his "innocence",' said Anthony. 'What happened?'

'We had a great time dining and dancing at the Grand Hotel in Stockholm on the night we arrived on our second visit. We had, arguably, been ordered that morning by both Sir Peter Maitland and Winston Churchill to enjoy our trip and we were obeying their orders with considerable enthusiasm and at considerable expense to someone's budget, I'm not sure whose.

'On the way back to our own rather less grand hotel, quite late at night, it became obvious we were being followed. We didn't know it at the time, but it was an SD team of five men in two cars who'd decided to finish the job of abducting me. The old town of Stockholm is a bit of a maze and we tried to evade our followers by dodging into the bottom of a narrow alley that had a lot of steps at its far end.

'They started shooting at us. I ran to the top of the alley and got hit by one of their cars as I emerged and was bundled into it. Bob, meanwhile, with seven rounds in the magazine of his Walther PPK, had shot and wounded one man at the bottom of the alley, where we'd entered it. His second shot missed. At this point, the car I was in was accelerating downhill in a narrow street in the dark with me unconscious on the floor in the back. Bob's third shot was one he later described as "wild". It hit the back of the car. With his fourth shot he killed another SD agent at the top of the alley. His fifth went through the rear window of the car and hit the back of the driver's head, killing him instantly. It must have been an amazing shot. He'd even remembered that although they drive on the left in Sweden, most cars are left-hand drive. The car lost control and crashed badly at the bottom of the hill. Bob got to the wreck and dragged me out, shooting and killing an SD man who tried to stop him in the process. That shot ignited petrol fumes that had been released, either by the crash or by his earlier "wild" shot, and the car blew up, though he got me clear. Another man in the front of the car had been injured in the crash and died in the fire.

'As I said, I wasn't conscious for most of this, but I pieced together what had happened partly from Bob's rather self-effacing account and partly from what I was told by the Swedish Security Service, who arrived on the scene just after the shooting stopped. Bob had just one round left in his Walther PPK by that point.'

'That is rather incredible,' said Anthony.

'I know,' said Monique. 'By my calculation at the time, with six rounds Bob shot and killed three men, caused the death of a fourth and wounded a fifth. That's how he lost what you described as his innocence and gained what I call a killer instinct. I've promised I'll never again accuse him of not having one.'

'And that's the man who knows I'm sharing a room with his fiancée?'

'Don't worry, he won't hold it against you.'

'I hope you're right, Monique. The car crash is presumably how you damaged your ribs?'

'Either that or by being hit by the car at the top of the alley. And my blonde wig was badly singed in the fire that followed the crash. I called her Ingrid.'

'Pardon?'

'Never mind, Anthony. Now it's your turn to tell me how you came by that look in your eyes.'

There was a long silence.

Monique sat up in bed in the darkness and pulled the bedding around her. 'It does help, you know, to share it with someone who understands.'

'I've never told anyone what happened,' said Anthony.

Monique thought it best to say nothing.

Then she heard the chair creak and sensed that Anthony had turned to face her.

His voice sounded tight as he spoke. 'The whole retreat was a shambles and I could tell you about any number of horrors I saw, from columns of French civilian refugees being bombed by Stukas or strafed by Messerschmitts to German and British tank crews being burned alive in their tanks. But what really convinced me that I wouldn't survive the retreat was something that happened three days before I arrived at Annette's father's farm.

'I commanded a rifle platoon, on paper with about thirty men. By this point, I had nearer twenty men, with the others dead, wounded or missing after days of intermittent action. There was no question of receiving replacements. It was dawn and we'd spent the night in temporary slit trenches just inside the edge of a wood that looked east down into a cultivated valley. Other units of the company my platoon was part of were on either side of us. It was eerily quiet, but we'd been told to expect an attack by a German panzer unit coming out of the woods on the far side of the valley with armoured infantry in support.

'We were all afraid. I certainly was. Our anti-tank weapons were few in number and not really up to the job of destroying the German tanks we'd encountered. Then, apparently out of nowhere, our positions were attacked by light bombers and when the sound of their engines and the bombs had died away, I realised I could hear tanks. Tanks have a very distinctive sound, a combination of their engines and their tracks. You nearly always hear them before you see them. There were a lot of them, and they weren't coming from the other side of the valley ahead of us, there were coming from behind us.

'To cut a long story short, we'd been outflanked. The Germans wanted to mop us up, sending tanks through the wood behind us, which shouldn't have been possible, followed by infantry. What followed was sheer hell. I have no idea how many men I killed. My memory is very blurry, but I know I killed enough to have kept me awake on too many nights since then. I was in a small trench with two of my men and a Panzer IV tank came right over the top of us, collapsing the trench in on us. I lost consciousness and only came to when I was being dug out by the survivors after the enemy had gone.

'It seems the Germans had decided they'd done enough to remove us as a threat and had gone back through the wood, moving ahead of us and blocking our line of retreat towards the coast. I was lucky. I was physically uninjured, while one of the men I was with in the trench had been completely buried and suffocated before he could be dug out. The other was run over by a tank track and there was very little left of him that was identifiable as being human.

'I lost half my remaining men in that engagement. We spent the next day working our way around the Germans who were between us and Lille so we could rejoin the main British Expeditionary Force, or what was left of it. Thankfully the Germans seemed to have paused their advance and we were able to get ahead of them.

'As I've told you, we were ordered to prepare defences at the farm where I met Annette. I knew by then that if I'd been a cat, I'd be on my ninth and final life and I think that was why there was such a desperate intensity to my feelings for her.'

'Thank you, Anthony. I hope it helped to tell me.'

'I don't know, to be honest, Monique. Don't you think we should get some sleep now?'

Monique heard the chair creak again and thought that Anthony must have turned away from her.

CHAPTER TWENTY-FOUR

Monique led the way through the stone porch that formed part of the rather fine main entrance of Dunkeld and Birnam station. Then she went into and through the deserted ticket office and onto the equally deserted platform beyond it, where she knew the train heading towards Perth would stop. A large railway clock on the outside wall of the main station building overlooking the platform showed that it was 7.10 a.m.

They hadn't had breakfast in the hotel as it had been too early. They had, however, found someone able to take payment in cash for their bill for the night and they'd left their overnight bags and the two Sten guns in the car, which was parked discreetly on a narrow side road next to the hotel. They'd agreed that leaving a military staff car outside the station might scare Helen away.

'You said last night that there was a waiting room with a good view of the platform,' said Monique.

'This is it here,' said Anthony. 'I'll wait inside as we agreed, while you stay on the platform.'

The weather had broken overnight and as well as the grey skies and the drizzle they'd encountered on the short walk from the hotel to the railway station, Monique found herself shivering in the chill wind that seemed to whip along the platform. At least this side was sheltered by a canopy that projected out almost as far as the tracks. Anyone waiting on the far side, for a train arriving from Perth, would be far more exposed to the elements unless they used the waiting room.

Monique found herself walking slowly along the platform in one direction before turning and walking back, then repeating the process. This was partly to give an illusion of warmth but, she realised, it was also due to nerves.

She could hear Sir Peter Maitland's words from the previous evening's meeting going round and round in her head: *'I do hope you are right about where Helen Erickson will be, Monique. There's a lot at stake.'* Monique very much hoped she was right, but, as she had for parts of the night, found herself thinking through various ways in which she might not be.

The clock on the platform had reached 7.25 a.m. when she heard a car door slam out in the car park, then another, and then the noise of a car pulling away. She wondered if the Soviets would be quite so brazen as to pull up at the main entrance. Or, if they had them here, it might only be a taxi. A couple of minutes later an elderly couple came out of the station building and onto the platform. The woman smiled a greeting at Monique while the man appeared not to notice her.

The tracks curved to the left not far beyond the north-western end of the platforms and Monique heard the approaching train well before she saw it. She was reminded of Anthony's description of approaching tanks. She looked around again. There was no one in sight other than the elderly couple.

A porter came out of the station building as the train came into view, belching steam and black smoke. It came to a halt and the elderly couple boarded the nearest carriage. No one got off. The porter blew a whistle and waved a flag and then, with a hiss and a momentary slip of its wheels, the engine eased forwards again, and the carriages followed it out of the station.

Monique wanted to protest, to call it back, to say there had been a mistake. It was only meant to leave after Helen had arrived to catch it and she had been able to talk to her. The silence that followed its departure seemed profound. Then she heard the waiting room door open behind her and turned to see Anthony, looking as worried as she felt, emerging from it.

'No sign of her!' he said.

Monique realised the porter was standing and watching them from only a few yards away. He was a wiry man with a grey beard who didn't look like he would see sixty again.

'Hello. You're the lady who was asking about passengers on the trains to Perth yesterday afternoon. And you, sir, were here when the later trains left. Is there something I can help you with?'

'Perhaps you can,' said Monique. 'We're with military intelligence and we're trying to find a young woman who's missing. Information we were given suggested she was intending to get on the train that's just left. Obviously, she didn't.'

'Aren't missing people more a matter for the police than for military intelligence?' the porter asked.

'We're working with Inspector Kennedy at Blairgowrie police station. I'm sure if you telephone the station, they can confirm who the captain and I are.'

'There's no need for that, ma'am. Does the young woman you are looking for have long blonde hair?'

'That's right. Have you seen her?'

'Perhaps. The woman I saw was wearing a beige raincoat and a black beret.'

'That sounds like her. Where was she?'

'It was all very odd. I was over on the down platform, the one over beyond the rails, for the arrival and departure of the 6.16 a.m. train from Perth. After I blew my whistle, this woman ran over to the front carriage carrying a suitcase. She opened a door and got in just as the train started to move. I'd not noticed her until then and I think she'd been hiding out of sight behind those bushes you can see over there. If she'd come in through the station and then crossed the footbridge, I'm sure I'd have seen her. I'm wondering if she got onto the down platform at its far end where it's quite close to a lane that runs under a bridge beneath the lines. There's a fence there, but if you were younger and more agile than me, it might be possible.'

'Where was that train going?' asked Monique.

'It was going to Blair Atholl which isn't far up the line. It would have terminated there a little after 7 a.m. and it will then form a stopping train calling at all the stations back to Perth a little later this morning. What you should know is that she could have connected at Blair Atholl with the fast train leaving there at 7.23 a.m. and going to Inverness. It runs directly from Perth to Blair Atholl so passed through here without stopping earlier.'

Monique could see Anthony looking at his watch and assumed he was thinking the same thing as her. She smiled at the porter. 'Thank you, you've been extremely helpful. How far is Blair Atholl by road?'

'I can't say exactly. By rail, it's 19 miles and 58 chains, but I suppose it's a little more than that by road once you've driven through Pitlochry and the Pass of Killiecrankie.'

'And how about Inverness?'

'Again, I can only give you the distance by rail, which is 102 miles and 52 chains.'

'What time is the train you mentioned due to arrive in Inverness?'

'10.18 a.m.'

'Thank you again. Anthony, we need to get moving!'

The porter held out an arm as if to stop Monique. 'You

should know you're not the first person this morning to be looking for that woman. When I came back across the footbridge after seeing off the 6.16 a.m. train, there was a man on the up platform, this platform, who asked if I'd seen a woman, and described her accurately. He wouldn't have seen her himself because she didn't enter by this side of the station and the train was already at the platform over there and blocking his view when she appeared. He had a foreign accent and I think he was here yesterday evening like you were, sir. I told him what I've just told you. I'm sorry if that wasn't the right thing to do, but there was no reason not to.'

'Does that mean he knows about Blair Atholl and the connection to Inverness?'

'It does, ma'am.'

'What did he look like?' asked Anthony.

'He had a beige raincoat on and a tweed cap. He was probably in his late thirties and had dark hair. I'd say he was average in size.'

'And do you know if he left in a car?'

'No, he didn't. He left the station but was back a minute or two later. He said the telephone box outside wasn't working. Apparently "Button B" was stuck in the pressed-in position and any coins he put in came straight back out. It was the first I'd heard of it. He asked where the next nearest telephone box was and I told him it was down at the bottom of Station Road, where it meets Perth Road. He left the station and when I followed, to check on the telephone box outside, I could see him running across the car park towards the top of Station Road.'

'How do we find Blair Atholl station when we get there?' asked Monique.

'You follow the main road toward Inverness through the centre of the village and turn left just after you pass the Atholl Arms Hotel. The station will be right in front of you.'

*

'I could kick myself,' said Monique, 'Helen Erickson is running rings around us.'

'If it's any consolation, Monique, she's running rings around the opposition, too.'

'According to the map, we need to go back into Dunkeld to pick up the main road north. That means turning right when we've got through Little Dunkeld. What worries me most, Anthony, is that there is still an opposition for Helen to run rings around. They must know by now that Viktor Ivanov is in police custody and there's no point pressing ahead with what they're doing. Yet the other man, apparently the one you saw yesterday, was at the station this morning. Perhaps most irritating of all is the thought that he ran down the street outside our bedroom window, not long before we'd have been up and about.'

'If I'd been awake, I'd have seen him from my chair,' said Anthony. 'I suppose we were at a disadvantage when compared with the Soviets because we'd heard the story Helen wanted us to hear, that she was going south to Perth and then England. The Soviets didn't know that, so had to keep watch at the station for trains going in both directions.'

Anthony drove over the substantial stone bridge that took them into Dunkeld. 'Helen obviously has a lead on us if she arrived at Blair Atholl a little after 7 a.m., and she'll now be on her way to Inverness, assuming that's really where she intends to go. Two things are worrying me, Monique. I only know the main road towards Inverness as far as Dalwhinnie, which is where we'd turn off to head west on the few occasions that I travelled to the Commando Basic Training Centre by road. Based on the timings and the distances the porter gave us, getting to Inverness railway station in time to meet Helen's train would mean averaging over 40 miles per hour all the way, which I frankly don't believe is remotely realistic.'

'What's the second thing worrying you?' asked Monique.

'What if this journey north is another feint? What if Helen really intends to travel back south from Blair Atholl, having thrown any pursuers off the trail? From what the porter said, she'd only need to hide on the train she went to Blair Atholl on and wait for it to form the train back to Perth. We know she has a copy of *Bradshaw's Guide* with her that would allow her to spot a possibility like that.'

'Don't you think that's just a little too convoluted?' asked Monique.

'I'd have thought what she's done already was fairly convoluted,' said Anthony. 'But she's done it.'

'That's true. Perhaps I should add to the list the two things worrying me.'

'What are they?' asked Anthony.

'The first is that even if we could get to Inverness before Helen's train arrived, assuming that's where she's gone, we don't really know what she looks like. Identifying an attractive blonde woman who looks like Veronica Lake might not have been a problem at Dunkeld and Birnam station. It could be a very different proposition at Inverness station.

'The second thing worrying me is this. What if the man in the tweed cap was keeping watch on the station while the

Soviet woman was staying nearby? I saw at least one hotel in Dunkeld that looked open. If you start with that assumption, they could be an hour or more ahead of us, which I assume would give them enough time to get to Inverness before Helen's train arrived. We saw no sign of the man hanging about near the phone box in Birnam, so either he was keeping out of sight, or the woman had already picked him up.'

'No guarantees, but I'd guess you'd get to Inverness fairly comfortably with an additional hour,' said Anthony.

'What makes it worse,' said Monique, 'is that the Soviets do know what Helen looks like from having followed her and would probably be able to spot her even if Inverness railway station is busy.'

'If you were in their shoes, wouldn't you be tempted just to check to see if Helen was at Blair Atholl station?' asked Anthony. 'If they were an hour ahead of us, they might have got there before the Inverness train left and while she was still there.'

Monique found that a deeply worrying thought. 'To my mind, we need to find out what we can at Blair Atholl station and then decide what we do from there. If Helen did go north then maybe we need to have her train met by the police in Inverness, though I don't like the idea.'

A little later, she looked up from the map. 'This is Ballinluig, which means we're about halfway to Blair Atholl.'

'Thanks, Monique. Distances do seem to stretch out when you've got no road signs to show where you are or distance markers to show how far you've come.'

Monique smiled. 'Talking of distances, what's a chain? The porter at the station talked about them.'

'It's a form of measurement. A chain is 22 yards and there

are 80 of them in a mile. I think it's mainly used by land surveyors and by the railways. And in cricket, of course. A cricket pitch is 22 yards or one chain in length.'

Monique laughed. 'Sometimes, living in Britain can be charmingly bizarre. I remember someone explaining to me in a pub in London what gills and fluid ounces and drams are. I'm not sure I remember what he said in any detail. Ah... but I do remember who it was who was telling me. It was Bill Douglas while he still thought his charm might get him what he wanted from me. When Bob finds whoever killed him, I hope I get a chance to thank them.'

'You want to thank the murderer?'

'That's right.'

*

The Atholl Arms Hotel was a large, imposing building standing at the far end of a line of fine houses set back from the left-hand side of the main road through Blair Atholl. The whole village seemed to be built from the same grey stone.

'What a pretty place,' said Monique.

'I suspect it would be even prettier in decent weather,' said Anthony. 'The rain seems to have become more persistent as we've headed north-west.' He turned left just beyond the hotel. 'It looks like this is the station car park. There's no dark blue van here, which is something.'

Monique got out of the car and led the way into the station building. The ticket office was empty, so she went out onto the platform beyond it. There was no one there either.

Back in the ticket office, she looked around again. Then she shouted. 'Hello, is anyone here?'

There were sounds of movement and a moment later a door opened and a man in his fifties wearing a railway uniform emerged. 'Hello, can I help you?'

'Do you work here?' asked Monique.

'I'm the station master, Graham Fisher.'

'We're with military intelligence.' Monique showed the man her security pass. 'Have a man and a woman been here this morning, asking about an attractive young blonde woman in a beige raincoat and a black beret? The woman probably did the talking and has a foreign accent.'

'Like yours?'

'I'm told she sounds a little like me, yes.'

'No. There was a young woman who looked like the one you described here earlier, but there's been no one asking after her. Not until now.'

'What can you tell me about her?'

'She got off the stopping train from Perth, which arrived on time at 7.04 a.m. and terminated here before moving off to the sidings. I think she must have gone into the waiting room over on the far platform, the down platform, to keep out of the rain. I was over there for the arrival of the fast train and saw her board it before it left at 7.23 a.m.'

'Do you know if she had a ticket?' asked Monique. 'I'm wondering if she was going to Inverness or to somewhere else. Perhaps she's going to get off somewhere this side of it or intends to travel beyond it.'

'No, sorry. As she was changing trains, checking her ticket would have been for the train guards.'

'Monique, come and look at this!'

Monique turned and saw that Anthony had moved to the far side of the ticket office, where he was looking at a poster on the wall, a map emblazoned with the title *'London, Midland and Scottish Railway Routes in Scotland'*. A network of red lines of varying thickness was laid out over a beige map of Scotland surrounded by blue sea.

She walked over towards him. 'What is it, Anthony?'

'Look at this line here. Mr Fisher, can you tell me what this is, please?'

The station master joined them in front of the map. 'It shows the steamer service from Kyle of Lochalsh to Portree on the Isle of Skye and then to Stornoway on the Isle of Lewis. It's shown on the map because some of our train services to Kyle are timed to connect with the steamers.'

Monique kept quiet. She knew exactly what Anthony was thinking, that Helen had misled everyone by saying she was going to find safety with her mother in England when in fact she was intending to find her way to her father in Stornoway. It made sense. It was him she'd sent a letter to.

'Can you tell us how you'd get to Kyle of Lochalsh from here by train and how that would connect with the steamer services?' asked Anthony.

'Certainly, come through to my office.'

The station master led the way through the door he'd emerged from. Beyond was a wood-panelled office with a large wooden desk and chair, a bookcase, and a fire burning in a fireplace. The room was hazy with strong-smelling pipe smoke.

'If you just bear with me a moment, I need to check the timetables to make sure nothing's changed very recently.' The station master took a thick volume out of the bookcase and sat at his desk, shuffling pages back and forth and making notes on a notepad.

'Right. You were asking about the young woman, so I

imagine you want to take as your starting point the train that left here for Inverness at 7.23 a.m. Is that right?'

Anthony nodded. 'Yes, it is.'

'That train should arrive in Inverness at 10.18 a.m. She will have to change there. There is then a train that leaves Inverness at 10.50 a.m. and gets into Dingwall at 11.47 a.m. She has another change there, before catching a train that leaves Dingwall at 12.30 p.m. and arrives in Kyle of Lochalsh at 3.15 p.m. The timetable says that train connects with a steamer to Portree and Stornoway, but it doesn't say what time the steamer sails.'

'Thank you,' said Monique, who had been taking notes. 'That's extremely helpful.'

'Does this woman live in the Hebrides or on the west coast?' asked the station master.

'No, why?'

'My sister lives in Gairloch, in Wester Ross. Pretty much the whole of the western side of the Highlands is a "Protected Area" under the 1939 Defence Regulations. That means anyone living there or travelling to the area needs a special pass, in addition to their National Identity Registration Card. For adults, it's a pink card, while children get a metal identification token to wear on a string around their neck with their name and address engraved on it.

'What that means in practice is that anyone boarding a train for Kyle of Lochalsh in Dingwall should have their protected area pass checked before they are allowed to travel. If that young woman doesn't have the correct pass, then she won't be allowed to get onto that train.'

'Thank you again,' said Monique. 'Do you mind if I borrow your office to discuss with my colleague what you've told us and then use your phone to make a phone call back to the people we report to?'

'Our phone lines go via the public switchboard, but you are welcome to make your call from here.'

CHAPTER TWENTY-FIVE

It didn't take Monique too long to get through to Miriam, Lieutenant Colonel Ferguson's secretary, but then it seemed to take an age for her to track down Bob. Monique realised that it was still quite early and wondered whether he was eating breakfast. The thought made her feel hungry. They still had some stale sandwiches left over from the previous evening in the brown paper bag in the car, but she'd not found the idea very appetising.

Finally, she heard a noise as he picked up the phone.

'Hello, Monique. Do you have Helen?'

'Not yet, Bob. But I know where she's going.'

There was a pause on the line.

Monique felt she had to fill the silence. 'I'm sorry, Bob. I know I said something very like that to you last night, and I know it's going to be hard for you to tell the other people who were at that meeting. But I am surer now. I need your help though.'

'Don't worry, Monique. I was just so certain you were going to tell me you had her that it took a moment to digest what you were saying. I'll certainly do anything I can to help. What do you need?'

Monique wondered if she could hear any disappointment or anger in his voice. She realised that while they might be planning their wedding, in some ways she still didn't know Bob very well.

She took a deep breath. 'I'm calling from the station master's office at Blair Atholl station. I'm aware this is an insecure line but am going to have to be quite open with you anyway. It seems that Helen was never intending to travel south to be with her mother. I'm guessing she only told people that to throw anyone following her off the scent. She caught a train travelling towards Inverness very early this morning, well before Anthony and I went to the station. She had to change here at Blair Atholl and is now on a train that is due to arrive in Inverness at 10.18 a.m. By the time we found that out, it was too late for us to drive to Inverness to meet the train. In any case, we don't know Helen by sight so might have missed her if the station was busy.'

'Do you want me to alert the police in Inverness to meet the train and identify Helen?'

'It's more complicated than that. I am sure that the man who was in custody in Blairgowrie must have contacted his people last night, though I haven't had a chance to confirm that. The problem is that it appears the other two members of the opposition team are still very much in the game. I don't understand why, as it's no longer possible for them to achieve what they want. Or what we believe they want. I don't know for sure, but I think it likely they are far enough ahead of Anthony and me to get to Inverness in time to meet the train and, unlike us, they do know Helen by sight.'

'You want me to have the Inverness police find and pick up the other two members of the opposition team at Inverness station?'

'Yes, please. Tell the police they're wanted in connection with a murder near Blairgowrie.'

Monique was relieved to hear Bob laugh.

'You know, if you'd not mentioned it, I might not have thought of telling them that! Seriously, though, you'd better tell me everything you know about their appearance and any other information that might help the police.'

Monique did so.

'What about Helen?' Bob asked.

'I'm in two minds about her. If the Inverness police can take her into some sort of protective custody when she arrives, that would be good, but we only have a description that could easily apply to other young women in Inverness. There's also the risk of them simply scaring her off. It might help to tell the Inverness police that Helen is almost certainly intending to catch a train in Inverness that's bound for Dingwall at 10.50 a.m. But they need to be clear that finding her is of secondary importance compared with arresting the rest of the opposition team.'

'You said you know where she's going.'

'I can't be certain, but I am fairly confident. I believe that when she gets to Dingwall, Helen intends to connect with a train leaving at 12.30 p.m. that is due to arrive in Kyle of Lochalsh on the west coast at 3.15 p.m. We've been told that before being allowed to board the train in Dingwall she'll need a special protected area pass, which I assume she won't have. But she seems very resourceful and as far as I can work out isn't likely to let anything like the lack of a security pass get in her way. There's some doubt about whether she's even got a train ticket.'

'Why would she want to go there? I mean, I'm sure it's lovely and I seem to remember from before the war that it's where you catch the ferry to the Isle of Skye. But it's an odd destination for a young woman trying to evade people who are following her.'

'The railway timetables show that the train that arrives at Kyle of Lochalsh at 3.15 p.m. is timed to connect with a steamer that goes to Stornoway in the Outer Hebrides.'

'Ah, I see! She's trying to get to her father. I suppose that makes sense. You've clearly got a plan. Are you simply hoping that if we can get the police in Inverness to lock up the rest of the opposition team, Helen will find her way to safety in Stornoway?'

'No, I've got something more active than that in mind. As soon as you and I finish this call, Anthony and I will set off to drive to Kyle of Lochalsh. We can't get to Inverness before Helen, but Anthony is confident that the changes of train she has to make will ensure we get to Kyle of Lochalsh before her.'

'You'll still have the problem of not knowing her by sight. I don't know, but I'd imagine things might be quite busy there.'

'That's where I need your help again. Do you remember that we travelled over to the west coast last November, between our two visits to Orkney?'

'Yes, I do.'

'And do you remember we were told that certain material was flown from England to RAF Stornoway before being transported by RAF launch to the place we were visiting?'

'I begin to see where this is going.'

'That's right, Bob. I need you to contact Helen's father. You told me he wanted to fly over to the mainland yesterday. I need him instead to make use of RAF Stornoway's launch to get to Kyle of Lochalsh before the train arrives at 3.15 p.m. Anthony measured it very roughly on a railway map of Scotland and reckons it's about 70 miles, which isn't trivial for a sea crossing, especially if the weather's as miserable on the west coast as it is here. But if their launch is up to transporting highly sensitive material to the mainland, we can hope it's up to getting him to Kyle of Lochalsh in time. That way there can be no possible problem recognising Helen or setting her at ease when she arrives.'

'I'll do that as soon as I've finished talking to you. I hope you don't mind my playing Devil's advocate for a moment, Monique, but what happens if Helen isn't on the train when it arrives? What if the Inverness police do identify her and take her into protective custody? What if they scare her into hiding in Inverness or into boarding a train heading somewhere else? What happens if she isn't allowed to board the train at Dingwall because she doesn't have the necessary security pass?'

'If she's not on the train when it arrives in Kyle of Lochalsh, I will ask her father to accompany Anthony and me and drive to Dingwall, and then if necessary to Inverness. That seems the best way of reuniting father and daughter. It would probably help if you were honest with the father about the uncertainties surrounding this, but I truly believe the most likely outcome is that she will be on the train when it arrives in Kyle of Lochalsh.'

*

Bob was able to reach Group Captain Erickson at RAF Stornoway rather more quickly than the previous time he'd called him. Tom Erickson was concerned that Helen hadn't yet been found but seemed relieved and almost childishly excited to be asked to help bring the search to an end himself.

It took Bob rather longer to identify and track down the head of Special Branch in the Inverness Burgh Police, an Inspector Grant. However, when he was able to talk to the man, he got the sense that Grant quickly understood what Bob was telling him and the importance of ensuring the two remaining

NKVD agents got no further than Inverness railway station. He also talked to Grant about Helen Erickson and again had the sense that he understood she was not to be his priority.

Then Grant surprised him by taking the initiative. 'Thank you for giving me the full picture, sir. I'm wondering whether, if we can identify Helen Erickson, the best course of action would be for us to keep a discreet watch on her but let her proceed without hindrance.'

'I can see the sense in that, inspector, though the information I have is that she's reacted very unpredictably whenever she's believed herself to be followed. She also appears to be very keen to avoid having anything to do with the police, for reasons I don't understand. I don't want your people scaring her into getting onto a train bound for Wick or Aberdeen rather than one going to Dingwall and from there to Kyle of Lochalsh.'

'Don't worry, sir. If we're able to identify Miss Erickson, then I'll keep an eye on her myself and you can be sure I'll do a better job of it than the Soviets appear to have done. If you agree, I can also ensure she doesn't fall foul of any checks on protected area documentation at Dingwall station. The people doing those checks report indirectly to me and it will be simple enough to overlook the carriage this woman is in or, if necessary, the whole train. I can then travel on the same Kyle of Lochalsh train as her to ensure there are no unforeseen problems. Even assuming we do detain the two NKVD agents in Inverness, I don't want anything to happen to Miss Erickson while she's on my patch.'

'Thank you. That's more than I was hoping for. It will certainly be neater if she gets to Kyle of Lochalsh on that train. What you're suggesting does seem to address the most obvious ways in which that might not happen. You'll need to keep a lookout for my people when you arrive, though.' Bob went on to describe Monique and Anthony.

As he put the phone down, Bob made a mental note to mention his favourable impression of Inspector Grant the next time he spoke to his father, a superintendent in the Edinburgh City Police and responsible, amongst other things, for Special Branch in the city.

Then he telephoned Inspector Kennedy in Blairgowrie and confirmed that Viktor Ivanov had contacted the Russian embassy in London the previous evening and was due to be picked up by them that afternoon, after further treatment to his broken wrist, which seemed more badly injured than at first thought.

*

Monique was acutely aware that in driving to Blair Atholl they'd disappeared off the edge of the known world, or at least that part of it shown on the one-inch scale maps the Argylls had given her at Stirling Castle. Anthony said he knew the way as far as the Commando Basic Training Centre at Achnacarry Castle near Spean Bridge, and that they could pick up maps of the rest of the journey to Kyle of Lochalsh from there. Monique was unhappy with the idea that they might get hopelessly lost in the absence of both road signs and maps. She felt she'd let Bob down once already today. She didn't want to do it a second time.

On the condition that she posted it back to him afterwards, the station master at Blair Atholl station lent Monique his copy of the *Automobile Association Touring Map of Scotland.* It was undated and its heavy use suggested it might be quite old, but it was better than nothing. It at least appeared to show the main roads and, with Anthony's help, she was able to trace their intended route. This seemed remarkably serpentine, divided into sections heading generally north-west, then south of west, then almost doubling back to go north-east, and then finally heading north-west again.

Monique asked Anthony to drive and as they climbed towards the Pass of Drumochter she was pleased to see the rain easing and then stopping and the cloud becoming a much lighter grey. Although Anthony knew the way, Monique found her attention divided between the mountain scenery they were driving through and the map she kept open on her lap.

'I was about to say that I'd never seen these mountains before,' said Monique. 'But looking at this map it seems I'm wrong. I've flown over them several times, I must also have travelled this way by rail when going up to Caithness last year, where I encountered Bob. And when travelling back, for that matter. I've also just noticed, on the next fold on the map to the east, that it shows Port Gordon, where I had my first sight of Scotland in September 1940.'

'Was that where you came ashore with two Abwehr spies after your seaplane landed off the coast?'

'It was. Two of us were arrested at the railway station there early the next morning. I remember very little about the journey down to London, but it was by rail, and I suppose we might have come this way.

'According to the map, we turn left a little beyond the Dalwhinnie Hotel, which must be quite remote to be shown on a map of this scale and can't be all that far ahead of us now. We go for eight miles on that road and then turn left again, at a place called Drumgask. Sorry, Anthony, I know you've used these roads before, but if I'm navigating, I can at least feel like I'm contributing.'

'Don't worry, Monique. It is helpful to have confirmation we're going the right way.'

'Oddly enough, we don't go far down that road before we pass another marked hotel, the Loch Laggan Hotel. Now I come to look at it, there are quite a few hotels marked on the map, despite its small scale. On this journey, we also pass the Invergarry Hotel, the Tomdoun Hotel and the Cluanie Bridge Inn. And if we are going to Achnacarry Castle, we pass the Gairlochy Inn. I suppose that's because whenever this was produced, the Automobile Association wanted to give their members a choice of places at which to dine and to stay, so hotels were as significant as medium-sized settlements.'

'Don't get your hopes up too much, Monique. I can tell you with certainty that a couple of the hotels you've just mentioned have been requisitioned for military use or are simply closed. And I'd not bet on finding lunch being served at any of the others either. I think we've got time in hand on this trip and I'm sure we can find something to eat, or at least some fresher sandwiches to take with us if you prefer, when we pick up more detailed maps at Achnacarry Castle.'

'The Commando Basic Training Centre is a few miles out of our way, isn't it?'

'Not many.'

'Let's see how we're doing for time when we get to Spean Bridge. This map will get us to Kyle of Lochalsh if necessary and I'd prefer to eat the stale sandwiches we've already got than fail to meet Helen for a second time today.'

'I accept that, but we're also going to need petrol and

Achnacarry Castle would allow us to kill several birds with one stone. Talking about our failure in Birnam this morning, how did the group captain take it?'

'It's hard to tell on the phone and I suppose by the standards of traditional courtships we haven't had all that long to get to know each other. But he seemed keen to help and wasn't obviously upset that we hadn't got Helen.'

'If it helps, Monique, I'm not sure you're right about traditional courtships. I never got seriously involved with anyone before the war, but I had friends who married women they might have been courting for far longer than you've known the group captain. I was never sure how well they really knew them, though. You need to remember that the group captain has supported you after what happened in Gothenburg, and you've supported him after what happened in Stockholm which, as we discussed last night, did change him. I'm sure that in some important ways you know each other far better than many couples who have been married for years.'

Monique found herself struggling to hold back tears and to conceal that was what she was doing. 'Thank you, Anthony. That does help.'

CHAPTER TWENTY-SIX

The rest of the morning seemed to pass interminably slowly for Bob. After his phone calls were done, he'd had a slightly awkward meeting with Sir Peter Maitland and Commodore Cunningham before they returned to London. As Monique had predicted, they'd not been happy that Helen Erickson was still at large, and they'd been doubly unhappy that two NKVD agents were still active. The only good news he'd had was confirmation that the blood staining the uniform they'd found was the right type for Bill Douglas.

Then Bob had gone to check on the progress in the search for the missing suspect. Lieutenant Colonel Ferguson was able to tell him that Corporal Peter Kerr had been seen by a man who knew him boarding a train bound for Edinburgh the previous afternoon. The police in Edinburgh were searching for him but had not yet found any trace of him.

Meanwhile, Lieutenant Commander Michael Dixon and Sergeants Gilbert Potter and Alan MacMillan had been talking to men who might have been in or around the Great Hall at about the time of the murder.

What was becoming clear was that this was a major task. It didn't take long to question each of the men, but there were hundreds of them to talk to and simply making sure the lists of interviewees were comprehensive was not straightforward.

With Bob taking an active part, they were able to split the interviews four ways but by lunchtime progress still seemed slow.

The four of them shared a sandwich lunch in the office they'd been loaned, and it was clear to Bob that the others felt as pessimistic about their prospects as he did. He tried to divert their attention by telling them how Monique and Anthony were getting on, though this seemed to have the same effect on them as, he admitted to himself, it had on him: of emphasising just how tedious their day had become. He got the sense that the others shared his view that they were spending a lot of time and effort looking for someone who it genuinely might be better not to find.

Bob found that idea rather shocking. But he couldn't get away from the sense that whatever the murderer's reasons for killing Bill Douglas, they were probably very good ones. The final thing feeding his doubts was a strong belief that whoever had killed Bill Douglas was highly unlikely to be any danger to anyone else.

But it was Bob's job to find the killer and he had to carry it out to the best of his abilities, despite his doubts.

He rang Inverness Burgh Police again. He knew Inspector Grant probably wouldn't be available, but Bob was able to talk to a Sergeant MacDonald, who said he reported to the inspector. The good news was that the police had with reasonable certainty been able to identify Helen Erickson when she got off her train in Inverness and he confirmed that she had subsequently boarded the 10.50 train to Dingwall. It seemed that Helen had a valid railway ticket for the journey from Blair Atholl to Kyle of Lochalsh when she arrived in Inverness. The sergeant said he thought that she must have purchased it from the guard on the train.

As planned, Inspector Grant had himself travelled on the Dingwall train and then intended to catch the train to Kyle of Lochalsh. Bob looked at his watch and realised that the train should already have left Dingwall, but he recognised how hard it must be for the police to keep up to date with things as they developed.

'You said that was the good news, sergeant. What's the bad news?'

'I'm afraid we found no trace of the two Soviet agents, sir. It wasn't for the want of trying. We had a dozen men in plain clothes in and around the station, so many we were very concerned we'd scare Miss Erickson away. Every pairing of a blonde woman and a dark-haired man was quietly stopped and questioned, as was every blonde woman of the right age on her own, and every man behaving in anything like a suspicious manner. We also combed the town centre for small dark blue vans and erected roadblocks after the train arrived to check for the van leaving. We caught a pickpocket in the station but, as I said, there was no sign of the two people we were looking for.'

'Is there any chance your operation was spotted by the Soviets, and they escaped?'

'Yes, sir, there has to be a chance of that, despite the roadblocks.'

'How far is it by road from Inverness to Dingwall and from Inverness to Kyle of Lochalsh?'

'It's a little more than 20 miles to Dingwall and about 80 miles to Kyle of Lochalsh.'

'Am I right in thinking that if the two Soviet agents did detect the police presence at Inverness station, they could have driven to Dingwall and got there well before the Kyle of Lochalsh train left, or that they could reach Kyle of Lochalsh by road before the train Miss Erickson will be on arrives?'

'They could get to Dingwall in plenty of time, sir. But remember that Inspector Grant was on that train with Miss Erickson, that he knows the Soviets are still at large, and that he is armed. Also, I'd have expected to have heard something by now if there had been a problem at Dingwall before the train left.'

'Is the inspector on his own?'

'Yes, sir. But he is very capable.'

'What about the chances of the Soviets getting to Kyle of Lochalsh in a car before the train arrives?'

'Ordinarily, sir, I'd have said they'd have no problem. But it would depend on the route they took. If they first went to Dingwall, they'd then probably take roads following the railway via Achnasheen. If they went that way today, they would have a problem because the ferry making the crossing of Loch Carron at Stromeferry broke down yesterday and I don't believe the service has been restored. The alternative route, down Loch Ness and then west to Kintail, is a similar distance, but wouldn't be any help if they'd set off on the northern route having first followed the train to Dingwall.'

'Very well, thank you.'

Bob put the phone down and sat back in his chair. Lieutenant Colonel Ferguson's secretary placed a cup of tea on the table in front of him.

'Is there a problem, sir?'

'Thank you. I'm just finding it a little frustrating to be such a long way from the action and unable to get any sort of clear picture of what's going on. With apologies, I think I need to talk to Group Captain Erickson's office at RAF Stornoway again.'

Bob wasn't surprised to find the group captain had set off for Kyle of Lochalsh rather earlier. However, as he had hoped, it was possible to have a message forwarded by radio to the launch for the group captain's attention. It was quite a simple message that he dictated over the phone: 'One. Helen is believed to have successfully boarded the train due to arrive at Kyle of Lochalsh at 3.15 p.m. Two. Unknown to her there is an armed Special Branch officer, Inspector Grant, on the train. Three. The two Soviet agents are unaccounted for and still at large. Four. Please pass this on to Madame Dubois on arrival at Kyle of Lochalsh.'

*

Although it was difficult to judge with any accuracy because of the indirectness of their route, in Monique's mind the Commando Basic Training Centre at Achnacarry Castle was roughly halfway between their starting point in Blair Atholl and their destination in Kyle of Lochalsh. They'd taken considerably less than half the available time to get there, so she consented to Anthony's proposal that they eat in the officers' mess at Achnacarry.

They were too early for lunch but there was some excellent chicken soup available which they ate with bread. Then they picked up some sandwiches to replace the stale ones in the car. Monique wasn't sure when they'd next be able to eat, so felt it best to be prepared.

Monique did see a couple of faces she remembered from her visit to Achnacarry Castle the previous year, though none so well she could attach names to them. She thought it was interesting to see how well-liked Anthony seemed to be amongst those who had been his fellow instructors at Achnacarry. A number went out of their way to shake his hand and say hello as he and Monique sorted out food for themselves, fuel for the car, and more detailed maps for the rest of their journey.

While they were eating, Anthony suggested they borrow a lorry-load of men from the commando training centre to follow them and help guard against any problems that might arise in Kyle of Lochalsh. Monique felt there was no need, though she could tell Anthony still thought it might help.

Even though she knew they had plenty of time left, Monique couldn't resist the impulse to look at her watch several times during their brief visit and she was relieved when they set off again, this time with her driving and Anthony navigating.

They didn't speak for a while and Monique wondered if Anthony had dozed off. If he had, he woke when they pulled up at a barrier across the main road at what seemed to be a bridge over a river. After showing their passes to the obviously bored soldiers manning the checkpoint, they were allowed to proceed.

Anthony unfolded one of the maps. 'This is Loch Oich on our right. That was the Laggan Swing Bridge across the Caledonian Canal back there where the checkpoint was. In about two miles the road curves to the left, away from the loch. We should then turn left at a hotel in Invergarry onto a road heading generally west. It seems that even on Ordnance Survey one-inch scale maps, navigating by hotels is a popular occupation.'

They encountered another military checkpoint a hundred yards after making the turn and again were allowed to pass after proving who they were.

'A little further south, at Achnacarry, everything north-west of the Caledonian Canal is in the protected area,' said Anthony. 'I think that's true here too. I've just got to change maps as we're inconveniently crossing over several map corners and edges. That's better. This one sees us along Glen Garry and then north-west to Glen Shiel.

'I've been along this road. We need to turn north at a settlement called Tomdoun. But if we went straight on along it, we'd end up at a tiny place called Kinloch Hourn. We sometimes used to drop lorry-loads of trainees from Achnacarry there and tell them to head into the mountains of the Knoydart peninsula, to see if they could find their way on foot back to the west end of Loch Arkaig and then to Achnacarry. It's a stunningly beautiful area but extremely remote and rather unforgiving in anything but fine weather.

'For quite a while now we'll be on single-track roads and driving them can be a bit of a challenge if you're not used to them. Do you want me to take over, Monique?'

'As I said before I set off for Stirling yesterday evening, I'll pretend you didn't ask me that, Anthony. I've just seen you drive the single-track road from Dalwhinnie to Spean Bridge and then to Achnacarry, and I watched Bob doing it last November when we went over to Gruinard Bay and back. The principles really don't seem that complicated. Being built differently than you between my legs doesn't necessarily make me a worse driver than you.'

'I'm sorry Monique.'

Anthony lapsed into silence, not speaking again until he told her to look out for an acute turning to the right, just beyond the Tomdoun Hotel. From there the road became quite mountainous. They met some traffic on the way but not a lot. Monique was pleased to find her belief that driving these roads was no more than applied common sense was borne out in practice.

Monique wasn't sure how far they'd gone when Anthony

told her to watch out for a T-junction ahead and turn left when they got to it.

'It looks like what the AA call on their map the Cluanie Bridge Inn is what the Ordnance Survey call the Cluanie Inn on theirs,' he said. 'There it is, coming up on the left. I'm not surprised to see the Ordnance Survey have it right. From here we descend through Glen Shiel to the head of Loch Duich, which is where I'll need to change maps again. To my mind, these mountains trump anything we've seen further south or east.'

Anthony unfolded the next map before Monique reached a junction at the bottom of the glen, a place with a lovely view of an open loch beyond them. The weather had continued to improve as they'd travelled north-west and the patches of blue sky between the mainly white clouds added to the attraction of the place.

'We're playing a game of map corners again now,' said Anthony. 'We turn right at the junction up ahead, which makes this place Shiel Bridge. We then follow Loch Duich to a village called Dornie. It seems that once we're there we use a ferry to cross an offshoot of the loch so we can continue west.'

Monique looked at her watch. She remembered from the smaller scale map that once they'd got to this point, they really didn't have much further to go and they still had plenty of time in hand. But two hours early seemed vastly better than two minutes late.

Anthony must have noticed and guessed what was on her mind. 'Don't worry Monique. If there's a queue for the ferry, we'll be able to claim military priority. And we've got the Sten guns if we need them.'

Monique smiled. 'I'm sure that would go down well with

residents.'

A little further on, the road climbed steeply to run high above the loch, offering amazing views across and along it. 'It's as well we do have time in hand,' said Monique. 'This road is fairly challenging.'

As they descended, Monique caught a glimpse of a castle on an island close to the shore of the loch and connected to it by a stone bridge. Monique slowed so they could look down on the castle from their high vantage point.

'That looks absolutely beautiful,' she said. 'But am I the only one who thinks the stonework looks like it's been standing for years rather than centuries?'

'I see what you mean, Monique, but it would be a great place to call home. According to the map, the village isn't far ahead and that's where we find the ferry.'

They drove into Dornie a short time later.

'Do you see what I see, Monique? It appears our fairy godmother has listened to our concerns about a ferry queue and replaced the ferry with a bridge. A toll bridge apparently, though as military personnel on duty we're exempt. It looks like the toll booth is closed anyway.'

As they crossed the bridge, Monique was relieved that they'd not be delayed by a ferry. 'Have you any idea how far we still have to go to Kyle of Lochalsh?'

'We've got another map change coming up, which doesn't help. Hang on. Yes, according to the AA Touring Map it's ten miles from the ferry, make that the bridge, to Kyle of Lochalsh. We stay roughly parallel with the north shore of what is now Loch Alsh as far as a place called Balmacara and then we do a loop inland and approach our destination along the shore from the north. The one-inch map shows a slipway for the vehicle ferry across to the Isle of Skye with, a little to its east, a pier that seems to have the railway station built on it. Presumably, that's how they make the connections between the trains and the steamers.'

'Hopefully, we'll be able to identify Group Captain Erickson's launch when it arrives, if it's not already arrived,' said Monique. 'I've never met the man but I'm hoping that there won't be many RAF group captains wandering around Kyle of Lochalsh today.'

*

Bob's first interview after he'd telephoned Inverness and then Stornoway proved less tedious than any of the earlier ones, though not in the way he'd hoped for. He'd decided they should carry out interviews in an informal setting wherever they found their interviewees. Corporal Andrew Watson worked as a supervisor in the canteen kitchen in the Palace. He was a large man in every sense and had on a clean white jacket, trousers and hat. Bob realised that there was no way this Cinderella was ever going to come close to fitting into the glass slipper, and certainly not into a pair of battledress trousers with a 31-to-32-inch waist. At this time of the afternoon, the main activity in the kitchen seemed to be finishing the lunch service and Corporal Watson suggested they talk in a corridor rather than in the kitchen itself.

Bob explained what he wanted in a way that was becoming very familiar, then went on to confirm he was talking to the correct man and discuss his background. Corporal Watson was 34 and was born and brought up in Helensburgh. Bob then confirmed that the man shared a twin room with another corporal on the top floor of the Great Hall.

'As I'm sure you are aware, we are investigating the murder of a man in the Douglas Gardens on Tuesday evening. Can you tell me what you were doing between 9.30 p.m. and 10.30 p.m. on Tuesday?'

'That's easy, sir. I was playing cards with two mates in the room I share with one of them. We started before 9 p.m. and went on until about 11 p.m. We're not subject to normal lights out rules, so weren't doing anything wrong.'

'Who were you playing with?'

'Corporal Peter Gray is the man I share the room with. He works at the firing range down in the Nether Bailey. The third man was Corporal Peter Kerr, who works in the quartermaster's office. He's in the room next door to ours. At present, he's got it to himself. I've not seen him since yesterday, come to think of it.'

'Corporal Kerr was with you the whole time?'

'He might have nipped out for a pee once. The tea we serve here goes straight through you. But he wasn't gone for more than a couple of minutes as the latrine is only at the end of the corridor.'

'Have you any idea what time this was?'

'No, sorry, though I think it was after lights out. As I said, he was hardly out for long enough to disturb the flow of the game.'

'Thank you, that's very helpful.'

Bob left the Palace and headed for the Nether Bailey. Corporal Gray wasn't on his list of people to interview, but he wanted to speak to him as quickly as possible to see if he confirmed what Corporal Watson had said.

It turned out that Gray wasn't only able to confirm what his roommate had told Bob, he was also able to say that Corporal Kerr had gone for his toilet break at just after 10.15 p.m. Bob thanked him and left the firing range.

As he walked back up towards the North Gate, he reflected on the fact that he no longer had any suspects at all. Whatever Corporal Peter Kerr's reason for not wanting to talk to military intelligence, it wasn't because he had killed Bill Douglas.

CHAPTER TWENTY-SEVEN

The train from Dingwall to Kyle of Lochalsh was busy. Helen had been able to find a seat on the forward-facing side of a compartment in the second of the five carriages of the train. She had a window seat while to her right were three men in naval uniform. The one nearest the corridor seemed more senior than the other two and had spread himself out and was snoring.

Sitting opposite Helen was a harassed-looking woman with two young and obviously bored children, a boy and a girl. Two more sailors occupied the rest of the bench seat on the far side of the compartment and had spent the journey smoking and playing cards on a leather case one of them had laid across his legs.

Helen had been out into the corridor once, to go to the rather smelly toilet at the end of the carriage. She'd found men standing in the area by the doors, as well as some in the corridor itself. One man wearing a fawn gabardine coat and a brown homburg hat was standing just outside their compartment and smoking, leaning so his back was pressed against the glass next to the sleeping sailor. Helen had squeezed past him when she went to the toilet, and she'd wondered if he might be watching her. When she returned, she got a better look at him and was relieved that he wasn't either of the men who had been following her

Helen had her copy of *Bradshaw's Guide* open on her lap and was following the journey. Although there were no names on the platforms, she knew from the time that the last stop had been called Achanalt and now the train was slowing down as it approached Achnasheen. She expected it to be larger because it was shown as a place on the map of Scotland that her mother had given her.

According to the timetable, it was an hour and twenty minutes from Achnasheen to Kyle of Lochalsh so there wasn't too much further to go. The timetable said the train connected with the Stornoway steamer, but she had no idea how long she'd have to wait. She was worried about whether she had enough money left for the steamer fare.

She'd considered hiding in the toilet on the train to Inverness to avoid the guard. But as she had the money it seemed only right to buy a ticket. And having a ticket certainly made things easier when changing trains in Inverness and Dingwall. She knew she ought to buy a ticket for the steamer too, but if it cost too much, she was sure she'd think of something. She knew that once she got to Stornoway, her father could pay for a ticket for her.

Helen hoped Duncan had been able to get back to the travellers' camp and to little Duncan and Betsy without any problem. He'd shown her how to get onto the northbound platform without going through the station or being seen by the man on the other platform, the man who'd followed her from London. She'd made Duncan promise not to tell anyone that she'd not caught the train she'd said she was going to catch.

Helen realised that the young girl from the opposite seat had got up and was now standing right in front of her. She had long red hair and looked to be about ten.

'What's in your book?' asked the girl.

'Maisie! Stop bothering the young lady and sit back down next to your brother.'

Helen looked up at the woman and smiled. 'It's OK, really.' She turned the *Bradshaw's Guide* round so it was facing the girl. 'Hello Maisie, I'm Helen. This is a book that shows all the railway timetables for the whole country. They publish a new one each month, so it's always up to date. My mother gave me this one because I'm making a long train journey for Easter. I've been using it so I would know how far I've come and how far I've got to go.'

'Where are you going?'

'I'm going to stay with my father, who is stationed on an island called Lewis in the Outer Hebrides. I'm travelling to Kyle of Lochalsh on the train and then I'm catching a steamer. What about you?'

'We live in Plockton,' said Maisie. 'We've been visiting our Granny and Grandad in Inverness. I wanted to stay for Easter, but Mummy wouldn't let us.' The child glanced round reproachfully at her mother, who smiled in an embarrassed way at Helen.

Helen thought it was best to change the subject. She noticed the girl had a circular brass pendant about the size of a half crown coin with something rather crudely inscribed on it, suspended around her neck on dark green cord. 'That's a pretty pendant you've got, Maisie. Where did you get that?'

'All my friends have one. So does Stuart, who might be my brother but certainly isn't my friend.'

The boy, who seemed a little younger, glared at Maisie and swung a leg as if to kick her. His mother slapped him.

'What's it for?' asked Helen.

'It's my identity token. It's for the war. It's got my name and address on it. You can only live where we do, or visit, if you have one. You must have one too, or you wouldn't have been allowed to get on the train.'

'Maisie, stop being rude!' The woman leaned forwards and

took a grip on the girl's upper arm. I'm sure Helen is old enough to have been issued with a protected area pass rather than an identity token. Come and sit down.'

'Do I have to?'

'Yes, you do. I've got some sweets in a bag, but you can only have one if you behave.' The woman smiled apologetically across the carriage.

Helen sat back and closed her eyes. It seemed she'd found her way onto a train going somewhere you were only meant to visit if you had a special security pass. If so, then things might get very tricky when she got to Kyle of Lochalsh.

CHAPTER TWENTY-EIGHT

'You were right about the timing, Anthony. We do have plenty in hand. Do you have any idea where we go now that we're here?' Monique had driven over a bridge crossing a railway line and into what was obviously Kyle of Lochalsh's main street. There were quite a few people about, many of them in naval uniform. She had to brake to avoid a pony and trap coming the other way that had pulled out to pass a lorry parked outside a shop.

'The one-inch map isn't that detailed,' said Anthony. 'As I said earlier, the railway station seems to be on a pier a little to the east of the centre of the village. There should be a left turn coming up in a moment that will take us there. If we go straight on, we come to the slipway for the ferry to the Isle of Skye.'

'Let's go there first,' said Monique. 'It might help give us an impression of how the place is laid out.'

Monique drove past the junction and then came to a halt when waved down by a man in a flat hat and dark blue pullover standing in the road. She wound down her window and smiled at him.

'Hello, ma'am. If you want to cross on the ferry, you'll need to pull up behind the black van on the left over there. That's the ferry queue and you can buy your tickets at the wooden booth on the right, opposite the head of the queue. We've only got five vehicles waiting at the moment, so you'll be on the third crossing.'

'No, thank you. We're not here for the ferry. We're just going to the end and then turning round.'

'There's a place to turn by the gate to the Station Hotel,

ma'am. You can't miss it. Well, you could, but then you'd have to swim. We had someone try that in a navy lorry last week. He said his brakes had failed. The lorry was in a pretty sorry state once the tide went out and they were able to winch it back onto the slipway.'

'Thank you. I'll be sure to keep out of the sea.'

Monique wound up her window and drove on slowly. The road broadened as it approached the top of the slipway and formed a junction with a drive leading through a gateway on the right.

She turned the car round. 'We're not going to be in anyone's way if I pull onto the verge over there, on the left just beyond the hotel gateway. Besides, if anyone objects then, as you pointed out earlier, we've got the Sten guns.'

Anthony smiled. 'We've got time for a cup of tea if you like and if they're open. I'll see if they are.'

Monique followed as Anthony led the way. The end of the hotel nearest the gate looked like a single-storey extension to the main building and had 'The Station Hotel' painted on the slates, she guessed where it might be most easily visible from the rest of the village and to anyone waiting for the Skye ferry. Anthony walked round to a door set in the side of a large porch built onto the front of the main part of the hotel and went in.

The hotel backed onto rising, wooded ground. In front of it, between it and the sea, was a lawned area bounded by a low white wooden fence at its forward edge. Monique walked over to the fence, which divided the lawn from a short rocky descent to the shore.

She thought this was an amazing spot in what was now nearly perfect weather, with largely blue skies and just enough in the way of white clouds to add interest. Off to the right, on what she assumed was the Isle of Skye, the horizon was magnificently mountainous. The most obvious mountains were rounded in shape but, beyond them, there was the hint of sharper and more jagged peaks.

Beneath the mountains, just visible beyond the rising ground to her right, was a lighthouse and an accompanying cottage on what was either a headland projecting from the mainland or an island.

There were several small islands set in the stretch of water ahead of her. On its far side was a village overlooked by a stump of a castle. She thought that must also be on the Isle of Skye. A boat was making its way towards Kyle of Lochalsh from the village on the far side. It appeared to have a hull on which someone had placed a piece of wooden roadway large enough for two cars and surrounded by railings. Or, as at present, large enough for a red van and a crowd of foot passengers.

When Monique turned to look back at the hotel, she saw the three-storey central block had a flat-roofed two-storey extension on the left-hand side as she was looking at it. The ground floor of the extension and part of the main block projected slightly forwards of the building and had large windows, behind which she could see an empty dining room. The absence of the usual criss-cross sticky tape from the glass suggested no one thought it likely this place would be bombed. The building was finished in a weathered grey harling and the whole width of the central block had been adorned with large white capital letters between the first and second-storey windows that again proclaimed the hotel's identity to the world.

Monique had the sense that Bob was hoping they might spend their honeymoon staying at the North British Hotel on

Princes Street in Edinburgh, drinking fine champagne, eating reasonable food, and enjoying excellent sex. Monique liked the idea but wondered if they might not get bored, of the champagne and the food at least, after a couple of days. If the Station Hotel in Kyle of Lochalsh was open for paying guests, then this would be a pretty good spot to come to for a total change from Edinburgh and their normal day-to-day lives. She resolved to find out if it offered accommodation before she left.

Monique realised that Anthony was walking across the lawn towards her.

'I'm afraid we're too late for lunch and too early for dinner,' he said. 'And the idea of afternoon tea seems not to have got this far. Hello, that looks like the ferry from Skye arriving. I'm not sure I'd be too keen to entrust a car I owned to it.'

When the ferry reached the slipway below the hotel, it was tied by one of its crew to a metal ring set in the stones. Then, with help from the man who had been managing the ferry queue, the roadway section was swung round, and ramps were lowered. The foot passengers disembarked and then the van drove off. As soon as the slipway was clear, two navy staff cars drove down it and up the ramps onto the ferry, followed by a handful of foot passengers. The roadway section was then swung back to align with the hull and the ferry set off for the crossing to Skye.

'Were those cars at the front of the queue when we drove past?' asked Anthony.

'I wasn't paying attention, to be honest. I was too busy following instructions and not driving into the sea.' Monique smiled. 'But if the military regularly jump the queue, I can see it causing resentment. Though having said that, private motorists aren't meant to have any petrol now anyway. Did you bring the map from the car? It's a wonderful view from here.'

Anthony unfolded the one-inch scale Ordnance Survey map so they could look at its topmost section, which covered the area they were in. He was able to confirm that much of what they were looking at, from the mountains to the village opposite, called Kyleakin, was on the Isle of Skye, and that the stretch of water in front of them was Kyle Akin. After some debate, they decided that the lighthouse Monique had noticed was on an island, though its symbol on the map was partly obscured by a thickly printed grid number.

'You also get a good view of the pier from here,' said Monique. You can see the railway station has been built out along it, though it's partly obscured by the steamer that's moored on this side.'

Anthony turned to look. 'I'm wondering why the Station Hotel is so removed from the railway station. Wouldn't it have made more sense to call it the Ferry Hotel?'

'That's true,' said Monique. 'The pier and the station seem busy, even though we've only got a partial view. You can just about make out the name *Lochness* on the prow of the steamer. There's a small military lorry being lifted aboard by the ship's crane. I suppose she must have a cargo hold in front of the bridge. There's another crane which looks to be on the quayside, lifting a load of sacks in a net over to the rear of the ship.'

The *Lochness* had a dark blue hull. There was rust staining that was obvious even from this distance, especially below the anchor and along the horizontal strip above the waterline that Monique imagined was intended to protect the hull if she was berthed too enthusiastically. The top of the hull and the superstructure were white. The single funnel was largely red, with a band around the top in a blue that matched the hull.

The sound of engines coming from over her right shoulder caused Monique to turn round.

'I think that this is Group Captain Erickson making his entrance,' said Anthony.

Monique watched as a beautifully sleek craft cruised past. Its hull was a rather darker blue than the steamer's and carried a very large Royal Air Force roundel surrounded by a yellow ring on the prow, with, even larger, the number 132, also in yellow, just behind it. The superstructure looked low and purposeful and was light grey.

'Let's see where he goes,' said Monique. 'We need to find him and say hello. First, though, I just need to pop into the hotel. I won't be a moment.'

*

Monique asked Anthony to drive. It took their security passes and her most winning smile to get them past the elderly railway employee manning the barrier at the top of the access road that sloped down to the railway station. There was no parking beyond the foot of the road, they were told, but there should be a space next to the wall near the bottom.

As they started to descend, Monique asked Anthony to stop for a moment. 'I just want to get a feeling for the layout of the place from what must be the best viewpoint over it.'

The pier seemed nearly as broad as it was long. They appeared to be on the only access road and the railway station, whose near end began not far from the bottom of the slope, extended a good way towards the far end of the pier. The station had a platform on either side of it, which Monique imagined would be used by passenger trains arriving from Dingwall. There were more railway tracks or sidings on both sides of the station, filling the available space between it and the quays on either side of the pier.

The *Lochness* was moored on the west side of the pier, the right-hand side as Monique was looking. Most of the considerable amount of activity she could see was on the quay next to the steamer or around several goods trains or parts of trains parked on lines between the station and the *Lochness.* There were more goods wagons, singly or connected, on the tracks on the other side of the station, together with a couple of passenger carriages.

A mast sticking up above the level of the far end of the pier, beyond the station, and two men manoeuvring a gangway on the quayside there, confirmed the impression Monique had had from her last sight of Group Captain Erickson's launch about where he was intending to moor it.

'Have you seen enough?' asked Anthony.

'Yes, thanks. Even though the steamer can't be due to depart soon, given the train meant to connect with it is still three-quarters of an hour away, the quay looks like an ants' nest from here. Finding Helen Erickson isn't going to be easy and it's bound to get busier once her train arrives.'

Anthony pulled away down the slope. 'Did you notice the additional pier a little to the east of this one, with a ship tied up to it? I'm wondering if that explains all the naval uniforms we've been seeing. Whatever that place is, it's not marked on the map. But then I suppose there's a great deal been built in the past few years that doesn't appear even on War Office editions of the Ordnance Survey maps.'

He turned the car round at the foot of the slope and drove a little way back up it to park between two other vehicles next to the wall on what was now the right-hand side of the access road.

Monique led the way along the station platform to its far end, again surprised at the number of people who were about. As she approached the gangway a tall, dark-haired man in his late forties came into sight making his way up it. The group captain's uniform he wore gave Monique a good idea of who he was.

'Group Captain Erickson? I'm pleased to meet you. I'm Monique Dubois from Military Intelligence, Section 11, and this is my colleague Captain Anthony Darlington. Call me Monique.' She shook hands with Erickson, while Anthony saluted.

'I'm pleased to meet you, too, Monique. I'm only sorry that my daughter's holiday arrangements have caused you so much trouble.'

'I think the apology should be the other way, sir. If Helen hadn't outwitted me at a railway station in Perthshire early this morning, this could all have been resolved there and you'd have had no need to make this journey.'

'It's not a problem. The RAF air-sea rescue unit based in Stornoway comes under my command and I've paid them very little attention since taking over. They provide a valuable service covering a large area of sea and have been very happy to demonstrate to me just what their high-speed launches are capable of. And please call me Tom. By the way, I have a message for you from Group Captain Sutherland.'

He reached into an inside pocket and pulled out a folded piece of paper which he handed to Monique. She opened it and saw a handwritten note.

'It was radioed to us while we were on our way,' said Erickson.

Monique glanced at Anthony. 'Bob says that, and I quote, "Helen is believed to have successfully boarded" the train that is due to arrive here at 3.15 p.m. I'm not sure why he'd have phrased it like that, but I think we can assume that if he'd subsequently found out she didn't board the train, he'd have sent a further message.

'He goes on to say that there is an armed Special Branch officer, an Inspector Grant, on the train and that Helen does not know of his presence. So far, so good, but he then goes on to say that, and I'll quote again, "the two Soviet agents are unaccounted for and still at large". That's not welcome news. I rather wish I'd taken you up on your suggestion we borrow men from the Commando Basic Training Centre, Anthony. This isn't turning out to be my best day for important decisions.'

'Perhaps I can help?' said Erickson. 'RAF Stornoway has a detachment of the RAF Regiment. They are intended mainly for airfield defence but have a full range of infantry skills. After Bob telephoned, I thought it best to cover all eventualities and asked for six volunteers. I may only be able to offer you five men as one appeared to be suffering from terminal seasickness the last time I saw him, but you are welcome to use them as you wish. This is very much your show, Monique. What do you want me to do, and what can my men do?'

'To my mind, the important thing to remember is that you are the only person here who can confidently recognise Helen. And you will of course immediately be recognised by her even though she won't be expecting to see you here. The area between the railway station and the moored steamer looks chaotic, and it can only get worse when the train arrives, with people getting off an unknown number of carriages. I think we need you where you stand the best chance of meeting her, which must be at the landward end of the gangway used to board the steamer.

'If you have two of your men with you, that will ensure that once you have met Helen you can bring her securely to this launch, which seems the safest place in the circumstances. Then I'd like two more of your men to be positioned at the foot of the road that climbs from near the inland end of the railway station. I don't know for certain that's the only road access to the pier, but it's the most obvious. I would suggest that the fifth man secures access to your launch.

'Anthony and I will be on the platform when the train arrives. We might be able to identify Helen, in which case we will keep an eye on her as she makes her way to you. Being there will also give us the best chance of contacting the Special Branch officer. I'm sure Bob will have given him our descriptions.'

'What about the Soviets?' asked Erickson.

'Ah, yes. With any luck they'll have evaporated into thin air, having realised that they cannot now achieve their objectives. But that was as true this morning as it is now, and we know they were still involved then. We also know from Bob's message that they weren't caught in Inverness, which was the next thing I was counting on. This is a long way of saying "I don't know". We will just have to be prepared to deal with anything that might arise.'

'Thank you for your honesty.'

'Are you armed, Tom?'

'No, and I'll stay that way. There will be a lot of people

about once the train arrives, including my daughter, and I think it's best if only people with real competence in handling guns are carrying them. I go through my mandatory training and refreshers, of course, but it's better for everyone if I'm not armed this afternoon. Do you want me to get my men off the launch so you can brief them, Monique?'

'Yes please, Tom.'

CHAPTER TWENTY-NINE

Helen spent part of the rest of the journey lost in the beautiful scenery she could see out of the window. After Achnashellach, the tracks followed the right-hand side of what her map of Scotland said was Glen Carron. That meant she could admire a loch with mountains rising steeply beyond it, and then a winding river in an equally glorious setting.

The railway line crossed the glen as it approached Strathcarron. After the train pulled out of the station, Helen realised that the good views were now on its other side, and she could only see them by looking across the smoky compartment and through the train's corridor, which was still partly obscured by the man leaning against the glass.

On her side of the train, the ground rose steeply. It relented briefly after the train pulled away from the next stop but then seemed to rise almost sheer, offering no views at all. The glimpses she could see through the train corridor made her regret she'd not found a carriage with seats on that side.

Helen thought she'd caught the woman sitting opposite glancing at her once or twice. She wondered if she had worked out from Helen's conversation with Maisie that she didn't have the security pass that she needed to be travelling to Kyle of Lochalsh. She tried to dismiss the idea, telling herself that she was simply imagining things. Nonetheless, when a guard slid open the compartment door as the train approached Stromeferry and asked to see everyone's tickets, Helen found she was holding her breath, waiting for the woman to say something. At least she had a ticket, she thought.

Nothing was said, but Helen was still deeply relieved when

the woman told Maisie and Stuart that they were nearly home and stood up to get their bags down from the netting luggage rack above their heads. The sailor who had been asleep had woken up and helped the woman down with her luggage, then offered to carry it to the door of the carriage and pass it out to her on the platform.

Maisie said goodbye to Helen as she followed her mother out of the compartment and Helen replied and smiled at the girl. Stuart looked round and pulled a tongue as he went out into the corridor.

Helen was surprised that none of the people standing in the corridor or at the ends of the carriage came in to take the vacant seats, then realised that with just fifteen minutes left until the train reached Kyle of Lochalsh, it probably wouldn't be worth anyone's while. Even the man in the corridor, leaning against the glass of their compartment, didn't appear to think it worth moving, and he must have seen the two children and their mother leave.

A few minutes after they left Plockton, Helen saw a man pass along the corridor from the direction of the front of the train who looked familiar. He glanced into the compartment as he walked by and then excused himself as he passed the man standing outside the compartment. Helen felt sure it was the man she'd seen that morning at Dunkeld and Birnam railway station, the one who'd followed her from London with the woman.

The man didn't reappear, but Helen began to feel more and more anxious as the train neared Kyle of Lochalsh. She told herself that at least this gave her something better to worry about than whether Maisie's mother had realised she didn't have a security pass, but that didn't help. When she glimpsed a church, she stood up to get her suitcase down. She put it on the seat she'd been sitting on and then opened it, putting away her *Bradshaw's Guide*. She decided to keep the map of Scotland in her handbag. She thought it might be useful on the steamer to help show where she was and what she could see.

When Helen sat down again, with the suitcase on the floor in front of her, she realised the train was pulling into a much larger station than anything she'd seen since Dingwall. The platform was on her side of the train, so she was able to watch as it came to a halt. She was pleased to see a freestanding sign had been placed on the platform with a large arrow pointing towards the front of the train and the words 'Portree and Stornoway steamers this way'.

She stayed seated until the five sailors left the compartment, turning to head towards the front of the train. Helen then stood up and followed. As she neared the end of the carriage and the door, she realised the man in the brown homburg hat who'd spent the journey outside her compartment was behind her. She looked around and caught his eye and smiled, nervously. He touched the brim of his hat in response.

*

Monique had also seen signs on the platform directing passengers to the steamer. She positioned herself close to the station building in line with the rear of the engine and the front of the tender. Everyone leaving the train to catch the steamer would have to pass her here. That would include Helen Erickson unless she was intending to fool everyone again.

Anthony was a little further along the platform, level with the front of the first carriage. He was standing in the middle of the platform, where disembarking passengers would have to flow past both sides of him. There were a few army uniforms on view, but no officers that she'd seen. This seemed the best way of getting Anthony noticed by the Special Branch inspector.

The train had obviously been quite full and many of those on board were heading for the steamer. Monique lost sight of Anthony for a moment in the crowd. When she had a clear view of him again, she saw he was standing with his head bowed towards a man in a light-coloured overcoat and a brown hat, who had a hand on Anthony's arm and was speaking to him. Anthony saw her looking at him and waved then pointed. She tried to make out who or what he was pointing at and realised that a young woman who matched Helen Erickson's description was just a few yards away from her and would pass her in a moment.

With Anthony and, she assumed, Inspector Grant behind Helen she decided to stay ahead of her and turned to walk with the flow of people. A railway porter a little beyond the engine was shouting for people wanting the Portree and Stornoway steamer and pointing to his left, her right, along the quayside formed by the end of the pier.

Monique looked round, careful not to catch Helen's eye. The young woman was now about ten yards behind her. She was reassured to see that Anthony and the Special Branch man were close behind Helen. A man wearing a flat hat and carrying a sack on his shoulder nearly bumped into Monique and cursed her for slowing down to turn round. An argument that drew attention to her was the last thing Monique needed so she simply turned and followed the crowd.

The flow of people slowed and divided to pass either side

of a railway goods wagon being rotated by three men on a turntable set into the surface of the quayside. The crowd was then directed to turn right again, this time apparently by a member of the steamer crew. The scene that greeted Monique on the far side of the goods train nearest the steamer was one of total pandemonium. Parts of the quayside were covered with piles of sacks, wooden boxes, barrels and wicker baskets. People were milling around everywhere. Some were queueing to board the vessel using the gangway. Others seemed to be seeing off friends and relations or just watching. A dozen young men in naval ratings' uniforms stood off to one side. Monique assumed they were waiting to board.

Group Captain Erickson stood close to the end of the gangway with two of his RAF Regiment airmen in their khaki uniforms and RAF berets. There was more cursing when Monique pushed ahead through the crowd, intending to get to Erickson to let him know his daughter was approaching.

She'd almost reached the group captain when she saw him look past her. His face lit up as she heard a cry of 'Daddy' from behind her that cut through the hubbub of voices, and she turned to see Helen stop with her mouth open and a look of shock on her face. Then the young woman pushed forwards.

Monique took a few steps away from the gangway and the most densely crowded area of the quayside. There was no point in her getting in the way any more than she had already. Suddenly there was a scream and Monique realised that someone had run into Helen from behind and knocked her over. She watched as the man who'd collided with the young woman bent down to pick up her suitcase and then set off in Monique's direction, with the crowd seeming to open in front of him as he ran. She stuck out a foot and the man tripped, stumbled and went down on one knee and his free hand, before regaining his balance.

Another figure ran past Monique and caught the man as he set off again, bringing him down hard on the stone quayside with a rugby tackle. The suitcase slid for a few feet on its own before coming to rest beside the wheel of an open goods wagon on the track nearest the steamer.

Monique ran over, pulling out her pistol, then crouched down to press it against the back of the head of the man who had knocked Helen over. 'Don't move.'

The second man stood up and dusted himself down rather theatrically. 'Hello. You must be Madame Dubois.'

'And you must be Inspector Grant. You don't happen to have a pair of handcuffs with you, by any chance?'

'Yes, but let's ask the constable here to use his.'

Monique realised a policeman was standing beside her. She wondered how she'd missed seeing him. Inspector Grant showed him something, presumably a warrant card, and the constable saluted.

The crowd had gone very quiet and, as the policeman applied his handcuffs, Monique could hear movement behind her. She turned round to see Anthony, Helen and the group captain approaching. The girl looked shaken. Monique replaced her pistol in her shoulder holster.

It was Helen who spoke first. 'That's the man I first saw in London, who's been following me. There are two others, a man and a woman.'

'Hello Helen, I'm Monique. Are you all right?'

The girl nodded.

'Good. I'm with military intelligence and I've been following you too, though you've done a very good job of staying one step ahead of me. The other man you mentioned has been arrested by the police, but I don't know where the woman is. Have you any idea why this man tried to take your suitcase?'

'No, none at all. And where is it? I thought he had it.'

Monique looked around. The suitcase was no longer by the wheel of the goods wagon, or anywhere else she could see. 'Anthony, you make sure Helen remains safe. Take her to the launch. Constable, can you get this man locked up securely somewhere? Inspector Grant, do you know if there are any ways out of here other than the road up from the station?'

'Sorry, Madame Dubois, Kyle of Lochalsh isn't somewhere I visit very often.'

'There's another way out on this side of the pier, ma'am.' Monique turned to see the constable pointing. 'If you go past the wooden buildings over there, beyond the end of the quay, then turn left to go between them and the rock cutting, you come onto Harbour Street. That leads up to the centre of the village.'

'Thank you. Inspector, you come with me.' Monique set off at a run, drawing her pistol again. As she turned the corner to go behind the wooden buildings, she saw a leather suitcase lying on the ground. She ran a little beyond it and was rewarded by a glimpse of a blonde woman who looked back at her as she got into the driver's side of a dark green saloon car parked on the street a hundred yards away. It then started and drove off.

Inspector Grant was just behind Monique. 'I do know that the police station is just up there. I'll get a car and go after her. There's only one road out that doesn't involve a ferry and there are security points on the roads leading into or out of the protected area. We can warn them to be on the lookout for her.'

'Right, thank you. I'll go and check on Helen. At least we know she's safe now.'

The inspector ran off. Monique returned to pick up the suitcase and then walked back onto the pier, avoiding the crowds on the steamer quay by walking between two lines of freight wagons a little nearer the station. At the far end of the pier, she found the group captain and four of his men with Anthony and Helen, standing by the gangway leading down to the RAF launch.

They all turned to face her as she approached.

Monique held up the suitcase. 'It was taken by the woman, who has driven off in a car. Inspector Grant has gone after her and the police will alert the protected area checkpoints. Is this your suitcase, Helen? The woman had abandoned it. Would you mind opening it and seeing if anything is missing?'

'Yes, it's mine,' said Helen. She took the suitcase from Monique, placed it on the quayside and opened it. 'Someone's been through it. Or that might just be it being dropped and then shaken by someone running. I don't think anything is missing, though.'

'Are you sure?'

'There wasn't all that much in here anyway. Hang on, this is rather odd.'

'What is?' asked Monique.

'I put my copy of *Bradshaw's Guide* in the suitcase as we were arriving at Kyle of Lochalsh station. Mother gave it to me when I met her in London on Monday in case I had any problems on the journey and needed to check train times. I'm sure she never realised it would see as much use as it has. That's what's odd, though. They're published every month so don't seem to be intended to last. Even after a couple of days' use, mine was showing signs of wear. I also used a pencil to mark some trains while I was at the travellers' camp. Ah, do you know about that?'

'Yes, we talked to Betsy and her Uncle Peter,' said Monique.

'Well look. This is table 748, which shows the trains from Dingwall to Kyle of Lochalsh. I put an arrow beneath the train that I wanted to catch. It's not there. This is the same book in the sense that it's the April 1943 edition of *Bradshaw's Guide*, but this one has less wear on the covers and the spine and the marks I made in it aren't there.'

'You're saying that your copy of *Bradshaw's Guide* was switched for a different copy of the same edition between you arriving at Kyle of Lochalsh and me retrieving the suitcase?'

'That's right.'

'I'm beginning to wonder whether the people following you were really after your copy of *Bradshaw's Guide* all along. It was important enough for them to chase you the length of the country for, and to carry a replacement with them in the hope you'd not notice that it had been exchanged.'

'Why would they do that?' asked Group Captain Erickson.

'I don't know, but I think it's important we find out. If that woman has Helen's copy of the guide, then we need to get it back. If she's given the chance to drive halfway across Scotland with it, then she might find a way of getting what she wants from it before she's caught. There's no point in our setting off in pursuit by car. Inspector Grant is already doing that, and anyway she's now got a lead on us. But the roads really aren't that good. Tom, do you know the main road heading inland from Kyle of Lochalsh?'

Group Captain Erickson nodded.

'Good. Do you think your high-speed launch can make it to the new bridge at Dornie before a car that's being driven as quickly as the road allows?'

'If you factor in the loop in the road to the north when leaving Kyle of Lochalsh, then yes, I do.'

'Good. I would like you and two of your men to take Helen somewhere safe, like the station master's office, while I borrow the other two and your launch and crew. Where's the fifth man, by the way?'

'I sent him with the policeman. I didn't want the prisoner escaping between here and the police station. Wouldn't it be best if we come with you?'

'No. I'd prefer Helen not to be involved. And we don't have time to argue.'

'Our Sten guns are still in the car,' said Anthony.

'There's no time to go and get them,' said Monique.

'We're not short of weapons on the launch, Monique,' said Group Captain Erickson.

CHAPTER THIRTY

Tom Erickson introduced the launch's captain as Flight Sergeant Mellor. He told the flight sergeant to comply with any instructions that Monique gave him and then retreated up the gangway to the quay. Monique was relieved he didn't try to press his case to come with them. She didn't want anyone on board who was senior enough to feel any responsibility for what she had in mind.

The gangway was swiftly pulled up onto the pier and the launch came to life with a deep throb from its engines that Monique could feel right through her feet and legs.

Monique and Anthony followed the flight sergeant down into the wheelhouse.

'I understand you want to go east, ma'am?'

'Yes, please. A Soviet agent is trying to escape in a car with material we need to recover, and I want to get to the new road bridge at Dornie before they do.'

'We need the same Admiralty chart I used when coming into Kyle of Lochalsh and it's already laid out on the table at the back here. Can you show me exactly where you want to be?'

Monique took a second to get used to the very different appearance of the chart compared with the maps she was familiar with. 'It looks ancient. Will it be reliable?'

'It's an 1859 chart that was resurveyed in 1901 and last updated in 1941. It will be fine for what we want, ma'am.'

'This is where we need to be,' said Monique, putting her finger on the paper. 'The chart shows the new bridge, so despite what I just said is more up to date than the Ordnance Survey map we used to get here. Do you see the slipway shown just south of the bridge on the west side? That would be the ideal place to land.'

'As you wish, ma'am. The depth of water should be fine, even in the side loch as we approach the slipway. It's a little before half tide and the tide is coming in, so we should have no problems.'

He spoke to the helmsman on the wheel and the launch pulled away from the quayside.

'You'll find it a little slow at first, Madame Dubois. The naval base just along the north shore of the loch from here is HMS *Trelawney*. There are anti-submarine nets strung right across Kyle Akin just ahead of us and we need to make our way carefully through the gap that's intended to allow navigation while keeping the Germans out. The nets are there to defend the naval base, but also to block access by enemy vessels to the sea route round the mainland side of the Isle of Skye.'

'What does the navy do here?' asked Anthony.

'HMS *Trelawney* is the shore base of the 1st Minelaying Squadron, sir. Since 1940 they've been building what they call the Northern Barrage, a series of defensive minefields between Greenland, Iceland, the Faroe Islands and Orkney. The mines come in by train, are loaded onto minelaying ships and then taken out into the Atlantic. It's quite a large operation.'

'Will it take us long to get past the anti-submarine nets?' asked Monique.

'No, we're clear of them now. Hold onto something.'

Monique grabbed the back of a fixed chair she'd been standing behind as the launch surged forwards and its nose rose out of the water.

'Good,' said Monique, raising her voice to be heard over

the increased noise, 'I was worried we might lose our race with our Soviet friend.'

'They'd need a good lead on us for that to happen,' said Flight Sergeant Mellor. 'You're lucky you're making this journey now and not a thousand years ago, though.'

'Why?'

'Did you notice a ruined castle over on the Isle of Skye side? It's called Castle Moil. According to legend, an earlier fortress on that site was home to a Viking princess who hung a chain between her castle and the mainland to enforce a toll she charged on any boats passing along Kyle Akin. She is remembered as "Saucy Mary" because... well.'

The flight sergeant looked embarrassed.

Monique smiled. 'You're going to have to tell me the rest of the story now you've got that far.'

'It's said that when a toll was paid, she would express her thanks by showing her bare breasts to the ship's crew. Hence the name "Saucy Mary".'

Monique laughed.

'It's not going to take us very long,' said the flight sergeant. 'If you need to make any preparations, now would be the time.'

'Where are the men from the RAF Regiment?' asked Monique.

'In the cabin, just through that hatch.'

Monique and Anthony went through into a larger cabin than she had expected. But then it needed to be able to accommodate both the crew and anyone who had been rescued, she supposed. Two men were seated and looked up as they entered. A third was lying on a bunk, apparently still unwell. Monique ignored him and explained to the other two what she wanted from them.

The group captain had come well equipped and having

ensured the two men had rifles and ammunition, Monique picked up a Thompson submachine gun while Anthony took a Sten gun.

Monique knew that they were close to their destination when the sound of the engines died down and the nose of the launch lowered. She was followed onto the deck by Anthony and by the two men from the RAF Regiment.

She found herself looking at a very different view of the castle they'd admired earlier as the launch cruised past it and into the mouth of the narrower offshoot loch, crossed by a bridge that also looked very different now than when they'd been driving over it. The central section of the bridge looked as if it was intended to lift to allow boats to pass underneath. She wondered if blocking the road by opening the bridge might be a better way of achieving the result she wanted but then realised there wouldn't be time to find whoever was responsible for opening it, still less persuade them to do so.

As they slowly approached the slipway on the west side of the offshoot loch, Flight Sergeant Mellor knelt on the deck at the front of the launch, looking down into the water and signalling by hand to the helmsman.

He looked round and saw Monique. 'I think we'll make it to the slipway without difficulty. We'll lower some fenders. With the tide rising we ought to be able to tie up while you are ashore.'

When the launch nosed up to the ferry slipway, the two RAF Regiment airmen jumped down onto it, one slipping and falling on seaweed before recovering. They then helped Anthony and Monique ashore.

Following Monique's directions, the two men ran the short distance along a disused road from the slipway to where it met its stone wall-lined replacement leading to the west end of the bridge, then a further hundred yards along the road towards Kyle of Lochalsh. They stopped close to the entrance to the grounds of what a sign on the frontage of the building said was the Loch Duich Hotel. Monique hadn't noticed the hotel when they'd driven along the road earlier and hoped there wouldn't be too many witnesses to what she expected to happen next.

Monique and Anthony followed the men but stopped where the road formed a sharp corner, not far from the end of the bridge. They waited for two Royal Navy lorries that had just driven over the bridge in the direction of Kyle of Lochalsh to pass before crossing the road to the inside of the corner.

Monique watched the lorries until they disappeared out of sight beyond the two RAF Regiment airmen and the hotel.

'In one sense this is better than I'd hoped for,' said Monique. 'Our men will try to flag down the green car. If the driver stops, fine. If she doesn't, then we are the fallback. You heard me tell those men not to fire. I don't want them firing in our direction or in the direction of the village and I don't want them involved in the shooting of a Soviet agent.'

'That seems wise,' said Anthony. 'I take it we will be less restrained if she doesn't stop? Presumably, that was why you told the men to take cover if the car went past them?'

'Yes. That's also why this spot works so well. I'd forgotten this corner in the road. It will inevitably slow down anyone coming towards the bridge in a hurry. If we stand here on the inside of the corner between the road and the wall, we'll be on the wrong side of the car for the driver, but the angles mean we'll be able to fire without endangering the two men or anyone in the village or the hotel.'

'You're determined to make sure she doesn't get past, aren't you Monique?'

'Oh, yes. One way or another. I'm sorry I can't explain to you why, Anthony. You'll just have to trust me.'

It seemed very quiet while they waited.

'What if the woman has gone to ground somewhere back towards Kyle of Lochalsh?' asked Anthony. 'I'd have thought she should have been here by now.'

'I agree. If she has gone to ground, we'll just have to find her.'

'Hang on,' said Anthony. 'I can hear a car coming.'

Monique watched as a dark green car came into view, travelling at speed.

'Are you sure this is the same car?' asked Anthony.

'It's the right type and colour but it was too far to read the registration plate. I'm sure I'll recognise the woman, though. Don't fire until I do.'

Monique took a deep breath as the two men she'd positioned stepped out into the road, one from either side, and raised their arms to signal the car to halt. It didn't change speed and the two men jumped back. One then ducked out of sight behind a wall forming part of the hotel entrance and the other ran over to join him.

Monique thought the driver was going to lose control of the car as it approached the corner but she braked hard and was able to slow down enough to start her turn. For a split-second Monique caught the eye of the blonde woman driving the car and then she fired, her bullets ripping into the bonnet and windscreen of the car and then its side. She heard Anthony fire as the car was alongside them and saw his bullets create a line of holes along both the front and back doors of the side nearest them.

The car never completed the turn, instead smashing at an angle into the stone wall on the far side of the road and coming to an instant halt.

'Last time I was involved in something like this, the car caught fire,' said Monique. 'We have to get Helen's original copy of *Bradshaw's Guide*, and quickly.'

She ran round the back of the car to the driver's side and saw that the front door was hanging open. The very obviously dead body of the blonde woman was lying with her lower legs still in the footwell while the rest of her body had collapsed out onto the verge. Blood was pouring from wounds in her head and torso.

'Bloody hell, you don't mess about, do you, ma'am?'

Monique realised the two RAF Regiment airmen had run back to the corner. One was standing on the verge and looking at the woman's body, apparently speechless, while the man who had spoken was looking at Monique with a shocked and angry expression.

'Can you go back to the launch, please, and ask the flight sergeant to wait for us?'

'You can't just leave her there like that, ma'am.'

'I'm hoping we don't have to. There should be a police car following her. There it is now.' Monique pointed back along the road. 'Now just return to the launch as I asked, please.'

Monique had been aware of Anthony opening the doors on the passenger side of the car and now he appeared round the back of it as she was gingerly checking the driver's pockets.

'There was a shoulder bag in the footwell on the passenger side,' he said. 'I couldn't see anything else in the car and the boot is full of what seems to be wireless equipment. He opened the bag and peered inside. There's a copy of *Bradshaw's Guide* in here. There are also some maps and other documents. Plus a couple of items of clothing.'

'Leave everything where it is. We'll take the bag and study the contents later. Give it to me, it doesn't match your uniform.' Monique flipped open a folded card she'd taken out of a wallet that she'd found in the driver's inside coat pocket, though only after she'd moved the woman's shoulder holster out of the way. 'Anthony, I'd like you to meet Helena Berdyaev. This identity card says that she was a first secretary at the Soviet embassy in London. I've never met her, but I have come across her work before and can tell you that she was believed to be quite senior in the NKVD's British operations.'

The police car stopped a few yards back along the road. Monique saw Inspector Grant get out of the driver's side while a young constable emerged from the passenger's side. She put the bag over her shoulder and slipped the wallet into her pocket, remembering too late that it had blood on it.

'You seem to have a gun in your hand every time we meet, Madame Dubois,' said the inspector. 'Only this time you've obviously used it.'

'I had men from the RAF Regiment try to wave her down, back by the hotel, and they had to jump clear to avoid being run down. We had no choice but to open fire to stop her. As a result, we have retrieved evidence which I believe may be of great importance to national security.'

'Is that what's in the shoulder bag?' asked the inspector.

'That's right.'

'Have you found anything that says who she was?'

At that moment the young constable came round to the driver's side of the car, saw the dead woman, and was immediately sick on the verge.

Monique pulled the wallet out of her pocket and held out the identity card for the inspector to look at.

'I assume you're going to keep that, too,' he said. He took out a notebook and copied the details down. 'The Soviet embassy isn't going to be very happy that you've shot one of its first secretaries.'

'She was with the NKVD, and they'll just have to learn to live with what's happened to her,' said Monique.

'I hope you don't mind my saying so, but this looks more like an Al Capone gangland execution than an intelligence operation, Madame Dubois. You're even carrying a proper Tommy gun.'

'Perhaps if you'd been a little less far behind her, we might have had more options,' said Monique.

The inspector smiled. 'That's fair comment, Madame Dubois. I don't think she was expecting to be pursued and she was going at a modest speed when we caught up with her, just before she reached Balmacara. She put her foot down hard then. We stayed with her until a mile or so back when she just about squeezed past two Royal Navy lorries coming the other way. We were less fortunate. They seemed disinclined to pull over for a police car and we had to reverse to a passing place to let them by.'

'These roads weren't designed for pursuit,' said Monique.

'I don't think they were designed at all, they just happened over time.' The inspector took a deep breath. 'Very well. I can't say this sits at all comfortably with me, but I suppose you want me to get someone to clean this mess up and explain what's happened here in a way that doesn't raise too many questions?'

'That would be helpful, inspector.'

'As you wish. I'll phone for assistance from the hotel. If

you are finished here, Madame Dubois, I suggest you get on your way. I assume that the boat over there is waiting for you?'

CHAPTER THIRTY-ONE

Little was said in the launch on the way back to Kyle of Lochalsh. The two men who had been ashore stayed out of the way, presumably in the cabin. Monique had the sense that the account of the killing of the Soviet agent that they'd given to the launch's crew before she reboarded the vessel didn't show her in a very good light.

As they arrived back at the pier, Monique saw that the *Lochness* had left and was making its way past the island lighthouse she'd noticed earlier.

Group Captain Erickson had, as Monique suggested, commandeered the station master's office. There was an RAF Regiment airman with a rifle standing outside the door. and the group captain was sitting drinking tea and eating biscuits with Helen when Monique and Anthony went in.

'Did you get to the bridge in time?' he asked.

'Yes, thank you. Please pass on my thanks to the crew of the launch and the men who came ashore with us. As they will doubtless tell you, it didn't end at all well and I think they may be a little shocked. We did secure Helen's original copy of *Bradshaw's Guide*, however, which I think may be what matters most. I will keep that. If Helen is returning to London by train after Easter, she can use the replacement provided by the woman who had been following her to plan the route.'

'What happens now?'

'First, I need Helen to give me a detailed account of everything that's happened to her on her journey so far. Captain Darlington and I will both take notes. Once we've done that and she's answered any supplementary questions we might have, you are free to do as you see fit. I imagine that will mean she can look forward to a ride in a high-speed RAF launch to Stornoway as the steamer's now left.'

Helen started quite falteringly but grew in confidence as she told her tale.

'What I don't understand,' said Helen, after she'd finished, 'is how one of the men got onto the train that brought me here from Dingwall. Had he followed me in Inverness and Dingwall?'

'I don't think so,' said Monique. 'We may never know, but my best guess is that he and the woman arrived in the area with some time to spare. Perhaps she dropped him at the station the woman and children got off at, Plockton, with instructions to board the train and try to locate you before it arrived in Kyle of Lochalsh.

'I think that we probably had this wrong all along. You should know that the people chasing you were Soviet agents. We assumed they were trying to kidnap you because your mother does secret work for the government and they wanted to blackmail her. As I said on the quayside earlier, I now think that this whole thing has really been about their getting their hands on your copy of *Bradshaw's Guide*, preferably in a way that meant you wouldn't notice the exchange.

'Helen, can you think of any opportunities they might have had to make the swap before they ran out of options and knocked you over on the quayside? I'm not sure why they waited so long.'

Helen sat back in her chair. 'As I've told you, the first time I really got worried was when someone tried the door of my compartment on the sleeper train from Kings Cross to Edinburgh. But they wouldn't have been able to swap the books without me knowing.'

'What if they'd knocked you out?' asked Anthony. 'If they'd taken your purse and your watch it would have looked like a robbery, and they'd have been able to swap the books. And that was before your copy got creased and marked, so you wouldn't have been able to tell.'

'Thank you, Anthony,' said Monique. 'That does make sense.'

'There was another opportunity after I arrived at Easter Crimond,' said Helen. 'My things were in the cottage and anyone watching must have known that I didn't have them with me when I went to the farmhouse. Why didn't they just sneak into the cottage and make the exchange while I was with everyone else, eating and talking?'

'You'd sent two of them off on the wrong train earlier that day,' said Anthony. 'Is it possible they'd not caught up? If the woman had the book and hadn't got to Easter Crimond by then, they wouldn't have been able to make the swap. Perhaps the woman and the other man only arrived later.'

'Yes, I see that,' said Helen. 'I didn't ask before, is Angus all right?'

'I'm sorry,' said Monique. 'He was killed by the Soviets. I don't know for sure, but I think he must have met them when he was returning to the farm from the travellers' camp. It's hardly any consolation but your Uncle George, Aunt Jemima and Ben are all safe, though they were locked in their pantry by the Soviets.'

'It's my fault Angus is dead, isn't it?' asked Helen, with tears in her eyes.

'No, it's not. He was a brave man who wanted to help. The only people to blame for what happened to him are the people who killed him.'

'What will happen to them?'

'The Soviets are our allies, in name at least. The police caught one man at Coupar Angus railway station. He'd crashed his car and broken his wrist but claimed diplomatic immunity and will not be punished for what he did. I imagine that the man arrested on the quayside earlier is already claiming diplomatic immunity and demanding that he be allowed to telephone the Soviet embassy.'

'What about the woman?' asked Helen. 'You told Daddy that when you went off in the launch it didn't end well. What did you mean?'

'She's dead. She refused to stop her car when some of your father's men instructed her to. I felt we had to do whatever was necessary to stop her getting away with the stolen copy of *Bradshaw's Guide*, so I shot her.'

'We both shot her,' said Anthony. 'It wasn't something Monique did on her own. Sometimes the world can be very unpleasant, and sometimes you need to do things you'd prefer not to do.'

'Thank you,' said Helen. 'I'm grateful to both of you. At least someone has paid for what happened to Angus.'

Monique saw a look of shock pass over the group captain's face. Mainly, though she was struck by the echoes in what Helen said of the reactions she'd heard, including her own, to Bill Douglas's murder. She thought it best not to tell Helen that the woman they'd killed near the end of the bridge at Dornie had been called Helena.

Monique turned to the group captain. 'There was something I wanted to discuss with Helen privately, Tom. Would you and Anthony mind waiting outside?'

'As you wish, Monique.' The group captain stood up and made for the door of the station master's office. Anthony followed without comment.

After Anthony had closed the door, Monique moved her chair a little closer to Helen. 'I wanted to talk to you on your own because I'd like you to tell me why you've been so reluctant to involve the police.'

'I'm sorry, I can't tell you.'

'Come on Helen. After all that you've been through over the past couple of days, whatever happened in London must pale into insignificance. Besides, I may be able to help.'

Monique held Helen's gaze for what seemed a long time before the young woman looked down.

'Very well. I'm studying to become a doctor at the London School of Medicine for Women, which is on Hunter Street in Bloomsbury. I live in a flat in a run-down terraced house on St Chad's Street, close to where it meets Argyle Square. It's got two bedrooms and I'm sharing with three other female medical students at the school. If you're not familiar with the area, then you need to know that Argyle Square has a reputation as a centre for prostitution.

'Three doors along from us is a large old pub, *The Holy Well,* which has a hotel on its upper floors. Only it's not a hotel, it's a brothel. Last Saturday night I was in the flat on my own, studying. There was a banging on the door and Molly, one of the two young women who live in a flat on the floor below us asked if I could come and help.

'I've known they were both prostitutes since not long after we moved into the flat, but they don't cause any trouble and it's a case of "live and let live". Molly wanted me to go with her to *The Holy Well* because, she said, a girl had been injured and the

307

doctor they usually rely on couldn't be reached. She'd come to our flat for help because she knew we were medical students.

'When I got there, I found a girl called Amanda had been beaten up by a client and was extremely distressed, as you'd expect. As far as I could tell she had no broken bones, but she was already developing black eyes and other bruising. She didn't want to be taken to hospital, and the woman who was in charge didn't want that either. There wasn't much I could do other than calm Amanda down and tell her to rest.

'As I was checking her over, a man came in. He was wearing a civilian overcoat but the woman running the place referred to him as "inspector". I'd say he was well into his forties. He asked a few questions about the man who had attacked the girl, and then asked who I was and why I was there. After he left, Amanda told me that he was a local police inspector who looked after the establishment. That apparently meant he offered protection from the law and, to some extent, from incidents like the one that had taken place. In return, he had the run of the place and had a particular taste for sex with the younger girls who worked there. She said he was a nasty piece of work – not the exact words she used - and that I should watch out for him.

'Next morning, Sunday, I was walking to get a bottle of milk from the corner shop when the same man, now wearing a police inspector's uniform, stopped me in the street. He told me that what I'd done at *The Holy Well* the previous night amounted to practising medicine without a licence. He knew I was a student at the London School of Medicine for Women and said that if he told them what I'd done I would be expelled. On the other hand, he said, if I agreed to sleep with him, then he could make the problem disappear completely.

'I hope I didn't show him how afraid and disgusted I was. I'm not exactly an innocent, but he's easily old enough to be my father and I found the idea utterly abhorrent. I told him I was going to be away from London over Easter, which was true as the arrangements had been in place for some time. He gave me a horrible smirk and said that he'd be in touch when I got back and was very much looking forward to seeing more of me.'

'And that's why you were so reluctant to involve the police when you realised you were being followed?' asked Monique.

'That's right. I know it made no sense, logically, but when I saw a policeman at Princes Street Station, all I could think was that Inspector Vincent was intending to rape me. I just wanted nothing to do with any of them.'

'Is that his name? Can you tell me anything else about him?'

'Yes, Inspector Vincent. He said I should call him "Theo" when he stopped me in the street. He's based at the police station in Grays Inn Road.'

'Look, Helen, I need you to trust me. You must understand that he has far, far more to lose than you if the story of his encounter with you at *The Holy Well* gets round. Besides, was what you did actually practising medicine anyway? It sounded to me like you were merely providing simple first aid and comfort.'

'That's what I've been thinking. But it doesn't help. He has the power and the uniform. Who's going to believe me?'

Monique smiled. 'I do, which is a good start. Don't worry about it and don't let it spoil your Easter. I promise you that Inspector Vincent won't bother you again.'

Monique again held Helen's gaze. Finally, the younger

woman smiled. 'Has anyone told you that you can be quite scary? I'm awfully pleased that you're on my side.'

When Monique left the station master's office, Group Captain Erickson was standing talking to Anthony on the platform. He turned to face her. 'I didn't want to ask this in front of Helen, but is my wife in trouble?'

'I don't know,' said Monique, 'but I hope not. I believe that the copy of *Bradshaw's Guide* she gave to Helen was somehow intended to be a means of providing information to the Soviets about the work she's doing. But think about this, would any mother knowingly expose her daughter to the dangers that Helen has faced?'

'No. Elizabeth is very unconventional in many ways. But she loves Helen and would never for an instant do anything to harm her.'

'In that case, I don't think she's in serious trouble, though I am sure she will need to answer some difficult questions.'

'What should I tell her if we talk?'

'Just that Helen is safe. Don't go into any details about what's happened and please don't mention the *Bradshaw's Guide*. And you should assume that any phone conversations the two of you have for some time to come will be monitored. I think that's all I can tell you.'

'Speaking of Helen being safe,' said Erickson, 'I'll telephone Jemima and George Moncrieff to let them know. Can I say anything to them about what's behind all this? They've had their lives turned upside down and their friend has been killed and I feel a responsibility for that.'

'None of this is your fault, any more than it's Helen's,' said Monique, 'and the less you say the better. I believe that the plan is for the Moncrieffs to stay with George's brother while things get sorted out at their farm. You would probably be best talking to Inspector Kennedy at Blairgowrie police station to find out how to make contact directly and to let him know your daughter is safe.'

'Thank you again, Monique. Bob is a lucky man.'

'What do you mean?'

'It's a small world. Bob's name came up in a conversation I had recently with an old friend. He told me that Bob had become engaged to a beautiful and mysterious lady who was on loan to MI11 from MI5. I'm guessing that's you. Congratulations.'

'Er, thank you.'

The group captain went back into the station master's office. Monique saw that Anthony had a broad grin on his face.

'What's so funny?' she asked.

'I'm not sure I've ever seen you embarrassed before, Monique.'

'Let's just be on our way. I'm hoping we can be back at Stirling Castle before it gets dark. It feels like it's been an enormously long day already.'

'I assume your chat with Helen was about her aversion to the police?'

'Yes, I'll tell you all about it on the way back.'

'Hang on, Monique,' said Anthony. 'Before we set off, there's one other thing that's particularly been troubling me.'

Monique had been waiting for him to ask about their shooting of Helena Berdyaev and her heart sank because she knew there was only a limited amount that she could tell him. 'What's that?' she asked.

'How did the Soviets know Helen was heading for Kyle of Lochalsh?' asked Anthony. 'They had enough information to know she was probably going to Inverness. But it was only because we visited Blair Atholl, saw the railway map on the wall and talked to the station master that we worked it out. I can't believe that Soviet agents based in London know Scotland any better than we do.'

Monique stopped on the station platform and looked around. There were some people about, but far fewer than earlier. The train Helen had arrived on was still standing at the platform, though the engine had been moved to the other end of it and turned round. She'd seen a sign that said the train would be leaving for Dingwall at 5.30 p.m. which perhaps explained why the station was still so relatively quiet.

'That had passed me by,' said Monique, 'but it is a very good question. Let's sit on this bench over here and see if there's any enlightenment to be had in Helena Berdyaev's shoulder bag.'

Monique and Anthony sat down, with the bag on the wooden bench between them.

Monique opened it up and looked inside. 'We should handle the *Bradshaw's Guide* as little as possible, but there is one thing I must check.' She took the book out of the bag and leafed through it. 'Good. There's an arrow in pencil beneath the 12.30 p.m. train from Dingwall to Kyle of Lochalsh on table 748. I wanted to be certain this really was Helen's copy.' She returned it to the bag. 'As you said at the bridge, there are maps and other documents in here too.'

Monique drew out a folded map. 'Oh, look, here's a copy of our old friend the *Automobile Association Touring Map of Scotland*. It seems identical to the one we borrowed in Blair Atholl, though in much better condition. At least we know how they navigated. The other map in the bag is a folded London &

North Eastern Railway map. Perhaps they picked it up at King's Cross Station before following Helen Erickson onto the sleeper train to Edinburgh? I'm not sure that answers your question, though, because I don't think LNER operates the routes that Helen has been using in Scotland.'

Anthony took the map from her and opened it up. 'Maybe not, but other operators' lines do appear, especially in Scotland. Scotland is tucked away in the top-left corner of the map and, in some ways, the smaller scale and lack of detail might have helped the Soviets. Looking at this, if you knew Helen had caught a northbound train from Dunkeld and Birnam and was probably heading for Inverness, her onward options are rather limited, essentially to Wick and Thurso or Kyle of Lochalsh. And the steamer routes are also shown, including the one from Kyle of Lochalsh to Stornoway. I'm sure the Soviets would have known Group Captain Erickson is based at RAF Stornoway and they'd have been able to work out as quickly as we did where Helen was intending to go.'

'But we needed help from the station master at Blair Atholl to work out how they might get there by train.'

'And Helena Berdyaev, like Helen Erickson, had a copy of *Bradshaw's Guide* available to her, the one she then swapped for this one. She could have looked up the services, just as Helen did, though perhaps more carefully as her copy remained pristine.'

'I'm wondering if that means the Soviets were behind us rather than ahead of us this morning,' said Monique. 'If Helena Berdyaev had been in a hotel in Dunkeld, and contactable by telephone, then they could have set off in pursuit not long after Helen's train left Dunkeld and Birnam. That's what we assumed in thinking they would meet her train in Inverness.

'But what if the woman was further away? We know she'd changed cars. What if she'd taken over the task of watching Coupar Angus railway station after Viktor Ivanov was arrested? What if she'd been somewhere else or not easily contactable by phone or out of range by radio? Perhaps the time they had left when they were able to meet up meant that they made the same decision we did and headed straight for Kyle of Lochalsh. They couldn't have been too far behind us if they had time to divert to Plockton so the man could meet the train. Perhaps they overtook us when we stopped at Achnacarry Castle?'

'Would they have been allowed to enter the protected area?' asked Anthony.

'We know they would have passed through two checkpoints on the way, as we did,' said Monique. 'Clearly, diplomatic papers issued by the embassy of an allied nation were sufficient to ensure they were allowed through. It's a shame I never thought to ask the men at those checkpoints if they'd already seen my blonde sister.' She saw the puzzled expression on Anthony's face and smiled. 'Uncle Peter at the travellers' camp said Helena Berdyaev and I could almost be sisters, apart from the colour of our hair. Anyway, the day's not getting any younger, let's move.'

It wasn't far to where they'd left the car.

'You can drive, Anthony. I think it should be my turn to admire the scenery.' Monique walked towards the left-hand side of the car while Anthony made his way round between the wall near the foot of the sloping access road to the station and the vehicle.

'Anthony, is there meant to be a trail of liquid on the ground behind the back wheel? That's a rhetorical question, by the way.'

Monique saw him duck down.

'Damn! It's the same on this side. Someone's cut the brake hose leading to the back wheel.'

Monique saw him move forwards.

'It's the same with the front wheel.' He came round to her side of the car and ducked down at its front and back. 'The brake hoses leading to all four wheels have been cut.'

'So why hasn't the car rolled back down the slope into the one behind it? And no, that's not a rhetorical question.'

'Because the handbrake uses a separate system to operate the drums on the rear wheels and that must still be working.'

Monique saw Anthony examine the vehicle behind theirs. Then he walked up the slope and looked at the one in front.

'It's just us, I'm afraid. It's fixable, but not quickly. I think we now know what Helena Berdyaev was doing after she dropped her colleague off at Plockton railway station and before two of the group captain's men took up guard here. I'm just not sure how she knew which car was ours, or who we were for that matter. You said you'd never met her, Monique.'

'I hadn't. But remember that last night you talked about a dark blue van picking up the second man after the last train left Dunkeld and Birnam station. You said you thought you'd also seen it earlier, when we first went to Birnam. I think I remember seeing it too but didn't pay it any attention. If we assume Helena Berdyaev was the driver of the van, then she'd have had a chance to see both of us when we were there and identify our car. She would also have seen you, perhaps more clearly, after the 7.52 p.m. train left.'

Monique paused to collect her thoughts before continuing. 'Let's assume she dropped her colleague off at Plockton, then drove here to Kyle of Lochalsh and parked on Harbour Street before walking to the station, where she kept watch. Depending on the timing, she could have seen us arrive, and where we parked. What better way of ensuring we'd not be able to follow her after she got Helen's copy of the guide? Would cutting the brake hoses have taken much effort?'

'No, a couple of minutes and a sharp knife would have done it. If you hadn't noticed the brake fluid on the ground, we'd probably have got to the junction at the top of the slope before discovering we couldn't stop and crashing.'

Monique laughed. 'It looks like Helena is still trying to take her revenge, even from beyond the grave.'

CHAPTER THIRTY-TWO

'Hello, Bob.'

'Where are you, Monique? Is Helen safe?'

'Yes, she is. Her father is taking her to Stornoway. The opposition have been dealt with and I believe I know what they were trying to achieve. I'm calling you from the headquarters at HMS *Trelawney,* which is a naval base here in Kyle of Lochalsh, but I can't go into any details on the telephone.'

'Are you coming back?'

'Yes, the navy are just organising a car and a driver for us. I still hope we can get back to Stirling Castle before it gets dark, but that may not be possible. If we have to finish the journey in the blackout then we may be quite late.'

'What's happened to your car?'

'I'll explain when we get back. How's it going at your end?'

'Not well. We've interviewed nearly everyone who was in or around the Great Hall at the time of the murder. We're struggling to cross-reference everything we've got. The only real development is that although the man I suspected remains missing, presumably hiding in Edinburgh because he knows we want to talk to him, I have established that he has a firm alibi for the time we are interested in. That leaves us without any suspects at all and without any clear idea of what to do next.'

'I'm sure something will turn up.'

'Perhaps. I'm looking forward to seeing you again, Monique.'

'Likewise, Bob.'

'I hope you've done nothing to make your ribs any worse

since I last saw you.'

Monique laughed. 'Don't get your hopes up too much, Bob. See you later.'

*

Monique was surprised to see an attractive young woman standing beside the naval staff car that was waiting for them outside the headquarters building at HMS *Trelawney*. Then she mentally ticked herself off for making the same assumption about women drivers that Anthony had.

The woman opened the boot and Monique placed her overnight case in it, beside the one already in there. She'd put Helena Berdyaev's shoulder bag in her overnight bag so it would be out of sight and relatively secure. They'd wrapped their Sten guns in overcoats to make them less obvious, but Monique's unravelled as she placed it behind the cases, and she saw the look of surprise on the driver's face as the submachine gun rolled out.

She watched as the young woman very obviously sized Anthony up while he was putting his bag and rather better concealed Sten gun in the boot. As it was wrapped in the same way as Monique's, it was perhaps a little obvious anyway. It might have been wishful thinking on her part, but Monique got the sense that Anthony shared a look with the young woman as she closed the boot. As his back was to her, Monique couldn't be sure.

Monique got into the back of the car and Anthony followed. 'Hello. I'm Monique Dubois and this is Captain Anthony Darlington. Have they told you that we need to go to Stirling Castle?'

'Yes, ma'am, they have. I've had time to pack an overnight bag. I'm Leading Wren Ruth Woodburn. Please call me Ruth.'

The young woman had short dark hair under her uniform cap and Monique smiled at her when she looked round. She seemed to be in her mid-twenties.

'Call me Monique, please.'

'Yes ma'am, Monique I mean.'

After they set off, Monique rapidly formed the impression that Leading Wren Woodburn was rather more competent than either Anthony or Monique herself when it came to driving on single-track roads. The car also felt more powerful than the one that they'd had to leave in the care of the Royal Navy.

'You're lucky you didn't want to travel any earlier,' said Ruth. 'I heard the road was blocked at Dornie, not far ahead of us, and they've not long cleared it.'

Monique asked Ruth to slow down as they approached the west end of the bridge at Dornie, then to pull over and stop at the end of the stub of old road leading to the ferry slipway. The dark green saloon car had been pushed a little way along the disused road and covered with a tarpaulin. She imagined the police intended to remove it when they could.

She got out and walked over to the car. The tarpaulin had been well tied down over much of the car and she saw no point disturbing it. Anything significant that she and Anthony had missed in the frantic few moments after it had crashed would have been removed by the police, as they had removed Helena Berdyaev's body.

As she walked back to the navy staff car, Monique saw that the stone wall on the outside of the corner had stood up well to having a car driven into it.

'Thank you, Ruth. We can press on now. I've not got any

other plans for stops or excursions.'

'Of course, Monique.'

Ruth pulled away and resumed her impressive rate of progress.

'Can I ask you a question, Monique?'

'Of course, though I don't promise you an answer.'

'That car we stopped at back there, the one that had hit the wall. Was it yours? I was just wondering why you needed to be driven to Stirling Castle.'

'No, we did have a car, but it had brake problems in Kyle of Lochalsh and would have taken too long to repair.'

'I couldn't help noticing that the tarpaulin they'd put over the car at the bridge left part of one door uncovered and it looked like it had bullet holes in it. I probably shouldn't ask, but were they connected with the Sten gun I saw you putting in the boot?'

'If I tell you, will you keep it to yourself?' asked Monique.

'Yes, I promise.'

'The simple and truthful answer is that the damage to the car had nothing to do with the gun you saw me putting in the boot. Or the other one you perhaps noticed Captain Darlington also put in there. There's another answer which is rather more complicated, and I'd prefer not to give you. It might help if you know that Captain Darlington and I are with a branch of military intelligence. I imagine it will be common knowledge in the village and at HMS *Trelawney* by the time you get back anyway, but that car was being driven by a Soviet agent, a woman.'

Monique saw Anthony raise his eyebrows. He obviously thought she was telling Ruth too much.

'Gosh, how exciting! Life at HMS *Trelawney* is deathly

boring most of the time.'

Monique leaned forwards in her seat. 'I was talking to some Wren officers based in Orkney last November who were telling me that at one time there were 600 men stationed in Orkney for every woman and that it had once been the best place on Earth to catch your man. They said more Wrens had arrived since then, but it was still a happy hunting ground.'

'The numbers are certainly in our favour in Kyle of Lochalsh,' said Ruth. 'But the choice is a bit limited in other ways. It would be fair to say that the Royal Navy doesn't go out of its way to post the cream of its recruits to HMS *Trelawney*. I know that doesn't reflect well on me, either, but I like to think I'm the exception that proves the rule. What's this idiot doing? Shit!'

Monique was thrown forwards against the back of the front passenger seat as Ruth braked hard and brought the car to a standstill. Then she wound down her window and swore, fluently and creatively, at the driver of a civilian lorry who had driven through a passing place he should have stopped in. Ruth edged the car forwards and forced him to reverse, then swore at him again as she passed.

'It makes you wonder how some of these people survive to get this far. I've seen that idiot before. He's local and really should know how to drive these roads.'

Monique settled back in her seat as Ruth regained speed. 'There must be social events and that sort of thing laid on?'

'There are, Monique. But the male naval ratings are usually about as interesting as cabbages and it's strictly "hands off" as far as the officers are concerned.'

'You don't have anyone special just now?' asked Monique.

'No, I don't. Do you? You're not wearing a wedding ring.'

Monique heard Anthony stifle a laugh.

'I'm engaged,' she said. 'But I don't wear my ring while I'm working.'

'Who are you engaged to?'

'He's a group captain in the RAF who also works in military intelligence. We first met properly last year.' Monique felt the need to change the subject. 'Surely Kyle of Lochalsh can't be as boring as you say? It looked lovely earlier.'

'Looks can be deceptive, Monique. I've heard it said that the last time anything interesting happened in Kyle of Lochalsh was in November 1940.'

'What happened then?' asked Monique.

'It was well before my time there, but a minelaying ship called HMS *Port Napier* dragged its anchor in a gale and ran aground in Loch Alsh. They got it afloat again but then a fire broke out while they were refuelling it. It was full of mines, and they evacuated Kyle of Lochalsh because of the danger the ship posed. It eventually blew up and sank, though sadly it failed to take the village with it.'

'Can I ask you a personal question, Ruth?' said Anthony.

'That rather depends on what it is, sir.'

Monique could see Ruth was smiling. She thought that Anthony, sitting behind the driver, probably couldn't.

'I'll be blunt,' said Anthony. 'You sound like you went to a good school. Why are you driving a car for the Royal Navy in Kyle of Lochalsh?'

'That's a long story, sir. But you're right. My parents have never been short of a bob or two and I went to Roedean School in Sussex. Afterwards, I was supposed to conform to their expectations and attend society functions and then find and marry an earl's oldest son. You know the sort of thing.'

'I never quite moved in those circles myself, but I'm guessing you chose not to conform to their expectations?'

'That's right, sir. My father's younger brother, never the most highly regarded member of the family, was very keen on motorcycle racing before the war. To my parent's absolute horror, I also got involved in building, repairing, and racing motorcycles. It pretty much took over my life.

'When the war came along, I wanted to do my bit and joined the Wrens. My parents insisted I apply to become an officer, but I wanted to do something practical. Partly because of that, and partly to spite my parents, I applied to become a motor mechanic and driver. I had a series of postings to naval bases in southern England which I thoroughly enjoyed, and which allowed me to develop my skills and enjoy the sort of social life Monique talked about in Orkney.

'Getting posted to HMS *Trelawney* late last year was a bit of a shock, to be honest, especially as it happened at the start of winter. I'd never been to Scotland before, and I love driving around the country. But I've already told you what I think of Kyle of Lochalsh. It's got so desperate that I'm even thinking of applying for a commission.'

'Why don't you?' asked Anthony.

'The thought of how much it would please my parents has held me back so far. Possibly not for much longer, though.'

The conversation lapsed and without the need to navigate or drive, Monique simply sat back and watched the scenery pass in what was now beautiful evening light.

*

'Monique! We're nearly there.'

Monique recognised Anthony's voice and, as she opened her eyes, she realised that they were in Stirling. She wasn't sure how long she'd slept but saw that it was getting dark.

'Thanks for completing the trip in daylight, Ruth,' she said. 'I wasn't looking forward to doing any of that in the blackout.'

'No, I'm grateful for that, too,' said Ruth. 'It always takes such an age to get anywhere in the dark. I'll need somewhere to put my head down tonight before driving back tomorrow.'

'I'll make sure we find you somewhere suitable and something to eat, even though it's late. I don't know what the female accommodation options might be. I think I've only seen one woman based at Stirling Castle, and she's the garrison commander's secretary, Miriam.'

She turned to Anthony. 'We also need to find Bob when we get back and give him a report. I suspect there might be some repercussions after today that we need to warn him about.'

Monique saw Anthony raise his finger to his lips and realised he was right.

Ruth must have seen him too, in her mirror. 'Don't worry, sir. You get very good at not listening to what's being said in the back of the car when you're doing this job. That's a lie really, because what you get good at is pretending that you're not listening or simply not there at all. I drove an admiral and a captain from Kyle of Lochalsh to Inverness a couple of months ago and could have told the Germans everything they needed to know about the positions of our ships in the Atlantic afterwards. I didn't of course.'

Monique leaned forwards. 'Ruth, you need to drive up to the top of this open area in front of the castle, where you can see the main gateway.'

She and Anthony showed their passes and Ruth drove on

324

after the guard waved them through.

'You turn right beyond the gateway through a stone arch. It's very tight,' said Monique. 'Then you follow the road up through another narrow stone arch. Beyond that, you turn right and find somewhere to park.'

'Will here do, Monique?'

'Perfect. Now I know I promised you food and a bed, but I need the two of you to stay here in the car while I go and find Bob.'

'I need the toilet, Monique,' said Ruth.

'I have to admit that I do too,' said Anthony.

'You know where they are, Anthony. Take Ruth into the building our office is in, then I'd like you both to come back to the car.'

Monique followed Anthony and Ruth into the building and went up the stairs. She pushed open the door of the office that MI11 had been loaned and stepped in. Bob and Michael Dixon looked up at her from their seats at the table, which was covered in sheets of paper. Sergeants Gilbert Potter and Alan MacMillan were standing to one side, looking at a blackboard that had been fixed to the wall since she was last in the room.

Bob stood up, looking very weary. 'Monique, you can't believe how pleased I am to see you.'

They embraced.

'I'm pleased to see you, too, Bob, but there's something we need to do now, before it gets properly dark. Can the four of you follow me outside?'

Monique led the way and found Ruth standing by the car.

'Can I introduce Leading Wren Ruth Woodburn to you all? Ruth, these two gentlemen are Group Captain Robert Sutherland and Lieutenant Commander Michael Dixon, both with Military Intelligence, Section 11. I'd also like to introduce Sergeant Gilbert Potter, who is with MI11 and Sergeant Alan MacMillan who is based at the Argyll and Sutherland Highlanders' depot here at Stirling Castle and is assisting us.'

Monique looked round. 'Good, here's Anthony. Right, I want to play a little game. Ruth, can you get into the driver's seat, please? Bob, I'd like you to get into the front passenger seat. Michael, can you get in the back, it doesn't matter which side. Can the rest of you stand here? We'll leave the doors on this side of the car open so you can all see and hear what we're doing. Now I'll get in the back as well.'

As Monique got into the car, she saw two soldiers walk past, obviously intrigued by what was going on.

There was silence in the car for a moment.

It was Monique who broke it. 'While we were driving up to the castle, Ruth said something that got me thinking. I want you all to imagine that we are in a car travelling from RAF Grangemouth to Stirling Castle. I'm Mrs Edith Burns, and I work in the Foreign Office. I'm anxious to get to the castle because my plane has been delayed and I'm worried I'm going to be late for dinner. I abhor being late.'

Bob laughed. 'Sorry, Monique, I know this is serious but that was a wonderful impression of Mrs Burns.'

Monique smiled. 'Michael, I'm afraid I've cast you as Bill Douglas, rapist and all-round utter bastard. You are spending the journey telling Mrs Burns about your family history in Castle Douglas in Galloway, your connections with the Black Douglas family and how the man you believe to be the brother of an ancestor of yours, the 8th Earl of Douglas, was murdered by King James II in Stirling Castle. You think you can upset Mrs Burns by going into the gruesome detail of the killing, so that's what you do. You conclude by telling her that if the dinner finishes before it gets dark you will visit the Douglas Gardens for the first time since you were 15 to look again at where the 8th Earl's body ended up after it had been thrown out of a window.

'Your turn, Bob. You are Alastair Warner. You hate Bill Douglas because he tried to ruin your career in SIS and nearly succeeded. You've spent the journey from London, via an unwanted stop in Carlisle because of an aircraft problem, trying to avoid the man and are now sitting in the front of the car and pretending to read a newspaper so you don't have to interact with him. Afterwards, you will say you tried not to take any notice of what he was saying, but it's obvious you've heard it all.

'I've not been closely involved in this investigation since yesterday afternoon, but I know that the thing that's stumped us is working out who might have known that Bill Douglas was planning to go to the Douglas Gardens, and who also knew his version of the story of the killing of the 8th Earl of Douglas. You've ruled out everyone who knew and that's left you high and dry.'

'That's a fair summary,' said Bob.

'Think about what you're missing Bob. Someone else knew all the details of the death of the 8th Earl, knew about Bill Douglas's family background and knew about his plan to visit the gardens after dinner.'

'Who was that?' asked Bob.

'Me, sir,' said Ruth.

'Good God!' said Bob. 'How could I have overlooked something so obvious? The driver of the car! Michael, Anthony, can you get hold of the orderly officer? Take Gilbert with you.

We need to know who was driving the car that brought Bill Douglas, Edith Burns and Alastair Warner from RAF Grangemouth on Tuesday. It ought to be memorable because the plane was late arriving and it would have been the last run of the day. I don't care whose evening we have to ruin but I need that man found tonight and brought to our office here to be interviewed.'

CHAPTER THIRTY-THREE

Monique asked Sergeant MacMillan to take Ruth to get something to eat and then to find her somewhere suitable to spend the night. She realised that the last thing she'd eaten herself had been the soup at Achnacarry Castle late that morning. They'd left the sandwiches they'd picked up there in the car that had been sabotaged in Kyle of Lochalsh.

Bob told Monique and Anthony to go to the officers' mess to see if there was anything to eat at this time of night. He said he wanted to interview the driver of the car himself, with just Michael present and Gilbert taking notes. Monique was relieved that he backed off when he saw how strongly she wanted to be there too. Anthony promised to bring her a sandwich back if he could find one.

Perhaps because it was so late, it took a little while for the regimental bureaucracy to identify Lance Corporal Ernest Watson as the man who had driven the car carrying Bill Douglas and his two companions to Stirling Castle on Tuesday.

Michael and Gilbert accompanied the orderly officer to find and detain the lance corporal while Bob and Monique went back to the office to check the record of MI11's interview of the man, assuming there had been one.

'Gilbert talked to him this morning,' said Bob, looking at a sheet of paper. 'Watson said that at the time of the murder he'd been in his room on the first floor of the Great Hall, reading. He said he has a twin room he'd normally share with another junior non-commissioned officer but that at present he has it to himself. That leaves him without an alibi, of course, but he comes from Oban and appears to have no reason to know Bill

Douglas. We left him in a large "undecided" pile. That was what we were trying to work our way through when you got back, Monique.

'Although I said we'd interview the man in here, that's not a good idea as we'd need to do something with all the paperwork we've generated and cover up the blackboard. Let's use the larger meeting room downstairs. I'm sure it won't be needed by anyone else at this time.'

Bob led Monique down the stairs to the meeting room, where they checked the blackout curtains were properly closed and turned on the light.

They'd left the door open, and Michael looked round it and then came in a few moments later. 'Lance Corporal Watson is in the corridor with Gilbert. Do you want to see him now?'

'How does he seem?' asked Bob

'Composed. Unsurprised. Resigned. I think that about sums him up.'

'Let's see what he's got to say for himself.'

Bob took the seat in the centre of the table on the opposite side of the room to the door. Monique sat to his right and Michael took the seat to his left. Gilbert came in behind Watson and at first stood by the door. Monique saw that Watson was an athletically built man and assumed Gilbert was making sure he didn't try to get away. The lance corporal took the central seat on the other side of the table. Then Gilbert sat in the chair nearest the door and took a notebook out of a pocket after he'd placed a package wrapped in brown paper on the table in front of him.

Bob introduced himself and the others from MI11 to the lance corporal. 'Would you confirm who you are, please?'

'I'm Lance Corporal Ernest Watson. I'm with the Argyll

and Sutherland Highlanders and I work in the motor transport section here at Stirling Castle. I'm 30 years old.'

Monique thought that Michael's assessment of the man had been spot on. There was something very calm, almost serene, about him.

'Thank you,' said Bob. 'I'm sure you know that we're investigating the murder of a man in the Douglas Gardens on Tuesday evening. Sergeant Potter, who just brought you in, interviewed you this morning. You told him that you were in your room, reading, at the time of the murder. We have reason to believe you weren't telling the truth. I'd therefore start by asking you the same question that he asked you earlier. Where were you between 9.30 p.m. and 10.30 p.m. on Tuesday?'

'It's quite late, sir, and I'm sure that you are as tired as I am. I'm not going to have a very comfortable bed tonight, but I'd like to get to it sooner rather than later. Would it help get this over with as quickly as possible if I told you that I killed Bill Douglas on Tuesday night and that I'm proud of what I did?'

'Thank you for that,' said Bob. 'But I'm still going to need you to tell me what happened in detail. I'd like you to start when you picked up three passengers who got off a delayed aircraft at RAF Grangemouth and brought them to Stirling Castle.'

'As you say, there were three of them. A woman who looked like a strict schoolteacher got in behind me. A man in his twenties got into the front passenger seat. And a man in his thirties in a flash suit who looked like a black market spiv got in the back seat on the left. The man in the front buried himself in a newspaper while the spiv in the back insisted on telling the schoolteacher all about himself, even though it was obvious she didn't want to hear what he had to say.

'The spiv told her that his name was Bill Douglas and that his family had lorded it over Castle Douglas in Galloway for centuries. He said he'd been brought up in the area and they still owned lots of land there which he was going to inherit when his father died. I started to listen more closely after that. He told the woman how he was descended from a man whose brother, another William Douglas, had been murdered in the 1400s by a Scottish king here in Stirling castle.

'Then he went on to describe the murder of this other William Douglas in gory detail. He said the king stabbed him in the neck and then in the body. Then a courtier cut his head open with a large axe. Then others who were present stabbed him many times before they threw the body out of a window. He said that the body ended up in what became the Douglas Gardens. He'd visited once, when he was 15, and hoped to visit later that evening, after the dinner they were both going to had finished and before it got dark.'

Monique leaned forwards. 'Why did you say you listened more closely when you heard where Bill Douglas came from and who his family were? You're from Oban, so you wouldn't know anyone in Castle Douglas.'

Lance Corporal Watson looked down at the table in front of him and said nothing. Monique watched as a tear ran down to the tip of his nose and then formed a drip before falling to the table in front of him.

When he looked up, she could see his eyes were red with tears. 'I recognise your voice,' he said. 'You were in the gardens that night, weren't you? I was hiding beneath the stone steps leading up to the door in the King's Old Building and I heard you come into the gardens. I didn't get much of a view of you even though you were very close to me at one point. When I heard you arguing with Bill Douglas, I came out to see if you needed help. You'd already put him on the ground and I only saw your back as you went down the passage. I knew I didn't have much time, so I ran over to Bill Douglas, hit his head as hard as I could with an axe and then used my knife to stab him in the neck and then in lots of other places. It just seemed so absolutely right to kill him in the same way that the Scottish king had killed his namesake, and in the same place.'

'What did you do then?' asked Monique.

'I threw the axe over the castle wall so it would end up on the cliffs on that side. I hoped no one would find it, but I know that someone has. Then I ran back along the wall walk to where I'd left a plank that I used to crawl across to the window at the far end of the Great Hall, to the room used as a store. Once there, I changed into my own uniform and returned to my room, which is only two doors along from the store. I knew the chances of anyone seeing me in the corridor were very small.'

Bob placed his hand on Monique's arm, so she didn't ask her next question.

Instead, it was Bob who spoke. 'Are you saying that your room is one of the others with a window looking out of the end of the Great Hall above that courtyard?'

'That's right, sir. I've been expecting you to come and arrest me ever since I heard you'd searched the rooms there and had worked out how the plank had been used to get to the wall walk.

Monique saw Michael look apologetically at Bob.

Bob looked back at Watson. 'As you say, lance corporal, the rooms there, including yours, were searched. You've said what you did with the axe. What about the knife?'

'He still had it with him, sir,' said Gilbert Potter. 'In a leg sheath like Captain Darlington's. I found it when I searched him. This is it here.' He touched the brown paper package he'd placed on the table at the start of the interview.

'Thank you, Sergeant Potter. Lance Corporal Watson, can you confirm that was the knife you used when you killed Bill Douglas?'

'Yes, sir, it was.'

'I've one more question about a point of detail,' said Bob. 'What did you intend to do with the bloodstained uniform you hid in the store?'

'I thought that when the fuss died down, I'd collect the uniform and gloves and burn them in one of the heating boilers in the castle. You found them before I had the chance.'

Bob looked to his right. 'Monique, do you want to continue?'

Monique took a moment to gather her thoughts. 'Lance Corporal Watson, we've talked about the car journey and about killing Bill Douglas and what you did immediately afterwards. What I was trying to understand a little earlier was why you said you'd found it particularly interesting when Bill Douglas told the woman in the car where he came from and who his family was. I thought you were from Oban, which is a long way from Castle Douglas.'

Monique again saw tears in Watson's eyes.

'May I call you Ernest?' she asked.

He nodded.

'Thank you, Ernest. We may have taken two days to identify you, but during that time we've found out a great deal about Bill Douglas. A little earlier I described him to someone as a rapist and all-round utter bastard. A couple of years ago he tried to ruin my reputation because I wouldn't sleep with him. That was what our argument in the gardens was about. During this investigation, I've also met a young woman he raped last Christmas and a young man whose career he tried to ruin. Monique looked at Bob and Michael. Has anything else come to light in the last day or so?'

Michael leaned forwards to look at her past Bob. 'There's a strong suggestion that it was only his family connections that stopped him being arrested for rape during the school summer holidays when he was seventeen.'

'Thank you, Michael,' said Monique. 'The question I want to ask you is this, Ernest. We know other people wanted Bill Douglas dead. Why did you want him dead so badly that you were the one who decided to do something about it?'

There was a long silence.

Then Lance Corporal Watson looked up. 'The girl he raped when he was seventeen was my older sister, Maria. We lived with our mother in Castle Douglas while our father was at sea with the merchant navy. Maria was fifteen at the time and worked as a shop assistant in a men's shoe shop. She said she'd met this charming boy from a good family but, within days, when she wouldn't do what he wanted, he forced her. She fell pregnant and died of complications in childbirth. The baby died too. I was twelve at the time and this left me as an only child. My mother took me to live in Oban to get away from the ghost of Maria. She never got over her anger that Bill Douglas escaped punishment for what he did. She died, my father said of a broken heart, two years later.'

There was another long pause before the lance corporal continued. 'When I heard that bastard boasting about his family in the back of the car, it was easy enough to work out who he was. All the ghosts came rushing back and I knew I had to kill him, and ideally in a way that was as close as possible to what had happened to his namesake back in the 1400s. I already had a good knife and getting an axe was easy. Sourcing a uniform to use wasn't much harder. The uniform store is just downstairs from my room, and I know someone who works in the quartermaster's office well enough to be able to borrow the key to it. I didn't know what time the dinner he'd talked about was due to end so went out at a little before 9 p.m., using the plank between the storeroom window and the wall walk. It was quite cramped in the hiding place I'd chosen but as you proved, ma'am, it did keep me quite well hidden.'

'Thank you, Lance Corporal Watson,' said Bob. 'I am truly sorry about your sister and her child, and your mother. I know it will be no consolation to you but during this investigation, I've heard from two different people who would like to thank you for killing Bill Douglas.'

'Make that three,' said Monique.

Bob continued. 'I don't think I've ever said this to anyone, either before the war as a policeman in Glasgow or since becoming an intelligence officer, but part of me wishes that we hadn't solved this case. I know you're no danger to anyone else. But it's my job to solve the cases that come my way and the best I can offer is the hope that when you come before a judge, they feel as I do about what you've done. I will certainly make sure that when you come to trial, other people with reasons for wanting Bill Douglas dead will be allowed to speak on your behalf.'

'Thank you for saying that, sir. To be honest, I'm pleased you've caught me. Now I'll get the chance to put on public record what Bill Douglas did to my sister Maria eighteen years ago. Nobody will be able to sweep it under the carpet this time.'

'I do have one final question,' said Bob. 'Was it Corporal Peter Kerr who lent you the key to the uniform store?'

'I'd prefer not to say, sir.'

'It's just that he's been missing since yesterday. He disappeared after he was told we wanted to speak to him.'

'He had no idea what I was planning, sir. I told him I wanted to do a quiet swap for something I'd damaged. He was just doing a friend a favour.'

'Thank you. It's helpful to have cleared that up. Sergeant Potter, can you take Lance Corporal Watson to the guardhouse, please? I think you'll be fine without an additional escort. We'll sort out the formalities in the morning.'

After Gilbert had led the lance corporal out of the room, Bob leaned back and exhaled noisily.

'I'm sorry Bob,' said Michael. 'I'd lost my bearings and had no idea we were so close to the decorating store when we detained Lance Corporal Watson in his room.'

'Don't worry about it, Michael. That pales into insignificance compared to my gaffe in not thinking about the driver of the car much sooner.' Bob pushed his chair back from the table and stood up. 'Does anyone know what time the officers' mess bar stops serving drinks? I've seldom felt more in need of a strong gin and tonic.'

CHAPTER THIRTY-FOUR

Are you going to tell me what Anthony was like in bed?' asked Bob. 'I hope you had a little more room than we've got tonight.'

Monique could hear in his voice the grin that she couldn't see in the darkness of her bedroom.

'Don't be wicked, Bob. I owe you half-a-crown because he insisted that he should sleep in a chair. Anyway, as I told you on Tuesday night, you're perfectly at liberty to go back to your allocated room and sleep by yourself if you don't like my bed.'

'But your bed has you in it, and I very much like that. How are your ribs?'

Monique laughed. 'They're up to what you've got in mind, Bob. But first I need to tell you about today. I think there might be repercussions and you need to know what happened.'

'Business before pleasure? I can live with that. What do I need to know?'

'We assumed from the beginning that someone was trying to kidnap Helen to allow Mrs Erickson to be blackmailed into revealing something about her work on Ultra. With hindsight, perhaps even at the time, that didn't make complete sense, but we had no better explanation for what was happening.'

'What do you mean about it not making sense?'

'It would be hard to conceal that Helen had disappeared. As soon as it was known, MI11 or MI5 or whoever would alert the people Mrs Erickson worked for that there was a problem and that she might have become a security risk. It would have meant that the mother was no longer of any use to the kidnappers and their whole operation would be a waste of time.'

'I see that,' said Bob. 'As you said, though, we had no better explanation.'

'I found a much better explanation today. Helen Erickson planned her railway journeys using the April 1943 edition of *Bradshaw's Guide* that she'd been given in London on Monday by her mother. That's how she managed to wrong-foot everyone so brilliantly.

'Today, on a crowded quayside in Kyle of Lochalsh, the remaining male Soviet agent grabbed Helen's suitcase. By the time I retrieved it, the woman had swapped Helen's copy of *Bradshaw's Guide* for an identical April 1943 edition of the guide and made off with it. The problem, from the Soviets' point of view, was that because of all of Helen's unplanned travels, her copy had seen more wear than it otherwise would have done, and she spotted the switch because the replacement was less obviously used.

'When Helen gave Anthony and me a detailed account of everything that had happened to her, it became clear that switching her copy of *Bradshaw's Guide* with an identical copy had been the objective of the Soviet operation all along. They made their first attempt on the sleeper from Kings Cross to Edinburgh but then they had problems being in the right place at the right time before Helen disappeared.'

The bed creaked as Bob rolled onto his back. 'I'm guessing that you think that something the Soviets want was concealed in the first copy of *Bradshaw's Guide* by Mrs Erickson before she gave it to Helen.'

'Perhaps not by Mrs Erickson, as that would have placed Helen in danger. But yes, I think there's something in that copy of the book that the Soviets want badly.'

'You said that the woman made off with the book, Monique. Did you get it back?'

'Yes, Bob, I did. It's still in her shoulder bag, inside my overnight case in the corner of the room.'

'You've not told me how you retrieved it,' said Bob. 'Is that where the repercussions you mentioned come in?'

'Yes,' said Monique. 'Having swapped the books, the female NKVD agent drove out of Kyle of Lochalsh with Special Branch in pursuit. I'd been told there was only one road out that didn't involve a ferry crossing, so borrowed Tom Erickson's high-speed launch and went east along a sea loch to cut the woman off at a bridge ten miles from Kyle of Lochalsh.

'Anthony and I had two of Tom Erickson's men from the RAF Regiment with us and they tried to flag the woman's car down as she approached the bridge. They had to jump out of the way to avoid being run down by her. Anthony and I were waiting nearer the bridge, where the road turns quite sharply. I positively identified the woman when she was very close to us, and I opened fire with a Thompson submachine gun. Anthony joined in with a Sten gun. The woman suffered multiple wounds and must have died instantly. The car crashed into a roadside wall. We then retrieved the woman's bag containing the book as well as a wallet with documents identifying her as Helena Berdyaev, a first secretary in the Soviet embassy in London and, as we know, quite senior in the NKVD's British operations.'

'Wasn't Helena Berdyaev the woman who was controlling the spy you identified at X Base at Gruinard Bay last November?' asked Bob.

'Yes, that's her. To be honest, I'm surprised she wasn't kicked out of the country after that, but it seems she wasn't.

The thing is this, Bob. I took that course of action because I believed that Ultra might be compromised if we didn't retrieve the book immediately. To anyone who knows nothing about Ultra, what I did could look, to say the least, heavy-handed. The two men from the RAF Regiment were on the scene very soon after the shooting happened, and it was obvious they weren't happy. Inspector Grant of the Special Branch in Inverness was driving the pursuing car and described what I'd done as an "Al Capone gangland execution" before rather reluctantly agreeing to clear things up.'

'What about Anthony?' asked Bob. 'He doesn't know about Ultra.'

'While we were waiting at the bridge, I told him that it was imperative that the woman didn't get past us, that I was sorry I couldn't explain why, and that he'd just have to trust me.'

'How did he take that?'

'Although we didn't share a bed last night, we did talk about some quite deep and dark things, in particular about how people get the shadows behind their eyes that I've got, and he's got, and you've had since that last night in Stockholm. I think he knows me well enough to trust me. Certainly, he didn't question what I asked him to join me in doing today or show any disquiet about it afterwards.'

'That's something, at least,' said Bob.

'Look, Bob, I need to ask you a favour.'

'What is it?'

'You said earlier that you want to sort out the formalities here in the morning. Do you mind if Anthony and I drive straight down to the office first thing in the morning to write our reports about our search for Helen Erickson and what happened to Helena Berdyaev? I'd forgotten tomorrow is

Friday, and Good Friday too. I want my report, and Anthony's, to be with Commodore Cunningham as quickly as possible, preferably before the Soviet embassy starts to complain too loudly about the death of a first secretary. I'm hoping that he doesn't observe bank holidays and I propose to hand-deliver copies of the reports to the commodore before the end of normal office hours tomorrow.'

'How will you do that?' asked Bob.

'I need a nice man with an aeroplane to fly me to RAF Northolt tomorrow afternoon.'

'I'd be happy to, Monique. Perhaps we could make a night of it in London, then fly back on Saturday morning?'

'I'm sorry, Bob. That's a lovely idea. But I've got something work-related in mind for tomorrow night. I need you to trust me and simply fly back north tomorrow without me. I'll stay with Yvette at her flat and make my own way by train on Saturday. And before you ask, she's still got Susan in her life and I've got you, so we will be sleeping in separate rooms.'

'All right. Can I ask what the work-related thing is that you want to do? Is it something I ought to know about?'

'I'm intending to use Yvette's MI5 connections to tidy up a loose end. And speaking of MI5, I haven't yet revealed the full extent of the favour I'm asking of you tomorrow afternoon.

'After I spoke to you and then Yvette from the naval base in Kyle of Lochalsh, I telephoned another contact in MI5. I had to be careful what I said, but we agreed that I needed to get what I'd recovered, the *Bradshaw's Guide* and possibly other material, to them for analysis as quickly as possible. I'd therefore like to call in briefly at RAF Kidlington in Oxfordshire on our way to Northolt.'

'Fair enough. That's somewhere I've never been.'

'I'm told it's got steel matting runways that should be long enough for a Mosquito.'

'Can I ask why you want to go to RAF Kidlington?' asked Bob.

'Because it's close to Blenheim Palace, which serves as MI5's headquarters. The technical people I need to look at what I've found are based there. Much of MI5 moved there in September 1940 after their previous headquarters in Wormwood Scrubs prison in London was bombed. You'd not be the first to make a "from a prison to a palace" joke at this point.'

'I'll not bother then,' said Bob. 'Changing the subject a little, the loss of a car in Kyle of Lochalsh might give Michael, Gilbert and I a problem getting back when we've finished here. You and Anthony will have taken the only car we now have. I'd ask Taffy Jenkins to drive up here to pick us up but as you know, he's on leave. I'm sure we can work something out to ensure we're not stranded.'

'That's something else I want to talk to you about, Bob. I know you let John return to his old unit in the Intelligence Corps in February because you felt that we didn't need two drivers in the office.'

'That's right. As I said at the time, my predecessor was driven everywhere. Now more of us prefer to do our own driving, it's much harder to justify having two men in the unit who do nothing beyond driving and providing, on paper at least, some added security.'

'Yet when our only remaining driver, Taffy Jenkins, goes on leave it can cause problems, as it has now,' said Monique.

'Where are you going with this, Monique?'

'What did you think of Leading Wren Ruth Woodburn?'

'The young woman who drove you and Anthony from Kyle of Lochalsh? I only met her briefly so it's hard to say. I must admit it took her just five minutes to see something I'd been failing to see for two days. I think I know the answer, but why do you ask?'

'She's trained as a motor mechanic and driver. I can tell you from direct experience that she's an exceptionally good driver. I imagine that she's a good motor mechanic too because before the war she built and raced motorcycles. She also hates her current posting in Kyle of Lochalsh. She hates it so much she's thinking of applying for a commission, something she's refused to do in the past mainly to spite her wealthy parents, who sent her to a very good school.'

'And you think she'd be a good fit for MI11?'

'I do. Apart from anything else, it would be good to have another woman in the office in addition to Joyce and the typists. I'd thought I might be able to involve her in some of what I'm doing, perhaps using her as an assistant as well as a driver.'

'Are those the only reasons?' asked Bob.

Monique realised that Bob wouldn't see her smile in the dark. 'I did get the sense earlier of just the slightest hint of a spark between her and Anthony.'

'You can't go round playing matchmaker, Monique. Besides, if we have another attractive young woman in the office, I suspect there's far more danger of her turning Michael's head than Anthony's.'

'I'm going to have to ask you to trust me about this, Bob. I know Michael had quite a reputation with the ladies before he met Betty in Orkney last November, but I've seen no signs of him straying since then, either before Betty moved down to Edinburgh or since.'

'Very well, though only on the condition that if this breaks up Michael and Betty's engagement it will be for you to take responsibility and explain to her why. See if you can find Ruth and have a word with her before you leave in the morning. If she responds positively, suggest she might want to run Michael, Gilbert and I to Craigiehall, probably around mid-morning, so she can see where we are based and, subject to the obvious security constraints, get a sense of what we do. She will then need to return to Kyle of Lochalsh, of course, but if she seems to like the idea, I'll see what I can do.'

'That's great Bob.' Monique leaned back and ran her hand down his chest.

'Hang on, Monique. Much as I want to move from business to pleasure as quickly as possible, there's another staffing issue I want to discuss with you.'

'What's that?'

'Gilbert Potter came to see me on Monday. He enjoys what he does in MI11 and likes working with Anthony. But he's due a promotion to staff sergeant and that could be delayed if he stays with us. His home regiment is the Coldstream Guards, and he wants to return to mainstream soldiering with them.'

'You can't stand in his way, Bob.'

'I've no intention of doing so, but I do need to find a replacement. What do you think of Sergeant Alan MacMillan?'

'He doesn't have the physical presence of Gilbert and I know who I'd back in a fight between the two of them. On the other hand, it might be good to have someone with us who was keen to do any background research we needed and from what I've seen of him I've been impressed. But I've been away from the castle for part of the investigation, so Michael might be better able to express an opinion.'

'I've already talked to him, and he was very positive about the idea. I've not yet had a chance to talk to Anthony Darlington, either about Gilbert leaving or about my proposed replacement. If he's also positive, then I will sound out Sergeant MacMillan. Now, if that's the conclusion of business, where were we?'

Monique felt Bob cup her right breast in his hand and lean over to kiss her, but they bumped noses in the dark and she felt him pull back.

'You do know that if we get married, we'll not be allowed to have sex anymore, don't you?' he asked.

Monique laughed. 'Just you try and stop me, Bob!'

CHAPTER THIRTY-FIVE

The following afternoon Bob and Monique flew to Kidlington in Oxfordshire in the Mosquito. Monique handed over Helena Berdyaev's shoulder bag and wallet to a man in a tweed suit and glasses who she only introduced to Bob as Charles. He'd walked over to the aircraft from a waiting civilian car as the propellors stopped turning.

Bob then took off for the much shorter flight to RAF Northolt. Monique seemed very preoccupied.

'Are you having second thoughts about what happened to the Soviet woman?' he asked.

'No, what I did was right. But I have been worrying about how it's going to look if Helen Erickson's original copy of *Bradshaw's Guide* turns out to be just that, a book of railway timetables, with no evidence of anything being added or hidden.'

At Northolt, Bob watched while Monique climbed down the ladder from the hatch in the floor of the Mosquito before reaching back up to push her flying gear through into the nose compartment of the aircraft, where it would be out of the way. She looked up at Bob from the open hatch and blew him a kiss. She then walked over to a waiting civilian car and hugged Yvette, who was standing beside it. Both waved to him as he started to taxi after restarting the engines.

Bob told himself that Anthony had trusted Monique enough to kill Helena Berdyaev without question. The trust that Monique was seeking from him by staying with Yvette was almost trivial in comparison. He knew their relationship was a thing of the past. Somehow, though, that didn't seem to help.

After a rather lonely flight north, Bob went for dinner in the officers' mess at RAF Turnhouse.

As he was driving back to the bungalow after dinner, he realised that he'd not even begun to write his report about Bill Douglas's murder at Stirling Castle and was going to have to go into the office the next day, Saturday, partly to try to get that done and partly to catch up with the mountain of other paperwork that had built up over the past few days.

Monique telephoned from Waverley Station when her train got in at 6.25 p.m. on Saturday. She said that she'd been on the train since before 10.00 a.m. that morning and was both hungry and thirsty. Bob took a taxi into the city and joined her for a pleasant evening at the North British Hotel.

As they sat drinking champagne after finishing their dinner, Bob saw Monique's face take on a serious expression.

'You're probably wondering what I was doing in London, aren't you?' she asked.

'Besides delivering your report? I knew you'd tell me if you wanted to.'

'I think I told you I was intending to use Yvette's MI5 connections to clear up a loose end.'

'You did.'

'You will recall that in my report I said Helen was being blackmailed by a police inspector in London, a man called Vincent. Last night Yvette and I had an interesting time visiting several brothels and other houses of ill-repute in the Argyle Square area of Bloomsbury. We collected quite a lot of anecdotal evidence about Inspector Vincent, who is well-known to several of the establishments and the women in them, especially the young ones. He's not the only policeman in the area offering "protection" in return for sexual favours, but he does seem particularly active.

'Early this morning we intercepted him while he was walking from the home he shares with his wife and two teenage daughters, neither much younger than the girls he seems to favour as sexual conquests, to his local shop. That seemed to have a nice circularity as that's how he approached Helen Erickson. I offered him two options. Either he resigned from the police and joined one of the armed services or details of his corrupt and immoral activities would find their way to the Metropolitan Police, to his family and to the newspapers.'

'How did he respond?' asked Bob.

'He seemed shocked. I'd half expected bluster and aggression from him, but he just caved in. After we'd spoken, he gave up on his shopping trip and turned and walked back in the direction of his home.'

'Do you think the Metropolitan Police would accept as evidence what a couple of MI5 agents, acting unofficially, said about Vincent? The force is not known for its incorruptibility, and I'd imagine that goes up to quite senior levels.'

'Probably not,' said Monique, 'and the police might also try to prevent the newspapers from printing the story. But after what we'd found out last night, Yvette and I knew enough to sound convincing. It also felt right to bluff him in exactly the way he had tried to bluff Helen Erickson.'

'I hope it works,' said Bob. 'If he simply calls your bluff, you may have a problem.'

'He won't,' said Monique. 'He's a coward as well as a bastard.'

Bob raised his champagne glass. 'Here's to you and Yvette for trying to help Helen Erickson.'

On Sunday, Monique surprised Bob by suggesting they

attend the Easter celebration of the Eucharist at St Mary's Dalmahoy, the church that Bob's mother had recommended to Monique for their wedding. Bob thought it could only be half-a-dozen miles from their bungalow in Corstorphine and he readily agreed.

The service was busier than Bob had expected and was led by the rector, a gentle man called Bernard. Bob had never been particularly religious and found his attention wandering as he took in the sheer beauty and character of the little church. He had been to a wedding of a friend there, some years earlier, but saw it with different eyes now it was being suggested for his own wedding. He hoped Monique liked it as much as he did.

The rector concluded with a few words about Easter. Bob had never really thought about it before. He knew the date changed from year to year but hadn't realised it was always the first Sunday following the full moon that occurs on or after the spring equinox. Tuesday, as he'd seen when being driven to Stirling Castle, had been a full moon.

Bob was more surprised to hear that today, the 25th of April, was the latest possible date on which Easter Sunday could ever fall. And still more surprised to hear that the last time it fell on this date had been in 1886, with the next being in 2038.

After the service, Bob realised that Monique hadn't followed him out of the church. People were still coming out, so he didn't try to go back in. Instead, he wandered over to look at something that had caught his attention when they'd arrived. On the edge of some trees not far from the church stood what seemed to be a very old stone cross slab through which someone had drilled a hole, obviously many centuries after the stone had originally been carved.

He heard a movement on the grass behind him as Monique reached around and put her hands over his eyes.

'Guess who?'

He turned and Monique stepped back, looking embarrassed.

'I'm sorry, Bob, I forgot.'

Bob laughed. 'Don't worry about it, Monique. It would have looked very odd to anyone else if you'd only covered my right eye. I'm pleased you were able to forget I don't use the other one. Anyway, what did you think of the church?'

'It's really beautiful and perfect for what we want. The small size is also just right. We're only going to be able to invite colleagues and your family and I don't want them rattling around in somewhere that's too big.'

'Does that worry you, Monique? I'm sorry we can't invite anyone on your side.'

'It's not a problem, Bob. All that matters to me is that you are there. Anyway, the reason I was delayed coming out was that I was arranging for us to come and meet with the rector on Tuesday evening, in the rectory cottage over there. You don't mind, do you?'

'Of course not.'

On Monday and Tuesday, Bob had the sense that Monique was waiting for a response to the reports that she and Anthony had written, but none came.

Little else happened, which gave Bob the chance to finally get on top of his paperwork, probably for the first time since before the second trip to Stockholm, nearly a month earlier.

The meeting on Tuesday evening with Bernard, the rector of St Mary's Dalmahoy, lasted far longer than Bob had expected.

Bob liked the man, but he realised that Monique's feelings

went rather further and that she'd seen something in Bernard that made her believe she could trust him completely. They spent a little time talking about Bob and his background, but most of it was occupied by Monique giving a complete and quite detailed account of her own life. Bob was surprised. He'd expected her to stick with the story of Monique Dubois, which wouldn't have taken very long at all.

When she finished, there was silence for a few moments.

It was Bernard who spoke first. 'I'm very grateful to you, Monique, for being so open and honest with me. Should I call you Monique, in light of what you've told me?'

'It's what I call her,' said Bob. 'And that's the name we'd both like Monique to be married under. It's also the name that will be on all the documentation necessary to allow her to be legally married.'

'Very well. If you'd simply come here as Robert Sutherland and Monique Dubois, I'd have been very happy to marry you. In some ways I'm even happier to marry you both now you've been so honest with me. As you said Bob, there will never be any question of the legality of the wedding anyway, with the proper documents in place. But to my mind, it adds a great deal to know the real woman who is getting married rather than the identity you've chosen to adopt, Monique.'

'That's what I was hoping you'd say,' said Monique. 'Are you sure there's nothing in my having been married twice before or the way I've spent my life that causes you a problem?'

'Technically, I should discuss with the bishop the question of marrying someone who has been married before, even a widow. However, I assume that the Monique who will be shown on the legal documents has not been married, despite her referring to herself as Madame Dubois. In these exceptional circumstances, I am happy simply to rely on the documentation. And as for how you've lived your life, well these are very strange times, and many people are living quite extraordinary lives.'

Monique beamed. 'We just need to set a date, then!'

CHAPTER THIRTY-SIX

The call came late on Thursday afternoon.

'Hello, is that Group Captain Sutherland? This is Commodore Cunningham's office. I've got the commodore on the line for you.'

Bob heard the click as the call was put through to his boss.

'Hello, sir, it's Bob Sutherland here.'

'Hello, Bob. I'm sorry about the short notice, but I need you down in London tomorrow morning. You should bring Madame Dubois, Lieutenant Commander Dixon and Captain Darlington with you. I appreciate some or all of you might have other plans for the day, but this is important, and I need all four of you here in my office.

'I know that your Mosquito can only seat two, so I've had someone arrange for an Avro Anson to pick you all up promptly at 7.30 a.m. tomorrow at RAF Turnhouse. From my own recent experience, I know that the flight time will depend on weather and wind, but when you arrive at RAF Northolt you will be met by two staff cars and brought here. I've arranged to be notified when your plane lands so I can organise things at this end.'

'Can I ask what it's about, sir?'

'All will be explained when you arrive. I'll see you then. You won't need overnight bags.'

There was another click, and the line went dead.

Bob had heard Anthony Darlington and Gilbert Potter leave the office a few moments earlier so lifted the sash window. When he saw them walking into view he shouted for Anthony to come back. Not dignified, perhaps, but effective. He liked the outlook from his office but had never previously appreciated the benefit of a first-floor location that overlooked the path between the main entrance and the car park.

After Bob had gathered Monique, Michael and Anthony in his office, he told them the news.

'Do you know what it's about, Bob?' asked Monique.

'I asked that. All he said was that everything will be explained when we arrive.'

'It has to be about Kyle of Lochalsh and Helena Berdyaev,' said Monique.

'If it were that, he wouldn't want me there as I was at Stirling Castle the whole time,' said Michael. 'It has to be something else.'

'There's no point in speculating,' said Bob. 'Let's just make sure we are all at RAF Turnhouse in time to catch our aircraft at 7.30 a.m. tomorrow, "promptly", as the commodore put it.'

*

Bob hadn't slept well and he knew that Monique hadn't either.

Their Avro Anson took off from RAF Turnhouse in reasonable weather, with a light wind from the west and a uniform layer of quite high cloud.

Bob didn't want to get involved in further pointless speculation about the purpose of their trip. He and Monique had done enough of that the previous evening. To remove himself from any discussion in the passenger cabin, he asked the pilot if he minded Bob acting as co-pilot.

Flight Sergeant North, as he introduced himself, seemed very happy to let someone else do the flying while he sat back to read that week's copy of *Flight* magazine.

Bob enjoyed flying the Avro Anson. The challenge of

operating an aircraft with a performance that, compared with the Mosquito, was very sedate was interesting and helped take his mind off the possible reasons for their trip.

Not sufficiently, though. Bob knew Monique was extremely worried about how the killing of Helena Berdyaev would be perceived. He was, too. After he'd read their reports, he had talked to Monique and Anthony separately and at length. To his mind, Monique had been right to decide that if the Soviet woman didn't stop when directed to do so, she had to be shot.

What worried him was his uncertainty about how others would see it. It would depend on what MI5 had made of what Monique had given them, but it might also depend on just how loudly the Soviet embassy in London was complaining about the killing of a first secretary.

The thing that worried him most about Commodore Cunningham's telephone call was the instruction that Michael Dixon should attend the meeting. The only possible reason Bob could think of for Michael being involved was if the decision had been taken to sack Bob as deputy head of MI11 and replace him, at least temporarily, with Michael.

As they flew further south the sun broke through the cloud in places, leaving an attractive patchwork on the ground below that did little to lift Bob's mood.

*

Bob and Monique said little to each other in the back of the car they shared from RAF Northolt into central London. Michael and Anthony were in a second car behind them. Bob didn't know the city very well, but over time had come to identify some of the landmarks. Different drivers seemed to prefer different routes but, as usual, the car turned right when it reached Westminster Abbey. A little further on it pulled over to the right-hand side of the road and stopped next to the kerb. Also as usual, this seemed to upset other motorists, in this case the driver of a bus who was having difficulty pulling out to pass them.

MI11's London offices were on the top floor of Sanctuary Buildings in Great Smith Street. Bob led the way into the building, noticing again that the board in the reception showing the varied list of occupiers made no mention of MI11.

The commodore's secretary smiled when Bob led the others into her office, which Bob took to be a good omen.

'The commodore is waiting for you, sir. Go straight through. Does everyone want tea?'

They all did. Bob took the offer to be another good omen.

Commodore Cunningham's office had outward-facing windows, something Bob had been told was highly prized in a building in which the alternative was windows that looked across grubby internal wells into other people's offices.

It also boasted a desk and a meeting table. The commodore was seated at the latter with Paul Gillespie, the man on loan from the Cabinet Office to Sir Peter Maitland's staff.

The commodore stood and smiled in greeting, which to Bob's mind was a third good omen.

'Sit down everyone. Thank you for coming at such short notice. Ah, here's the tea.'

There was a moment's silence after the commodore's secretary left the room.

'Right, to business. I think you all met Paul Gillespie at Stirling Castle. By the way, well done for catching Bill Douglas's killer, Bob. I gather it was, as you predicted, an act of revenge for something he'd done during, to borrow your memorable phrase, a lifelong career as an utter bastard.'

'Thank you, sir, though it took Monique and a Wren driver to point out what should already have been obvious to me.'

'Well done to all of you. I've also been asked to pass on my thanks for the recommendations you made about the crew of the German aircraft that landed up in Aberdeen. I understand it was flown down to the Royal Aircraft Establishment in Farnborough by an RAF crew later last week, with a heavy escort of Spitfires to ensure no one on the ground or in the air got the wrong idea and took a shot at it.

'It's early days yet but they think that what they've discovered about the radar, with considerable assistance from the Luftwaffe crew, could be a huge help in working out how to defend our bombers over Germany.'

Bob could sense that Monique was becoming impatient at the way the meeting was heading off on odd tangents.

'I'm grateful for you telling me, sir, but none of this is really why we're here, is it?'

'No, that's true,' said the commodore. 'I should say that Paul Gillespie is here on behalf of Sir Peter Maitland.'

'Sir Peter sends his apologies,' said Gillespie. 'He wanted to be here himself but has had to meet the prime minister about another matter.'

'The reason I've asked you all down today,' said the commodore, 'is to discuss Monique and Anthony's pursuit of Miss Erickson across Scotland and the way it ended.'

Bob saw Monique glance at him. She'd obviously noticed the commodore's use of their first names and shared Bob's view that this was perhaps another good omen.

'I've read both of your reports, as have Paul and Sir Peter.

Did you read each other's?'

'I read Anthony's, sir,' said Monique. 'Obviously, I couldn't show him mine.'

'Yes, well we'll come to that in a moment. Indeed, perhaps we should deal with it now because otherwise this will become a very awkward meeting very quickly.'

He turned to the Cabinet Office man. 'Paul, this is the part of the meeting that Sir Peter was going to cover. Could you do the honours, please?'

Paul Gillespie shifted forwards in his chair and placed his hands, one on top of the other, on the table in front of him. 'What I am about to tell you is intended for Lieutenant Commander Dixon and Captain Darlington. I am telling you because Commodore Cunningham has convinced Sir Peter that we should. I am telling Captain Darlington so you can understand the context of what happened last week, and Lieutenant Commander Dixon because otherwise you would be surrounded in the organisation by people who knew what I am about to reveal, and that could place you in a very difficult position.

'I will keep it brief and only cover the essential points because I know that the group captain and Madame Dubois will fill in the details and explain the implications afterwards.

'I very much hope that neither of you has heard of a classification called Ultra Secret. "Ultra" is a code word for a form of intelligence whose existence cannot ever be revealed to the Germans. We have found ways to decrypt signals sent by the Germans using a family of different electro-mechanical cipher machines, often called Enigma machines, which the enemy believe to be totally secure. What this means is that a large proportion of the coded messages sent within and between elements of the German military and their state apparatus can be read and understood by us.

'There are some constraints. It takes time and effort and skill on our side, and part of the problem is that there is just so much traffic, but it is still a war-winning weapon so long as we can prevent the Germans from finding out that their communications are insecure. That means restricting the number of people who know about Ultra. Maintaining security also means being very careful about how we respond to intercepts. If we found out that a pack of U-boats was planning to attack a particular convoy, for example, flooding the area with warships could easily compromise Ultra. Some very hard decisions have had to be made.'

Bob glanced at Michael and Anthony's faces and saw this sinking in.

Paul Gillespie continued. 'The reason why Madame Dubois couldn't show you her report, Captain Darlington, was that she was aware that Mrs Erickson, Helen Erickson's mother, was working on Ultra and mentioned this in what she wrote as it was central to decisions she took. Mrs Erickson is a mathematician involved at the very sharp end of the decryption process.'

'And that was why we turned a car into a colander at the bridge at Dornie?' asked Anthony. 'I'm pleased but not surprised that my trust in you was justified, Monique.'

'That rather depends on whether MI5 found anything of interest in Helen Erickson's original copy of *Bradshaw's Guide*,' said Monique.

'They did,' said Paul Gillespie. 'The back two pages were stuck together. It looked like a printer's error. But when our people prised them apart, they discovered a series of photographic microdots stuck to one of the two facing pages. They are still working on them but believe that between them they provide a fairly good guide to what we've achieved through Ultra and how we do it.'

'Don't the Soviets know already?' asked Bob.

'They might have some of the pieces, but it seems they don't know how we've assembled them or what we are capable of as a result. Some of the initial work on cracking German cipher machines was done in Poland in the early 1930s and word of that must have reached the Soviets. Because of Ultra, we were fully aware of the Germans' preparations for their invasion of the USSR in June 1941. We tried to warn the Soviets without revealing the source of our intelligence but Stalin thought it was a trick. He soon found out that it wasn't.'

'Why was a copy of *Bradshaw's Guide* given to Helen Erickson chosen as the preferred way of transmitting this information?' asked Monique. 'It seems indirect and inefficient and inherently prone to failure.'

'That's a very good question,' said Paul Gillespie. 'We don't at present believe that Mrs Erickson is a Soviet spy. However, she has formed a clandestine and, shall we say, very close relationship with a male colleague who has been under suspicion and surveillance for some months. Their relationship was so clandestine that our surveillance had not picked up their night-time visits to one another's rooms.

'The presence of the surveillance also begs the question of how this male colleague sourced the means to take the photographs and process the microdots, but if he had any idea that he was under suspicion it does perhaps help explain why he didn't use a dead letter box or just post the material via the ordinary mail. He has now been arrested and Mrs Erickson is also being questioned. She is being rather more helpful than he is. She says she had the copy of *Bradshaw's Guide* for several days before giving it to her daughter. She kept it in her room in the house she shares with this man and with a number of other important civilian staff who work at Bletchley Park...'

Commodore Cunningham coughed, pointedly.

'Indeed,' continued Paul Gillespie. 'The exact location was a detail you were not meant to know. Anyway, it seems most likely that the mother had a copy of *Bradshaw's Guide* in her room for long enough for the man to doctor it without her knowing. And before you ask how he was able to tell the Soviets to look for a copy of *Bradshaw's Guide* being carried by Helen Erickson without also being able to pass on the material to them and save everyone a great deal of trouble, we don't yet know.'

'What this amounts to,' said Bob, 'is a total vindication of Monique's decision to stop Helena Berdyaev at any cost at the end of that bridge.'

Bob saw Monique flash a grateful glance at him.

'Oh, it's even better than that,' said Commodore Cunningham, smiling. 'Also in the shoulder bag you found at the scene, Monique, as well as Helen Erickson's original copy of *Bradshaw's Guide* and the maps you mentioned in your report, was an empty stamped and unsealed envelope, addressed to a vicar in Wimbledon. As an aside, I'd say that we previously had no idea there was anything untoward about him, but we now think he is part of a ring of Soviet agents in London.

'We have also received a report about what happened that day written by Inspector Grant, who is with Special Branch in Inverness. It would be a fair summary to say that the inspector was deeply unhappy about your actions in stopping the car and killing Helena Berdyaev, Monique. Perhaps his reaction is understandable as he knows nothing about Ultra but, as you are aware, we don't agree with him. More relevantly, the inspector confirmed in his report what both of you said in those you wrote, that his police car was quite some distance behind the Soviet car when it got to the bridge.

'Given the lead she had, if you had not been there, we believe it would have been perfectly possible for Helena Berdyaev to stop at a post box in Dornie, rip the back two pages out of the *Bradshaw's Guide* complete with the microdots, put them in the envelope, and post it. She could then have disposed of the rest of the guide in the next convenient loch. After that, she could have gone on her way with no evidence remaining of what had happened. You thought it was vital that you stopped Helena Berdyaev's car there and then, Monique, and you were right.'

'Thank you, sir,' said Monique.

'Wouldn't Helena Berdyaev's best course of action have been to post her letter to the vicar while she was still in Kyle of Lochalsh?' asked Michael.

'You'd think so, wouldn't you?' said the commodore. 'And perhaps, with hindsight, it would have been. But having sabotaged the car Monique and Anthony were driving, perhaps she thought she only needed to get clear of the village. Inspector Grant said in his report that she was driving as if she didn't expect to be pursued when he caught up with her. With no pursuit, her first point of danger would have been when she came upon a protected area checkpoint, and she could have ripped the pages out and posted the letter anywhere before then. She'd have realised her mistake when the inspector came up behind her before she reached the first settlement on her route, so she couldn't post the letter there. The lead she had on the police when she got to Dornie because of the incident with the Royal Navy lorries would have offered her best and perhaps her only chance.

'It goes without saying that the Soviet embassy is not best pleased about all of this, but they know they've been caught red-handed trying to steal the crown jewels and, at the end of the day, they are realists. Helena Berdyaev came close to being deported after that business you were involved in last November, so she should have been much more careful.'

Monique smiled. 'I think her real problem was that she was comprehensively outwitted by a very mature young woman called Helen. As we all were, for that matter.'

'The young lady's maturity may be about to be tested,' said Commodore Cunningham. 'I suspect her parents' marriage is about to encounter a very rough patch.'

Bob had been thinking much the same thing.

Paul Gillespie sat back in his chair. 'You should know that there's been a development concerning another matter you mentioned in your report, Monique. You said that Helen Erickson had been reluctant to involve the police when she feared she was being followed because of an incident with an Inspector Vincent here in London. Specifically, he was trying to blackmail her into having sex with him. That might have been difficult to resolve. I know you believed her, Monique, but it would still have been the young lady's word against his and he had an unblemished record. That might of course have said more about the low standards of some of his senior officers than his own high standards.'

'You used the past tense,' said Bob. 'You said "he had".'

'Indeed,' said Gillespie. 'Last Saturday afternoon Inspector Vincent was on duty at Grays Inn Road police station. At 2.25 p.m., not long after the start of his shift, he signed a revolver out of the station armoury. Then he went back to his office and blew his brains out with it. He left a note addressed to his wife that had a one-word message: *"Sorry."* He's not going to trouble Miss Erickson again.'

For Bob, the shock felt almost physical. He looked at Monique, who was looking back at him with an odd expression he couldn't read. He realised that she already knew and wished she'd warned him.

It was Commodore Cunningham who broke the silence. 'Monique, I'm sorry, but I must ask. I know you were in London on the afternoon of the previous day because you delivered your report and Captain Darlington's to me personally. Do you know anything about what happened to Inspector Vincent?'

Monique looked at the Commodore, now without any expression at all on her face. 'I spent most of last Saturday on a train from King's Cross to Waverley Station, sir. It left London at 9.50 a.m. and arrived in Edinburgh at 6.25 p.m. I'd imagine that at 2.25 p.m. I was probably somewhere in Yorkshire.'

Bob felt that Monique's failure to properly answer the commodore's question must have been as obvious to everyone else in the room as it was to him.

'I'm sure you could prove that if called upon to do so,' said the commodore. 'And it seems the police are satisfied that the inspector's demise was a straightforward suicide with no one else involved. Perhaps he just had a sudden, if rather belated, attack of conscience? I suppose we will never know. Very well, I think that concludes our meeting.'

Bob took a deep breath before standing up to leave with the others.

*

Bob touched Monique's arm in the corridor outside the commodore's office and she paused as Michael and Anthony headed for the lift.

'You might have told me about Vincent,' he said, quietly.

'I'm sorry, Bob. I thought we were going to have much bigger problems than him and I didn't want to add to your worries or distract you. Yvette heard what he'd done on Monday and rang me to let me know. It seems Vincent was even more of a coward than I'd thought and chose a third option that hadn't crossed my mind.'

EPILOGUE

The two staff cars were waiting for them, parked on the near side of Great Smith Street. They were now facing the right way for the traffic but were still causing an obstruction, this time to a brewer's horse-drawn cart which was unable to pass because of traffic coming the other way.

The pavement was quite narrow. Bob followed Monique out of the main entrance of Sanctuary Buildings and towards the front car, which had stopped directly opposite the doorway.

There were a few pedestrians on the street but Bob took little notice of them. As Monique started to open the back door of the car Bob caught a glimpse out of the corner of his good right eye of a man in a coat a few yards away who had come to a sudden halt. When Bob turned his head, he could see the man's gaze was fixed on Monique and there was a look of hatred on his face. Time seemed to slow right down. Bob realised that the man was raising a gun, a large weapon with a wooden stock, a metal barrel and a hefty drum magazine.

At the same time, he heard someone to his right, a man, shout, 'Look out Monique!'

Bob flung himself forwards and grabbed Monique, just as she was starting to turn to her right in response to the warning. He heard three shots in very quick succession, then he and Monique bounced off the side of the car and fell to the kerb before ending up partly in the gutter by the car's back wheel, with him on top of her. As they landed, he heard the deafening noise of a short burst of fire from an automatic weapon that sounded extremely close.

A woman screamed and Bob heard police whistles being

blown and the whinnies of frightened horses. When he lifted his head and looked around, he saw that the man with the gun was lying motionless on the pavement. Beyond him stood Michael Dixon with a pistol in his hand and a look of horror on his face. Slightly further away, standing beside the back of the second car, was Anthony Darlington, frozen, with his pistol partly drawn.

'Thank you, Bob,' said Monique, 'I'm grateful. But can you get off me now? Next time you ask me how my ribs are, I'll remind you of this moment.'

Bob stood and then helped Monique up, seeing her grimace and move her left arm around to cradle the right side of her chest.

'Everyone back in the building, immediately!'

Bob saw Anthony Darlington push Michael Dixon in the direction of the doorway to get him moving.

Anthony strode over and picked up the weapon the man had been holding, then reached down to feel the side of the man's neck. He turned to Bob and Monique and shouted, 'Come on you two, get off the street!'

Michael walked past Anthony to take Monique's arm. Bob saw her shake him off and bend down to look at the dead man's face. Then she allowed Michael to lead her back into Sanctuary Buildings.

'You too, sir!' said Anthony, pulling at his arm.

'Hang on Anthony. He was after Monique and she's safe. I want to know what just happened.'

'Our friend here pulled a gun from under his coat. It's a Soviet submachine gun called a PPSh-41 unless I'm very much mistaken, though it's also known as a "burp gun" because of its extremely high rate of fire and the noise it makes. Michael recognised the threat first and shot him three times in the back before he could bring his gun to bear on Monique. I was very slow off the mark, I'm afraid. The man must have pulled the trigger as a reflex as he died. It's as well you got Monique on the ground because the bullets that he fired passed over you and went into the rear corner of the front car, which as a result isn't going anywhere anytime soon. Now please get back inside until we know what we're dealing with.'

Anthony crouched down beside the man. As Bob went back into the building, Anthony rolled the man to one side, as if to check his pockets.

Inside, Bob saw that Michael and Monique were standing in a corner, off to one side of the reception area. Monique was holding Michael's arm and talking to him.

Anthony came in a few moments later and Bob watched as he removed the drum magazine from the submachine gun and checked the weapon was safe, before slinging it over his shoulder. Then Commodore Cunningham and a man in an army major's uniform and carrying a Sten gun emerged from the lift.

The commodore looked around. 'Are you all safe?'

'Yes, sir, said Anthony. We're all fine. There's a dead man on the pavement outside but I can confirm the two drivers are also safe and I saw no sign of anyone else having been hit by stray rounds fired by this thing.' He held up the gun. 'One of the cars is in a poor way, though.'

'Can you tell us what happened?' asked the commodore. 'This is Major Shoesmith, by the way, who looks after security here.'

Anthony told them.

'Thank you, Anthony,' said the commodore. 'Now I think we should return to the top floor and decide how to proceed.'

Bob followed the others into the lift, which took them back to the top of the building. In the corridor outside the commodore's office, he saw Anthony give Major Shoesmith a wallet that he'd opened to show the major something inside it.

'Could you excuse me for a few minutes, commodore?' asked the major.

'Of course,' said Commodore Cunningham. 'Let's go through to my office. I'll take a collective statement from the four of you.'

The commodore asked his secretary to take notes in shorthand and it didn't take long to put together a full account of what had happened.

After his secretary had left, the commodore sat back in his chair and looked at Monique. 'I think you should all wait here until we've established whether there's any remaining threat to you out there.'

'There isn't going to be, commodore,' said Monique.

'How do you know?'

'I recognised the dead man. I met him just before he was led off to the police station in Kyle of Lochalsh. Helen Erickson said he was the one who was with Helena Berdyaev in London before they both followed her onto the sleeper to Edinburgh. I think his attempt on my life was a result of a very personal grievance against me. A burp gun is a ludicrous weapon to choose if you want to kill someone on a city street. It's heavy and unwieldy and hard to conceal. If he'd simply used a pistol, and I'll bet he was carrying one, then I'd be dead. The only possible reason for him to want to use a burp gun to kill me would be as a symbolic act of revenge for the death of Helena Berdyaev, who I killed with a submachine gun.'

'You were right about the pistol, Monique,' said Anthony.

He took one from his army officers' raincoat pocket, removed the magazine, and placed it on the commodore's meeting table. 'He had this in a shoulder holster. On the other hand, remember that it wasn't you alone who shot Helena Berdyaev.'

'True, but it was my operation and my decision, and it was me he saw most clearly at Kyle of Lochalsh. I have no idea of the man's name, but I suspect that when you identify him, he'll turn out to have been the lover of Helena Berdyaev. I'm sure he was acting in a purely personal capacity and alone when he tried to kill me. The important question for you, commodore, is how he knew I would be here this morning. It suggests your security is not as good as it ought to be.'

'That's true, Monique, and the thought had crossed my mind.'

At that moment Major Shoesmith came back into the office. 'The police and some of my people have sealed off Great Smith Street. Captain Darlington passed me the dead man's wallet containing his identity documents and I've just had a chat with our friends in MI5. The documents show he was called Maxim Kozlov and MI5 says he is known to be NKVD and that he worked closely with Helena Berdyaev, who I understand was killed in a recent MI11 operation.'

'Did they say if Maxim Kozlov and Helena Berdyaev were known to do anything else closely together?' asked Monique.

'Sorry, I didn't ask, and they didn't mention it. Is it important?'

'It would simply have confirmed something I'm sure of anyway,' said Monique. She looked at her watch. 'I think we should be on our way.'

'What if there's still a second would-be assassin out there?' asked the commodore.

'I'm betting there isn't, sir.'

'You're betting your life on it.'

'I know, sir.'

Bob saw Commodore Cunningham look at him, obviously wanting him to reason with or overrule Monique.

'I saw the look on Kozlov's face when he raised his gun,' said Bob. 'I'm sure Monique is right.'

'Very well. I'll see if I can find you a second car to replace the one that was damaged.'

'I've got a better idea, commodore,' said Monique. 'I've got sore ribs and could do with a drink of something stronger than tea. Bob has a hole in the knee of his uniform trousers, and I suspect wouldn't say no to a gin and tonic. And Michael very definitely needs a drink.'

Bob looked down at his legs to see that Monique was right.

'What I have in mind is this,' continued Monique. 'There's a grand old pub about halfway along Victoria Street, on the right. Do you know it?'

'The Albert? Yes, of course.'

'The four of us can squeeze into the one remaining staff car outside. Unless things have changed in London recently, the Albert will already be open. We can go and have a drink or two there. I promise I won't let Bob fly the plane on the way back to Scotland later. Would you mind getting your secretary to telephone RAF Northolt to say we might be a bit delayed?

*

Bob felt slightly guilty about leaving the driver waiting for them outside the pub. But the man said he could park just round the corner and was happy reading.

The Albert wasn't busy, though it was already quite smoky. Monique led the way into the pub and then to a booth to one side of the open area in front of the bar, beside a window that had been heavily taped to protect against blast damage.

She turned to face him. 'Bob, you're paying, and Anthony and I will fetch the drinks. Michael, you sit down. Bob, you too, but only after you've got your wallet out.'

Monique had been right in predicting that Bob would want a gin and tonic. She returned with one, and a large whisky for Michael. Anthony brought a gin and tonic for her and a pint of bitter for himself. Bob noticed that Michael's hand shook slightly when he picked up his drink.

'I suggested coming here because I did think we could all do with a drink after what just happened,' said Monique. 'First, though, I would like to propose two toasts. The first is to Michael, who saved my life and lost his virginity today.'

'Hang on, that's a little rich,' said Michael, smiling.

'Fair enough, your innocence then. It never really gets any easier killing someone, but you do learn to cope with it a little better as time goes by. It leaves its mark on you, though, as you've probably noticed with Anthony and me, and more recently with Bob. I hope what happened outside Sanctuary Buildings a little while ago doesn't prey on your mind, but if it does, please remember that I'm only alive because of what you did, and probably Bob too.'

Monique lifted her glass. 'With that in mind, let's drink a toast to Michael's lost innocence!'

They all raised their glasses and then drank.

'You talked about two toasts,' said Bob.

'Ah, yes. The second one may be more controversial, but as you are my friends, I'd be grateful if you'd join me anyway. I chose this pub instead of any of the others in the area because it has memories for me from my time in London. Some of them are good and some are less so. The worst was the night that Bill Douglas told me he would denounce me as a German spy if I didn't sleep with him. We were sitting in this very booth, which was why I chose it just now when I saw it was empty. As you know, I poured his drink over his head and left. We all now know that what he tried to do to me was just one relatively minor act in, to follow the commodore's lead in borrowing Bob's phrase, a lifelong career as an utter bastard.'

Monique looked around to see if anyone was within hearing and lowered her voice to ensure privacy. 'It seems Bill Douglas was not unique and that the lately departed Inspector Theo Vincent was cut from the same cloth. My second toast, therefore, is to both Bill Douglas and Theo Vincent. May the pair of them rot in hell!'

Monique held up her glass and the others clinked it with theirs before drinking.

AUTHOR'S NOTE

This book is a work of fiction and should be read as such. Except as noted below, all characters are fictional and any resemblances to real people, either living or dead, are purely coincidental.

Likewise, many of the events that are described in this book are the products of the author's imagination. Others did take place.

Let's start with the characters. Some of the military and intelligence personnel who appear between the pages of this book occupy posts that existed at the time, but they are all fictional. This is significant because the military units and intelligence organisations mentioned were usually doing what I describe them as doing at the time the action takes place. Minor characters are also entirely invented, as are members of Military Intelligence, Section 11, such as Anthony Darlington: though I did borrow his name from a lovely man I worked with many years ago who had, in a previous life, been a senior army officer.

Some characters could be associated with real people because of their roles, such as the officers of the Argyll and Sutherland Highlanders based at Stirling Castle, the defecting crew of the Luftwaffe aircraft and the rector of St Mary's Dalmahoy. Again, the characters who play those roles in this book are not based on their real-life counterparts and are fictional, as are the Erickson and Moncrieff families and the Soviet agents.

The real King James II of Scotland did murder the real 8th Earl of Douglas at Stirling Castle in 1452, as (repeatedly) described in this book, and the historical sources are set out accurately. The latter's brother, the 9th Earl, did then rise in revolt before being exiled. The story of the Sir William Douglas of the late 1700s and his role in establishing Castle Douglas (and his falsely claimed connection back to the Black Douglases) is generally as described. Bill Douglas is an invented character, however, and the family story after the late 1700s is fictional.

Group Captain Robert Sutherland is also an invented character, though he has a career in the Royal Air Force that will be recognised by anyone familiar with the life and achievements of Squadron Leader Archibald McKellar, DSO, DFC and Bar. Bob Sutherland's family background and pre-war employment were very different to Archibald McKellar's, but the two share an eminent list of achievements during the Battle of Britain. Squadron Leader McKellar was tragically killed when he was shot down on the 1st of November 1940, whereas the fictional Group Captain Sutherland was only wounded when he was shot down on the same day, allowing him to play a leading role in this book and its four predecessors.

And Madame Monique Dubois? She is a fictional alias for a real woman. The real Vera Eriksen, or Vera Schalburg, or take your pick from any number of other aliases, had a story that was both complex and very dark. She disappeared during the war after the two German spies she landed with at Port Gordon on the Moray Firth were tried and executed by the British for espionage.

A hint of Monique's story emerges from the pages of this book but to get a fuller picture you should read my first novel, *Eyes Turned Skywards*.

Military Intelligence, Section 11, or MI11, was a real

organisation that had a role in maintaining military security. Its organisation and other aspects of its operations described in this book are entirely fictional. Sanctuary Buildings in London exists, and at the time was much as described, though its use by MI11 is fictional.

The Security Service (MI5) and the Secret Intelligence Service (SIS or MI6) both existed, and both continue to exist at the time of writing. They both, along with the Foreign Office, suffered from infiltration by Soviet agents between the 1930s and the 1950s, most notably by a group known as the 'Cambridge Five' who were active for many years. Sir Peter Maitland's conference at Stirling Castle is an attempt to uncover their fictional counterparts.

Trains play a large part in this book. The sometimes convoluted and rather odd train services that are used by Helen Erickson are taken directly from the timetables set out in the June 1943 edition of *Bradshaw's Guide*, being the nearest I could get my hands on to the April 1943 edition that Helen uses to plan her journeys.

The role of Bletchley Park in intercepting German communications encrypted by Enigma machines was much as briefly outlined here, as was the reference to the project as 'Ultra'.

The crew of a radar-equipped Ju 88 did defect to RAF Dyce as described in the book, though this happened on the 9th of May 1943. I moved the date to the 20th of April 1943 simply to fit in with the story. The significance of the defection was every bit as large as is suggested in the book.

Let's now turn to places that appear in this book. In writing about locations, I referred constantly to Ordnance Survey one-inch scale maps re-issued and updated by the War Office during

World War Two. They can be viewed on the National Library of Scotland's website. The same source allowed me to refer to the 1936 *Automobile Association touring map of Scotland* that is used by Monique and Anthony for part of their journey, and by Helena Berdyaev.

Princes Street Station in Edinburgh no longer exists but was much as described here. The same is true of Coupar Angus and Blairgowrie railway stations.

Easter Crimond is fictional. It draws on elements of other places that lie a little to the west of Blairgowrie. To suit the story, I have made significant changes to the landscape to the west of the town. The descriptions of the travellers' camp and of the way of life of travellers during the war draw on information gleaned from Duncan Williamson's classic book *The Horsieman.*

Dunkeld and Birnam railway station still exists, though it was almost completely cut off from the village of Birnam by the building of a section of the A9 in the late 1970s. Descriptions of the station and village before the new road was built are based on visits, maps and old aerial photographs. The Station Hotel in Birnam found in this book occupies a building that is now the Merryburn Hotel. This has only existed since the 1960s when it was converted from a shop, which is what the building would have been in 1943. Old maps show that Birnam had a gasworks, which explains the presence of a gas light in Monique and Anthony's room in the Station Hotel.

The roads in the Highlands used by Monique and Anthony in this book were much as described, and many were single-track. The course of the main road from Invergarry to the Cluanie Inn was changed very significantly after the war by a hydroelectric scheme that greatly expanded Loch Loyne. A bridge was opened at Dornie in 1940 to replace the ferry in use until then. The bridge did not appear on War Office editions of Ordnance Survey maps for some time afterwards, though it did appear on the relevant Admiralty chart almost immediately. The 1940 bridge was replaced by the one you see today in 1990. An entirely new stretch of road along Loch Alsh from Balmacara to Kyle of Lochalsh was built in the 1980s and another was built along the shore south-east of Dornie.

The Kyle of Lochalsh described in this book came from old photographs backed up by personal visits. The train arriving at 3.15 p.m. from Dingwall was timetabled to connect with a steamer to Portree and Stornoway, and this route was served by the SS *Lochness*. The chaotic quayside scenes described in this book came directly from photographs taken at the time.

The Station Hotel in Kyle of Lochalsh did overlook the ferry slipway. It was greatly expanded and renamed the Lochalsh Hotel in the 1950s. HMS *Trelawney* was an important naval base in Kyle of Lochalsh during the war and supported minelaying operations in the Atlantic. The Loch Duich Hotel existed and was converted into apartments in relatively recent times. It was used as the venue for the celebrations when the first bridge at Dornie opened in 1940.

The Stirling Castle of 1943 was a very different place from the Stirling Castle of today. It was changed very significantly when converted by the army into barracks in the early 1800s and efforts to reverse those changes in the years since the war have had even more far-reaching effects on the castle. The 1943 Stirling Castle described in this book is generally accurate, including the gym block in the ditch in front of the castle's outer defences and the firing range in the Nether Bailey. And the Great Hall was, as described, converted into barracks to accommodate 400 troops. Having said that, many of the details in this book are conjecture, with assumptions necessarily made, for example, about internal layouts and about the positions of doors and windows in the 1943 castle based on what is visible today.

St Mary's Dalmahoy is a beautiful little church a little to the west of Edinburgh. It is much as described in this book and seems an ideal venue for Bob and Monique's wedding as both of my daughters were married there.

The Albert is a splendid public house on London's Victoria Street. It does not appear to have changed significantly since the 1940s, though the same cannot be said for the rest of Victoria Street.

The London School of Medicine for Women did exist and was on Hunter Street in Bloomsbury. St Chad's Street exists, and nearby Argyle Square did have an undesirable reputation during the war and for some time afterwards. *The Holy Well* is an invented establishment, though its name is inspired by an ancient holy well in the area dedicated to St Chad.

Money features at several points during the story. It's worth noting that £1 in 1943 was the equivalent of a little more than £50 at the time of writing, so Helena Berdyaev's offer of £5 for information about Helen in the travellers' camp would be worth over £250 today.

To conclude, in my view a fiction writer should create a world that feels right to his or her readers. When the world in question is as far removed in so many ways, some predictable and others not, as 1943 is from today, then it is inevitable that false assumptions will be made, and facts will be misunderstood. If you find factual errors within this book I apologise and can only hope that they have not got in the way of your enjoyment of the story.